NIGHT RUNNERS OF THE WINTER SEAS

JOHN APPLEBY

Ink & Laser Press
Duncan, British Columbia
2024

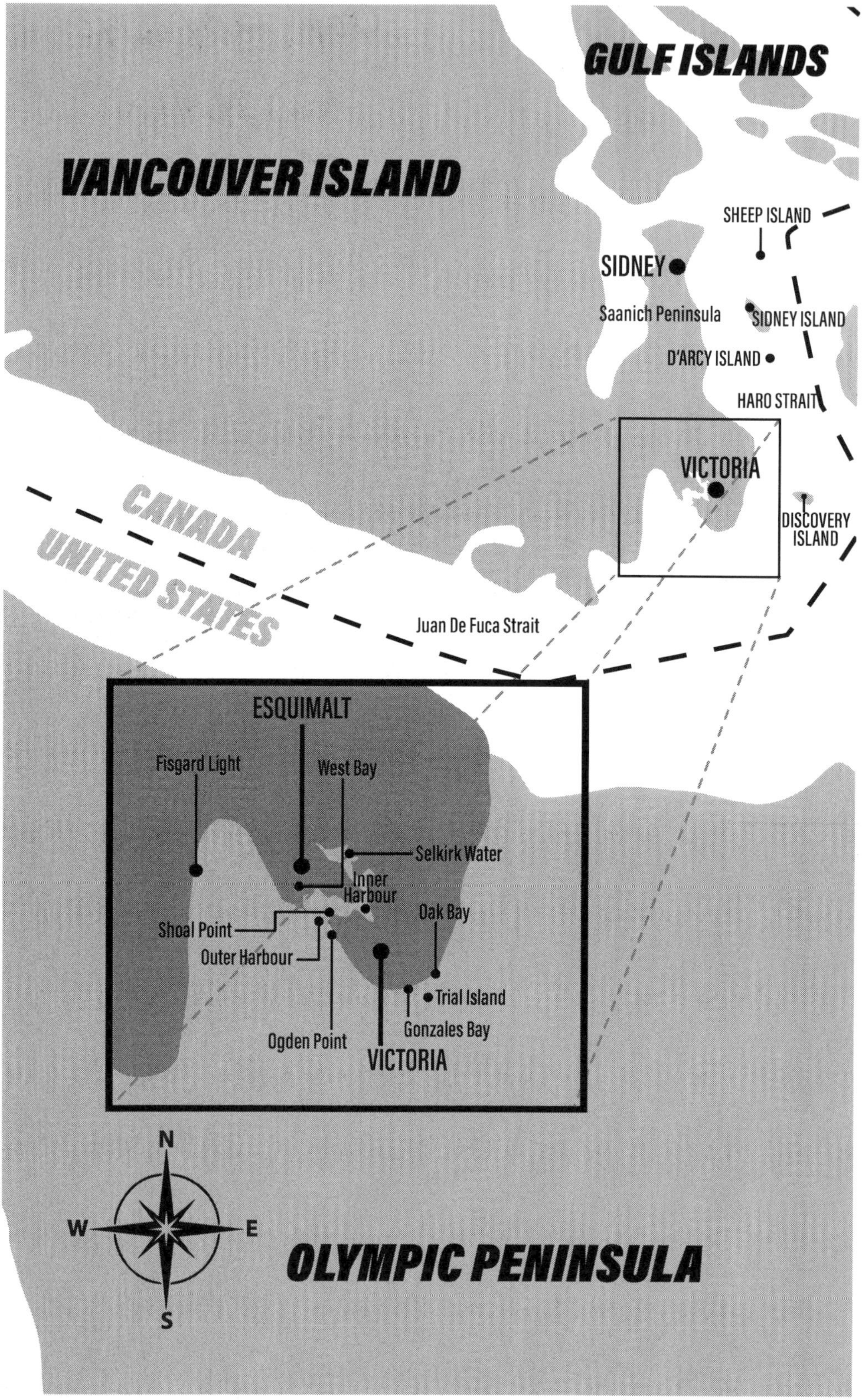
GULF ISLANDS
VANCOUVER ISLAND
SHEEP ISLAND
SIDNEY
Saanich Peninsula
SIDNEY ISLAND
D'ARCY ISLAND
HARO STRAIT
VICTORIA
DISCOVERY ISLAND
CANADA
UNITED STATES
Juan De Fuca Strait
ESQUIMALT
Fisgard Light
West Bay
Selkirk Water
Inner Harbour
Oak Bay
Shoal Point
Outer Harbour
Trial Island
Gonzales Bay
Ogden Point
VICTORIA
N
W
E
S
OLYMPIC PENINSULA

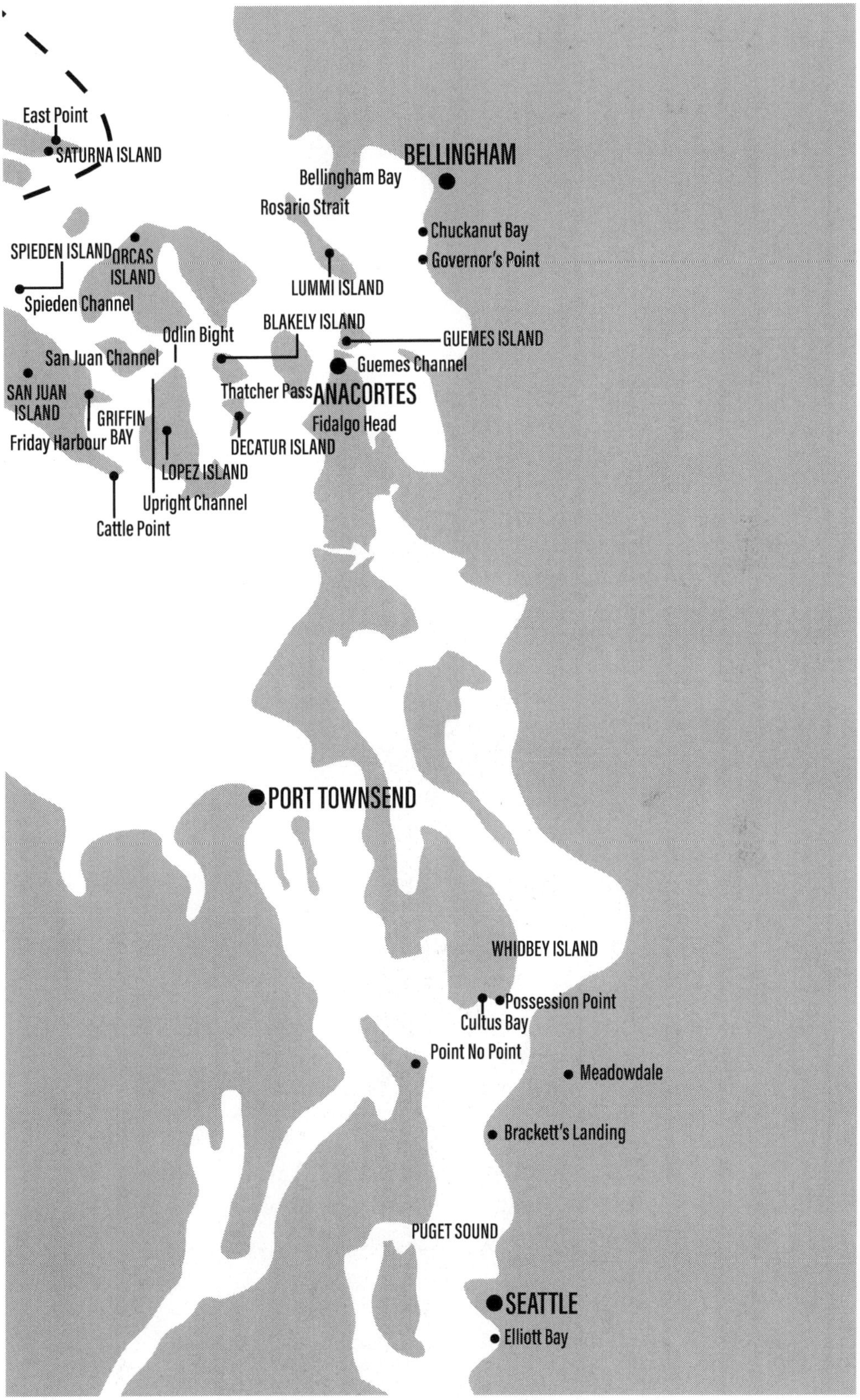
East Point
SATURNA ISLAND
BELLINGHAM
Bellingham Bay
Rosario Strait
Chuckanut Bay
Governor's Point
SPIEDEN ISLAND
ORCAS ISLAND
LUMMI ISLAND
Spieden Channel
BLAKELY ISLAND
Odlin Bight
GUEMES ISLAND
San Juan Channel
Guemes Channel
SAN JUAN ISLAND
Thatcher Pass
ANACORTES
GRIFFIN BAY
Fidalgo Head
Friday Harbour
DECATUR ISLAND
LOPEZ ISLAND
Upright Channel
Cattle Point
PORT TOWNSEND
WHIDBEY ISLAND
Possession Point
Cultus Bay
Point No Point
Meadowdale
Brackett's Landing
PUGET SOUND
SEATTLE
Elliott Bay

ISBN 978-1-7383825-0-7

Cover Image: *Night Runners of the Winter Seas* by Nora Bryant
Cover Design: Judith Appleby
Map: Maple Bay Graphics

Printed and bound in Canada by
Ink & Laser Press
Duncan, British Columbia

This book is dedicated to
Judith Appleby

Prologue

Thursday 12th April 1917

The machine gun fire was loud. On the bridge, the Captain, Commander Rexford, and the First Lieutenant, John Duthie trained binoculars on the headland to the southeast. HMS Cabot Cove *still lay about the same distance from the shore, hove to and drifting slightly to the southwest. Dugald McPherson checked back along each side. The screens had stayed in place, her lines disguised, the davits where the Patrol Boats were slung still hidden. There was another burst of gunfire, then the sound of an explosion.*

"What's Arundel got himself into now?" asked the captain.

"That was either a mine or a torpedo." Duthie retrained his glasses on a spot further inland. "There's no glow or smoke."

Commander Rexford turned around. "What's our position, Pilot?"

McPherson took a bearing. One on the west end of the chalk cliffs on the Jaslund Peninsula, another on the tallest church tower in the town of Glowe. Back in the chartroom, he ran the bearings on the chart and wrote the results in a small black pocketbook.

"We've drifted a mile from our last fix but we're still eleven miles from shore, sir."

Commander Rexford nodded. "Slow ahead," he told the First Lieutenant. "Course, northeast by east."

"Northeast by east," repeated the quartermaster at the wheel.

"Hear anything, Number One?" Rexford asked.

"No more gunfire, anyway," said Lieutenant Duthie, his glasses still focused on the shore.

McPherson picked up his glasses and swept them

in a full circle.

"Deck there!" The lookout in the crow's nest atop the foremast hailed. "Ship clearing the headland."

McPherson halted his sweep and picked up the new vessel. "Looks like a ferry, sir." Rexford waited for a moment as the vessel made open water. "Swedish Flag—nothing for us there."

Another ten minutes passed. "Small craft coming across her stern. One o'clock, heading toward us," Duthie said.

Three sets of binoculars swung left and held on the boat.

"It's Arundel. Engine sounds a bit rough," said McPherson.

"Just one head showing in the cockpit," said Rexford.

They watched for another five minutes as the boat approached.

"Pilot, as soon as we've got him inboard, set a course due north. We'll stay on it 'til we're over the horizon and change our profile again."

"Aye aye, sir!" said McPherson, moving to stand behind the quartermaster.

"Looks like they took a lot of bullets," Duthie said. "God! What happened?"

He refocused his binoculars. "There's a couple of people down on the deck at the aft end of the cockpit. Peter's got the helm. Looks like he's okay. He's heading for the starboard side."

The coxswain was already organizing the lifting crew at the boat davits. McPherson
leaned over the starboard bridge railing. "Cox'n!" he shouted, "Boat coming alongside, looks like wounded on board—stand by to bring them up."

The captain came up beside him and called out, "I'm coming down." He headed for the companionway. "John, come with me," he told the First Lieutenant. "Pilot, get underway as soon as we get the boat inboard."

McPherson rang the engine telegraph to Standby and checked the bridge crew. "When we go, we'll steer due north," he told the Quartermaster. The man nodded. Both bridge lookouts were in position on the wings. He hailed the seaman in the crow's nest. "Any more traffic around the headland?"

"No." The lookout paused, then shouted, "All clear, all points."

McPherson went back to the starboard bridge wing and looked down into the well. The coxswain had sent a man down with the fall lines. He stepped onto the boat and clipped the first line onto a shackle. Someone from the boat crew clipped on the second. The ship's winch took the strain, and the patrol boat came easily out of the water, swung inboard and onto its chocks.

Its windshield was shattered, the machine gun dismounted, and the torpedo was gone. Blood covered the cockpit deck and there was someone else, a woman, bending over a bleeding body. As the deck party secured the boat, McPherson rang the telegraph for Half Speed. "Steer north," he told the Quartermaster and increased to Full Speed when they picked up out the turn.

Lieutenant Duthie ran back up to the bridge. "The captain says set course for Portsmouth. We'll worry about changing our looks after dark. He'll be with Peter and his passenger and the rest of us will stand watches. You have the conn. Wilkes was badly shot up. He doesn't look too good. Leading Seaman Logan's okay, although how he kept that motor running is beyond me."

McPherson nodded. "Who's the woman?" he asked.

"No idea! The captain had her and Peter taken to his cabin as soon as they were aboard. Someone's going to have to tell me what she was doing on the boat and how she learned to plug bullet holes in people."

Chapter 1

Tuesday, August 19th, 1919

The tiny station was called Hope. A train sat quietly as the morning sunlight made its first appearance on the ridge lines of the hills to the east. The river, with its waters calm in late summer, flowed off to the right. A red signal light glowed on the other side where the track curved away. A few passengers alighted. A couple got on at the rear carriage.

McPherson was the sole passenger in the dining car. The waiter showed him to a table.

"Are we on time?"

"Yes sir," replied the man as he handed him the menu, "but we have to stay here until the Silk Train goes by."

The Silk Train was the connection to the fastest ships on the Pacific. From Hong Kong to Vancouver, their holds carried as much raw silk as they had space for. The Silk Trains, once loaded and dispatched, had absolute priority on the tracks.

He ordered breakfast and watched the morning sun creeping down the hillsides, the light spreading further into the valley. There was movement behind the screen of trees on the riverbank. A plume of white smoke rose and flattened over their tops as whatever was causing it moved rapidly toward them. A large light on the front of the locomotive came into view, speeding up to the curve in the track. He felt the dining car vibrate as the rest of the train appeared. It came abreast of them, gave off a sustained roar and flashed past.

They pulled back out onto the main line and the train rattled and lurched over the points. Three hours later, the brakes squealed as it came to a halt at the station in Vancouver.

McPherson glimpsed the harbour wharves through parked freight cars. Masts and booms of ocean-going freighters lit by the mid-morning sun, not as many ships as he remembered from pre-war years. The green of the North Shore mountains contrasted in the distance. He called a porter to carry his trunk over to a taxi. At the terminal, the ticket clerk gave him a boarding time of nine o'clock that evening for the night boat to Victoria. He pulled out his notebook and ran over the list of shipping line offices.

Canadian Pacific Steamships was nearest at the head of the stairs. He asked the young woman behind the reception desk for the Marine Superintendent, Captain Troup, waiting barely five minutes before being ushered into the inner office.

"You've been active, it would seem," said the older man, pointing to the row of medal ribbons on McPherson's jacket.

"Glad to be less so now, sir. I'm hoping the real world can take me back soon."

"I hope so too; we're a bit short of ships between the government not giving us any back and losing the *Princess Sophia* last year.

"I heard about that. What happened?"

"She grounded on Vanderbilt Reef. Sank with all on board lost." Troup paused and took a couple of deep breaths. "Might not have happened if you'd been on the bridge. Anyway, it's left us with fewer bridge billets, and until we get more ships, we can only tell you that we'll give you a place sometime in the next year or so."

"I saw the silk train go by up near Hope, so that trade's still working. Any spare spaces on the Pacific side?"

"The company office in London makes those appointments. Unless you have a certificate to allow you to navigate foreign-going vessels, you won't qualify for that sort of appointment."

"No, I don't—I had lots of offshore bridge time but I was too busy keeping my head down to get someone to record it properly."

"Let us know where to find you and I'll be in touch as soon as I can."

"Thanks for seeing me. I'm on the night boat tonight to get over to Esquimalt so I'll be found at General Delivery, Victoria for the foreseeable future."

"I'll give you a note to the purser on the *Victoria*; she's on the run tonight, and he'll give you a stateroom. It'll be a bit more peaceful than having to put up with the rackety crowd on that run," said Troup. As McPherson folded the note carefully inside the front cover of his notebook he nodded to the book and added, "At least you haven't forgotten everything I taught you."

"No, sir. They've served me well," he grinned. "I might even be able to write my memoirs if I ever do anything interesting in this life."

"Speaking of interesting," said Troup, "you probably won't get too far into local society before someone asks you whether you want to carry some special cargoes into the States. They're usually referring to liquor, which is banned in the state of Washington and about to be banned throughout the States. It's a risky trade and the people doing the asking usually want to keep their involvement at a safe distance."

McPherson got up and they shook hands. "They want someone else to take the risks," Troup went on. "Be careful if someone raises the issue; apart from the risks of carrying illegal loads, there's always the danger of being arrested and charged in the States. That might cause problems when you go into one of their ports as a merchant seaman."

"Seems like there's some extensive planning that's been happening while the war was on," said McPherson.

"That, and there's a fair amount of money coming into the province to run the trade. I suspect every one of our trains coming into Vancouver is carrying stock to feed it. Some of our most august citizens have their noses buried in the business, so don't be overly impressed by the
eminence of whoever raises the point."

"Thanks for the warning, sir. I hadn't heard about that particular trade."

"We'll have to wait a good year or so for general cargoes to pick up and there's a good deal of activity planned for the lumber business, but it's not showing yet."

Downstairs at the terminal café, he bought a copy of the *Vancouver News Herald* and found a table large enough to spread it out. The international sections held little interest; those stories about events in which he had been involved had information he knew to be wrong. In a couple of them he sensed the hand of former naval colleagues. Obvious misinformation was presented as fact. Ships' arrivals and departures were more interesting, but local traffic seemed as quiet as he had guessed from looking out of the train window.

After lunch, he squeezed himself into one of a rank of telephone booths in the cavernous waiting hall. He took down the directory, balanced it on his knee and copied the names and addresses of every additional ship's agent he could find. He spent the next two hours telephoning the most likely potential employers to see if he could get an appointment to see someone. No one said yes.

Many things had changed since 1914, but by 1919, the night boat from Vancouver to Victoria was not one of them. Since it left Vancouver at midnight and took a leisurely seven hours to get to its destination, it carried more than its share of people to whom daylight was either of no importance or even unwelcome. Loggers who had blown the last of their money used the boat to get back to work then returned to repeat the process. Shadowy couples arrived in separate taxis and surreptitiously found their way to the same cabin. Salesmen clutched sample bags in the lounges snatching sleep as they tried to wind up enthusiasm for their morning calls. Policemen herded shackled miscreants up the forward gangway and down into some special hole below decks. Sailors and soldiers with kit bags matching them in size found comfortable nests well away from the prying eyes of non-commissioned officers alert for any sign of military indiscipline. In fact, the night boat carried just about everyone except the rich and respectable, who found more comfortable ways of travelling.

The *S.S. Princess Victoria* had come into service in 1903 and was exclusively used on the run between Vancouver, Seattle, and Victoria. McPherson had worked the run occasionally but had been too junior to be regularly assigned. Just after he joined the navy in August 1914, the ship had rammed and sunk an American ship of similar size. The weather had been foggy, and even with extra lookouts and the ship's whistle sounding at regular intervals the accident had happened. When he heard about it, McPherson had wondered what he might have done to avoid the same fate, a thought which had stayed with him in every navigation decision he had made since.

He boarded as early as he could. Troup's note got him a stateroom and he asked the Chief Steward who the deck officers were; he knew none of them. He found his cabin and settled down for the night in very familiar surroundings, waking briefly to the thrum of the propellers through the hull as the ship reversed away from the dock, swayed slightly, and turned. After that he slept lightly, registering every course change until five o'clock, when the ship turned out of Active Pass. He sat up and took in the spectacular image of the rising sun reflecting on the hills of North Pender Island on the port side and the trees and farms of Saltspring Island on the other. Only five years earlier, these had been his life as he conned ships up and down the straits. He got up and approached the day with his customary precision. Spotting Coal Island in the distance meant they were two hours out of Victoria, and it was time to eat. His nose led him to the dining salon.

As he stepped through the door, he saw another naval officer seated at a table in a back corner with his face in the shadows. His jacket was thrown over a chair opposite and the cuffs showed the wavy rings of a Lieutenant in the Royal Canadian Navy Volunteer Reserve. McPherson came closer. The uniform was new, but the owner seemed to have lost interest in it. There was only a vestige of a knife-edge crease on the trousers, and the shoes had scuffed uppers despite unworn soles. On the seat beside him were a greatcoat and a travelling bag piled carelessly under a cap. It was the tunic which caught his attention. Two rows of medal ribbons ran out from the Distinguished Service Cross. Its owner was something other than a run-of-the-mill, returning serviceman who had enjoyed a comfortable war in command of a large oak desk. When he stopped in front of him, McPherson recognized Peter Arundel.

He kicked Arundel's ankle and stepped back quickly. Arundel opened his eyes and reached down to his belt for something that was no longer there. He looked up and visibly relaxed.

"Pilot," he said, using the term for the ship's navigator.

"Kid," replied McPherson, using a similar term for a junior officer before he had a chance to get above himself. "Looks like you've been around a bit."

Arundel's hair was dark and longer than a naval officer's should be. It highlighted the lines around his eyes, seated deep in dark sockets. They had not been that way the last time McPherson had seen him.

"So have you," said Arundel, looking at McPherson's jacket.

"You on the train yesterday?"

"No, I've been in Vancouver a few days."

Both were silent for a moment, each waiting for the other to say something. Naval officers who had been on secret operations stayed quiet about them in public. It was an unspoken rule that allowed them not to lie but did limit topics of conversation.

"Should be able to get something to eat here," said McPherson, using code to bring them back to the present. He looked over his shoulder and found a steward making himself unobtrusive. The man, wise in ways of drunks and madmen who sometimes needed awakening, had kept his distance. Now it was safe, he came over to the table with a coffee pot and two cups on a tray.

"Sir?" He took their order and left.

"Where now?" asked Arundel.

"No idea," replied McPherson. "I called into a few shipping company offices in Vancouver yesterday, but trade's a bit quiet." He looked over his shoulder to make sure no one was in earshot. "You learn anything useful after you left the ship?"

"I didn't learn a lot after that. Certainly nothing that'll be much use in peacetime."

"What looks like a possibility?"

"Don't have much choice, really. My father's

insurance business needs someone to take it over. It was to be my brother's, but he died at Vimy so it's up to me now."

Their breakfast came and the conversation lagged for a few minutes. None of the tables near them was occupied, so McPherson brought up what was uppermost in both their minds. "That was a confused time," he said.

"The whole time in the Baltic or just the last part?"

"It was odd from the start. It was only by the time we came to the last part with you and your lady friend that it was all batty enough to seem normal." He didn't say what Arundel already knew – that is, if normal was life on *HMS Cabot Cove*, an armed merchant ship, assigned to the Baltic for clandestine operations sailing between hostile and neutral waters, changing her appearance every week, while Arundel and two others piloted her motorboats, dropping agents in inconspicuous locations or making high-speed raids on small ports.

Arundel grinned. "I think our survival was mostly due to your navigating skills, occasionally supported by things you found in the little black notebook that permanently lived in your left-hand jacket pocket."

McPherson leaned back in his chair and took a ruminative sip from his coffee cup. "Bit cold." He signaled the steward. "Warm this up, will you please?"

"That'll be fifty cents, sir."

McPherson looked up sharply, "Really?"

"Perhaps not, sir," said the man as he hurriedly retreated and came back quickly with the pot in his hand.

"He can't have been on this run for long otherwise he'd know better than to try that on."

"Why?" asked Arundel.

"It's a trick they use on the American run. He'll

pocket the money because the company doesn't charge for extra coffee. On a busy run, he'll make another ten dollars a day, about four times his daily wage. He obviously doesn't know much about naval uniforms."

"Helps to know what people get up to then," said Arundel.

"As I kept telling you, keep your eyes open for details."

"And write them down in your notebook." Arundel pulled a small, hard- backed one from his inside jacket pocket.

"You didn't forget everything. Funny, the man who taught me about notebooks just made the same comment to me. What about that girl you picked off the coast? What happened to her?"

"Tatania? The captain hustled us into his cabin where Duthie finished patching me up. I didn't wake up until we were dropped overside in Portsmouth. Cars picked us up and delivered us to separate places in London. Never saw her after that." He changed the subject. "Speaking of the *Cabot Cove*, tell me how the captain fit in. I never worked out why he spent more time decoding messages in his cabin than he did on the bridge."

"I don't know much about him either. Rexford was another reservist called back to the service for the war. John Duthie was sent to turn the Merchant Navy's crew into something the Royal Navy liked better. That meant I had to do everything on the ship that didn't have anything to do with the war." McPherson grinned at the memory. "It's why when you and those other young lunatics arrived to pilot those noisy patrol boats, I had to teach you all everything you'd ignored on your Midshipman's course, like the realities of navigation."

"We weren't that bad, surely," protested Arundel.

"You hadn't the sea time that comes with watch-keeping on a large warship. None of you knew what you didn't know. Remember when I asked what you'd been doing? Your answer didn't give me much comfort."

"Odd jobs for a port captain, dogsbody on a destroyer in the Channel Fleet for a month then off to Coastal Motorboats." Arundel grinned as he said it.

"All time under your keel, I suppose. I last remember you being lifted aboard after bringing that shot-up patrol boat back alongside. What happened?"

"I picked up the lady and there was a submarine on the surface between us and open water. Wilkes was hit when we closed on it, and I got winged after we let our torpedo go. We hit the sub but it wasn't an easy runback. Our passenger did what she could for Wilkes, and Leading Seaman Logan, our steady-handed Newfoundlander mechanic, patched me up so I could get us back to the ship.

"At least you'd learned enough navigation to get back."

Arundel smiled. "I suppose I had, if I could read the compass with a bullet hole in me and set a course on a chart blowing around the cockpit. I guessed the drift well enough and avoided enough rocks to find the ship in the early morning."

"Barring the bullet holes, it's not that different from navigating a coastal ship around here."

"Glad to know I measured up."

"I was on the bridge when you came in and that's where I stayed for the next fifty-six hours, napping in the captain's chair between course changes and stopping to put Wilkes over the side. When we docked, I saw you and the lady leave, then I went to sleep and didn't see much else for another twenty-four hours. Where did you get to?"

"The Admiralty car took me to my uncle's house in London. They gave me these." Arundel pointed to his jacket. "After that I was back to dogsbody jobs on a destroyer. What about you?"

"When I came out of my bunk, there was a summons to the Admiralty and an innocuous-looking admiral took us to Buckingham Palace. I went there with Leading Seaman Logan. The king pinned the Distinguished Service Cross on me and the Conspicuous Gallantry Medal on Logan. We got back to the ship and found that the captain had got Logan promoted to Petty Officer. The ship stayed alongside and all but its regular crew were dispersed."

"A few were posted to the same destroyer as me."

"I hoped for a posting closer to home, but they told me that my experience providing support for small boat operations would help them plan an operation in the Caspian Sea. The Russian Revolution made them worry about the safety of India. The government wanted to secure the back door, and that involved shipping twelve Coastal Motorboats overland. I took Logan with me. He wasn't happy because he wanted to get back to Newfoundland, but the navy didn't have that many spare small boat mechanics. The choice was coming with me or going back to the Baltic. He chose me because it looked like it might not be quite as dangerous."

"The newspapers said it became a shooting war," said Arundel.

"It was just getting into its stride after we finished all the planning, but the Commodore commanding the operation wouldn't let me go. He kept saying I was essential to its success and managed to promote me as a consolation prize. I got out in June as more Royal Navy officers became available. I pointed out that my shoulders had the only pair of Canada flashes in Northwest Persia and that, with the big war over, they should let me go home. The Commodore agreed and sent me on my way. I went back to London and after some admiral debriefed me at the Admiralty, I was sent round to Buckingham Palace again and the

King gave me this." McPherson pointed to the ribbon of the Distinguished Service Order.

"Who was the admiral?"

"Romilly. Said he has a niece out here called Arundel. Relative of yours?"

"He's my mother's uncle."

McPherson nodded. "He was wearing civilian clothes, and everybody called him Sir." He looked out over to the shoreline of the Saanich Peninsula starting to unfold outside. "Not much seems to have changed."

"No," agreed Arundel.

The waterfront houses of Sidney appeared through the windows off the starboard quarter. McPherson noticed a small boat coming rapidly round two small islands from American waters on their port side. They heard the snarl of its motor as it cut very close to their bow, heading for the channel between two islands which lay ahead of them.

"Some toy sailor out early," said McPherson disdainfully. "It's only the idiots that go that close to islands in these waters."

"You sound like you know them well," said Arundel.

"Should do. I spent eight years on coastal steamers learning not to make mistakes before I went into the navy."

"What's the problem with that island?"

"Sheep Island? Same as with most of the others around here—rocks. Sometimes you're lucky and the tide gives you a little room, but unless you know exactly where you are, stay away. I thought you told me you knew these waters?"

"Not in that detail. Do you know the name of every rock around here?"

"Used to. I'll have to spend some time reminding myself. That one in particular, and the three behind it, Brethour, Domville and Gooch—we used them to remind ourselves that the American border was on the other side. It wasn't a major concern but remember what I kept drilling into you: at sea you leave nothing to chance, unlike that half-wit we just saw. What do you think he was doing out this early?"

"More likely he was out late," said Arundel noncommittally.

They spent the rest of the trip chatting idly about old acquaintances until the ship pulled into Victoria's Inner Harbour. McPherson looked out with professional interest as they rounded the point before easing up to the terminal.

"Good bit of traffic around."

"Where are you going now?" asked Arundel.

"Over to the Dockyard and the demobilization office. I'll probably spend the weekend at the wardroom. You?"

"I'll be going home from here." Arundel detached himself from the chair, swept his battered cap onto his head, pulled on his jacket, grasped his luggage, and headed for the door. McPherson was a little slower and came out behind him.

Arundel stopped and said, "My parents are putting on a bit of a party on Sunday afternoon. I can pick you up at the wardroom at half past one if you'd like to join us. There's likely to be a few local people, and if I know my mother, a few girls—she's been hinting that it's time for me to settle down. I'd appreciate a bit of help in managing them."

"Thank you. I don't know if I'd be much of a subject of interest to the ladies, but I'd like to come anyway."

Arundel strode off and lost himself in the crowd while McPherson went off to reclaim his trunk and find a taxi.

Chapter 2

Victoria, Wednesday, August 20th, 1919

McPherson waited for his trunk to be loaded on the rear carrier rack of a cab. Across Belleville Street was the soaring bulk of the British Columbia Legislature. Its massive green dome shone bright in the morning sun. The last time he had seen it was in November 1914, when the ship was going in the other direction. For all the time he had been away, the memory of it had done duty as a picture of home.

"Dockyard, please," he said to the driver.

The harbour had not changed too much. It was packed with just about anything that would float. On the north side, the gentry maintained their respectable cruising boats moored to the Yacht Club wharf. Working boats of every kind competed for space, and for all that he could see, no sign of war remained.

The Empress Hotel was still busy with tourists and had yet to change them for a complement of farmers from the Prairies who used it to avoid the vigorous winters at home. Victoria had maintained its usual appearance, unlike any in his experience. Its combination of mild climate and seaboard location attracted many retirees from other British colonies. Its architecture was distinctive and had its own unique combination of imported and cultivated native vegetation. The first hint of autumn had begun to turn leaves on the Garry Oaks brown.

The cab angled over to Wharf Street and along the Inner harbour toward the Bay Street Bridge. The Outer Harbour and the terminal with the ferry still berthed there disappeared on his left.

The taxi, which he recognized as a Crossley, was like the cars used by the naval staff on shore. They jolted through the streets, out of Victoria and into the adjacent town of Esquimalt. The naval dockyard sat on its western side. They stopped at the main gate, guarded by a solitary policeman. McPherson's uniform satisfied him, and he waved them into a warren of narrow lanes which eventually led to the wardroom, the home of local, unmarried officers and their transient counterparts in every British naval dockyard throughout the world.

The driver unloaded his trunk and found a hand truck to wheel it into the reception area. McPherson paid him and turned to the naval rating manning the reception desk. "I'll be here for a few days, I expect," he said, handing over his travel documents.

"Very good, sir," said the man. "Have you been here before?"

"Not for a while," replied McPherson. He signed the register and took his key.

"Lunch is served between eleven hundred and thirteen hundred hours," the sailor commenced in practiced patter. "Dinner from seventeen hundred to nineteen hundred, breakfast from six hundred to eight hundred; extra messing is seventy-five cents a day payable when you leave. Laundry is done daily, and shoes are done overnight. "Boots" charges 10 cents a pair. There's a barber in the barracks, but most gentlemen prefer to go into town. The trams leave the main gate every half hour on the hour and the half hour; local route information is at the stops. There's a direct telephone to the taxi company over there," he pointed to a corner of the lobby. "Do you want your trunk taken up to your room or put in storage?"

"I'll have it upstairs please," McPherson replied. "Where's the demob office?"

"Entrance at the east side of the headquarters building located by 'A' Jetty. It's open from nine hundred hours to twelve hundred and then from thirteen hundred to sixteen hundred."

McPherson left his luggage and walked down to the headquarters building. The dockyard was a silent place with very few people moving about. It had a level of tidiness that said more about disuse than naval activity. Most of the buildings he passed had shut doors and closed windows. He saw little movement around the headquarters building except a sign by the front door pointing the way to the entrance of the Demobilization Office located inconspicuously at the side.

Inside was a large room with four petty officers behind a counter and an elderly Lieutenant Commander seated behind a desk. One of the Petty Officers looked up from the seaman facing him across the counter. "Sir," he said, pointing toward the officer behind the desk.

McPherson walked over, handing his discharge letter and pay book to the older man, who said, "I'm Strang. Good morning." He wore the straight rings of the regular navy on the white background of the Paymaster Branch. He had an English accent and his well-worn medal ribbons were for campaigns of the previous century. The gold rings were tarnished but the Canada flashes on his shoulders were much newer and showed him as another transplant from the Royal Navy, without whom the infant Royal Canadian Navy could never have been started. Strang reached into his desk drawer and extracted a printed form. He spread out the form on the desk.

"And to you," said McPherson, watching him.

"Been around a bit, I see," Strang continued as he riffled through the pay book. "Seems like the Royal

Navy paid you at their rates. They're less than ours so we're going to need your book for a few days to work out how much you're owed. I can't promise anything until Monday, but we're not too busy at the moment, otherwise we'd have to hang on to you for weeks. I can give you your gratuity money now as well as the pay we owe you since you last drew something from the RN. I can also give you an allowance for clothing, but you'll find that, at Victoria prices, it's not enough to buy anything decent. You'll have to suit yourself to suit yourself."

McPherson smiled at the well-worn joke, hoping that this genial old war-horse would keep enough pressure on his equally venerable assistants to move his complicated release along. Commander Strang wrote rapidly across the form in front of him, dried the ink on his desk blotter and gave it and the pay book back to him.

"Take this to the cashier and come back to see us on Monday morning," he said. "You can show the cashier's slip to the wardroom and tell them you'll be with us 'til then. Enjoy yourself for the weekend, but don't spend all the money. Except for the reconciliation we'll give you next week, that's all there is. You will stay on the Reserve List unless you do something to get thrown off it, so you can write "RCNR" after your name until you die, and then put it on your gravestone."

"What else does that mean?" asked McPherson.

"I'm told it means that the navy can come and get you whenever it wants. It has this arrangement with the people who issue your maritime certificate, something to do with the sealed orders that are always in every British Empire merchant ship's safe. Do you have any thoughts about the future?"

"Not many," McPherson replied. "Canadian Pacific will be taking me back, but not for a while yet. That was all I knew before the war, but after the last five years, perhaps it's time to look somewhere else."

"You've got the next few days to think about it, anyway," said Strang.

McPherson thanked him and walked over to the cashier's window on the other side of the room. The man, an elderly Petty Officer with Pay Writer's badges on his lapels, took the form and paybook. He peered at them over half-frame glasses, took another form and laboriously wrote numbers against preprinted entries. He totaled the amount, reached into his cash drawer and counted out six hundred seventy-three dollars and thirty-eight cents. He took McPherson's paybook and entered the details. He pushed the money across the counter and said, "Like the Commander said, we'll need your book until Monday to work out what's owing, so come to see us then in the morning."

McPherson left the office and walked back to the wardroom, a little unsure as to what to do with the rest of the day. Hunger reminded him of the time, and he went straight into the dining room. A single table set for eight indicated the communal nature of the place, but today he was alone. The window beside the table was open and he savoured the warm breeze carrying a scent of the ocean. He took a chair giving him a view of the water's edge as a waitress, a wartime departure from the steward of tradition, placed a bowl of soup in front of him.

After lunch he wandered into the anteroom. The newspapers were mounted on wooden strips which discouraged residents from taking them out of the room. In addition to *The Times* and *The Scotsman*, the racks held *The Globe* from Toronto and *The Gazette* from Montreal. McPherson wanted the local paper and found *The Victoria Colonist* in its own separate rack.

The Colonist had broad coverage of international and local news. He slogged through European stories covering the remnants of the war he had just left,

American legislation and the visit of the Prince of Wales to Canada. There was little maritime news except a notice that the Royal Northwest Mounted Police were assuming a coastal patrol role. For a moment he thought of applying to join them but discounted it immediately. Without any friends on the inside, he would have to start at the bottom. It would be years before he advanced to any higher rank. The one thing he knew about the national police force was that its lower members were badly paid.

Other parts of the newspaper were more helpful, particularly advertisements for clothing stores and places to live. None of the places to rent appealed to him so he turned to information about stores. The paymaster had been right, the thirty-five-dollar clothes allowance would not take him too far. His major choice, before he bought anything, was what he should dress himself to do.

The clock on the mantel shelf chimed eight bells in the afternoon watch, sixteen hundred hours in the modern navy. Halfway through the chimes, another officer came in, a man of about his own age wearing the straight stripes of the regular navy. He nodded to McPherson and said, "John Ellis. I'm the officer of the watch."

"Dugald McPherson."

"Passing through?"

"Demob."

"Shouldn't have too much difficulty in landing somewhere," said Ellis, looking at the interlaced rank stripes on McPherson's sleeve. "Everyone wants proper seamen, not us naval versions."

"Not yet they don't," replied McPherson. "I came in yesterday and things are going to be quiet for a while." Ellis's jacket had the shadow of a ring stitched above his top one. "You seem to be staying in."

"Not much choice, really. I was in the first class of midshipmen here in 1910 and thought I could make a decent career out of it. I had a good war, finished as a Lieutenant Commander, but then went back to the rank I started with in 1914. I don't know anything but the Navy and I have a wife with a youngster on the way."

McPherson was lost for a reply. The ribbon of the Distinguished Service Cross was on Ellis's jacket. The old phrase "What do you do when the band stops playing?" ran through his mind.

Ellis slouched morosely over to the rack of newspapers, pulled out one that McPherson had just put down, and riffled through the pages for a few minutes.

"I'm not sure I'd know what to do with myself in civilian life. There's too much confusion out there. I don't see much in the way of jobs; trade unions are on strike all over the place and Canada doesn't seem to know what to do with itself. Half the countries in Europe have turfed their monarchies and the Americans are lecturing everyone about how to put everything back together. The only thing this paper's talking about are the tours underway by royalty and army commanders telling us how well the army did. I spent the whole war on British ships with RN types sniffing about colonials. I got this," he said, pointing to the Distinguished Service Cross, "for a fairly violent cutting-out raid on a UBoat and all they could say was, 'What else can you expect from a cowboy?' Now we're demobilizing so fast that we couldn't defend the coast from a bunch of Boy Scouts on a raft. I'll let brighter people do the thinking—they all say we've finished the war to end all wars so I might just as well stay in the navy, take their money and hope they're right."

McPherson thought Ellis had been saving the speech up for an uncritical audience so he did not respond. He saw no sense in pointing out that his own prospects as a professional seaman seemed to be about as limited.

Chapter 3

He went to sleep feeling uneasy. For the first time in weeks, and one of the few times in years, he was not in something that was moving. He opened his window but even the light breeze that came in off the water was not enough to settle him. Ariadne's half-remembered face came to him before sleep did; Ariadne, an unexpected encounter in the Portsmouth library. He had been looking for some information on the Caspian Sea and found the public library. She was the librarian, and he, needing to keep quiet about his work, had to make several trips to put together the information he wanted. They got closer over the weeks as she asked more about Canada than what he was doing in the library. Inevitably, their curiosity overcame their reticence – hers at getting involved with someone who might die, and him the admonition of his mother about avoiding fornication. There were two blissful weeks before he left, and the likelihood of making it permanent when he got back. By the time he did, the Spanish flu epidemic raging worldwide had taken her.

The bells sounded from the clock in the anteroom. It was automatic that he woke at the chime of two bells in the morning watch, marking five o'clock in the morning. He slid out of bed and entered the dining room fifteen minutes later.

Breakfast was fast and the morning paper was in the anteroom in time for his coffee although there was not much maritime information in it. Canadian Pacific

Steamships advertised that it was reducing its coastal fares. A wooden schooner had been launched from a local shipyard, but its owners and planned base of operations were Norwegian. He was disappointed that the yard was not building anything more modern. Internationally, cargoes were backing up in Shanghai because of a dispute between China and Japan, and ships were being diverted from other routes to ease the blockage. Professionally, there was nothing encouraging for him at all.

The reception area had roughly-printed maps of the city, so he took one, using the back of it to list all the places he had to visit: the clothing stores; the bank where he had left his account in 1914; and the warehouse where his few possessions were stored in a large wooden box.

The streetcar rattled through the streets of Esquimalt, and he caught the familiar smell of Victoria's air, a unique combination of salt laden breeze and cedar from the sawmills along the Gorge waterway, all overlaid with a whiff of browning leaves.

The streets were lined with overhanging trees and gardens spilled onto the rim of the sidewalks. They went over the Bay Street Bridge, which straddled the industrial waterfront of West Bay. Here the Gorge and its sawmills pointed the way to Portage Inlet, a long finger which reached about four miles into the outer reaches of the settlements surrounding the city. McPherson got off when they came to Wharf Street at the Inner Harbour. He walked up Humboldt Street with the Empress Hotel to his right. On his left, newly built on the promontory at the intersection with Gordon Street, was a large four-story building that appeared luxurious, but had nothing on the outside to identify it.

He crossed over Douglas Street and followed Humboldt until he came to a medium-sized, single-storey brick building marked with a weathered sign that said *Vickers Storage*. A small wicket gate set into the left carriage door led him into a covered forecourt. A man, whom he did not remember, stood behind an improvised office counter formed where the upper half of the entrance door swung backwards.

"I'm Dugald McPherson. I left a box here in October 1914 and I'd like to get into it."

The man peered at him for a moment and walked to the back of the office, returning with a large ledger, "1914" painted in white on the cover. McPherson, reading the entries for October upside down, saw his signature about a third of the way from the top. He pointed it out to the clerk, who looked at him with irritation.

"We'll need some more money," he said. "You paid for two years when you dropped it off and you sent twenty dollars in 1916. That covered you until October last year. How long do you want to leave it for?"

"I don't know at the moment. I got back yesterday; I should have a better idea in a couple of months."

"Pay us ten dollars to cover it until the end of October and we'll give you a few more months if you need it. I'll get the box down now and you can get into it whenever you need to."

"You should also have some journals which I posted here while I was away," McPherson said as he handed over ten dollars and took a receipt in return. He went inside and the clerk locked the door behind him.

"You're careful around here," McPherson said.

"The boss insists on it. We keep shipments for the Hudson's Bay Company here when they run out of space."

"Furs or trade goods?" asked McPherson with professional interest, wondering why Hudson's Bay would ever run out of dockside space.

"Don't know what it is," said the clerk. "I just move it around." Limping, he pushed a hand truck down a side aisle lit with a dim electric light, checking numbers on bays of shelving stacked four levels from the floor on both sides. When he stopped, McPherson looked up and saw the end of his canvas-covered box on the top shelf. The clerk pulled a roof mounted gantry into position and hooked a ladder to a railing that ran the length of the ceiling. He climbed slowly up the ladder until he could reach over and clip two chains to a frame under the box. When he came back down, he told McPherson to move back, and then he pulled hard on the lead line. A loud click sounded in the enclosed space as the two chains tightened against the side of the box. The clerk pulled the line, and with a ratcheting sound, the box was lowered onto the hand truck.

"Great seamanship," said McPherson.

"I was at sea for thirty years, all of it in sail and the last ten as Bosun." The clerk lost his irritation with the compliment. "Getting cargo out of the hold and landing it at some place where there wasn't a wharf was all part of the job. It's good to have a job where I can use some of the skills, in spite of the rheumatism," he said as he pushed the truck back in the direction of the office.

McPherson moved out of his way, and as the truck went by, he brushed against the goods stacked under a tarpaulin on the lower shelf. The movement was enough to cause the cover to slip and he saw the distinctive design on a case of *Buchans's White Label Whiskey* stacked above two others on the rack. The clerk caught the flash of colour and reached over to replace the cover. Neither man said anything about it.

"I can put this close to the door so you can get it easy."

"That'll be good—thanks," said McPherson.

The clerk wheeled the truck next to an empty slot and slid the box onto the shelf.

"The place looks a bit better run than it was when I left my things here," observed McPherson.

"My boss bought it in 1916 and hired me to organize it. He's a ship master and I sailed with him."

"What's his name? I might know him."

"Ephram Chambers."

"Heard of him, never sailed with him." McPherson reached into his pocket for a quarter and handed it to the clerk. "What's your name? I'll be in here a bit until I settle on what I'm doing."

"Thank you, sir, it's Joe. I'll get the box with your other books," he said.

McPherson unlocked the lid and recoiled slightly at the pungent smell of moth balls. He had packed the box with his customary precision. On the top was a fitted tray containing a large envelope with all the essential documents of his life: a photograph of his now-dead parents in a cardboard folder; his baptismal certificate; his maritime qualification certificates from the Board of Trade in London; and his account passbook issued by the Bank of New Caledonia. Below the envelope were his journals. Under the tray were the civilian clothes he had thought worth keeping when he left. He took off his jacket and, wincing again at the smell, he tried on each one in turn. His merchant navy jacket with the two rings of a second officer above the cuffs no longer fitted across his chest, nor did his only civilian suit, his watch-keeper's coat and even his oilskin foul-weather gear. The sole exceptions to the array of misfits were his storm hat, his merchant navy cap with the Canadian Pacific badge on the front, a couple of woolen toques, and his sea boots.

As the pile of discarded garments grew, so did the problem of what to do with them. He wrapped everything in the oilskin and repacked the remainder, took his bank passbook out and locked the box. On his way out through the office to pick up his package of notebooks, he asked Joe for ideas. After a few moments' thought, Joe mentioned the Salvation Army.

"Should have thought of that myself,"

McPherson said. He hefted the package, nodded to Joe, and walked back down Humboldt Street. Every sailor and most servicemen were drawn instinctively to the 'Sally Ann.' It was the place which was always there when he was in port, whether for the tea urn going twenty-four hours a day, or just a quiet place to sit with religion kept quietly in the background. It was time he looked after it, he thought, and he asked a passing policeman where their temple was to be found. Naturally, it was in the scruffiest part of town at the foot of Yates Street, well within reach of the waterfront.

When he got there, he threw his package on the counter and announced: "Seaman's clothes that shrunk while I was away."

"Common problem," said the attendant. "Did you check the pockets?"

"No," said McPherson, momentarily irritated with himself. He unwrapped the package and went through every garment. In the side pocket of his oilskin trousers, he felt a lump, which, when extracted, was his clasp knife, its four-inch blade and marlin spike folded into the handle.

"Thank you for reminding me," he said ruefully.

He came out of the temple and walked up Yates Street, past the bank where the poet Robert Service had worked before heading to the Yukon and fame. At his own bank he handed over his passbook to a teller who excused himself and went to the back of the banking hall where he leafed through a file box and pulled out a card. He called over another man who leafed through another box. The second man came back to him said quietly, "Would you step over here, please, sir?" He pointed to a counter on the other side of the hall. There, the banker said, "Your account has no entries corresponding to this passbook, Commander."

McPherson had not earned promotions and medals by losing the initiative in the face of difficulties.

He reached over the counter and took his passbook from the man and looked down at him for a few seconds. He said in a slightly louder voice, "Mister whatever-your-name-is, you have a serious predicament." Two people standing at the other end of the counter looked up.

"My name is Morris, Commander. Would you wait here while I get the manager?"

McPherson leaned back against the counter as the other man walked quickly to an office in the corner of the hall.

"Commander McPherson?" said a voice behind him, a moment later.

McPherson turned and saw a middle-aged man, a little shorter than himself, formally dressed in a black morning coat and striped trousers, with an expression that suggested he found minor matters beneath him. "I am the manager; my name is Armitage. I'm informed that there is some confusion with your account."

"I am not aware of any confusion about my account," he replied in a voice loud enough to be heard by people in the bank. "You seem to have the contents of it."

Armitage's eyes flickered around the hall. "Perhaps my office would be more comfortable," he said, and opened the gate in the counter to let McPherson pass through. The manager's office was spartan and the chair for visitors was uncomfortable enough to discourage long conversations. McPherson sat down, opened his passbook, and placed it in front of the bank manager, keeping it firmly in his grip.

"You see here that my last entry at this bank was on the first of October, 1914, and that, here," he took several sheets from his wallet and laid them out across the open passbook, "are the records of ten telegraph transfers I made from your branch in London between then and last month. Now you're telling me you can't find the money. That is not confusion; it's a very serious problem for you. My reckoning is that the account should have just over one thousand, two hundred and eighty dollars in it, depending on the exchange rate for English pounds."

"That is a record of transfers, indeed, Commander, but we have no way of knowing what directions you might have given to our London branch," replied the banker.

McPherson stayed silent for a moment. When he spoke again, it was a naval officer addressing a subordinate.

"Mr. Armitage, I have just returned to Victoria for the first time since I made the last transaction at this bank and your acknowledgment of this passbook is proof enough that the account exists. I would have had no need to give instructions to send the money to another account or to withdraw them, and nor, as you can see, have I obtained any cheques that would allow me to make any payments out of it. I have spent the last five years in the employment of a large organization which would not exist if it lost records. I expect no less of you."

He stood up and turned toward the door. "That money came in here and someone put it somewhere, so you need to go back through your records for the last five years and find it. I'll be back here on Monday morning. I trust you will have the matter cleared up by then."

"If you would be good enough to leave your passbook with us, we can be sure of getting the dates right," said Armitage tentatively.

McPherson stared at him and held out the passbook open at the last page. Without a word, the banker copied the details into his journal.

He walked out onto Government Street very conscious of both his depleted wardrobe and now reduced funds. In spite of the confidence he'd assumed while talking to the bank manager, he was not certain that things would be straightened out by Monday. His days on the naval payroll were dwindling. He could keep wearing his uniform, but in a city full of demobilized servicemen, he would just stand out as someone who had not made the jump away from wartime life. He was thankful he had the cash from the naval paymaster, but with his carefully amassed reserve gone, he was uncomfortable with his diminishing options.

He walked up Government Street past a couple of clothing stores which were of some interest. It was useful to think of wearing clothes "suitable for gentlemen" as the advertisements put it, but his problem was where he would wear them. Formal suits for the office were common displays, along with tweed suits for less formal occasions. Blue or striped blazers with white flannel trousers were there, but they were marked down to denote the end of their season.

In England the men wore suits with long tailed coats. He thought about the suits worn by diplomats. Those in the Baltic were muffled up for Scandinavian winters, and in the Mediterranean lightened for the semi-tropics. Nothing seemed to give a good example for the oncoming fall and winter in Victoria. He came to a shop on the corner of a small alley leading off the street with *F. & W. Cartwright* discreetly written at the base the front window and, on the inside, a broad array of choices.

An elderly assistant allowed him to walk the length of a display rack before saying, "Good morning, Commander. Do you have any particular preferences"?

"No," he replied. "I've not worn civilian clothes for many years and I'm not sure what I should be looking for."

"You're certainly not alone in that at this time, sir. I presume you're back quite recently."

"Yesterday."

"A little soon to be precise about what the

future holds, perhaps."

"Yes."

"We hear that the maritime world is taking some time to sort itself out."

"You seem well-informed."

"We've been in business here for almost fifty years, so we've seen many officers make the transition to civilian life, and back again to the service for that matter."

McPherson looked at the man a little closer. Though he was a little stooped and his hair was quite white, his suit was perfectly cut and only embellished by a tape measure hanging around his neck.

"I should be listening to any suggestions you might have, then."

"Thank you, sir, we might find a way to be helpful. Do you plan to return to a former employer?"

"Hopefully so. Canadian Pacific Steamships."

"Ah, yes, it may be a little while, then."

"You are well-informed."

"We clothe gentlemen who keep us so. Our prices are a little above the allowance that the government provides, but not excessively so. I presume that when you return to the company's service, you will need seagoing apparel at that time."

McPherson had never considered that he was dressed in 'apparel', but now he had stepped up a few notches in the navy, he was considered to have done the same in civilian life. "Yes, but I think I can have my uniforms modified to meet the need."

"May I suggest not, sir. Your naval uniforms, presumably tailored by Gieves of London," he looked over the fitting with an expert eye, "would inevitably show the marks of your wartime rank picked off the sleeves. I doubt that Captain Troup would find that acceptable. When they call you to go back, we can fit you out on reasonable terms. I suggest you keep your uniforms against the day the navy will call again."

"Very well, then. Where do I start? When I had my uniforms done, Gieves had a large ready-made stock and finished them by hand."

"We have the same, sir. Perhaps you could remove your tunic and we can do a little measuring."

McPherson complied and remarked, "I had a twenty-nine-inch waist when I got to London; I don't suppose it's changed much."

The clothier wrapped a tape measure around his waist. "The particular garments we have here of that size might be a little tight on you, but I think we can manage. What sort of circles do you see yourself moving in?"

"Certainly not the height of society, anyway—people's offices, the odd lunch and the occasional dinner, perhaps."

"If I might ask, sir—some maritime gentlemen are availing themselves of employment in smaller coastal vessels. Would that be something you might be considering?"

"I have absolutely no idea."

"Against the possibility, sir, may I suggest a boating jacket and some flannel trousers?
I'm told that some social occasions involving Americans are periodically involved, and, as always, we must be prepared to show them a good example. In any event, the same garb would be useful at informal local events."

Eventually they settled on a grey suit with a waistcoat, a selection of shirts both hard- and soft-collared, a pair of ties, a tweed hunting jacket, a double-breasted blazer which the tailor called a boating jacket, and light grey trousers. In addition, he took a Burberry trench coat as defense against Victoria's autumn and winter gales. An informal soft-brim hat and a tweed cap were, the shop man assured him, becoming quite acceptable for a gentleman to wear on an everyday basis. He also bought a soft-sided canvas travelling bag, which the tailor said would withstand being stowed in small boat lockers.

"Everything will be ready for you on Tuesday at noon, if you would be kind enough to leave a deposit now."

McPherson took twenty-five dollars from his notecase and put them on the counter. "Do I ask for you when I return?"

"By all means, sir. I'm usually here. My name is Cartwright, and I own the shop."

"Not the original, I take it."

"No, sir, that was my father and my uncle, and if I should be absent for some reason, my nephew will be pleased to help."

As he left the store, McPherson had a momentary thought that there was some depth to commercial life in the city which had never involved him before he left. He also thought that the tailor was the most circumspect of anyone he had met in referring to the liquor trade—and that probably meant that the trade was widespread enough that it might be his only alternative.

Chapter 4

Sunday, August 24th, 1919

Peter Arundel drove up to the wardroom door a little before half-past one. Unexpectedly, he too wore his uniform.

"Can't stand to get rid of it either?" commented McPherson.

"It's one of those events. The clothing stores around here have all the fashionable modern stuff, but it looks a bit frilly, and I don't like the alternative of looking like my father. The stuff I have for daytime is good for the office, but weekends are another matter."

"I can understand that. I never wore much other than sea-going clothes since I was fourteen, and even if I get back on someone's bridge, I still need to get something a little less stiff. As it happens, even the minimal amount I had doesn't fit either, so it all got dropped at the Salvation Army. I went to Cartwright's on Thursday, and they had enough to start me off."

"You out of the navy yet?"

"Not quite; I spent too much time in the hands of the Royal Navy and the paperwork hasn't all caught up. Just as well—the bank I relied on to keep everything safe has a problem recognizing me."

"Which one is that?"

"The Bank of New Caledonia. The manager is called Armitage. We had a rather direct conversation where I told him I'd be back on Monday and expected him to have the problem solved. In the meantime, I spent a good part of the last two days looking for places to work on shore and thought about places to live as well."

"Nothing turn up yet?"

"No, everyone's in the same position as Canadian Pacific. The government's still hanging on to the ships they requisitioned for the war, and no one I talked to has a lot of optimism for what's to happen on the coast in the next couple of years."

McPherson looked idly out of the left-hand window at the passing houses. "It all looks quite comfortable around here still."

"Victoria doesn't change much."

"Not so far anyway - unlike every other part of the known world."

The car lurched a little over the tram tracks.

"Nice car," said McPherson as he looked around the inside. A mark on the dashboard resembled an inverted arrow. "Speaking of the government untangling itself from equipment, looks like the British government used to own this."

"Very true. It's a Crossley—the British Army used a lot of them. The car manufacturers weren't too keen on them flooding the market in England while they were trying to sell new ones, or so the story went. My father and his cousin put a small organization together to collect them in France and ship them over here. It won't work for much longer because we'll probably be switching over to drive on the other side of the road like the Americans."

"The taxi I took on Wednesday looked similar," said McPherson.

"They were the first to need cars and we were able to supply them here and in Vancouver."

"What happens when the rules change, and we move to the right side of the road?"

"It'll be a problem in the cities, but not much of

a one outside; most of the roads in the province are still one lane tracks. If we have any cars left to sell, there's always Japan, Australia and India, they'll keep to the left."

"Not back to England?"

"No, that would probably not be wise. The arrangements we made circumvented some rules and it's better to keep them out of sight and not remind anyone of their existence."

McPherson said nothing. He had long known of ships' captains who loaded cargoes unofficially and off manifest. It seemed the habit was catching amongst this city's leading citizens. They ran slowly down Esquimalt Road toward the Bay Street bridge; there they picked up a little speed and the air rushing past the canvas top made conversation difficult. Arundel threaded the car inexpertly through the town traffic as they turned onto Douglas Street.

"Been driving long?" asked McPherson as they narrowly missed a pedestrian and stopped momentarily to allow another car to maneuver around them.

"Started on Thursday. It's a bit different than piloting a boat. More levers and pedals."

"Hopefully you'll get the hang of it before too long." McPherson gazed over the panorama to their right. "I must have looked at this sight hundreds of times from a ship's bridge, but I never stopped to think of it as beautiful."

"I never thought you were the sort to consider anything other than the running of the ship."

"I never gave myself the time. It's only when you've spent a few years with people trying to kill you that you need to stop and look around a bit." A whisper of a sea breeze came in from behind them and brought with it more of the distinctive late-summer smell. "You don't find this anywhere else that I've been."

Arundel looked at him quizzically. "I never thought much about it."

"When you're young, you don't have a lot to compare it against. All the houses look windswept," said McPherson, changing the subject. "I've spent all my time on this stretch of coast keeping as much sea room as I could find, but it never occurred to me that the folks on shore would be as hunkered down as I was."

"Didn't you spend any time on shore?"

"Not a lot. Victoria was always a place for quick turnarounds. Until I went into the navy, I lived on whatever ship I worked on. If I came ashore, it was because I'd had enough of the cook and needed a change. I was looking for the Sally Ann on Friday and couldn't find it from the shore side—had to ask a policeman for directions."

"No drinks, no women?"

"I've seen enough drunks on the bridges of ships that I haven't wanted to imitate them, and I found out early that trying to navigate with a hangover was as bad as being roaring drunk. As to women—mind your own business."

Arundel wisely changed tack and pointed out to sea. "These waters were where I learned to handle small boats. On a clear day it was easy enough to get out there looking for salmon or ling cod, or leaving a few crab traps out, but the weather could turn quickly and some of the tidal currents around the islands could get you into trouble if you weren't set up properly."

"So I remember you telling the skipper when you came aboard *Cabot Cove.* I confess I thought you were embroidering it a bit, but I guess it all worked out. I'm still wondering whether I want to look at the sea or to find a place as far away from it as possible."

Arundel swung the car onto a crescent with comfortable-looking houses on both sides and stopped in the driveway of one of the larger ones.

"Is that a choice you need to make now?" he asked after shutting off the engine.

"No," replied McPherson, "provided I can get my bank sorted out and some sort of a job to do. This is the first time in my life I've ever been at a loose end."

McPherson stepped out of the car and followed Arundel into the house. They came into a spacious wood-paneled entrance hall with glass-paned doors. Arundel showed McPherson into a cloak room where his hat joined many civilian ones.

"Welcome, Commander," said a man coming out of the reception room.

"Lieutenant Commander Dugald McPherson, my father, Major Michael Arundel."

"Major Arundel, it's good of you to ask me over," said McPherson, smiling.

Michael Arundel was smaller than his son and dressed in a lightweight grey suit of a type favoured by Englishmen in colonial settings. His tie, which McPherson knew to symbolize the Royal Engineers, stood out prominently against a cream-coloured shirt and marked him, as if proof were needed, as an army officer.

"I take it this is not your first time in Victoria," said Michael.

McPherson recognized the oblique probing technique that Michael was using to get him to indicate his social standing and whether he could be trusted alone with the family silverware.

"No, it isn't, although, as I was telling Peter in the car coming over here, my previous life afloat only gave me short stays in any port, including this one."

"Who did you sail with?"

"I was apprenticed with Canadian Pacific and was rated Second Officer before I went to the navy."

"Captain Troup must have been impressed with you; most of the Second Officers I've seen are much older."

"I was fortunate."

McPherson presumed he had passed the test because he was ushered into the reception room with Peter. The space was well-filled with people. French doors gave access to a large terrace, at the edge of which the waters of the bay were clearly visible. Inside the door a woman was standing at the front of the room, a tightly-packed crowd gathered beyond her.

"Come and meet my wife. Cynthia, this is Commander McPherson. Captain Troup appears to think most highly of him."

A coded social message that said that Michael was sufficiently satisfied with him to let him wander unaccompanied among their guests.

"Mrs. Arundel, thank you for inviting me. I met your uncle, Admiral Romilly, in London."

"He was well, I hope."

"Yes, he was."

"We seem to have lost my son," she said, looking around the room.

Message received—the Admiral was no topic for discussion. McPherson looked behind her to see what Arundel was doing and saw him talking to his father.

The older man was looking around the room, and following the direction of his head, McPherson saw his bank manager, Armitage, standing with a group of people beside the fireplace. Michael Arundel walked over, and the two men turned to face the wall for a private discussion.

McPherson continued to chat with Cynthia Arundel about innocuous events in London. When the two by the fireplace turned back, Armitage looked over at McPherson, and after Michael had gone back to Peter, came over to him.

"Commander. Nice to see you here. We're still trying to clear up the small problem we discussed on Friday. I'll have some more information on Monday."

"Thank you, Mr. Armitage. I'll see you then."

Armitage gave him an unctuous smile and went

back to his companions by the fireplace.

"How reassuring," said Cynthia, who had been following the movements of her husband. McPherson thought Mrs. Arundel understood the context of the discussion without the benefit of any explanation. "Commander, a drink?" she asked.

"Thank you, no."

"A teetotaler?"

"Not in that sense, Mrs. Arundel, I've seen too many drunks on ships' bridges, and I had to step in occasionally to keep us off the rocks. It's just not anything I ever started.

"Clever you. I wish there were a few more with that idea. Come and meet some people. Are you married?"

"No."

"Some of the young women here will be pleased." She took him over to where a group of young people were standing.

"Dugald McPherson, this is Mar Fraser and Millie Anstruthers. You might know Millie's father, Captain Anstruthers; apparently, we borrowed him from the Royal Navy for the war."

This was the first time that he had had to take in the change that had happened in social circles where, now, introductions did not begin with 'Miss.' "I have met him, but he was at the top end of the hierarchy when I was at the other."

"He's not really too frightening," said Millie, "and he's around here somewhere."

"Hello, man," said Mar. "You're quite a rarity." She was swaying slightly; her speech was a little slurred. "There are so few men left, you know, and some of the ones that came back have had bits shot off them. Do you have any bits that were shot off you? Some of the men I've met have lost really serious bits." She snickered. "The only thing they can be used for now are monks."

McPherson was new to this kind of conversation. His interactions with women prior to the war had been the rather stilted discussions between ship's officer and lady passenger; most of them during the war had been similarly formal. The only exception had been Ariadne, where their relationship had started because he had needed her expertise.

Mar Fraser, obviously drunk, knowledgeable about male anatomy and gripped by the effects of tragedy, was a problem he had not met. He fell back on the naval officer's principal defence when faced with a difficult social challenge and looked for someone to bring another drink. A waitress was passing with a tray, and he took two glasses and handed one to each woman. Millie gave him a severe look, deftly took the full glass away from Mar and handed it back to the waitress.

"Do you have a cigarette?" asked Mar.

"Yes," he replied, reaching into his inside pocket and pulling out a battered metal case. He turned it quickly in his hand to avoid showing the obvious circular dent on one side, the legacy of a bullet which had ricocheted off the cockpit railing of his motorboat. It was a conversation he did not want to start. He pushed the catch and offered the contents to each woman, then took one himself. Mar fitted hers into a long holder and pulled out a lighter from her purse but failed to match the end of it with the lighter.

"Not used to women smoking, I'll bet," she said.

"Not much," replied McPherson diplomatically.

"Not even in London?"

"Perhaps once in a while," he said. "Let me help." He took the lighter from her and lit the cigarette, then lit Millie's and his own. "We get used to doing this sort of thing on the ship's deck in a stiff breeze," he explained, handing the lighter back. Millie looked at him gratefully and looked across the room to Cynthia for some help.

"Mar, my dear, I need a little help in the dining room," said Cynthia, coming over. She ushered the younger woman away.

Millie watched her go. "Mar was engaged to their older son, Nicholas."

"Peter told me he died at Vimy," he said.

"A captain in the 16th Battalion," she replied.

"That unit drew a lot of men from here. There must be a few bereaved families around."

He sniffed at his drink and changed the subject abruptly. "Pimm's Number One, the mixer of choice," he said. "It shows up at every cocktail party I've ever been to." He put the glass down.

"You must have been confined to the navy," said Millie. "Now they use it to avoid sharing whiskey. Besides, booze is supposedly illegal here at the moment, so the Pimm's camouflages the gin they mix with it."

"Illegal? I seemed to have missed that."

"Since 1917, but you'd never realize it from looking at this lot." She pointed around the room. "There's half the principal legislators in the province in this room, not to mention senior police officers and Michael Arundel's business crowd."

"Influential," he said.

"Very much so," she replied, "and all grateful to be able to indulge themselves without having to follow the same rules as the common herd. The Americans are going for the same thing; the state of Washington has been fooling about with it for years and the entire country goes on it in October."

"You seem well-informed on the subject."

"Talk of it is inescapable. You had an interesting time of it over the last few years," she said, looking at his medal ribbons.

"The navy's very kind when it comes to recognizing normal service," he said.

"Must have changed since my father's day," she

replied.

"Are you a regular in this crowd?"

"Only with my father," she said. "My mother died some years ago, so since 1914, when he went back into the navy, I've done hostess duty." She looked at the crowd milling about the room. "This is a little different from the usual naval mob; there, I usually get treated as if I were my mother." She smiled and her eyes crinkled a little at the edges showing him that it was a comparatively common occurrence.

"This certainly isn't a naval mob," said McPherson. "Apart from Peter, I seem to be the only one in a uniform of any kind."

"You do rather stand out. I hope you have a good run of excuses handy so you can avoid telling people what you did to earn those medals like you just did with me."

"I'm hoping too many people around here don't know as much as you do."

"Don't bet on it. Victoria is a military town. Any man under the age of thirty probably just took off a uniform, and anyone over fifty probably used to have one. The Arundels are well-connected in some surprising places—come and meet a few."

They moved around the room and Millie introduced him to the people she knew. Most of the young women were in their mid- to late-twenties, and there were more of them than he expected. Most of his contemporaries running off to the war had put their lives on hold for four years and the casualty lists had kept the numbers unbalanced.

Peter Arundel appeared and joined them as they went from group to group. McPherson was relieved that most of the younger men kept the conversation to talk of pre-war days.

Several of the older men wanted to talk about his war. This was a conversation for which, at least, he was ready. His natural reserve was supported by the memory of his last discussion with Vice Admiral Sir James Romilly, with whom McPherson had a lot more to do than he had admitted to Arundel. The Admiral was an intense man of medium height who, when out of uniform, which he usually was, could be mistaken for a minor accountant. The incisive message that he gave McPherson before leaving England was fresh in his memory.

"The war is over now, McPherson, at least your part of it is, so please accept both my thanks and that of His Majesty. Go home to that pleasant place of your birth. Find a girl to marry and something to do and settle down. Don't talk about what you've done for us, or I'll get to hear about it sooner than you think. Forget about us if you can and don't ever be tempted to get back into the business for yourself or anyone else. When the government moves large sums of other people's money around, it's a matter of state. If you do it, it's piracy. I will hear about it and I will personally land on you like several tons of bricks. Do you understand?"

"Yes, sir," he had replied.

The Admiral's admonition hung heavily and for the few social occasions involved so far, he had put together a series of stories about naval situations and people which were sufficiently generic. They were close enough to what he could have done and gave him a decent cover for any event. When he met a former naval officer, he managed to keep the other man talking about his own experiences long enough to fill the time.

With the Admiral in mind, he asked Peter, "Is your family close with the Romillys?"

"Close enough, given the distance," Peter replied. "My parents keep pushing me to develop a closer relationship with his son, John, who's about my age—a right prat, from the few times I've met him."

On their way round the edge of the crowd,

heading for the terrace, they caught up with Peter's father talking quietly to a man about ten years older than his son.

"Peter, Commander McPherson, this is Harry Calhoun from Seattle."

"Harry," said Arundel politely.

Calhoun was about Peter's size and dressed in a flamboyant suit that set him well apart from the other men in the room.

"You must be glad to be home," was Calhoun's innocuous opening.

"Indeed so," said Arundel, with the constrained politeness of the British naval officer forced into conversation with someone totally unknown to him. McPherson stayed quietly in the background.

"What now?" asked Calhoun.

"Back to the family business," said Arundel, not wanting to share details with a stranger.

"I've just bought a yacht," said Calhoun. "Not sure I really know how to handle it. If you've nothing better to do, perhaps you could give me a hand." He smiled and melted into the crowd.

"Interesting man," said Millie. "I don't know too many people who can buy a yacht. Must be more money around in America than there is here."

"Some people did quite well supplying American forces during the war." A tall, middle- aged man, dressed a little more formally than most of the younger guests, appeared at Millie's side.

"Hello, Father," she said.

"Sir," said McPherson and Peter simultaneously.

"Nice to see you both," said Captain Anstruthers. He looked at McPherson. "Getting settled back into home life?"

"Hopefully," said McPherson. "You look a little less formal than when we last met."

"Still tying up some loose ends, but I should be

contemplating my garden on a full-time basis in a couple of months."

"I've been in the wardroom for the last few days," said McPherson. "There didn't seem to be a lot going on."

"No," said Anstruthers, "we're handing a couple of jobs back to the Provincial Police and some more to the Royal Canadian Mounted Police, as they will be calling it next year. That's about all the government seems to want us to do."

"What happened to the Royal Northwest Mounted Police?"

"To be amalgamated with the Dominion Police to form this new lot."

"Don't we want to defend the coast?"

"Apparently not—we might officially get in the way of people running liquor down to the States."

McPherson recognized the thread of a privileged conversation. Obviously Millie was part of it as her father's confidante; Michael Arundel had membership judging by the eminence of the guest list at his party, and he and Peter were apparently considered safe. He decided to stay quiet and let information roll toward him at a rate that the others thought was comfortable. He was surprised that Peter kept quiet as well; usually junior officers with a couple of drinks inside them got a bit noisier.

"Come and see me before you leave the dockyard," said Anstruthers.

"Sir," said McPherson as the captain excused himself.

"What are you going to do to keep yourself occupied, Peter?" asked Millie.

"Father's insurance business, I suspect."

"It's fairly steady, I should think," she said with some interest.

"There's a lot to learn. I may go somewhere for a few deep breaths before I settle down."

"On your own?"
"For the moment, yes."

Chapter 5

McPherson was relieved when the crowd started to thin out. The last guests said their cheerful goodbyes with the occasional young woman favouring him with a last lingering look. He undid his jacket and sank gratefully into a chair beside Peter on the terrace. Michael and Cynthia joined them.

"Well," said Michael, "that lot certainly put a dent in my supplies." He didn't seem to be too concerned and put a full tumbler of whiskey into his son's hand.

"I'll see to the dinner," said Cynthia.

Peter sipped the whiskey appreciatively. "Better stuff than that gin you were handing around," he told his father.

"Yes, it is."

"Who's Harry Calhoun?"

"Have you heard of Prohibition in the United States?" Michael asked.

"Something about it. Half the people at the party were talking about it. The Americans must be mad."

"Mad they may be," replied Michael, "but there's a large number of people down there who don't want anything to do with it and they're the ones who will buy any amount of alcohol we can get to them. Our worthy leaders tried the same thing here while you were away. It's collapsing in a heap."

"We?" Peter raised his eyebrows.

Michael grinned and looked levelly at his son. "I might be going to give you another shock. The money I made selling those cars needed to be invested somewhere, so I took a bit and put it into a company called Consolidated Exporters. We sell whiskey and any other kind of drink the Americans want to buy."

"I had to ask enough stupid questions on my way through the ranks of the navy," said Peter, "that I don't mind doing the same of you. How do you sell it to them?"

"We make it a point not to know—officially. People like Harry Calhoun buy loads from us and we consign them, ostensibly, to places up the B.C. coast. Once they leave our wharf, we simply presume they get there, although, to be truthful, if people in the metropolis of Bowen Island drank everything we sent them, they'd be dead before the next shipment arrived. Even for the legendary capacity of Canadians, that's too much."

"What does Harry do, then?"

"I really don't know exactly," said his father. "He picks up from us in Victoria. We have a much larger operation in Vancouver and there's a very different crowd who do business with us there."

"How long have you been involved?" asked his son.

"Not long. The legislation covering all of the United States just became final although several states have been going that way for a while."

"Isn't it illegal to sell to them?"

"Not in Canada, as long as we pay the nineteen dollars a case in excise taxes."

"So, our government gets its share."

"More than its share. Nothing like a politician when it comes to creative taxation."

"What happened to you in the last four years, Father? When I left, you were the model of respectability. I come back to find you selling used cars with a dodgy history and whiskey under the counter."

McPherson thought it was time to see if they wanted him around for the detailed conversation. He leaned forward in his chair.

"Peter, I should probably be getting back to the wardroom."

"By all means stay, Commander; you might find all this of interest," said Michael. "As you have probably found, there's not a lot going on here commercially as we get ourselves straightened out from the war. Things have changed a lot and the rules that prevailed before the war have been adjusted somewhat."

McPherson smiled and sat back. "Thank you, sir. I'm looking for something to be interested in; there seems to be a shortage of available ships' bridges."

"Good show. Let's talk about it over dinner. We'll call you for it in half an hour or so." He got up and went inside.

Peter and McPherson sat quietly and looked over the terrace railing to the water lapping at the rocks that rimmed Gonzales Bay. A wooden stairway ran diagonally down the cliff to a floating dock at its base.

"Is this where you kept your boat?" asked McPherson.

"Yes, although I hid mine at a neighbour's place across the bay. My parents didn't object to the boat as much as they did the time I spent in it, so I had to think of excuses as to why I wasn't around."

"It must have been a lot of time. You were quite the expert when you showed up on *Cabot Cove*."

"Lots of rocks and currents close to home, and I had to deal with most of them if I wanted fish. That was the price the neighbour charged for hiding my boat."

"What did you catch?"

"I had a bit of a route and most of it was in a five-mile radius. Salmon, of course, and crab from that island over there." He pointed to an outcrop showing black against the water, reflecting red from the sun setting behind them. "Rock cod, too, if the tide was right; they stick close to the shore and those rocks below don't leave much room for mistakes."

"Your boat have an engine?"

"Yes, but it was old, and unless I was careful, it would stop at the least convenient time. I carried spare parts as well as oars and a sail."

"If your parents didn't like the time you spent on the boat, how did you explain away the fish?"

"After giving some to the neighbours who helped with the boat and swearing our cook to secrecy, I sold the rest. The money paid for the fuel and repairs and left some over for other things my parents didn't like either." McPherson guessed he was not getting the full story and confirmed it when Arundel changed the subject. "You must have had a few good fishing spots up and down the coast."

"A few, I suppose; I didn't pay too much attention, really, since the cook fed us. If you're the junior hand, someone finds work for you if you're within reach, so I didn't have a lot of spare time. If I had any, I usually had things to do inland."

"What did you do with your time?"

"Went to the library, mostly; I haven't a lot of formal education, so every time I had an exam to write, I needed to brush up on some basic knowledge, and after that I just wandered the shelves and picked up books that looked interesting. I got to know the librarians, and once I could work out the questions, they started to give me more help. I still do that."

"Probably learned a lot more that was useful than I ever did from any of the schools my parents sent me to."

"I wasn't going to live the kind of life they seem to expect you to."

"My brother was to be the respectable one. I

was happy with the idea I'd pick my own path."

"Looks like you're going to have to follow the family path now. You don't seem too excited about it."

"About all I can remember of discussions on the subject is that excitement in insurance is usually a bad thing."

"It's not unlike the sea; peacetime ships' officers work very hard to stay away from excitement. You told Millie you're not about to settle down—does that mean you're not staying here?"

"It means I don't want to be the alternative that Millie's looking for." They both sat quietly until Cynthia came out and called them in for dinner.

The dining salons of Canadian Pacific's Coastal Steamships, particularly those on the triangle run that linked Victoria, Seattle, and Vancouver, were certainly the equal of any ship afloat, and of many first-class hotels. The naval messes ashore had a penchant for silver candlesticks, serving dishes, and table utensils. Their walls were usually adorned with paintings, mostly very large and depicting storms, battles, and admirals of previous centuries. Despite all that, McPherson's experience of formal dining with a family was limited.

The Arundel dining room walls had landscapes, many of places along the coast of Vancouver Island, but no portraits. McPherson was a little surprised. He had thought the family to be a branch of distinguished lineage and expected to see pictures of eminent forebears gazing down. The furnishings were substantial but did not seem to be very old. McPherson had imagined that wealthy families carried their furniture from generation to generation, but the Arundels seemed to have assembled their possessions recently.

The dining room table was long. Michael took his place at one end, and Cynthia took the other. Peter and McPherson faced each other on opposite long sides. Michael passed around a decanter, explaining to both Arundel and McPherson, "We ran out of our stock from France half-way through the war, so rather than pay the rather extravagant prices that they asked, we started to import from Chile. It helps to use one's insurance associates to enhance one's own trade, and their reds and whites are quite drinkable. Pisco is their version of brandy. I know you don't indulge, Commander, but with your permission, I'll pass it in front of Peter's nose."

Unlike the navy, the Arundels did not say grace before meals, and the meal was served by a single maid who withdrew after serving a delicately arranged light salad. Michael opened the conversation by telling McPherson, "It is kind of you to join us, given the experience you must have had with our son on your ship."

McPherson's strength had never been light-hearted banter, but he did his best. "I could say he was not that much trouble, but then you might ask for details." He smiled and hoped the conversation would go in another direction.

"True, but it's good to see you anyway. Would you consider making Victoria your home?"

"As much a possibility as anywhere, I suppose; I've been a seaman since I was fourteen and I went with the ship. When I started, I was on any run they wanted from Seattle to Juneau and every port in between."

"And in the Navy?" McPherson hesitated before answering. He could admit to any location where Arundel had been, but nothing afterward.

"The Baltic, of course, and before that, a fleet destroyer in the Mediterranean; they kept me on anything involving close coastal work. After the Baltic I did odd jobs and navigation training."

"And now?"

"As I was telling Peter, the shipping world is a bit quiet and will likely stay that way for a few months yet."

"Things are equally so on shore," said Michael. "We're all waiting to see how the world unfolds. It's the biggest change we've seen in generations. The Russian, German, Austrian and Ottoman empires are no more. Britain and France are bleeding, and America has discovered its strength. Lots of the people we used to trade with are bankrupt, although much of the money they used to possess is available through London banks. Our job in Canada now is to see where we fit in."

"Are we discussing politics or business?" asked Peter.

"Politicians look after themselves; we have to stay a few steps ahead of them to make a living," replied Michael.

McPherson had not reckoned on a dinner party opening with a succinct discussion on world affairs. Even as a merchant seaman, his part in the economy had been very much a middleman. Someone organized his route to pick up cargoes and someone else did something with them after he had unloaded them. Gossip among the officers on the bridge and shipping agents kept him well aware of where his loads were to be found, and where the money came from to pay for them. "That probably accounts for the lack of interest in getting anything seagoing moving," he said. "If there was any freight to be had, Canadian Pacific would have us pulling rafts to move it. Now they're quite happy to wait for the government to release ships from wartime use."

"In the decayed empires of Europe, people are looking for something to eat; over here, particularly in America, they're looking for something to drink," said Michael. The conversation lapsed to allow the maid to clear the salad plates. She replaced them with a cold salmon dish garnished with mayonnaise that McPherson had never seen before, even when the ship's chef had excelled himself. "It's certainly the best market available to us now," he continued after the maid left.

"I can see that there are people who don't like the idea of Prohibition, but there must have been enough people who wanted it to make the case for the law to be passed," commented Peter.

His father thought for a moment. "I don't pretend to understand Americans, but I can say that in every society there are people, large numbers of them, whose faith is conformity. If someone makes a loud noise about something, they'll go along with it just for a quiet life. There are others who see themselves as the shapers of society. In the case of Prohibition, it's the collection of noisy do-gooders who've claimed the moral high ground. People like that will always be with us; it's just the cause they use to justify themselves that changes."

"Most states seem to be full of breweries and distilleries, and California, in particular, produces a lot of wine. There must be a lot of people who are about to lose their jobs," said Peter.

"I don't think their government cares, any more than our government did here when they tried the same move a couple of years ago—which theoretically remains in force."

"Presumably the drinkers among them are reacting like those who were here this afternoon," observed McPherson.

"Very perceptive of you," said Michael. "British Columbia had to make so many exceptions to the law to get any support for it, and then the man they picked to enforce it was arrested for using forty-five thousand dollars of the province's money to import train-car loads of rye whiskey from Ontario. He organized the process so that no one could find either the whiskey or the proceeds of its sale. The miscreant is in prison for a short time saying nothing, and will, I suppose, enjoy the proceeds on his release."

"The man got his position by lobbying for the legislation, and then ran it to his own advantage. Sometimes I don't think we elect the brightest political leaders," added Cynthia. "It's either that or they're involved somehow."

Michael grinned. "The discussion I was having with Harry Calhoun this afternoon was about how to make our arrangement a little more efficient."

"I wondered what his connection was," said Peter. "He seems a little different from your usual run of acquaintances."

"It's not just empires that have changed," Cynthia put in.

"Your mother's right," said Michael. We justify our business by telling the government we're consigning our shipments to one of the islands up the coast. They don't question the reality of it, because if they did, they'd lose the money from the excise tax and then need to find some other way of making up the revenue."

"It sounds like there's a fairly large organization involved," said McPherson.

"Liquor is just another commodity that has been added to existing trade routes, with, of course, the advantage that the Americans can't add tariffs to it," said Michael.

McPherson thought through the possibilities. Their losses must be mounting and if they're only playing on the sidelines of the business, they are going to have to change the way they run things. "I assume you're directly involved." McPherson put his fork down, "and, since I'm here, I'm assuming you're wanting me to be involved in some way."

"Consolidated Exporters handles the merchandise, and they have a policy of replacing stock that's lost in transit for any reason. We organize the dollars to meet that need," said Michael.

"How does Harry Calhoun fit in?" asked Peter.

"He buys from Consolidated Exporters, and at the moment he has more customers than he can supply. The company finds him to be a reliable partner and would like to help him."

"What causes a supply problem?"

"In this case, it's an issue with the kind of boats he's using and the people he's using to crew them. At first, traders could get by with any old boat they could lay their hands on. Now the authorities have improved their ability to intercept cargoes on land and the Coast Guard is more in evidence than it used to be. There's also some raiding of cargoes on both the sea and on shore. The men doing the running need a little more speed, a lot more skill, and boats that are easier to unload. We want to cut down on the cargo losses, as well."

McPherson now knew why he had been invited to stay, but despite the details coming out, thought he was getting less than a full story.

Dinner finished at eleven o' clock, and after a desultory conversation about the Victoria social scene Peter took McPherson out to the car. He drove slowly enough to let them talk.

"Enjoy yourself?" he asked.

"I suppose so. It's the first time I've been in that sort of company. Is there anyone in the city who does anything except send liquor southward?"

"Oh yes, people work in the law, banking, coal mining, lumber, fishing, and ranching in the interior. Most of the conventional stuff is like shipping—very quiet at the moment. A lot of them work for the government, collect pensions, or live off investments or money sent out by families somewhere else. Getting involved with people in the liquor trade gives them some excitement. A few of them are investors in my father's insurance pool."

"I doubt your family is there for the excitement. I take it that your apparent surprise at hearing of your father's range of business activities was window dressing for my benefit?"

Arundel grinned. "Yes, it was. We were only sure of your discretion when you stayed to hear the details."

"And the greatest need is to pick up speed in delivering the trade goods?"

"Yes."

"Which is something with which I, together with you, have had some recent experience." McPherson looked out over the straits and paused. "Is this a job offer?"

"It's certainly a suggestion that you could come in with us."

"Doing what, precisely?"

"At the moment we deliver stock to Calhoun's agent, who picks it up in Victoria and takes it down to Seattle. He uses a converted fishing boat which takes a biggish load but goes slowly. He's lost a few loads to hijackers and government agents when he lands, and we have to meet the cost of insuring the loss. Also, I think the man he uses is an awful navigator and he's come back a few times with the load still on board because he got lost. We're looking for ways to do it better."

"You're telling me a lot about your family business. You seem pretty sure I'll join you."

"We hope you will, but nothing I've told you couldn't be discovered in any bar in Victoria, except, of course, the real details of the rum trade operations. The men who're doing it never say anything about it to anyone."

"As I'm certain you've already realized, you have two problems. The first is the kind of boat you use, and the second is the people you use to crew it."

"In a nutshell, yes."

"What do you want me to do that you can't do for yourself?"

"Let's start with the boat."

McPherson thought for a moment and looked out at the houses lining the darkened streets. "We just spent a few years running fast boats in difficult jobs. Wouldn't be that different, I suppose. Have to work out what kind of a boat we need. I've seen enough boats that people tried to adapt from the purpose for which they were built, and it rarely works well."

"Does that mean you're in?"

McPherson's immediate prospects were limited. The bank had lost his money, and the choice was doing something essentially illegal or finding something quite different—and as Arundel had pointed out, everything was quiet.

"I might just as well give this some consideration," he said after a minute. "Who runs the show? Harry Calhoun?"

"At the moment, yes."

"Um," said McPherson noncommittally, "that might not be too good—doing something illegal for someone I don't know."

"We would probably take over that part of it and leave Calhoun as the man we deliver to."

"Again, doing something illegal for someone I don't really know."

"You know us."

"I had you on my ship for a year as a highly irresponsible young officer Your father, I met today. This is not a long-standing association." They drove for a few blocks in silence. "However," said McPherson, "In the short term I need money and I need something to do, so until the bank problem is sorted out and until the shipping business improves, I might as well come in with you."

"As you saw today, business circles in Victoria are quite small. They allow people of influence to make their views known to one another and avoid misunderstandings becoming unmanageable, so if there's a problem, we can get help."

"Let's hope it applies to operations in areas of questionable legality."

Even as he said it, McPherson thought wryly of the change that had come over him during five years in the navy. The young second officer of 1914 could not have dissembled his phrasing as neatly as the Lieutenant Commander of 1919 found easy, nor would he ever have considered a job like this. They rumbled back over the Bay Street Bridge. The Gorge Inlet reflected the occasional light from the shore, showing its watery way up through the west side of the city.

"Where do you think we need to start?" asked Arundel.

"Depends on what 'start' means."

"Finding the right boat for the job and delivering to Harry Calhoun."

"There seems to be a lot missing from that statement. If Calhoun is the buyer, is he the only buyer? What happens to the less-than-reliable man who's doing the work now? Is he still in the picture, and are we an addition to the operation? Also, I know where you sit in all of this, but I'm not sure where I fit in, apart from lending some expertise in boat handling."

"I think my father was hoping you would run the American delivery side."

"The risky bit, you mean." McPherson stayed quiet until they came to the dockyard gate where the policeman on the barrier raised it and saluted when he saw McPherson's uniform cap. As they came up to the wardroom entrance, Arundel stalled the car.

"You need lots more practice at this," remarked McPherson, "and I still need lots more details."

"Why don't we talk it over tomorrow?"

"I'm still trying to organize my way out of the navy. Perhaps I can call you when I'm clear."

McPherson got out of the car and watched as the car lurched away into the darkness. "Every time we get close to the details, the discussion is interrupted," he thought.

Chapter 6

Monday, August 25th, 1919

By five forty-five, McPherson was outside. The first signs of dawn appeared behind the ridge overshadowing the harbour. The dry-dock on the south side was empty. The one ship that lay alongside the jetty was clean, which said more about its infrequent sailings than it did about its efficient crew.

After about an hour of picking his way past vacant buildings, empty piers, and an undisturbed foreshore, he was ready for breakfast, and headed for the wardroom. The dockyard officer of the watch was there before him and nodded politely.

"On the way out?"

"Hopefully so, once I finish with the demob office."

The man looked at the stripes on McPherson's sleeves. "Back to the folks you were with before?"

"Not for a while. We need to sort out some ships first. You?"

"I'm still making up my mind. There's little enough to do outside, and a reliable salary pays for a lot of boredom."

McPherson smiled as he reached for the morning newspaper. "Something in that, I suppose." He opened the paper. The man took the hint and left him to it.

The Hapsburg rule in Hungary was coming to

an end, and German money had made a major inroad in Mexico over the last couple of years. He wondered how much of it had come loose from the fall of European empires and found its way into Canada. A small article, datelined Russia, caught his eye. The regime of Admiral Kolchak, who had been the direct beneficiary of his operations in the Caspian Sea, was failing.

The newer, twin-engine patrol boats they had used there might be useful for what the Arundels had in mind. The business idea was far enough away from their use in the Caspian that the consequences of ignoring Admiral Romilly's unequivocal homily about keeping his mouth shut probably would not arise. Their boats had done well over forty knots, faster than anything in local waters. He mulled over the concept as he finished his coffee, and walked down to the demobilization office to, with any luck, become a civilian.

He was the only one in the office, but every staff member had his head down and appeared to be busy doing something. Strang looked up from his desk and called him over.

"Had a good weekend, did you?"

"Well enough."

"We owe you seven thousand, six hundred and forty-eight dollars, and fifty cents."

McPherson sat back and had to wait for a moment or two before he could reply. "That's more than I expected."

"I can share it out around the office, if you prefer."

McPherson dutifully smiled at another shopworn joke. "I'll find a way to manage with it."

Strang reached into his lower desk drawer and pulled out a stiff-backed ledger holding a stack of blank cheques. He laboriously filled out the counterfoil page then repeated the process with the cheque itself. As

Strang scratched away at another form, McPherson had some time to let the information settle in.

It was enough money to buy a house in one of the better parts of town. He could sit in it, if he wanted, and wait for jobs to appear. He could travel and look at possibilities in other parts of the globe. Added to the money that Armitage had implied would likely reappear, his immediate concerns had evaporated.

Strang blotted the ink on the second form and looked up. He tore the cheque out of the register and passed it and the form to him.

"That's your discharge from active service. Unless you resign, you will remain in your present rank, as an officer in the Royal Canadian Naval Reserve. Do you have an address where you can be reached in the event that his Majesty has further use for your services?"

"I don't. I'll use General Delivery, Victoria for the time being."

"When you get something of longer duration, write to this address," he said, pointing to the top of the form. "You can wear your uniform on a daily basis for the next thirty days and stay in the wardroom for another couple of nights. The navy will send you a note about annual training requirements, but that probably won't come for a few months yet, and it really is just a way of keeping the reserve list up to date. There usually will be no need to report in personally. If circumstances require you to go active, they'll probably be obvious enough from the newspapers. Good luck, and with any amount of equally good fortune, we probably won't see you again."

McPherson went upstairs to the second floor of the headquarters building and walked down to an office at the end of the hall. He tucked his hat under his left arm and tapped on the door.

"Come in."

He opened the door. "Sir," he said.

"McPherson. Sit down."

Anstruthers' office had a view over the Straits of Juan de Fuca, the lighthouse at the harbour entrance in the foreground, Trial Island in the middle distance. Before the war, the water between them would have been full of ships and other watercraft, but today the sea was empty.

"All finished at the pay office and set to leave us?"

"Looks like it, sir. There may a bit of paper catching up in the next few months, but I'll look like a civilian tomorrow."

"Enjoy yourself yesterday?"

"Very different from places I've been before."

"Know the Arundels well?"

"First time I've been to their house, sir. I had young Peter on board my ship for a while in '16 and '17."

Anstruthers grunted but did not push the point. "They're very well-connected, both here and in London. You might consider being very careful in any dealings you have with them. They look after their own interests first, and anyone involved with them is only useful so long as he contributes to the job they have at hand."

McPherson sat back in his chair. "I did find the eminence of the company a little overwhelming."

"That's a good start, anyway. I've spent my life in the Royal Navy, and all of it has been keeping trade routes open. Some of the skullduggery I've seen British traders initiate has been enough to start local wars, and I used a lot of my time finishing them before too much damage was done. I've seen many people like the Arundels before, and I've had to use my ship's guns to get a few of them out of problems they caused."

"The government must have been irritated, sir."

"Usually not. Someone in London was making

money out of the incident, and the only reason to keep an expensive navy was to help them make more money."

"I suppose now the war is over it will be back to normal, then," McPherson said.

"Whatever 'normal' means. The imperial government leaned on Canada earlier this century to take more responsibility for its own defence. That meant forming the Royal Canadian Navy, amongst other things, but the Canadian government is dragging its heels on fleshing it out, especially after the war. The Arundels seem to have been well-organized for the end of hostilities."

He paused and looked out of the window for a moment. "I was surprised to see Harry Calhoun there yesterday. Harry is well below their usual social set, so it may be that Arundel needs some more quick money to get something else going. The business he had with surplus government motor cars seems to have run its course. My guess is he won't take unnecessary risks for longer than he has to, so be careful you aren't his path out of them. The one thing I learned when I was stationed in Hong Kong is that the more gentlemanly the manners, the bigger the pirate there is behind. It's an unusual thing to find an engineer officer doing—they're usually quite conservative, so he deserves careful attention for that reason alone. What did they offer you?" The captain inserted the question deftly.

"Nothing definite, just asked some questions about coastal navigation," McPherson replied, noting the warning but keeping the details of the evening conversation to himself.

"They often find a way to do you a favour just so you feel a sense of obligation to them. It's a form of gentle persuasion that works well for them."

McPherson thought of his absent bank account followed by the convenient job offer. Was that a coincidence?

"Remember that, in their view, you're not part of the family, just someone to be used for as long as it's convenient They'll make absolutely sure you only know what is absolutely necessary about their affairs, so whatever they offer you it's only a minor part of the whole story. I'm glad my daughter grew up in the knowledge of the risks out there. You may have noticed she's likely to be more impressed by a chartered accountant than a modern-day adventurer."

"I enjoyed meeting her," said McPherson neutrally.

The captain stood up. "I hope we'll see each other again," he said, ending the conversation.

McPherson got up, pulled himself to attention and put his hat back under his arm. "Thank you, sir."

He walked over to the wardroom. Although money would not be an immediate problem, without employment it could disappear fast enough. And without a cushion, there would be nothing to help if he were ill or injured. He was no longer a twenty-two-year-old with no cares. He needed to find a reliable bank to keep it safe for him.

Yesterday's exposure to the Arundel family and friends gave him alternatives. The newspaper had advertisements for houses that were now within his grasp. The thought of making a firm shore base was something new but nothing in Victoria would be of much use if he had to leave.

He reached the door of the wardroom as the lobby clock was chiming eight bells for noon, and he went into the dining room for lunch. The room was empty, but before long the morose officer of the watch joined him.

"All settled?" he asked.

"Yes. I'll ship out after lunch."

"Sure you wouldn't like a few days free room and board?"

"Thanks for the suggestion, but I've a room

booked in town. It's probably wise to keep my nose as close to the waterfront as possible."

"I'll get the duty driver to run you down, then; all he does is sleep."

Chapter 7

"Strathcona Hotel, please," he told the driver after they collected his box from Vickers Storage. He checked in while the driver took the box from the back of the car. The hotel room was comfortable, much larger than any ship's cabin he had lived in with space for his bag, trunk, and storage box. He could stay there for as long as he wanted, and he was grateful that he could afford something better than the dockside flophouses or indifferent boarding houses he had used in earlier days.

He sat back and took the cheque from his pocket. The experience with the bank and the money missing from his account had given him an unwelcome sense of vulnerability, and like any other unexpected attack, caused him to think about how he would defend himself against something similar in the future. If he took the Arundels up on their offer, albeit temporarily until something else turned up, it could be lucrative. There was definitely personal risk involved, so how much would that be worth?

He jumped up, stuffed the cheque back in his pocket, and left the hotel. If he was going to sea again he would need to replace the seagoing clothing he had taken to the Salvation Army. His visit to the elegant Cartwright's had not included any robust working gear. The Hudson's Bay Company warehouse was on Wharf Street; what it may have lacked in sophistication, it made up for in efficiency. The clerk readily assessed his size once he said what he wanted, and in ten minutes he had two pairs of canvas trousers, two mackinaw shirts, and a set of oilskins packed into a duffel bag ready to take out. He told the clerk he would be back later to collect it and headed for the bank. When he got there, he asked for Armitage and was quickly shown into his office.

"Good morning, Commander." Armitage sounded a little too hearty. "I'm pleased that we managed to sort your problem out."

"So you can let me have my money?"

"Not quite at the moment—when your first remittance came through, we inadvertently transferred your account to our London office. Please accept our most sincere apologies. I have wired them this morning to return your information and we should have everything straightened out in a few weeks."

McPherson groaned, "A few weeks? What if I should need the money sooner than that?"

"The bank would be pleased to extend an overdraft should it be necessary."

"I've never had an overdraft, but I understand you would charge me for the privilege."

"Indeed so, Commander."

"I don't really have the inclination to argue at the moment, but I will remember this exchange and it doesn't leave me a good opinion of your bank. I will be back weekly to find out how this process is proceeding." He walked out onto Government Street very certain the Bank of New Caledonia was no place to deposit his newly acquired cheque.

He remembered the bank he had passed earlier where the poet Robert Service had worked and got through the front door just before the three o'clock closing. Once again, his uniform made him a respectable prospect, and a clerk hurriedly ushered him into the manager's office.

The man stood up as he came in. "Good

afternoon, Commander. I'm John Bannister."

"Dugald McPherson." He took the envelope from his inside pocket and extracted the cheque. "I'd like to open an account," he said, laying it on the manager's desk.

"This is a very large sum, indeed."

"I spent a long time waiting for it."

"Do you have an account with us anywhere else?"

"No. Why do you ask?"

"We like to know our customers, and this is a comparatively large sum to come in from the street to a bank where you are not known."

"I have an account with another bank, but the service has been less than satisfactory, so I thought I would try you."

"Indeed, Commander McPherson. Were you referred to us?"

"No. Should I have been?"

"Not necessarily. What was the nature of your dissatisfaction with the other bank?"

"Do you wish to open an account for me or not?" McPherson reached across the desk to pick up the cheque.

"Certainly, Commander, certainly." Bannister hurriedly pulled a form from his desk drawer.

"Address?"

"I don't have one yet. I'll get a post office box in the next few days. It's likely enough that I'll stay in Victoria, so for the moment I'm at General Delivery."

"The cheque will take three days to clear, so you won't be able to draw any money from the account until after then. What would you like to do with the money?"

"Leave it in the account," he replied, puzzled. "What else is there?"

"We can offer you some choices which would give you a better investment return than a simple account can offer."

"I'll think about that later when I'm more certain about what I'll be doing."

"Do you have a job to go to?" said Bannister, pulling a passbook and an envelope with blank cheques from his desk drawer.

"Probably not for a year or so. Most of the companies I have spoken to are waiting for ships to either come back from the war or get built to replace war losses."

"So I hear. Would you be interested in some small boat work?"

"How small?"

"Some of our customers have gone into coastal freight delivery in a small way."

Was there anyone in this city not pushing bottles into the States? "Thanks for the suggestion, but I have enough money to last for a little while, so I'll take a bit of a rest for a few weeks before doing anything." He left the bank thinking that Bannister would probably try to find him before he saw the need to do the reverse.

The cheques and the account papers were sticking out of his pockets. He was uncomfortable at the lack of the trim appearance expected of naval officers in public. He already owned a battered canvas case which he used to carry rolled charts and his sextant, but it was large, obvious, and inconvenient for daily use. He went into Cartwright's.

"I need something to carry these," he said, spreading the loose items across the counter in front of the owner. "Is there a case I can use to carry documents?"

"Yes, of course, Commander," said Cartwright. He produced a slim, black, buckled bag from a drawer behind him. "I think this will be suitable. It's quite weatherproof. While you're here, we've finished the boating jacket and one pair of grey trousers. Perhaps you can take them now, together with a pair of shirts and the trench coat."

"I'm surprised," said McPherson, as he pulled out his wallet to count out the money. "You're almost the only person in Victoria who hasn't mentioned, directly or obliquely, the potential for getting involved in the liquor delivery business."

"Tailors, Commander, are by profession, discreet," said Wilson, smiling.

Back at the hotel, he called Arundel from a public telephone in the lobby. Arundel answered immediately and asked, "Do you know the Belmont Club?"

"I know of it, but I wasn't in those circles when I left here," McPherson replied.

"Neither was I, and the place has a new building, so even if you knew the old one, it wouldn't help. It's on Gordon Street, opposite the Empress Hotel. I'll see you there in an hour."

He thought about changing out of his uniform, but he had no idea what the right dress for visitors to this particular club might be. He had been to many similar establishments in London as a guest of members. He had found that each had its own rules of conduct, and in particular, appropriate dress. Wartime had allowed ordinary uniforms to be worn at all times of the day. In his brief stay in the city, he had taken out a membership in the Naval and Military Club. The Belmont Club was similar, so presumably shared some of the same rules.

He dropped his case in his room and opened his box. He sorted through the notebooks which had been his constant companions since his first days at sea. He looked for the ones likely to have details for Puget Sound and the Gulf Islands and leafed through them for any information that might be useful. He quickly realized that information gained from piloting a coastal steamer between large ports left a number of gaps compared to what was needed to run smaller vessels close to shore. For a moment he wished he had spent some time on fishing boats or running tugs pulling log booms. He was thankful he had remembered to make notes on navigational hazards of all kinds, as they posed as much danger to large craft as they did to small ones. He had also noted places where he might meet other ships. Three quarters of an hour went quickly, and he had only enough time for a quick look over his collection. He took out his current notebook and put it in the side pocket of his jacket.

The Belmont Club was the large building he had noticed on the corner of Gordon and Humboldt Streets, and was just over a block away from his hotel. He recalled hearing discussion among his more eminent passengers of its new building being opened in 1913. At that time no one had seen the need to introduce an acting second officer for membership, which was fortunate because the fees would have been beyond him. He walked down the steep hill of Gordon Street to the stairway leading up to the club's ornate entrance. The name appeared nowhere on the outside of the building; many London clubs had been similarly unidentified. One hall porter had explained to him that anyone who had business inside would know what it was. It seemed he was reaching into the world of social acceptability. He pushed open the door and found Arundel waiting for him on the other side of a second door.

"Drink?" said Arundel, leading the way into a lounge directly behind the lobby. They sat down at a corner table.

"Soda water, please."

'You won't mind taking on a job delivering liquor to other people when you don't drink it yourself?"

"I haven't agreed to take on the job yet, but no, it's their choice, not mine."

"It's probably time to talk about some details, then."

Arundel signaled a steward and asked for a whiskey and a soda water siphon with a second tumbler. McPherson pulled out his notebook.

"Better put that away; there's an obscure rule in here that business can't be discussed in the dining room or lounges," said Arundel.

"In heaven's name, why?" asked McPherson.

"I have no idea," replied Arundel. "It probably has something to do with some less-discerning members in earlier times using the cachet of the club to push some less-than-reliable propositions."

"Like rum-running, for example?"

"Worse than that—probably something unprofitable, or even outright fraudulent."

"So, where do we start?" said McPherson. "We were going to talk about Harry Calhoun, and where you fit in. Exactly what sort of operation are we to run, and what would be my part?"

Arundel added some soda to his whiskey, sat back in his chair and paused for a few moments before replying. McPherson saw with approval that he filled the tumbler to the top.

"Harry is the man in Seattle we sell to."

"Does he buy from other people as well? And how do you deliver to him now?"

"I don't know all the details. When we met on the boat last week, I had stopped over in Vancouver for a couple of days, and all I know about the business is what my father has told me since last Thursday. My brother was supposed to be the one taking over. I've been having a fairly intensive exposure to a number of bits of it that I didn't know existed until last week." He paused and took another sip of his whiskey. "The rum-running business is profitable, and we can't afford to ignore it. We've been keeping Harry supplied as much to keep other people out of the trade as to keep him in it. The men we have been employing have been a pretty mixed bunch, and because the opposition hasn't been too well organized, we've been able to keep things going."

"What's changed, and who's the opposition?" asked McPherson.

Arundel painted a haphazard picture of operations. An assortment of slow and cumbersome fishing boats and pleasure craft which were prone to run out of fuel, hijacked boats and loads, indifferent navigators and unhappy investors. "Altogether, it's organization that's lacking. That boat we saw from the ferry was one of ours and he came back without delivering the load."

"You obviously need better boats and better crews," said McPherson. "Tell me where I fit in, and then we can talk about boats."

"We have about five people running boats for us now, all going directly into Puget Sound. There are other people doing a much larger trade by stationing large vessels off the Washington, Oregon, and California coasts which supply smaller craft that deliver to shore. There's a good market for us in Puget Sound, but we need to move more merchandise, and to be competitive, we need to do it reliably." Arundel stopped and swirled the whiskey in his glass for a moment. "Some of the people we use now won't be too happy if we stop using them, but that might be the only alternative. My father cobbled together an agreement with his acquaintances in the trade to divide Puget Sound between them. We deal with Harry, and other people here deal with his competitors. It's important that we avoid going head-to-head with one another, but some of his competitors do take pot shots at us."

"You need to think of ways to avoid battles," said McPherson. "What about the American government?"

"The American Coast Guard has one cutter in

the Sound; it's a converted tug called the *Arcata* that does about twelve knots and carries a one pounder gun. The captain isn't slow to use if someone doesn't heave-to when hailed."

"Twelve knots is enough to match most fishing boats, but not anything that goes faster and stays out of gun range. Of course, the best thing is to avoid having him see you at all."

"Spoken like a good naval tactician—which is why we would like you to take over the running of the business in the Sound."

"Why not you? It's your family. I assume there's a lot of money involved—why bring in someone from outside? I could do some work to put the right kind of boat together and train someone to run it—you, for example—and leave you to it."

"The family, that being my parents and remnants remaining in England, appear to have decided that my commercial contributions are to be land-based from now on."

"And out of gun range, too, presumably?"

"Certainly sea-borne, anyway."

"So, how much?"

"Four hundred dollars a month starting today, with an additional eleven dollars a case for anything you deliver yourself, plus four dollars for every case delivered by any other boat you succeed in adding into our business."

McPherson sat back in his chair while he took in the details of the offer. It was a lot of money, about three times as much as he would earn with Canadian Pacific. "You're either making an enormous amount of money in this business, or you have a very large problem indeed. I really don't want to get involved if it's an all-out shooting war out there."

"It'll be like the Baltic where we spent a lot of time using your superior seamanship skills to keep us out of trouble," replied Arundel, topping up

McPherson's drink with the soda siphon. "Do you still have that ability to flatten someone who tries to hit you?" he asked.

"I had to use it on a couple of occasions in the last year. Is that a necessary skill?"

"It's more useful than continuing a fist or a knife fight. Harry and the people he's using haven't learned it."

"Interesting way of looking at things. How much will you be involved? Would I work for you or your father?"

"My father runs the business. I'm just his errand boy."

"I'd like to see more of the delivery end, and then I'll have a better idea of the kind of boat that could be used. The Coastal Motorboats we had in the Baltic might serve as a model, although chucking booze over the side is a bit different than firing torpedoes."

"We could round up Harry and use his yacht for a leisurely run to Seattle and back."

"Was that the reason for this conversation?"

Arundel did not answer but said, "Harry's at the Driard Hotel on View Street. He uses the dining room instead of an office. Let's go and see him."

"Dugald wants to see a little more of the operation," said Arundel when they found Harry sitting at a table at the back. "He'd like to know more about the Seattle end."

"Why don't we take a run down in the *Eloise?*" Harry said.

"When can we leave?" asked Arundel.

"Right now all right with you?"

McPherson looked at his watch. "It's just over sixty-five nautical miles, so as long as neither of you mind an overnighter, that's fine with me, but I need to get out of this uniform, so I'll need to go back to my hotel and get some gear. I'd like to look over the boat before we go, so I think leaving tomorrow morning would be better. On the way, we should take some time poking around the Sound and look at some of the places along the coast we might want to use for deliveries."

"The boat's docked at the Victoria Yacht Club wharf in the inner harbour," said Harry.

He had the evening to leaf through every one of his books for pointers on Puget Sound. When he shed his uniform, it occurred to him that this might be for the last time.

Chapter 8

Tuesday, August 26th, 1919

The next morning, McPherson slipped his notebook into the large side pocket of his new jacket and loaded a bag for overnight. The warm August air cut the need for heavy clothes, but he reached into his trunk and took out his watch-keeping hat. The peak would cut the glare from sunlight on the water. He felt strange as he made his ununiformed way across Douglas Street and down Fort Street to the harbour. Calhoun's yacht stood out, larger than he expected; one hundred and twenty-five feet long, two decks above the waterline, and a covered wheelhouse. It had a large funnel amidships, and masts fore and aft. He cast a critical eye over every surface and fitting in sight and was pleased to see that everything was clean; equipment that should be snugged down had been, and there were no loose ropes or other hazards in sight.

"You can stop the inspection now, Pilot."

Arundel's voice came down from the upper deck. "Harry has a crew to look after things."

"That's reassuring," said McPherson, continuing his examination.

"The steward'll show you the way up here."

A middle-aged Chinese man stepped out of a doorway to the deck in front of the gangway. "This way, sir," he said, pointing to a companionway leading up to the promenade deck behind the bridge. He led the way through a door into the wheelhouse, and as McPherson looked around at its impressive fittings, asked whether he would like a coffee or a stronger drink.

"Neither, for the moment, thank you," replied McPherson, looking directly at Calhoun. "Ready to take a run down to Seattle?"

"So Peter tells me," replied Calhoun with a slight smile.

McPherson grinned back as he cast a rapid professional survey over the spotless wheelhouse. "Nice ship. Presumably she cruises at about eighteen knots?" he asked.

"Yes," Calhoun replied. "The US navy owned her until a couple of months ago, and they only had her for the duration of the war. Before that she was someone's yacht. She has a triple expansion steam engine, and most people buying boats this size are going for diesel or high-speed gas engines. The price was right and she's in good shape."

"Biggish for an amateur sailor. You conn her yourself?"

"Most of the time; we only run her between Seattle and Victoria, sometimes to smaller ports or Vancouver, and only in daylight. I don't know much about navigation, but I have a *Puget Sound Pilot...*" he picked up a book from the ledge in front of the wheel and waved it, "...to tell me about tides and places to avoid. Then I have a couple of crewmen—Yang, who you met on the way in who triples as steward, cook and deckhand, and Welland, the engineer, who looks after the ship."

"Where are your charts?"

"Over there behind you in the cabinet under the table, but I don't have too many."

McPherson looked where Calhoun was pointing and went over to the table. He opened the drawer and riffled through the stock.

"There's not much here about the coast beyond Seattle. How did you get here?"

"We came in daylight, and Yang found Victoria quite easily."

"I won't be leaving with you unless you're carrying a full set of charts for Vancouver Island, the Southern coast of British Columbia and the Olympic Peninsula, including all of Puget Sound."

"Why do we need them?" asked Calhoun.

"You haven't done much sailing, have you? Every ship, particularly one this size, needs to carry charts for all the waters within the range of its fuel tanks. Once you're out there, the weather can close down, and you have no idea where you are. Even if you slow down to ten knots and avoid hitting a rock somewhere, you can be sixty miles in another direction before the weather clears. Before the war, I spent all my working life in these waters, and I never take them for granted. Nor does anyone else who plans to be alive beyond the end of the next week."

Calhoun looked back at him and paused for a moment. "Where do we get them?"

"The Dominion Government Marine and Fisheries Office. It's in the Customs Building on Wharf Street."

"I guess you know what charts to ask for."

"I do."

"Will you get them for me?"

McPherson looked at his watch. "They're probably open now. Peter, will you come with me? There'll be about fifty sheets, and we'll get spares for the ones that get used a lot." He looked back at Calhoun. "It'll probably cost about twenty-five cents a sheet. Oddly enough, I never had to buy them myself; the company always provided them. Now Peter can." He searched around the bridge for something to carry them in and found a large canvas bag behind the chart cabinet.

"Someone used this to stock up at some point," he said, and he beat the accumulated debris of years from both inside and out.

They left the yacht and walked up to Wharf Street. The Government Marine office overlooked the harbour and was open.

"I don't know why, when they open at nine, they always have to close at three," said McPherson. "They're not overworked." They went inside and McPherson asked the clerk for a catalogue. He took out his notebook and meticulously copied the reference numbers and titles of the sheets that they wanted. He asked Arundel to hand him an order form from the rack on the counter. He transcribed the list equally carefully and rechecked his list before handing it over to the man behind the counter. The attendant ran the list against another of his own.

"I can give you everything you want, sir, except those covering Bellingham and Whidbey Island. There seems to have been a bit of a rush on those recently. We won't be bringing in any more of the American charts; we've asked the local ships' chandlers to take over supplying them."

McPherson grunted and marked the absent ones in his notebook with a precise "X." The clerk was missing his left arm yet managed to deftly extract each chart and place it on the top of the chest before reaching into the drawer for another. McPherson had Arundel leaf through them and recheck them against his list.

Together they rolled up the charts and tied them with twine. McPherson left it to Arundel to pay and carry the load. "I'll lay you odds that clerk there lost an arm in France and was lucky enough to get back here before the rush. He got that job before a bunch of similarly injured men came looking for the same one."

"Lucky it wasn't one of us who lost the arm," replied Arundel. "I'll remember that when we start taking more risks."

At the yacht, Arundel unrolled the bundle onto the chart table. They resorted them and stowed them in the shallow drawers under the surface, then went down to the saloon on the deck below, where Calhoun was leafing through a boating magazine.

"Looking for a new one?" asked Arundel.

"Not really; it's just that with you and McPherson talking about marine things, I need to learn what the words mean."

"I told you Dugald was keen on details and doesn't take any chances he doesn't need to."

"What are you likely to want to do in Seattle? Drink? Find women?" Calhoun asked, looking at McPherson.

"I don't drink, and my fiancée died last year. I'm not looking for a replacement just yet."

"Not a lot of monks in this business."

"All I care about is making a living until a proper job shows up, and then I'll leave you to it," said McPherson.

"Again—what do you expect to do in Seattle?"

"Meet some of the people involved, think about what kind of a boat we will need, get some idea of where to deliver."

"I'll tell you where to deliver."

"It hasn't worked too well so far with you trying to run the boats and pick up on land as well," said Arundel. "Your men either get lost or get picked off by your competition. We've had to replace four loads under the insurance agreement, and you've missed another five because the delivery boat went somewhere else. It's not a good start to a business. We can work with you if you agree to let us handle the deliveries. You concentrate on picking up the load from the beach. That means Dugald will tell you where he's going to deliver and how, and when he wants the pickup done. Besides, both of us are used to running boats at night, and the likelihood is that all our deliveries will be done then, too," said Arundel.

Calhoun was silent for a moment, covering up some obvious irritation. "Most of the people I use to pick up don't like being ordered about."

Arundel gave him a level stare. "You'd better let them know that Dugald is a hard man, and a smart one too. If anyone has worries, make sure they tell him. Dugald will listen and then make the decision."

"What's that book you're carrying?" said Calhoun looking from Arundel to McPherson.

"Notes I made about navigating Puget Sound before the war."

"Won't have changed much in two years."

McPherson gave him a cold stare. "You Americans seem to forget that we were at it since 1914."

"Sorry—just a slip."

McPherson slapped his notebook on the small table beside Calhoun, and himself into the chair between him and Arundel.

"It's not particularly detailed, because on the trips I took down there the officers on the bridge were fairly experienced and the route was well-marked. All the notes I took had more to do with the harbours, and we probably won't be going into the larger ones; still, if we're going down there, I can make some use of them. When are we leaving?"

"Now, I suppose," replied Calhoun.

"It's just over six hours point to point," said McPherson. "On the way down, I'd like to go closer to the east side of the Sound and look at some likely landing sites."

Calhoun called Yang into the saloon. "We're casting off now. Is everything ready?"

The steward nodded. "You want me to steer the boat?" he asked in a heavily accented voice.

"Mr. McPherson here will be in the

wheelhouse; he'll tell you what to do."

Yang glanced at McPherson with an expressionless look and said nothing. McPherson said, "Come up when you've secured the lines. I'd like to see your engine room before we go anywhere."

They went out onto the deck and through a doorway located amidships. The companionway on the other side was narrow and Calhoun led the way calling out, "Welland!" as they went down.

The engine room was spotless, and every loose item stowed in its correct place. The boiler was fired, and the engine shaft was quietly rotating. McPherson grunted his approval as Calhoun said, "Welland, this is Mr. McPherson; he and Mr. Arundel here are coming down to Seattle with us. Mr. McPherson will be conning the ship."

The engineer stepped over the shaft tunnel and came up to them with an oil can in his left hand and a wiping cloth in the other. "Welland," said McPherson, "we've met."

"Yes, sir, I was with Canadian Pacific as an apprentice."

McPherson grunted again and looked around. "You keep a good engine room."

"Thank you, sir."

"We'll be ringing down in a few minutes."

Back in the wheelhouse, McPherson took the wheel while Arundel went to the wing overlooking the wharf. Yang was standing by the bow line.

"We'll cast off the stern lines first," said McPherson.

"Why are you doing that?" Calhoun asked him.

"It's better to let the stern swing free before engaging the propeller. The tide's ebbing, and with the stern clear of the dock, there's more room to move once the wheel's hard over—besides, then I'm less likely to grind your paint work."

"Cast off aft!" Arundel called over the side and

watched Yang move slowly to complete the task. "Cast off forrard!" and Yang moved equally slowly.

McPherson sat on his frustration and moved back to the wheel. He rang "Slow Astern" on the engine telegraph. Welland proved more alert than Yang; the propeller bit into the water and the ship moved backwards. As soon as their motion was measurable, McPherson rang "Slow Ahead" and swung the wheel over to pick up a course that would take them clear of Colville Island, an ambitiously named rock poking out of the water about fifty yards off their starboard bow, and about the same distance from the northern shore of the harbour.

"She'll go a lot faster," said Calhoun.

"Not until I can see what's coming the other way she won't, and there's local traffic I wouldn't trust not to hit us, so keeping the speed down until we're out of the harbour is the rule." The edge in his voice discouraged more comments.

Arundel moved to the front of the wheelhouse and swept his eyes from side to side, and for anything that might be coming from astern. McPherson leaned forward as they came abreast of the island and looked round Shoal Point on the other side of the channel. He eased the wheel to port, keeping the ship to the starboard side of the harbour entrance, and headed out to the Straits of Juan de Fuca.

As they came out past the breakwater at the harbour mouth, McPherson told Calhoun, who was leaning against the chart table, "If you want Yang to get a little instruction on ship handling, you might get him up here now."

Calhoun called down the companionway to the saloon, "Yang, time to go to work." The steward came to the wheelhouse and McPherson gave him space behind the wheel.

"Mr. Calhoun says you brought the ship in here. Did you do it on the compass?" He pointed at the binnacle directly in front of them. "Or did you do it by sight?"

"I know what to look for."

"Nothing wrong with that on a clear day in good weather, but I've been telling Mr. Calhoun that it's better to know what to do if it gets dark or the weather gets worse." The steward nodded. "Can you read this?" He pointed at the compass card spinning in the binnacle. "What direction are we headed?"

"South by south-west."

"And if I tell you to head south-east by east, show me on the card what the new heading is." Yang did it. "Seems you know a little more than Mr. Calhoun thinks you know."

"Mr. Calhoun happy for me to be steward."

"You're the quartermaster, I'm the officer of the watch, okay? We'll come round to east by south-east in about four minutes. Listen for me to say, 'Turn now!'"

Yang nodded and McPherson picked up a pair of binoculars, slung the strap round his neck, and moved back a little and off to one side. He stood with his feet apart, hands clasped at his back and eyes scanning the waters ahead, savouring the moment they put their bow into the Straits. It was months since he had been on the helm of a ship, and he was very glad to be back. The late-August morning fog was well-dissipated, and the shore was clearly visible on both sides of the Straits. He gave Yang a heading eastward to the mouth of Puget Sound. The others watched from the back of the wheelhouse while he made small adjustments to the course to offset the effect of light rollers, pushed by a freshening westerly which lifted the stern and would have made for a slightly uncomfortable motion.

"We'll change our track a few points to south," he told Yang, and pointed to the chart. "Keep the headland at Fort Worden off the starboard bow." Without taking his eyes off the waters ahead of them, he took a pace back and spoke to Calhoun and Arundel. "We'll turn southeast by Port Townsend and head down the east side of the sound." The other two nodded.

McPherson tapped Yang on the shoulder and told him to turn around so he could see their wake. It traced a wavy line behind them. "Once you get used to the ship, you'll learn the way the hull plays in the water. Every ship is different, and just keeping the course straight on the heading doesn't mean that she'll hold a straight line through the water. There are sea currents, wind gusts, and the hull itself isn't entirely true, so you have to keep checking. It's my responsibility as the watchkeeper to keep a lookout, and yours as a helmsman to feel the ways of the ship." He turned and told the others, "It never hurts to keep training seamen,"

"Old habits never die, Pilot," said Arundel.

"Pilot?" asked Calhoun.

"Second Officers in the merchant service are the ship's navigator, that's why they're called 'Pilot.' The navy picked up the idea and loaded the job onto the Second Lieutenant," Arundel told him.

"If you keep training Yang, he won't want to be a steward anymore," said Calhoun.

McPherson grinned. "You're the one who needs him to steer the boat."

"I was thinking we could have a Canadian boat meet one of ours and transfer loads at sea." Calhoun came back to a less sensitive topic.

"You're suggesting that a boat handler with indifferent skills can find another one in the middle of the night and transship a breakable cargo, with the prospect that the Coast Guard will show up at any time and start shooting at them. That might work later when everyone's had a little more experience, but it's too much of a risk now," said McPherson. "I think it would be better if we figured out the right boat to go into the

Sound, meet shore parties, and transfer loads there."

"Our investors are more than a little concerned about losses now. We need to run fewer risks," said Arundel.

"How do you want to do it?" asked Calhoun.

McPherson replied, "It's less a matter of the kind of boat than what we want it to do. It's going to have to run as fast full as it does empty. It should have a crew of two and be easy to unload. Fuel might be a problem on a long run there and back, so it might have to have two or three engines—one, possibly two, for speed, and one for cruising. If we're running in the winter, it'll have to be stable in choppy seas, and the hull will need protection from floating logs."

Every few minutes he put the binoculars to his eyes and swept the course ahead. "Seen anything likely?"

"No," replied Arundel. "I've seen a few advertisements in magazines, *Motor Boating* for one, but there doesn't seem to be anything for sale around here that would fit us. I've a few ideas about what might go into one, but having one built might be difficult."

McPherson half heard the conversation while he relished the salt-laden breeze cutting through the open wheelhouse window. The ship pitched a little as it crossed a light roller. He tapped Yang on the shoulder and pointed astern. The ship's track weaved a little.

"When those rollers come in off the port bow, steer into them a little and ease back once we're through." He pointed at the compass. "It's put us a point off our course."

Yang nodded and kept his eyes on the compass until McPherson touched his shoulder again and pointed out a floating log before he ordered a course adjustment to avoid it. Yang grinned as the pair of them slowly started to develop the teamwork necessary to run a ship along a busy waterway. McPherson was satisfied that the steward was safe to handle the wheel and moved the engine telegraph lever to "Full." The ship picked up a measurable bow wave and Oak Bay became visible off their port bow.

McPherson moved back another pace so he could talk to the other two without raising his voice. "Peter and I talked about the coastal motorboats we used in the war. The most recent versions have two aeroplane engines, and unlike the earlier ones, a reverse gear. They're equipped with two torpedoes fired over the stern and the hulls are hydroplanes. We thought of trying to lay our hands on a surplus one, but by the time we located something suitable, got it out here and put it to use, we'd probably lose a full season, and that assumes no complications in transportation and fitting out."

"We need to be running in October; I have customers already," said Calhoun, "and if we don't start supplying them soon, someone else will. Can you get a boat ready by then?"

"Not a long time to get one built and tested. I'd prefer a lot longer," replied McPherson.

"If we have to, we can use another boat. What about this one?" said Arundel, pointing round the wheelhouse.

"She's not too fast and she's pretty obvious, plus she's been seen in the Sound and everyone who counts knows she belongs to me."

"You could think about picking up a fish packer," put in McPherson. "There are usually one or two available and the prices aren't too bad. They have space in the hold and tanks for a few days' steaming. Later on, and only if we have enough experienced crews, we might be able to use it as a tender so the fast one doesn't have to be directly connected with the trade at both ends."

"What do you mean, both ends?" said Arundel.

"We'll have to decide whether we want to be

seen in Victoria Harbour picking up loads at the wharf – too many eyes around town and if someone sees us leave, they can be waiting along the route or at the other end," said McPherson.

"We could try having a boat pick up at the Consolidated Exporters warehouse on Wharf Street, run the stuff out to a place offshore on the Canadian side, transfer the load, and run on from there. I don't have anywhere in mind at the moment, though," said Arundel, looking alternately at the passing coastline and the chart.

"Right there!" McPherson put down his binoculars and pointed to Discovery Island just off Oak Bay.

"Why there?" The small island and the lack of cover or any apparent anchorage did not impress Arundel.

"It's deceptive," McPherson replied. "Why don't we swing inshore a little and have a look?"

"Things have changed since the last time I was here," said Arundel, looking through a pair of binoculars he took from the chart table. "Someone's built a little lodge and put some mooring floats out in front of it."

McPherson took the glasses from him and scanned the shorelines. "The anchorage gives reasonable cover from both the westerlies and the southeasters. There's room on either side of the float for the pickup boat to moor on one side and the runner on the other, or for the two to raft up and transfer the load directly."

"I see what you mean," said Arundel. McPherson conned *Eloise* out of the channel to the east of the island and Arundel asked him, "Is this the only place where we can make the switch? If we're moving stuff two or three times a week, we don't want to establish a pattern."

"There are a couple of other places we can use,"

said McPherson. "D'Arcy Island or East Point on Saturna are two possibles. We can find others if we need them, but those give us decent transfer points, and a place to get something to eat if we have to wait out some weather or a passing patrol boat."

The breeze from the southeast picked up and caught *Eloise* on her stern quarter. The deck heaved as Arundel steadied himself on the chart table and looked at the coastal charts. He mulled over some of the alternatives for transshipment and safe harbour if they needed some. "There's also South Pender Island," he said. "It has a deep anchorage at Bedwell Harbour—we could think about that."

"Not if you're expecting a southeaster even a little stronger than this breeze," said McPherson. "They come right up the throat and send you onto the rocks at the head. There's a little cove inside that's safe enough if you don't have to come out during the blow, but otherwise it's just like Browning Harbour on the other side of the island—really risky in the wrong conditions.

"Think about it for a while," said Calhoun. "When can you be ready to make the first run?"

"If we're to get a boat built for the purpose," replied McPherson, "I'll have to get a design roughed out and get it to a proper draughtsman to complete. I think I know what we want for engines. Seattle might be a good place to look around. I don't know how long a yard will take to put something like this together, even assuming that the right materials are available in Victoria or Vancouver. I'm guessing it will be at least two months, providing everything goes without a hitch."

"Better lay on another boat then," said Arundel. "We can't wait that long. A fish packer, even with a decent engine, can only do ten knots at most, but it will work temporarily. Can we arrange a drop fairly close to the border? Anacortes would be good, or a few other places on Fidalgo Island just south of the border. We could stay in Canadian waters until we're off the southern tip of Saturna Island and then cut over, make the drop and then get home quickly."

"Okay," said Calhoun. "I'll talk to the customers."

"What about the Coast Guard?" asked Arundel.

"The *Arcata* and her twelve knots could still give us trouble," said McPherson. "That's why we'll have to deliver at night and move the merchandise in the winter."

"Any use having anyone on shore tell us where the cutters are?" asked Arundel.

"Difficult to get the message passed except by phone," said Calhoun.

"That won't help if we're at sea. What about shore patrols?" asked McPherson.

"They're there, but they take local cops along with them. They don't like the federal men any more than we do so we usually get a tip. But we have to be careful because the Feds'll shoot without asking any questions."

McPherson concentrated on piloting the boat while he let the information sink in. He studied the chart as they cut through the water, noting landmarks, and imagining how they might look on a dark night with a heavy sea and crosswinds. They turned due south toward Seattle and McPherson took the wheel to let Yang return to being a steward. In the late summer light winds, they made good time down the Sound. He pointed off the starboard bow where darker shapes showed against the waves. "These are some of the places where ocean currents tend to concentrate the driftwood and other debris. There's rocks hidden below the surface, and they'll block the entrance to harbours you think are deep enough."

Calhoun nodded. "I'll take your point about charts."

"How do we connect with customers, and how would I know we have the right one in the dark?" asked McPherson after they were settled onto the new course, and after he had looked again at the chart and landmarks.

"Simple," said Calhoun. "When they make the deal, we tear a dollar bill across—the customer keeps one half and I give you the other. You match them up on the beach before you start to unload."

"Does the customer always pay in Victoria?"

"Usually, unless I know him very well and then we collect the cash on the beach."

"If the boat's carrying one hundred and twenty-five cases and I'm collecting the whole lot, that's close to $10,000 each time. That's a lot of money to have out in the open. Besides, it'll be dark, and I won't be able to see it, let alone count it," said McPherson.

"If it's the wrong amount, that's my problem," said Calhoun.

"Glad you plan to trust us that much," replied Arundel.

"I will until I have reason not to."

McPherson kept his mind on the helm for a while and marked possible locations along the shoreline they could examine on the way back. "Still a lot of fishing boats out here," he said, putting his notebook away. "Could provide cover for us with the fish still running into the fall."

"Keep it in mind if you find them out there. It might work in the evening when they head back to Bellingham, but won't be much use after midnight," said Calhoun.

"There's still the need to spot the people who want to take the money or the load," said Arundel.

"You'll just have to keep something heavy in the boat to discourage them," said Calhoun.

"I can't say I'm too keen on carrying much in the way of armament," said McPherson.

"Why's that?' asked Calhoun. "There's too much booze and money out there to stop some people wanting to get their hands on both."

"Have you ever tried having a gunfight in the middle of the night? The boat's moving, there's no light, and you don't know who you're shooting at. And every time you fire, your muzzle flash lets everyone know where you are," replied McPherson.

"Didn't think of it that way," said Calhoun.

"Besides, I don't want to be getting into a gunfight with the Coast Guard or one of your police forces."

"You are a Canadian, aren't you." Calhoun stated.

"I don't mind carrying a shotgun to repel boarders at close range, but I think we'll concentrate on staying out of trouble as much as possible—and when the new boat's finished, we'll rely on speed and handling. Besides," said McPherson, "I've managed to flatten the occasional man who came at me with a weapon."

"You're the captain," said Calhoun. He did not sound convinced.

They went the rest of the way in silence. McPherson periodically consulted the *Pacific Coastal Pilot* and took some bearings on some of the bays, rivers, and harbour mouths they passed. Twice he had Arundel take the wheel after he had swung the boat temporarily to a new heading while he wrote in his notebook.

Yang served lunch, and with it, a hefty portion of Scotch. Arundel, as well as McPherson, turned down the drink.

"Don't you imbibe, either?" Calhoun asked.

"Not much," said Arundel, "and never while I'm on the wheel."

"I'm astounded," said Calhoun. "I thought that was what kept the Royal Navy going."

"Perhaps it does for some," said Arundel noncommittally, "but I like to feel the way the ship moves, and I can't do that if I'm swaying around myself."

Calhoun turned back to Yang. "Keep the booze out of sight when we dock and the Customs come on board. We wouldn't want to embarrass anyone," he said.

"Won't they let it stay in bond?" asked Arundel.

"The less they connect me in any way with booze, the better," said Calhoun. "If they were to put it in bond, someone would want to write down a record of it and God only knows what happens to bits of paper that end up in government files. For all I know, some enforcer will dig it out and link me with the brand name and start something. This way, Yang will feed the Customs guy from what looks like his own private stock. The government man thinks he's getting away with something by putting one over on me, so he goes away doubly happy."

Calhoun moved over to the chart table and started stowing the charts in the drawer. "That reminds me—Welland's a drinker, and once he starts, he doesn't stop until he falls over. Yang makes sure he doesn't do any damage to the boat, but that means we're not going anywhere for a couple of days."

"We have a couple of days here, then? Would have been good to know that beforehand," said McPherson.

"Yes, today and tomorrow. What might you have in mind to do?"

McPherson looked at Arundel. "If we've decided we need a fast boat, we'll probably need aeroplane engines. We could look around Seattle," he said. "What do you think, Peter?"

"Boeing's just down the road, I believe," said Arundel. "There have to be a few people dealing in surplus engines around."

"Do you have enough time for that?" Calhoun replied.

"Likely enough," said McPherson.

"You can catch me at the Alexis," said Calhoun, turning towards the companionway. "I'll book you each a room there."

Chapter 9

Calhoun went down to the main deck and stepped off onto the dock. McPherson watched him walk up the gangway to the street and turned to Arundel. "Presumably you knew about this and didn't see fit to mention it? A bad decision. Is there anything else you haven't told me?"

Arundel looked at the deck. "The Boeing Airplane Company is doing a major upgrade on some wartime DH4 fighters to convert them for the US mail service; there should be a few Liberty engines about—410 horsepower, 12-cylinder. The biggest advantage to using one of those is that over twenty thousand were manufactured, so parts should be easy to find. I also think that, since newer models are out now, the Liberties should be fairly cheap."

"How did you come by that information?"

"Usual place. My father."

"Those engines will certainly provide the power we'll need. Let's forget you just put a foot badly wrong and carry on, for the moment at least. Question is, then—how do we choose? I'm comfortable enough buying one that looks in good shape, but if there's anything wrong with it beyond how it looks, I'm likely to be lost."

"I can manage. We had the Fiats and Thorneycrofts in our boats in enough pieces to know about the things in principle."

"I didn't get close enough to that part of things

to know too much; I'm glad you did even if you're not going to be around when we're using them. Apart from anything else, I'm not too keen either on getting my nice new clothes all grimed up by rummaging around an engine shop when I don't know what I should be looking for. Let's talk to Calhoun's engineer before he gets in the sauce. Whatever he knows about high-speed engines is more than I do, and at the very least, he can give us the questions we need to ask other people. He might even have a couple of pairs of overalls we can borrow."

They went down to the engine room and looked for Welland, whom they finally found next to a cup of tea in a small eating area next to the galley.

"How much do you know about gas engines in boats?" asked Arundel.

"Some."

"We need to put together a fast one."

"Going into business with the boss?"

"Something like that."

"Depends on what kind of boat and what kind of engine and what kind of propeller."

"We've both run fast boats, but we don't have anything like them here, so we need to start afresh," said McPherson.

"What kind of boats?"

"Most recently, fifty-five-foot coastal patrol boats with two aeroplane engines; either Fiats or Thorneycrofts," said McPherson.

"Please understand, gentlemen, that I make no claim to expertise here nor do I know those engines. I've heard of that type of boat, but I've never seen one. People wanting speed boats usually put big car engines in them, but getting twenty knots out of them is considered fast. Most craft are around twenty feet, and they're toys; they shouldn't go out in any kind of a sea. I don't know much about Mr. Calhoun's business, but I guess it runs year-round, so any boat you have will need to run through the winter. I know you're both seamen, but I think you've only sailed on deck. You'll either have to learn to fix a problem with the engine, or you'll fetch up on a rock somewhere. Do I have you right?"

"Mostly so," said McPherson, "but we need to start somewhere, and soon. There are a bunch of aeroplane engines available now and we can probably get them cheaper than ones from a car."

"Likely enough," said the engineer, "so let's talk about some basic rules. What I know about aeroplane engines is they run at almost full speed all the time and car engines don't. When you want to slow down you turn the engine off. When you want to restart it, the prop is still spinning, so you throw the switch, and it lights up again. You can't do that in a boat. Most engines I've heard of have a liquid cooling system, but they all depend on the outside air going up against a small radiator to operate. I'm thinking you'll need to put one close to the outside of the boat to be effective."

"We're thinking of using a couple of Liberties," said Arundel.

"Two," replied the engineer. "Double the fun. Remember, you're using these motors in a different way than they were designed for, so the reliability they might have had in the air is going to be less for what you're doing. The way you use them involves sometimes running the engine at less than full speed. When it goes at a lower speed than it's supposed to, the plugs will foul up and you'll need to stop, take them out and clean them. That's no fun if you have any kind of a sea running. You also have to keep the engine lubricated, and that means maintaining oil pressure. Your oil pump runs off the engine—if the speed's too low, the pressure drops and your engine stops."

"That's helpful," said McPherson. "You've given us a lot to think about. One more question: do you have some overalls we could borrow?"

"I do," said Welland, walking over to a

cupboard. "I'd also suggest you stop somewhere along the way and get a pair of gloves each, otherwise your hands will look like mine." He held up his grime-encrusted fingers.

McPherson took the overalls and loaded them into a sack. "Thanks, Jock," he said, and he and Arundel went up to the wharf.

"Jock?" asked Arundel. "Where did you get his first name from?"

"I didn't," replied McPherson. "Scotsmen are fairly common amongst merchant ship engineers. Sooner or later, they all answer to "Jock."

An hour later, they walked up the steep hill from the waterfront to the Alexis Hotel on First Avenue. They asked for Calhoun at the reception desk and the clerk checked their names against a list under the counter, then pointed to the left. The only door there was marked "Laundry." On the other side, a staircase led down to another door, which revealed a tastefully decorated lounge. An enormous bar took up a large part of one side and the air was filled with cigar smoke. Calhoun was sitting at a table toward the back with a clear view of the door. He was with two large men, deep in conversation with one of them. The other sat slumped in his chair and glowered down at the table. A striking, dark-haired young woman sat on his other side. It had all the aura of a very exclusive club and was largely occupied by well-dressed men with attractive women companions.

"Some prohibition!" said Arundel as they took chairs between the girl and Calhoun. A waiter appeared at his elbow and looked inquiringly at them. "Whiskey and soda, please," he said. McPherson shook his head and the waiter left as quietly as he had arrived.

"You do drink," said Calhoun.

"When it's a suitable time," Arundel answered.

"And you don't," said the morose one,

truculently, to McPherson who had picked the seat beside him.

Before McPherson could answer Calhoun interjected, pointing to the man on his right. "This is Jim White, one of my better customers. This is his daughter, Maureen, and on your other side is Mike Burnand."

McPherson smiled at Maureen, then turned to White, nodded and said, "Harry says we'll be delivering to you."

"He says you have ideas of your own about where to deliver. You need to know that if you do business with me, you bring the stuff to where I want it," said White aggressively.

"Depends how badly you want it," said McPherson. "What I've heard so far is that you've not been getting a lot of your stuff. That's either because you don't know how to signal a boat in at night, or because the man driving the boat doesn't know where to find you."

"You damn Limeys – you want to deliver booze to us, and you don't even drink it," said Burnand, leaning forward in his chair.

"We're Canadian, and we're seamen. We deliver things," said McPherson. Arundel's drink arrived; he sat quietly sipping while the others sparred.

The girl leaned over and told them quietly, "Mike ran a boat for my father. He's not happy to be replaced." McPherson and Arundel nodded. Burnand lurched to his feet.

"Let's move back. This isn't going to work out well," said Arundel to Maureen and signaled Calhoun and White to do the same.

McPherson didn't move. White said, "Mike'll flatten you, Dugald."

"Doubt it," said McPherson.

"You're still a lousy Limey," said Burnand, swinging his left fist at McPherson's head.

McPherson grabbed Burnand's arm before the fist connected, pulled it round and sent Burnand spinning until his face slammed into the wall, levering himself out of the chair as he did so. He twisted Burnand's arm up behind his head, bent down and said, softly, "That was very stupid. I'm going to let you go in a moment, and we're going to walk quietly over to that door behind me. After that, you're leaving." He let Burnand get up, then led him across the room to the door, opened it and gently pushed him out.

McPherson came back to the table. "It's always the drunks that try it."

"The sober ones have more sense," said Arundel.

"We'd have got a whole lot less attention if your man hadn't started something," said Calhoun to White.

"He wouldn't have had to if you guys didn't want to change the delivery arrangements." White's voice was getting loud enough to cause some nearby heads to turn.

McPherson said quietly, "You, Peter and Harry should stay here and sort out the details. Get them to bring you some sandwiches to mop up some of the liquor. Perhaps Maureen and I can go upstairs to the restaurant and get some dinner, then we'll join you again. That should give you enough time." McPherson looked at Maureen. "Are you ready for dinner?"

"Apparently so."

They stood up. "How do we get out of here—back through the laundry?" asked McPherson.

"Follow me, Admiral!" she laughed, and led the way to the corner where her father and Calhoun had disappeared. Behind the curtains was a door, then a short passage lit by a single bare bulb leading to a small courtyard; a short alley took them out onto First Avenue, where they could enter the hotel lobby again and from there, the restaurant.

"Come here often, I see," he said.

"I have to—my father needs someone to see him home."

"Downstairs operates pretty openly. I've heard about all the raids; don't you get arrested for being here?"

"If they raided this place there wouldn't be a senior policeman to process the charges, a District Attorney to prosecute, or a judge around to hear the case."

"I suppose I shouldn't be surprised," he said.

They were shown to a table and he automatically held out her chair in the manner he had copied from more socially-adept naval officers. He tried to adjust to the unfamiliar presence of a pretty woman across from him. It had been almost two years since he had left Ariadne in Portsmouth, but he still wasn't ready for another woman to take her place, no matter how attractive and intelligent.

Maureen smiled at him with a hint of curiosity in her eyes. "You're a little different from the men who usually turn up with my father."

"Who turns up with your father?"

"Mostly loud and brash types."

"Sorry, I'm just a recently discharged naval officer. I haven't had time to get loud and my betters wouldn't have let me be brash."

"You and your friend look like you had a share in some hard action."

"How can you tell?"

"Apart from you flattening one of my father's less-genteel acquaintances, you both have what my grandfather called 'gunfighter's eyes.' You seem to be on watch all the time, and you're certainly ready to take action."

"Your grandfather had interesting powers of observation; he must have led an exciting life. I'm really not that romantic a character—my friend is much closer to the type."

"Do tell me some details, and more about your friend. You know him well?"

"Wartime acquaintance, mostly. He's the one with the rich family and does all the business with your father." He paused for a moment. "This is really the first time I've been off the dock in Seattle. Would you show me around a little before we join your father at the yacht?"

She looked at him appraisingly before she replied, "It's probably not as attractive as some of the places you've been to."

"It's probably better than most," he replied.

"Really?" she said. "You must tell me about some of those."

"Well," he said, "for a start, the weather's better here."

"You've not been here in the winter, then."

"Can't be any worse than Victoria in a southeaster," he replied.

While they ate, Maureen gently probed him about Arundel. He told her some of the stories, but kept them light enough to encourage her to talk a little about her life. For a brief moment he wondered what Admiral Romilly would make of the career he was contemplating but decided that as long as they included gin in their loads, he would probably approve.

After dinner, they went back through the Laundry door. White turned to face them angrily. "What the hell took you so long?"

McPherson ignored him. "Get everything straightened out?" he said levelly.

"You leave her alone in the future, you slimy bastard. You hear?" McPherson said nothing. "You hear?" screamed White.

"Mr. White, you have nothing to be concerned about," said McPherson very quietly, and looked at him directly. White sat down.

Calhoun said quickly, "Jim agrees to the first few deliveries being made at the north end of the Sound."

"All right." said McPherson, looking at Calhoun. "Still set on using the torn dollar bill system?"

White said, "Why bother with that? Dugald will recognize me."

"It'll be a dark night, probably raining, and maybe a bit of a sea running," said McPherson. "I'll be at the wheel so you'll have the crewman to deal with, and under those conditions, neither of you would recognize your own mother at any distance over two feet."

Calhoun said, "Okay, Jim, we'll set up the delivery arrangements and come down here again. Dugald will be using a temporary boat, probably a fish packer, for the delivery so the transfer's not going to be as quick as the fast boat will be. You might want to keep that in mind."

White gave them a hard look. "Remember, we're paying for on-time, complete deliveries. You aren't the only runners on the coast and if you can't do it, we'll find someone who can."

"Sure Jim," said Calhoun easily, "and you remember that we're looking for a clean handover. We don't want to find the beach full of cops and ourselves in the middle of a gunfight, so keep your more talkative guys on ice for a few days before the delivery. Otherwise, we work with someone else, too."

"Well then, if we're all agreed," said McPherson neutrally, "perhaps we can call it a night. Peter, I'll see you first thing to look for those engines."

The next morning, McPherson and Arundel waved down a taxi in front of the hotel and headed south of the city to where Boeing's plant overlooked Elliot Bay, picking up some gloves on the way. They found a scrap dealer at the end of a shabby alleyway leading away from the back gate of the Boeing yard. His office was a shed on the other side of a door inset in a large gate, with *Finnerty's* painted along the top. Large sheds occupied the lot and sounds of a machine shop came out of one immediately opposite them.

McPherson looked through the gate. "We're not exactly equipped to go rummaging through old aeroplane engines, especially since we don't know where we're going or really what we're looking at when we find it."

"You're telling me we need a plan, Pilot."

"... and some preparation."

"Meaning what?"

"We're looking for an engine which neither of us have ever seen before. The ones we used to have were modified by someone else to use in boats and neither of us know the details of how it was done. At a guess, I'd say we need to find someone who knows something about cooling and lubrication for a start, and whether we want to put a gear box on it so the boat can go backwards. On a steam or diesel, the engine itself can do that, but a petrol one can't. There's a bit more to this than just fixing an engine on the fly. That being said, other people might have the idea about using these engines to do the same thing. If we can get them for scrap price now, we should do it." McPherson pulled on his coveralls and led the way into the yard.

Finnerty himself occupied a surprisingly tidy desk in the middle of piles of filing boxes. In addition to the engines he was scavenging from Boeing, he had two hundred still in their crates. They told him they wanted a pair to power a sawmill and would take another pair for spare parts. The dealer asked for two thousand dollars for four new ones. Arundel did the negotiating while McPherson opened each crate and supported the dealing effort by keeping a sour look on his face as he ran his fingers over the grease. Arundel did not bargain particularly hard to avoid drawing too much attention but knocked the price down to fifteen hundred dollars for form's sake.

"Give him half the money now," said McPherson, out of Finnerty's hearing, "and he'll get the rest on delivery. These things weigh just under eight hundred and fifty pounds each, so we need a truck and crew to move them. Keep the other half of the money and take a taxi back to the yacht. When you get there tell Welland to clear space in the hold. I'll stay with the load and ride back with it."

Arundel paid Finnerty and used his telephone to call a cab. McPherson waited for the dealer to find a truck, then supervised the loading; he was pleased to have the overalls because the carrier's truck was even dirtier than the scrap yard. Finnerty came along for the second half of his money. By the time they got back, it was late afternoon. Welland had rigged a chain hoist from the aft mast gaff and braced it to take the extra weight of each engine. White and Maureen had arrived and they all watched as the load was stowed. Arundel handed over the rest of the money and Finnerty left, grumbling only slightly about how little he'd been paid for a full day's work. Yang helped McPherson and Arundel clean off the grease that had, inevitably, stuck to their clothes, and when they were presentable again, Maureen suggested dinner.

"We could go to Doc Hamilton's," she said. "Perhaps I can round up a couple of friends so there's at least the possibility of intelligent conversation." Her father attempted an indulgent smile, but it died from a withering glance by his daughter.

"Who or what is Doc Hamilton?" asked Arundel.

"It's about the best speakeasy in Seattle," said Maureen. "It's like the hotel with the right people eating there. The cops go and break up other places."

White looked uncomfortable with the suggestion that they should eat together, but since his daughter had made it, he gave in with an attempt at good grace. He made a telephone call from the dock office for his car to come and pick them up. Maureen made two phone calls to some girlfriends to round out the party. Twenty minutes later, a car with a chauffeur at the wheel arrived and White told the driver to head for Doc Hamilton's.

The maitre d' greeted White effusively at the door and showed them to a discreet table where they could see the other customers without being too obvious. When her friends arrived, Maureen took charge of the seating arrangements. She put herself between Arundel and Calhoun with one of her girlfriends on Arundel's other side. McPherson was across from her. She shunted her father as far away from herself as possible with the other girlfriend to keep him occupied. The arrangement offered the only privacy that she could expect for conversation with Arundel.

"It's well patronized," commented McPherson.

"The leading lights of the community need a place to relax," she said.

"Leading lights?" he said.

"At these prices, they're the only ones who can afford it," she replied.

Arundel pointed at the table, set conventionally for an extensive meal, but with two coffee cups and one teacup at each place. "We'll be floating in coffee by the time we leave," he said.

"The one on the right is for the before dinner drink, the teacup is for the wine, and the last coffee cup is for brandy—or even coffee if you want it," she said.

"I wondered where all the stuff was drunk," McPherson said.

The waiter appeared and ostentatiously put bottles of soda water and ginger ale on the table together with a bucket of ice. He asked for their drink orders in a conspiratorial tone and filled them from coffee carafes carried on a trolley.

McPherson surprised him by reaching for the soda water. "Forgive me for asking," he said, turning to Calhoun, "but with places like this and the Smoking Room at the hotel, and with the amount of material brought in from Canada and, presumably, the stuff that people make themselves, just who is it here who supports prohibition?"

Calhoun replied, with his Irish accent becoming more pronounced as he drank more, "You've heard the saying that rules are for the obedience of fools and the guidance of wise men?" He paused and gestured around the room. "Behold the fount of wisdom."

Everyone laughed and White added, "There are a lot of folks who don't care one way or another about booze, but they do care about the government being the one to tell them whether they can or can't have a drink."

"So why can't the law be overturned?" asked Arundel.

"Churches!" said Calhoun cheerfully. "No one wants to be the first to take them on publicly. Mind you, without the moralizing harpies pushing Christian Temperance, and the drunken hypocrites that inhabit pulpits, we'd be out of business. Naturally, we support their efforts and contribute to the campaigns of all the politicians who rail away against the demon rum. If we didn't, we'd be selling booze at half the price or less."

"As a matter of fact," said Melissa, the girl sitting at Arundel's left, "I see several of the noisier ones here tonight."

"As well as the husbands of some of the temperance ladies—they must have a meeting going on somewhere," said Maureen.

"Hope it ends soon," said Janet, the other girl who had joined them. "Some of those guys get their hands all over the place after two drinks."

Arundel lifted his coffee cup. "Here's to

hypocrisy! Who else is here, then? It can't be all politicians and angels fluttering down to perdition."

White looked around the room. "There's Roy Olmstead, for one." McPherson saw a well-dressed man with a shining face and a glow of self-satisfaction. "He's a Lieutenant on the Seattle Police Force. We reckon his salary is insignificant now with all the money from the booze he's moving around. He never gets charged, mostly because all the town's leading citizens are on his customer list. I heard a rumour he's netting $200,000 a month now."

"Is he competition?" asked Arundel.

"Yes and no," said White. "At the moment, there's enough business for everyone, but if we cross his turf, he can get nasty, and he has enough government contacts to turn some heat on us. He won't let his guys get involved in anything else but booze, though. No girls, no guns, no drugs, no gambling."

The dinner was good and the conversation cheerful. White continued to look at Arundel warily, but Maureen kept up a flow of local gossip. Calhoun had settled on a cheerful plateau and kept up a breezy banter with the girls. McPherson just listened and watched and started to think the four hundred dollars he had agreed to was a little too insignificant for the risks involved.

They got up to leave, and while White made a show of paying the bill, McPherson noticed Maureen brush against Arundel and whisper something in his ear. The party broke up noisily outside and Calhoun hailed a taxi for himself, McPherson, and Arundel to go back to the hotel.

"Okay then, Jim," Calhoun said as it drew up beside them. "I'll see you in Victoria at the end of the month and we'll set up deliveries to start the next week. You pick the location, but for the first month or so, and until we get a fast boat and we're happy it's working right, we'll stick to the northeast sector of the Sound."

"That'll work for me." White got into his car with the three girls.

McPherson, Arundel, and Calhoun were silent in the taxi on the way back to the hotel, each man deep in his own thoughts. It wasn't until they reached their floor and the elevator car, with its operator, had disappeared, that Calhoun turned to Arundel and spoke. "Watch what you get up to with that girl. Jim's got plans for her and I don't think they include you."

McPherson held Arundel back as Calhoun disappeared into his room. "We don't want to wreck a perfectly good business arrangement over this, right?"

Arundel looked at him and said quietly, "I'm taken, actually."

"Make sure she knows it," said McPherson.

Chapter 10

Thursday, August 28th, 1919

McPherson was awake at his usual five o'clock and after breakfast in the hotel strolled around the awakening city and down to the waterfront. He was already in the wheelhouse with a chart spread out on the table recording details in his notebook when Arundel arrived.

"Anyone else about?" Arundel asked.

"Yang's in the saloon with coffee going," said McPherson, putting the chart away and pulling out another. "Otherwise, we have a hung-over engineer, and I haven't seen Harry. Interesting combination for the crew. An owner who doesn't know anything about boats, a steward who has the helm but doesn't know anything about navigation, and a drunk engineer." He made some more notes from the chart, then slotted it neatly in the rack beneath the table. "Let's go to the foredeck where we can talk without being overheard."

When they were leaning comfortably against the railing, McPherson said, "If I'm to be involved, we need to be clear on who runs what. I see the job now as picking up alcohol from somewhere, that someone has paid for. I deliver the merchandise to somewhere on the American side of the border, and someone else will pay for it on delivery. I then have a bunch of money from another country which has to be given to yet another someone. It really all needs to be a little tighter. You want me to take the risks that your mother won't have you doing, and I have to work with an American who's ignorant of the basics of the sea, doesn't have an organization put together and needs me to do all the work to get it running."

Arundel was silent for a moment. "How do you want to run it?"

"Before we go there, let's talk about money. If the rumours about Olmstead netting $200,000 a month are even half true, there's more in this business than the four hundred a month you've offered me. Four thousand a month with the same delivery payments would be more reasonable."

"That's my father's decision."

"I'll talk to him when we get back. Another thing—Harry's no use in this operation the way it's set up now, and Jim isn't any better. We can try it out, but it would be good to have a back-up plan."

McPherson kept his gaze steady while Arundel thought of an answer. "Those are questions I have to take back to my father," he said, finally. "We're not that closely involved with the day-to-day operations either."

It was almost noon before Calhoun had organized the yacht to get away. He alternately yelled instructions to Yang about the state of ship supplies and called for Welland to "Start the damn engine."

"Are you guys going to keep loafing around down there?" he roared to McPherson and Arundel, leaning over the bridge rail above their heads.

"With you in a moment," called Arundel, after glancing at McPherson for approval.

McPherson said, "We'll talk specific details with Harry when we get up on the bridge. Then we'll see how it goes."

Arundel nodded agreement as they went up the companionway to the upper deck. This time it was

Calhoun who took the wheel.

"Know what you're doing, Harry?" asked McPherson.

"Yes," was the hesitant reply. "I'm going to have Yang cast off the lines. I'll call for 'Slow Ahead,' steer her through the traffic, and head for Victoria."

"You might think of doing it differently. The tide is running, and if this were a larger vessel, you'd probably choose to wait for the ebb, but we can try this. First, make sure there's no traffic ahead and no one coming up on your port quarter. If you haven't got a lookout, walk over and do it yourself, but we've got Peter." He grinned at Arundel. "Peter, will you do the port side lookout?"

Arundel moved over, checked, and said, "Clear."

McPherson moved over to stand by the wheel. "Now put on two points of port helm and ring for 'Slow Astern,' then cast off the aft lines." He waited until Calhoun had done it, then said, "When you see the bow lines start to tighten, cast off, ring for 'Slow Ahead,' and put another two points of port helm on. Give three short blasts on your whistle and then take her out slowly; that way, as I told you when we left Victoria, you're less likely to scrape bits off your bow paint with the wharf."

Calhoun gave three long blasts on the whistle as he called for Yang to cast off.

"Careful with the whistle—that signal means you're in distress." McPherson waited until the boat was clear of the dock and said, "When you get into the fairway, you can pick up your course. I'd suggest north, north-west by north for the moment." He pointed at the compass card in the binnacle.

They ran out slowly with Calhoun picking nervously at the wheel.

McPherson stood well behind him. "Check again for anyone coming up on your port quarter and ease her into the fairway."

Calhoun adjusted the course slightly. "When do I increase speed?" he asked.

"When you're sure that no one's in the way. Use Peter to look."

"All clear," said Arundel without being asked.

Calhoun rang down for Half Speed. "I never did anything like this before and we always managed to get places."

"Probably luck was with you. I'm a sailor. I never trust to luck. Ring down for Full Speed when you're on course."

He motioned Arundel forward to replace him and moved to the back of the wheelhouse. "Depending on traffic, we could ease the heading to three hundred and forty degrees until we have to go by Whidbey Island," he said.

Calhoun's enthusiasm for steering the ship evaporated with the boredom of keeping the same course and having to keep a steady lookout over the compass card. He turned and looked down the companionway into the saloon and called, "Yang!" When the steward appeared, he pointed at the wheel.

"Hold the course at north by northwest," he said authoritatively. Yang nodded and when Calhoun had turned away, looked at McPherson for confirmation. McPherson grinned and nodded back. Calhoun stepped back to where McPherson was standing. "Are you ready to come and work for me?"

"Not at the moment. There're a few things I need to clear up."

"What's there to be worked out?"

"Quite a lot. Boats, times, and money for a start. Why don't you tell me about what you want done, and I'll think about it and let you know? Let's start by talking about how much liquor you want to move in, say, a month."

"I'd like a minimum of five hundred cases a

week, preferably a thousand."

"Have you thought about what you would want as a boat to carry all that? This one?" McPherson waved his arm around the wheelhouse.

"We could, I suppose. The stuff could be stored on the deck, and we could use the thing on the mast at the back to swing the load onto shore." Calhoun gestured vaguely to the aft end of the ship.

"I think you're referring to the gaff on the aft mast. How would you plan to move the payload to a place where the hoist can reach it so that it can be swung ashore? And where on the shore would you plan to land it? This ship only works properly if you have a dock, or if you transfer the load to a smaller boat that takes it inshore. We're starting to talk about a fairly large crew. Someone needs to be in the wheelhouse conning the ship and keeping a look out."

McPherson pointed to the port side railing. "You just saw what's involved in moving the boat out of harbour. Your engineer really can't leave the engine room because he has to be there for any signals from the wheelhouse." Calhoun grunted. "Someone has to run the gaff, and one or two men are needed to haul cases to a place where they can be offloaded. Your shore boat needs to be manned, and the ship's going to have to stay in position for as long as it takes to move the stuff ashore. That means the ship's going to be vulnerable to a Coast Guard cutter."

A scowl started to appear on Calhoun's face. McPherson carried on. "That's just on the American side. How do you plan to pick up the stuff in Canada? Peter tells me your existing efforts have had uneven results—to put it kindly. And while we're on that subject, how do you plan to run the shore operation? Five hundred caseloads need something big to move them. You tell me the Seattle Police aren't that keen on chasing down the trade, but there must be others who are trying to stop it. Large trucks moving around might just be noticed."

"Well, we agree it might be a good idea to move the stuff at night." Calhoun did not sound as sure of himself.

"And you think that might be less obvious? Peter and I have time on small naval craft. It's a specialty all its own. This part of the operation is almost the same, but we don't want people getting excited or being too obvious. The people who do best in the shipping business leave the actual moving part to people who know what they're doing, and here that means sailors. I'm prepared to do that part." He stopped and called over to Arundel, "Peter, can you step back here a moment?" Arundel nodded. McPherson tapped Yang on the shoulder. "Mr. Arundel has the deck." He turned to Calhoun. "Did you see that?" he asked. "You never make a change on the bridge without telling everyone who's affected. It'll take you a long time to learn that and all the other things we took years to learn." He moved up to where Arundel could hear him. "I'm about to tell Harry how I'm prepared to get involved." He turned back to Calhoun.

"I'll run the delivery operation, and for the foreseeable future, I'll have the final say on the places and times where and when we deliver. There are places all the way up and down the coast that will work and others which won't because of tides, currents, rocks, and weather." He pulled his notebook from his pocket. "I've been making notes from the chart. I'll work for the Arundels," he went on. "You pay for the merchandise any way you want, but if I have to pick up the payment on the beach, it'll be in a sealed bag and you people can work out later if it's the right amount."

"As long as I get the number of cases I want on each run," said Calhoun petulantly.

"Five hundred cases are not much of a load if they're packed and swung outboard on a gantry from a ship to a dock. It's different if it's a bunch of individual cases landed on a beach, using a dinghy to transship from a boat a hundred yards offshore," said McPherson. "When we get back to Victoria, we'll take our notes from this trip and use them to organize some information the shore people can use. In the meantime, you can pick some men who look like they might be reliable, and above all, tell them if they're wanting to shoot people at night, muzzle flashes will tell everyone where they are."

For a while no one said anything as they moved steadily northward. Whidbey Island appeared ahead, and Arundel used a folded chart to show Yang their position. "We're going to have to go a little to the west when we get up by the island. Let's call it three hundred and fifty-five degrees. I'll tell you when." He pointed to the compass card and left the chart clipped to a board beside the wheel. Yang nodded and Arundel stood back.

"You sailors have your own way of doing things," said Calhoun.

"It's mostly to avoid hitting things that are bigger than we are," replied McPherson. "Let's let Yang do the course change and then we can have some coffee. I'll take the helm and you and Arundel can talk the business side of things. I've told you what I'm concerned about; add to that the kind of boats we'd need to use. You two can talk about how things will get paid for, and I'll let you know if I like my part in it."

Arundel ordered the course change, and as they came abreast of the south end of Whidbey Island, McPherson took the wheel. Yang went down the companionway to the galley. Arundel and Calhoun stood at the back of the wheelhouse talking quietly. McPherson stood comfortably behind the wheel, enjoying the feel of the ship beneath him. Yang brought him coffee and sandwiches and set the tray on a ledge behind the windscreen. McPherson breathed in the salt-laden air and watched the shoreline uncover on either side of the channel. He missed the simplicity of commercial life afloat, and idly wondered, again, why he should run the risks of an illegal trade. Then he thought about four thousand a month.

He unfolded the chart and looked for possible landing areas. Not wanting to mark up the chart, he pulled out his pen and notebook, also tossing up answers to all the variables he could think of that affected the new business. Their major market was Seattle, and the men moving the loads into it would want to keep their drive into the city as short as possible. Their short run would mean a longer one for him, which meant higher risks of interception by the Coast Guard and more fuel required. The more fuel he carried, the less space for cargo.

Calhoun's voice interrupted his calculations. "What about those four engines you loaded yesterday?"

"They were available, so it seemed like a good idea to get them while we were there," replied Arundel.

Calhoun said, "I don't want White or anyone else on this end to know too much about how we're equipped. It's good enough for them to know that we arrive on time and he hands over the payment."

"I agree with that. Do we have anyone involved other than you, me, McPherson, and the crew of the *Eloise*?"

"One or two; I haven't found the right guys to do the shore handling yet," said Calhoun.

"That's all your affair. We just need to talk to them about how they handle things on the beach." Calhoun looked out of the wheelhouse window and said nothing.

McPherson put his notebook back in his pocket and turned to them. "Look," he said, "I don't mind not knowing about details that don't concern me, but I'm going to be riding on that boat, so I want things on the shore to run smoothly. It'll mean that we have to put some time into training them."

Calhoun looked back at him and said, "I'm glad you like the idea of a fish packer to run cargoes. After we lost the last cargo, I bought one and I hired the guy who sold it to me to be the crew. He's a Swede—Ollie Lindstrom—and everyone thinks he still owns the boat. No one in Victoria will know who he is if he's there just occasionally and loads the crates into the packer. Anyone who cares to think about it'll think it's going to a camp up the coast."

"Do you have it in mind that this fellow will have a piece of the operation? Because if you do, I want to approve him, and if I don't like him—forget it!" McPherson's voice was firm.

"Hope you're not going to be difficult," said Calhoun.

"Where the boat is concerned, yes! A fish packer's another slow boat that gets more vulnerable the deeper it gets into Puget Sound. It has some good uses if it's run the right way by the right man. We have to think our operation through. We pick up in Victoria and we don't want to be obvious about it. We go directly to a delivery point, preferably on the American side. A rule of thumb is, the slower the boat, the shorter the run. We've some ideas about a fast boat and those engines to put in it if we decide we need them."

Calhoun sighed. "Fine," he said. "I'll leave it at that. You two are better boat handlers than I would ever be and have the nerve to go with it. As far as I can tell, you're probably honest, but since I've met so few people with that quality, I can't be sure whether my instincts are right. Let's hope you like Ollie, or I'll have to find someone else. What about the engines? Will they fit in a packer?"

"No," said Arundel, "they're aeroplane engines. They'll need a specialized installation and boat design to work properly."

"Like what?"

"A bunch of technical things we haven't worked

out yet."

"Any idea how you're going to do all this?" Calhoun asked slowly.

"Frankly, no, not at the moment, but I know enough people around who do, so I don't see too much of a problem."

"I'm glad of that much," said Calhoun. "I wouldn't know where to start."

"What now?" asked Calhoun as the other two started down the gangplank in Victoria Harbour.

"I'll send a carrier to take those engines," said Arundel, looking back. "My father will be in touch about the money arrangements." McPherson and Arundel walked in silence up the walkway to the wharf and from there to Store Street. "What now with you, Pilot?" asked Arundel.

"Depends on what kind of an operation gets set up. That chat I had with Calhoun told me he knew even less about the business than I thought. We can't even be sure he has much of an organization to pick up the stuff when we deliver it. Doesn't surprise me that you had a bunch of loads go astray. Keep Calhoun occupied for the next few days until we have some firmer plans. "Meanwhile, we need to find a fast boat that can deliver a hundred cases or more—we'll probably have to build it. Plan on a crew of two, and if the other man isn't to be you, we need to find someone who's capable. I'm going to put some information together so the next time we meet, at least one of us will know what he's talking about. Shall I drop by tomorrow evening? I should have some ideas by then."

"Let's do that, Pilot. I'll call you at the hotel if I need you, but if you don't hear from me, I'll pick you up tomorrow at six. I'll beard the old man in his office and tell him what we've done. Then I'll go and find somewhere to store those engines."

Chapter 11

Friday, August 29th, 1919

McPherson felt better after unloading his frustration on Arundel and had a good night. The next morning, he turned his thoughts to the information he needed. He headed for the Victoria Public library, a familiar building at the corner of Yates and Blanshard Streets. In earlier years, he had burrowed deep into its musty stacks as he sought to make up the gaps in his mathematical education before taking the exams for his maritime tickets.

The librarians had given him much help in the past as he stumbled around the need to describe the information he needed. He remembered a widow called Mrs. Barclay, who was usually stationed behind the front desk. Mrs. Barclay was not at the desk, however; instead, her old position was occupied by a younger woman who, when he approached, was looking intently down at a reference book. The name plate on the desk under the heading 'Duty Librarian' said, 'Mrs. Hemmingson.'

"Would you tell me where I can find the section on marine reference material, please, Mrs. Hemmingson?" he asked. She looked up and he came face to face with the most stunningly beautiful apparition he had ever seen. Her hair was a light red, her complexion clear, and her eyes were the most striking deep green.

"On the second floor to the left as you reach the top of the stairs. It's in the second set of stacks up against the wall." Her voice had a faint Irish lilt.

He smiled, turned, and headed for the stairs. Half-way up, he had a thought and turned back. "I have some notes to make, and I should have brought a bigger book; do you have some paper I can scratch something on? I'd be happy to pay for it, if necessary."

"We do not keep writing supplies for our patrons' use."

"I'm sorry to be an inconvenience, but I've just come back from active service, and I need some information to put me back into the civilian way of doing things. I have to meet someone this evening, and I'd like to show up looking like I know something."

The woman looked at him and seemed about to sharply dismiss the request. She stopped and looked around to see if there was anyone within hearing distance; there wasn't. "Don't make a habit of this," she said quietly, and reached under the counter for a thin sheaf of unlined office writing paper. "Today we close at four o'clock; if you have to come back tomorrow, you'll need to be properly equipped."

She passed the paper over. Her wedding ring was on her right hand, an increasingly common practice among the widows of war casualties. "Thank you, Mrs. Hemmingson," he said as he turned back to go up the stairs. For the next two hours, he rummaged through the books and magazines for anything he could find on boats that might fit their purpose.

"You seem to have emptied several shelves," said a gentle voice behind him.

McPherson looked up from the book in front of him. "Mrs. Hemmingson," he said. "Indeed, I have. I'm thinking it's almost time to leave."

"We closed half an hour ago, Mr...?"

"McPherson, ma'am, Dugald McPherson. I'm

sorry to be keeping you. I'll put all these away."

"One reason we librarians remain employed is that we re-shelve books. We find that if we let our patrons do it, books disappear into the wrong places and are often never seen again." She scooped an armful, and looking at the numbers on the spines, expertly shuffled them and placed them in their respective shelves.

McPherson very much wanted to keep her talking. Her accent and tone were precise and implied an intelligence that reminded him of his lost Ariadne. "Perhaps I can hand them to you in the order I think they came in, and you can re-shelve them?" he asked.

"We could try," she said.

He took the first pile that lay before him and looked at the Dewey Decimal numbers on the spines. He shuffled them into an order that seemed logical and handed the top five to her. She looked at them. "Not bad for a first try," she said, and reshuffled a pair before putting them on a shelf. "You have the makings of a librarian; I could take your name and address to pass on to the Head Librarian, and she could call you in the event of a vacancy occurring."

"A kind, thought ma'am, but I'm a sailor, and even now I've been home from the sea a little too long." Dugald smiled.

"So it seems," she said, looking at the assembled titles, "but all of these are about small boats. Is there a living to be made among them?"

He did not want to open a discussion about rum-running with a perfect stranger, no matter how attractive. "The market for ships' officers on both the coastal and the offshore runs is a bit limited at the moment, so I thought I'd look at smaller boats whose owners might need some expert guidance."

"I'm surprised none of our prospective rumrunners have made you an offer." Was there no one in this town who was not hanging around the periphery of this trade?

"Nothing yet," he said cheerfully. "You seem to be well-informed."

"This is a library. People come in here to get information about things they don't know enough about. So far, you're the only one with almost a good reason."

"Thank you for that compliment anyway. May I help with the rest of the books?" He took up another armload. "What do the index numbers printed on the spines mean?" he said. He knew the system perfectly, but it seemed a good way to prolong the conversation.

"They're developed for libraries to categorize books by subject matter and allows us to add additional books on the topic when they become available. When libraries first carried books about ships, most of the material was related to sail. As steam engines were added, and later diesels and petrol, we were able to identify them and put them next to the earlier ones on the shelves. Looking to the future, we'll be able to accommodate new technical developments for ships, aeroplanes, and automobiles. It's called the Dewey Decimal System."

He shuffled the books that were resting on his forearm and handed them to her. "I'm sorry—I'm keeping you from closing up."

"Actually, I shooed the last patron out before I came up to see what a mess you'd made up here."

"Then I'm doubly sorry for keeping you from going home." He picked up the last pile of books and put them in order.

"You can always come back," she said.

"I'll have to. The only things I've managed to find so far lead to more questions." They went down the front steps together and went in separate directions.

Walking into the hotel, he realized that he was less interested in the books than he was in Mrs.

Hemmingson. The desk clerk handed him a message from Arundel, suggesting a pickup at six o'clock. He telephoned the house and passed a message through the maid agreeing to the arrangement. He had just enough time to go to his room and rummage through the books in his trunk for some of his notes on earlier voyages through Puget Sound. He felt a twinge of regret that he had not insisted on bringing the charts of the area back.

Arundel was outside on time and his driving had not improved. He announced his arrival with the motor racing and the gears grinding as he maneuvered the car alongside the curb.

"It's good that you do better with boats," McPherson said, as he got into the car.

"Criticize me after you've learned to drive," said Arundel.

"I've learned," he said. Arundel lurched into the path of an oncoming car and only avoided a collision by spinning the steering wheel at the last possible moment. "I can only consider the possibility of taking it up again if we get to your parent's place alive."

At the house, Michael came directly to the point. "Peter says you have reservations about Harry."

"Life on the water is complicated and you have to know what you're doing. Harry doesn't." McPherson pointed to the bay below them. "Moving around the coast involves conning a small vessel into a beach like this, and having to contend, as Peter well knows, with winds, tides, inshore currents, waves, sharply-shelving beaches, and a few rocks. There's also drifting logs in the open waters of the Straits, which, considering he'd be operating at night and often in bad weather, could cause more damage than the guns of any Coast Guard cutter." He smiled as Cynthia gave him a glass of soda water. "I've spent the afternoon at the library looking at our choices for boats that will do everything we need. I found nothing designed for our use, so we'll need to figure out something else."

"How much information did the library have? It wouldn't be a place I would think has the sort of information we need," said Michael.

"It has a fair amount, and the librarian was most helpful," said McPherson.

"Unusual," said Peter with a hint of a smirk. "They usually seem to be some dried-up old dear that tells you to be quiet."

"This one wasn't. She was quite well-informed, and even asked me if I'd been approached by any of the local rumrunners who might need my skills."

"Times are changing; who was this paragon of modern womanhood?" asked Peter.

"A Mrs. Hemmingson."

There was a slight pause as Peter and Michael looked at one another. "As it happens, she's one of our neighbours. She lives across the bay," said Michael.

"She wasn't at your gathering on Sunday?" said McPherson.

"No," said Michael. "She has a small son and I suspect that keeps her quite busy. Still, let's get on with our present concerns. We had rather planned our operations around Harry. Admittedly the people he picked to do the work haven't been all that successful. We assumed that was down to a lack of experience, and that it would improve in due course. You seem to be telling us it's not likely to get better."

"I think you may find that Harry is better left to organize the shore operations. Even then, Peter will have to spend some time teaching the crew how to pick up cargo from an unstable platform, and the ways they can move around at night to avoid people who want to stop them."

"Peter?" asked Michael, raising his eyebrows. "I thought that's why we were bringing you in."

"Oh," said McPherson, "I thought I was going to be the other half of the operation."

"So did I," said Peter.

"I think we need to go back a few steps, then," said Michael.

McPherson immediately thought of Captain Anstruthers's warning about large parts of his career being spent in turning his guns on targets generated by the likes of the Arundels. Trade was still the primary interest of the British Empire, and the Royal Navy was the instrument that kept it flowing. Running questionable material into Puget Sound in 1919 might not be a major part of British trade, but without the Royal Navy to provide protection, the Arundels still looked for hard men to take the risks to keep it moving.

"Perhaps you can tell us how you want it to go," said McPherson. He saw how this was unfolding with the Arundel desire to keep Peter out of the dangerous part but needing to get the business going quickly.

"We're really peripheral participants in the trade, and because our part is mostly concerned with insuring loads, we have a big interest in keeping losses to a minimum. As insurers, we can only participate in the legal portions of the business; we can't be involved in activities that the Americans, in this case, consider illegal. That's why loads picked up in Victoria are consigned to points on the British Columbia coast. Any losses that we are called upon to cover occur, obviously, before they reach their legal destination."

"An interesting challenge, Father," said Peter. "You're losing money on loads because Harry's incompetent, and you can't put a safer alternative in place because you can't be directly involved. And yet, you're sitting here with us discussing a direct solution."

"A puzzle indeed, my boy."

McPherson recognized the offer being thrown down; he was being given the opportunity to volunteer. Peter was to be left out of the picture for any personal involvement. If that were to be the case, it would be McPherson carrying the entire risk. This was the time for more money to be offered. His experience in hundreds of shipboard negotiations had taught him that the first one to speak after an offer was made would lose the advantage. He said nothing and looked at Michael as if awaiting the answer to the puzzle to be revealed.

"Do you have the answer?" asked Peter.

A wisp of irritation crossed Michael's face. McPherson glanced innocuously from one to the other realizing that they hadn't rehearsed this play.

"I understand Harry now owns a slow-moving, but large-enough boat to pick up merchandise in Victoria," said Michael. "The previous owner remains on board, so as far as anyone knows, he's still the owner. The manifest will show a location up the coast, and the load can be transshipped to another boat for delivery south of the border." Michael looked expectantly at McPherson, who met his gaze blankly before looking over at Peter. MacPherson noted how hard he was working to get this going. There was more here than just insurance.

"But Harry's not the man for that part of the operation," said Peter.

"Dugald," said Michael. "You're quiet."

Knowing he'd got him now, McPherson said, "He's not the man for any part of the operations and his boat is no better. We still need to see if the new one will work."

"My main concern is that the loads have to be protected from both the authorities and our competitors," said Michael. "You two have more experience with defending yourselves in the modern world than I do. What needs to be done?" Again, he looked at McPherson for an answer.

"Peter has more experience in this sort of thing. He did all the work moving up and down the coast and dealing with people delivering loads. He should tell us what's needed."

Michael allowed his irritation to show. "Perhaps you can let us know how you see your role."

"You've told me about your business worries. I have the skills to solve them. I'm interested in your offer. I've given Peter a price. Will that be satisfactory?"

"Yes, I'm glad we got that far," said Michael.

"There's a lot of money being made by people like Roy Olmstead, and presumably you want Harry to do that well," McPherson went on. "If you're Harry's sole supplier and he wants up to a thousand cases a month, at a hundred cases a load, you're going to have to give him up to ten loads a month. That sort of schedule means a two-day turnaround, and that means," he paused and looked at Peter, "that the boat's movements are predictable and a bit riskier. A larger boat would solve that problem but would require more time and people on shore and, probably, bigger crews on the boat."

He stopped and let the message sink in. "But back to the preferred boat—we need someone who can both design and build one to take advantage of those aeroplane engines Peter bought in Seattle." He took out his notes. "Today at the library, I listed our primary requirements: speed, range, carrying capacity, and sea worthiness. And you need to get into business as soon as possible."

"I'm pleased you're using the word 'our,'" said Michael.

McPherson smiled and carried on. "I'm a merchant seaman, so ease of loading and unloading are also important. This is a large and specialized kind of shipment and we have to consider how we'd unload. The longer we hang about in one place, the more obvious we'd be." He took a sip of his soda water and waited for comments.

"Where do we go from here, then?" asked Michael finally.

"I've found a few more publications. I'll spend

the next few days going through them and I'm sure I'll narrow our choices down."

"Thank you, Dugald," said Peter. "I take it you mean that information is available, and although it's possible we could take this information and work it into a set of plans for a boat we could use, it's better done by someone who knows what he's doing."

"You're right, and that especially includes getting someone to install the engines properly," said McPherson.

"It doesn't seem likely that Harry's customers are going to wait for him to sort out his problems, so it means that while we take the time to find the proper boat for this trade, we need to use something that's less than perfect to get going. We'll tell Harry we'll do business with him if we take over the Victoria operation and deliver loads to him in Puget Sound. If we're using a slow boat, deliveries are going to be at the north end, preferably not much further south than Bellingham. Later, with the faster boat, we'll work deeper into the Sound."

"If we have to do more than ten deliveries every month, we're still going to need another boat," said Michael.

"... and plan different routes and tactics. If we're not the only people delivering in the neighbourhood, the traffic's going to be heavy," added McPherson.

"That's a lot to take in all at once," said Michael, looking out over the bay.

"Unless you have someone in mind who wants to get into the delivery business, I'd suggest you buy Harry's fish packer and hire his crewman," said McPherson, "although it wouldn't surprise me if Harry slips him a few dollars to pass on information about the way we do business. If you decide on a new boat, you pay for the construction and the operating costs. I'm prepared to do most of the boat handling, but Peter has to do the work teaching Harry how to run the shore parties. And as I told Peter..." he looked at the younger man, "it would be wise to think of a back-up plan if Harry doesn't work out. Perhaps this Roy Olmstead would work with us."

Michael leaned back in his chair and took a ruminative sip of his whiskey. "That's something to think about, but for now, let's work with what we've got. Provided Harry's prepared to go with the amended plan, we have no objection to the arrangements you have proposed. We should, for caution's sake, camouflage the ownership of the boats, but that's not an insoluble problem. As far as operations are concerned, we should ensure that no direct link appears between us and Harry."

McPherson had a momentary thought that the "us" in this description would probably not include him.

"The Canadian government," Michael continued, "is happy collecting its excise tax on material taken out of bond. There's enough margin in our pricing to accommodate them. If we were to try to ship material and make it look as if it was going to Mexico, for example, the government would stay uninvolved, but it's in our interest to keep them satisfied. I'll speak to Harry about his boat and latest employee." He looked over at McPherson. "Perhaps you can refine the details of an appropriate boat and use Peter to help find the right people to build it."

"In that case, I'm back to the library for the next while."

"We should still be cautious in letting anyone become aware of our plans. There's a lot of money at stake—too much, in fact, to assume that everyone will stay honest," said Michael.

"I appreciate your concern, sir, but since I've arrived in town, I've had bankers, naval officers, warehouse keepers, a tailor, and a librarian ask me if I'm planning to enter the trade. I've made the decision to do it at least until something better comes along—longer if I have a good reason to stay. I was accustomed to a fair amount of larceny amongst officers and others on ships, although I was too junior to be offered or permitted a share of it—I'm only surprised to find the same practice in the higher parts of society."

A gong sounded from the dining room. Discussion lapsed when they went in for dinner. As before, Mrs. Arundel kept the dinner conversation light and largely focused on the lesser misadventures of Victoria society. McPherson thought that Michael had asked her to avoid discussion of serious matters.

He said goodnight to Peter outside the hotel and watched the car lurch away. Some things in life did not fit together properly. Arundel, a boat handler of exceptional skill, could not master the lesser complexities of an automobile. A city of apparent virtue had its leading citizens heavily involved in an illegal trade. And a beautiful, intelligent woman of some social standing was working in a library.

Back in his room he sat in a chair and ran his mind over the events of the day. How many other people were skirting rules? That stack of liquor, for example, stored in the out-of-the-way warehouse where his trunk had lain untouched for the last five years. Liquor was usually kept in bonded warehouses and did not spend much time in any kind of interim storage; the stuff he had seen looked like it had been in this warehouse for years.

Chapter 12

Monday, September 1st, 1919

He went back to the library. Mrs. Hemmingson looked up as he came through the door. "You, again!" she said. "I'm not sure we have any more material beyond that which you hauled out already."

"This time I brought a fresh notebook," he replied. "It should be good for a few hours."

"Go to it," she said.

He went back upstairs to the same table. He opened his book, took two facing pages and divided the left-side page into three sections—hull, engineering, and operations. He slowly examined the books on the shelves and the contents pages of the magazines. He listed the relevant information carefully under the applicable heading and posed questions on the facing page, and then started to sift through the piles on the table in front of him.

"It looks like you've outlasted all today's customers as well," said the gentle Irish voice behind him. He looked up. Mrs. Hemmingson was standing at the head of the stairs.

"I can't say I've found any more answers than I did two days ago, but at least I seem to have refined the questions a little more," he replied.

"Well, the answers will have to wait until tomorrow, but at least you can help cleaning up the mess you've left here."

"I thought I was being careful with the piles. They're all roughly in the order I took them down."

"Roughly is an adequate description," she said. "Here, take this pile and hold them while I see if the order makes any sense at all."

He scooped the pile up with the spines facing outwards admiring her deft movements as she riffled through the books and rearranged them expertly before replacing them on the shelves.

"That was impressive," he said. "In my world we'd call it shipshape," he added clumsily.

She looked at him with a smile playing at the edges of her eyes. "If I had to wait for you to do it, my son would be starving to death before I got home."

"A responsibility I could not bear, Mrs. Hemmingson."

"Your consideration is most welcome, Mr. McPherson. If you have no answers, I presume you will be returning?" she asked.

"I will. Tomorrow, in fact, and would I be permitted to invite you to lunch?"

"You might ask, but my acceptance would depend on how likely you are to stay with your books for so long as to prevent me from actually eating. Today you worked all through the lunch hour."

He looked at his watch and tried to find something clever to say. He failed.

He came up the library steps at two minutes before noon the next day and stood unobtrusively off to one side of the door.

"Sailors, it seems, keep good time, although I half expected you to come barging up to the desk," Mrs. Hemmingson said as she came out.

"I thought it wise to be circumspect and not give your colleagues cause for twittering."

"Thank you. Men are not always so sensitive.

As a widow, and especially now in this more permissive post-war era, I don't have to contend with the social constraints that would have governed me meeting you five years ago. However, Victoria's social circles are small, and even now, if I'm to be seen in the company of a man, especially an attractive one, it's as well to have a good reason."

"I've never been called attractive," he finally managed to spit out. He turned to be on the outside of the sidewalk as they walked over to the intersection.

"Well now, you needn't let it go to your head."

"I'll try." He smiled and asked, "Is the restaurant in the Dominion Hotel satisfactory for lunch?" he asked.

"I've never been in it," she replied. "Restaurant lunches don't form a large part of my life."

"It's across the road."

"I know, I've seen it."

He grinned at the rebuke, and as they reached the other side of the road, deftly shifted his position so that he was again on the outside. He leaned forward and opened the door for her to walk in ahead of him. The dining room lay on their right as they came in and McPherson steered her over to the reception desk. The room was crowded.

"Is lunch possible in the short time I have available?" she asked.

"I've reserved a table," said McPherson, and he gave his name to the woman at the desk.

"Thank you, Commander," said the hostess, and she led them to a table against the wall, away from the mainstream of dining room traffic. He pulled a chair out for Mrs. Hemmingson after asking which direction she preferred to face and sat down opposite. They opened their menus.

"Commander?" she asked.

"Lieutenant Commander, actually. I'm technically still in the service. They transferred me to the Reserve without asking. In London, staff in restaurants are quite fond of titles, and it's useful when you're looking for something that might be scarce—like a table at a busy restaurant at lunch time."

The waitress took their orders.

"What would you have said if I had objected to the choice?"

"Pointed out that time was not in our favour, said that all their neighbouring alternatives were dirty, and, if you had persisted, I would have been pleased to find that I had learned something about you."

"Someone has prepared you well for the challenges of life."

"Less a matter of preparation than opportunities for observation of the ways of others. My parents had no social standing and I've been at sea since I was fourteen. Any learning I can claim came from libraries."

"And from librarians over lunch, it sounds like."

"Not as often as you might think. Presumably you have the opportunity to pass on knowledge to clients with similar deficiencies every now and then?"

"I mentioned to Madge, the clerk who's relieving me, that one of our more enthusiastic readers has offered to buy my lunch for me if I give him some notes to help in some research. She asked if it was 'the big seafaring-looking man.' I said it was, and she said we might just as well help out the good-lookers as the ugly ones. I said I'd return the favour if she gets someone other than the usual boring man with a permanent runny nose, and she said she'd cover an extra half-hour for me."

"Ýou're very different from the usual librarian," was all he could manage to reply.

"It may be because I wear sleeve coverings to protect my cuffs from the dust and spilled ink that make us recognizable. Besides," she went on, "I haven't been doing the job for that long. It was a few years before I felt comfortable leaving my son with someone else."

"How old is he?"

"Four."

"My fiancée didn't live long enough for us to marry and have children. She died while I was still away. She was a librarian." He smiled slightly.

"I should have guessed. What were you looking to find out when you met her?"

He paused slightly to make sure he said nothing that would cause the Admiral to come looking for him. "A minor thing, really. I needed some information on the landward side of some Mediterranean ports. It was easier to see if it was available locally than making the run up to the Admiralty in London." He was a little surprised at how easily the lie ran off his tongue.

The waitress arrived with their lunch, giving them the opportunity to change the course of the conversation.

"Are you finding everything you need now?" Mrs. Hemmingson asked after a little while.

"I've lots of raw information about hull designs and engines," he said, "but I need to spend some time putting it together."

"You never did answer my question about our local rumrunners. They're the only people who talk much about small, fast boats."

He looked at her levelly. "It seems like this city has two kinds of people: those who are involved and never say anything about it; and those who aren't and say a lot."

"You're not the only one to come in and look at books—most of them give up after half an hour."

He needed to talk to someone, and this gentle-voiced woman, with her ready wit and keen sense of observation, might at least be an impartial commentator.

"I do have an offer, and with conventional seagoing jobs being in very short supply, I'm taking it."

"Anyone I'm likely to know? My late husband was well-connected. Before he died, I was a regular attender at local society functions."

"One of your neighbours, actually. The Arundels."

It was Mrs. Hemmingson's turn to pause. "Yes, I know them slightly. My husband had some dealings with Major Arundel, but since his death, we haven't socialized. How much do you know about them?"

"Not much. Peter was an officer on my ship for a short while, but he was assigned away. An old Royal Navy officer in Esquimalt told me to be careful of them, but that was more a matter of the fact that he knew the type rather than the people concerned."

"Was that Captain Anstruthers?"

"Yes. Does everyone know everyone else in this town?" McPherson took a sip of water and looked around the room.

"In certain social circles, yes. They also know all the details of each other's misadventures and make a point of not talking about them. The Arundels are fairly typical—they're well connected, but my husband said something went wrong in London before they came here. He didn't elaborate."

"Good background for the rum-running business perhaps; it skirts legality in Canada and is outright illegal in its principal market." He changed the subject rapidly. "Do you have misadventures?"

"One or two, and I don't talk about them, either" she said, looking at him directly.

"I must be the only person in the city without a past, but I'm certainly not the only one concerned about a future."

"What would that be if you had a choice?"

"Something unexciting, like a deck officer on a coastal passenger ship, hoping to become the captain at some point, with a nice little house ashore and a family in it."

"That's a full life."

"I need to get on the other side of the next few months to even hope it might be possible."

"Can't you just wait for something to turn up?" she asked.

"I could, but doing nothing would be difficult. Besides, what I've seen of the rum trade so far isn't that different from what I've been doing for the last few years, so any risks should be manageable." He put his fork down, finished with his lunch, but not willing to let go of this conversation. "Tell me about yourself. I can tell you're Irish."

"I'm not much in local social prominence, either, without my late husband," she said. "I went out to India as a maid for the family of a General. I was pleased enough to leave Ireland—all I faced there was a life like my mother's, patching up whoever I married when he came back from an evening out bashing someone."

"Doesn't sound like some of the lads were too successful at it."

"Some of them could bash back—and I hate unnecessary violence. India looked like an alternative that was far enough away I'd never have to come back."

"So how did you end up here?"

"There came a little problem when the General took too close an interest in me. When his wife saw the way things were going, she dismissed me. It was fortunate that my husband was acquainted with the family and was about to retire and leave India. He suggested a practical solution, and despite the twenty-five-year difference in our ages, I agreed. He was very much a gentleman, and I was an Irish farm girl polished up for domestic service. We came here and fitted in very well. He had a little money, sufficient to buy the house across the bay from the Arundels. He knew what wines to buy, and I knew what order the glasses were placed on the table. What about you?"

"Not that different from me, really. My father was a Scot, of the sort that the Hudson's Bay Company think is ideal to manage its interests in the far-flung reaches of Canada. He and my mother married the day before they caught the boat, and they moved from one remote place to another. I was born near what's now Dawson in the Yukon, and my brother was born and died in Fort Chipewyan in Northern Alberta. Any schooling I got was from my mother, basic reading from the bible and the Hudson's Bay catalogue. When I was fourteen, we came out to Prince Rupert and I saw the sea for the first time. After that, I didn't want to go back to my parents' life, and I was big enough to convince the captain of a coastal freighter that I'd make a deckhand. That was in 1905, and aside from the war, that's been my life so far."

She said nothing as she toyed with the remnants of her lunch. "Do let me know how it works out, Commander. I'm always interested in the outcome of the information people find in the library."

"Regular lunchtime meetings?" he suggested. "And my name is Dugald."

"Then I am Emmaline."

Later, McPherson sat in his room and laid out all his notes on the table. His first was the paper that Emmaline had given him, with a list of books about ship design. The entries in his notebook covered articles in magazines and needed refining. As a merchant seaman, his first instinct was to build the boat around the cargo hold. This boat would have to allow rapid unloading of crates of bottles by hand on a rolling deck.

He made a rough sketch of both a top and a side view of a possible design and closed his book. He was acutely aware that he now had more questions and still faced the need to find someone with answers. On the positive side, Arundel and he probably had more experience than anyone locally in running a boat like this.

He went down to the lobby and phoned the Arundel house. Peter's mother told him her son was at the Belmont Club and suggested he join him there. McPherson smiled and told her, "I think he'll have too good a start on me. I'll call in the morning."

Chapter 13

Wednesday, September 3rd, 1919

The next morning, he telephoned Arundel again. To his initial question, Peter told him, "There's a Japanese family named Takahashi in Rock Bay who run a good business. It's a father and son, and they build really solid fishing boats. I'll meet you there."

McPherson found him waiting outside the boatyard. They walked in together and Arundel said, "I don't suppose they know too much about aeroplane engines but there'll be a mechanic around who knows enough about speedboats to help with the technical problems. I bought my boat from these people a couple of years before the war. Hiro's the father and Akihiro, his son."

The office was at one end of a dilapidated shed overlooking the slipway, where a battered ninety-foot seiner was hauled out. The yard looked well used, but McPherson, with his singular concern about tidiness, saw that all tools were in their right place and wood was stacked in order of size. He couldn't see any paint or other flammable material lying around. A small boy with a broom was aggressively attacking a buildup of dust in a corner of the yard.

"Ohayō, Takahashi-san" said Arundel, nodding his head to the old man who came out of the office door. "Hi, Aki," he said to the younger man following him.

Aki came out and shook Arundel's hand. "Heard you were on the way back. Had quite a time, I'm told."

"Bit of a one. You?" asked Arundel.

"Navy didn't want me, so I volunteered to patrol up and down the coast in our own boat."

"Takahashi-san doesn't speak much English, but he can follow the conversation," Arundel explained to McPherson. "Aki and I have hung around together for years."

McPherson shook hands with the two men and held out his open notebook. Both the old man and his son looked attentively at the sketch.

"You want us to build this, Pete?" asked the son.

"Yeah, Aki."

"Better come in the office." The four of them squeezed in. "Without going in too deeply about why you want something like this, what do you want to do with it?"

"We'll usually tie up at a wharf, but we'll be running it up the occasional beach. It'll be a fast boat, with a crew of two," replied Arundel.

"Do you have a copy of the hull design for something like this?" asked Aki.

"No," said McPherson, "but I've had something like it out of the water enough that I was able to sketch the lines. I estimated the draft and guessed the additional allowance needed for the propeller shafts and the rudder."

"Between us," Arundel replied, "we can probably remember enough to give intelligent directions to a boat builder. One detail I don't remember is the angle the engine was mounted so that the forepart was higher than the stern. The propeller shaft was mounted at the same angle so there was no need to make any changes where it came out of the hull. That worked in a war ship, where all we carried was a torpedo that lay in its trough over the deck and pointed back over the transom. I'm not sure it would work for a boat that has to carry the maximum payload possible." Aki and his father made a couple of comments to each other and the old man nodded.

"I sailed with a few old seamen who thought of engineers as an unpleasant and usually greasy necessity," said McPherson. "I'm not like that, but I'm still not familiar enough with mechanical things. I've worked beside marine mechanics, but I was always too busy to pay much attention to anything beyond my own job."

He leaned over and unfolded a paper from inside the cover of his book and laid it on the counter. "We have the two Liberty engines, which I've sketched in here," he pointed, "but I can't work out how running the pair of them would give us enough speed to justify all the fuel they'd drink—and then there's the question of reliability. The hull design has to match the engine, give us the carrying capacity, and be unloadable by hand in the time likely to be available to the shore parties. It also has to be maneuverable close to shore, and able to be operated by just me and one other crewman."

"You surely do like your lists, don't you?" said Arundel.

"There's more; we have to think about getting the load to land. We don't want to rely on the shore crews to come out to us. It'll be safer to keep things in our hands as much as possible. We carried a dinghy to serve as a utility craft. They were useful enough, but Petty Officer Logan, our Newfoundlander mechanic, didn't like their quality or design. He kept on saying that if anyone in the navy was capable of thinking clearly, they would have used a dory."

"I remember him saying it," said Arundel. "I never did look up what one was. Any idea what it looks like?" He raised his eyebrows at Aki who shook his head. "We can see if any of the other local builders can help."

"I did already," said McPherson. "There was a picture but not much detail. On the main craft, I've estimated a fifty-foot hull with a seven-foot beam. That would give us enough stability for running and unloading cargo. We could get those by flaring the hull on a wide angle back from the stem and flattening out the keel slightly at the stern. The forepart of the hull should have a deep vee at the bow to cut through the water, with the line of the keel changed to give enough lift for the speed we want in rough waters."

McPherson paused while he riffled through some pages in his book. "We also have to consider," he went on, "that for moving a boat at high speed, in the dark, through waters full of floating logs, we'll need some defence if we hit something. A steel runner down the ridge of the keel and plates fitted over the planks at the bow below and just above the waterline might work. Above all, the boat has to run as fast full as it does empty, because its primary purpose is to avoid trouble."

"Not much in the yard at the moment except repairs," said Aki. "Probably can manage the hull. Not sure about the engines. What weight of loads and what size?" he asked.

"Wooden cases about this size," said Arundel holding his hands about eighteen inches apart.

"You taking it out in the weather?"

"Yes."

"Needs to have a bit of extra in the hull in case you hit something," said Aki. "Don't want it falling apart because we forgot to put the right bit on." He reached up to where a roll of brown wrapping paper was mounted on the wall and cut off a three-foot length, which he clipped to a table folded down below it. He carefully copied an enlarged version of Dugald's drawing onto it. For the next two hours he, Arundel and McPherson discussed details which he carefully added to the master plan. McPherson meticulously copied each change and new piece of information into his notebook.

Silently, the old man took a piece of two-foot-long, six-inch square, yellow cedar. He marked the outer dimensions along the side with a thick pencil and started to carve. As the others talked, a small replica of half the hull came alive in his hands. McPherson took it and turned it over and over, looking at it from every angle. He passed it to Arundel, who did the same. The model was virtually the same shape as Aki had drawn.

"Looks like we have a start," said Aki. "I went to school to learn how to be a draftsman, but my dad keeps turning out things like this, so I only have to do a take-off for estimating the materials. That just leaves us with managing the kind of power you want."

He went out of the office and climbed up the ladder leaning against the seiner on the slipway and called to someone down into the hold. McPherson went back to his notebook and leafed through the material he had copied down about engines, while Arundel just kept turning the exquisite model in his hands. Neither of them looked up until Aki reappeared with a man behind him.

"I'd hoped I had seen the last of you gentlemen," the newcomer said.

McPherson looked up and grinned. "Now you're here, you can tell us what a dory is."

"Petty Officer Logan! More than that, you can tell us how to fit motors in this boat," said Arundel. "After that, you can tell us what you're doing here."

"Better give me some details, then," replied Logan.

"As Takahashi-san and Aki will have guessed and are too polite to comment on, we want this boat as a rumrunner. Dugald has gone over every piece of information he can find on hulls and motors, but we're short on real expertise as to what to use and how to set it up. We took the opportunity to pick up some new Liberties in Seattle a few days ago because aeroplane motors are going cheaply at the moment. If we decide to use them, we don't have to buy when everyone else wants them, and if they don't work, we'll sell them."

Logan looked over the notes Aki had made and looked at the model Hiro had carved. "Yeah, I've got a few ideas, but I'd prefer to do a bit of thinking first. Can I copy some of this?"

"Yes," said McPherson, without looking at Arundel.

Logan wiped his hands on a piece of cotton waste and then used the space between the tips of his thumb and forefinger to measure off a two-foot length of paper from the roll above the desk. He took Hiro's carved half model, and with the same thick pencil traced the lengthwise and stern piece shape of the hull on the paper. He then added a sketch of the bow looking at it from the front, and carefully copied the estimated dimensions Aki and McPherson had agreed on. He folded the paper lengthwise and refolded it like a concertina, giving himself some pages where he could copy the rest of the information without smearing it with the incipient dirt that lay around the carefully maintained workshop.

"That was interesting, PO," said Arundel, watching the process.

"Pays to be careful, and it's not Petty Officer anymore, sir. The name's Jeff." He looked over at Hiro. "I should have that seiner fixed in an hour or so. I guess you want me to look at this then." He waved the folded paper. "Tomorrow morning alright?" he asked.

"Back here at this time, then," said McPherson. He and Arundel went back out to the street. "Sounds like you know the Takahashis well."

"Aki and I spent a lot of time together when we were kids. He had an old boat and we used to go out to some of the islands and fish. We'd sell the catch, and after a while I had enough money to buy a boat of my own. I'd bring it in here when it needed any fixing I hadn't learned to do myself."

"That where you learned to stay away from rocks?"

"Mostly."

"I'm assuming you're happy with paying for this."

"Within reason, yes. How much will we need?"

"I haven't a comparison, so it's just an estimate, but since we already have the main engines and the design, ask the Takehashis what they can do. Based on what I've seen, I'd say seven thousand dollars is a likely price."

"That should be acceptable."

McPherson changed the subject. "When is your father likely to have sorted the packer out with Harry?"

"He went to see him at the yacht last night and wasn't back when I went out to the club."

"Do you live in the place?"

"I get a room there when we go late; it saves disturbing everyone when I get home."

"You don't have much to do, then."

"Not very much. My parents are still going on about the insurance business and not taking the risks we took for the last few years. There's a few things that need looking at for insurance, but some other people have to make up their minds first before we can do our bit."

Chapter 14

Thursday, September 4th,1919

They met at the shipyard office, but with five of them needing room to work, it was too crowded. Logan suggested they use the cabin of the seiner hauled up on the slipway beside the office building. It was cramped, but at least it had a table that would hold all of them. Aki pinned his plan up on the rear bulkhead and spoke for his father.

"There's nothing like the boat you want on the water at the moment, and everything you want to do with it has to be worked up from something else. You're going to be carrying a pretty heavy weight. We haven't worked out precisely how much, but it means that the cargo area has to be clear for unloading. When you've unloaded, the weight of the wheelhouse and engines are going to pull the bow down, so the hull design has to counteract this. We think a step in the hull about a third of the way back would, with enough power when the bow rises, offset the loss of weight in the stern and leave a smaller bit of the hull in the water. Depending how the engines perform, we should get a maximum speed of about thirty knots, but there's a lot of guesswork in there." His father took his pencil and made an adjustment to the profile of the hull.

"The engines," Aki went on, "would fit best toward the bow of the craft in their own compartment located on the centre line forward of the control position. That would leave space for the hatch to come off easily and leave access to the entire compartment for servicing. The payload would lie astern of the cockpit, with the canvas hatch cover folded up behind it. A windscreen and a folding canvas cover would protect the cockpit. They can be battened into place when the weather turns bad.

"We'll use an oak frame with double planking on the hull, with fir on the outside and yellow cedar inside; for additional strength, we'll glue canvas between each layer."

"In the Baltic, rocks were our biggest worry, and around here they're worse," said Arundel.

"We could put copper sheathing along the length of the hull up to the waterline as well as steel plate reinforcement at the forward edge of the keel and on the flare of the bows, but it will be a matter of weight distribution. We'll need to offset the weight of the engines and the metal on the hull. We should also put the propellers in cages. They'll protect both them and the shafts from floating debris, and rocks if you don't hit them too hard." Aki drew the lines on the plan.

While they were talking, Logan had pulled out his peculiarly folded pad and was making notes on one of the open pages.

"Jeff?" prompted McPherson.

"While you've been adding weight to the hull, I've been thinking about what you'll need to push it, and how much fuel you'll need to do it. Leaving aside the fuel for a moment," the burr of his Newfoundlander's accent grew more pronounced as he moved deeper into his explanation, "you'll need enough power to lift the hull onto the step even at the lower end of your cruising speed. If you just use the aeroplane engines you have stored in the warehouse over there, they won't be at their best if you use them as your only source of power."

"Why? We did well enough in the Baltic." Arundel pulled the drawing over to have a closer look.

"In a way, yes, mostly because you were doing the driving and I was doing the fixing. There, we only had one load, the torpedo, and usually we didn't fire it—if we even took it in the first place. You probably didn't notice how many modifications we made on the fly to make sure the cooling and lubrication systems worked. You're going to need a reverse gear for the sort of thing you want to do now. The new patrol boats have two engines, both for additional power and in case one of them stops."

"We can go back to the design, then."

Logan took a deep breath while he was thinking through his answer and then spoke slowly and quite deliberately. "I think three engines would be the best—the two Liberties you have together with a fairly big diesel, which should be able to move you at cruising speed. It's going to mean three props out the stern, but the diesel can also serve as a starter for the Liberties. The thing that looks like it might be complicated with Liberties, although I've never seen them running, is that the torque from them would cause the boat to list to starboard. The engine runs the propeller clockwise, unless it can be geared to run it the other way. If you have two engines turning the propellers in the same direction, at speed you'll cause it to list at a greater angle, or even flip over. If we run the propeller on the port engine counter-clockwise it should take that problem away—I think. Just before I left Newfoundland in June, I talked to Mr. Platford of Rolls Royce, who was servicing the Vickers Vimy Captains Alcock and Brown were using to fly across the Atlantic. I asked him how they were dealing with this problem, because an aeroplane going sideways isn't much use. He told me about setting the two propellers to run in opposite directions."

"Three engines are a lot of weight forward,"

said McPherson.

"Yes," said Logan, looking at Hiro. "It probably means the diesel should be mounted forward, and the two Liberties behind the control position on either side of the cockpit. It'll be a bit chummy for two crewmen in there as well, so we may have to move them a bit aft. The control position would be at deck level to keep the boat's profile as low as possible. We've a bit more work to do on it." He paused and thought some more. "You should have double rudders. If you just have one, the power of two engines driving through a turn could break it. We have to give some thought to the controls, too. They're likely to be complicated enough that you won't be able to leave the cockpit until you're well away from rocks and traffic."

"How much?" asked Arundel, turning to Aki.

"I can give you half of your estimate tomorrow; that should get you started." Aki looked at his father who gave an almost imperceptible nod.

"Okay," he said.

"How long to get the boat finished?"

"After this seiner is finished, we have nothing in hand. Depending on the mechanical things, we can probably get it ready for testing by the first week in December."

Aki and Hiro left the cabin and expertly picked their way over the debris on the deck outside. McPherson turned to Logan. "What brought you out here?" he asked. "I thought you were wedded to the Rock."

"So I was, but when I got out of the service, there was even less to do there than there is here. You people had talked about this wonderful place where the weather was marvelous and the trees dripped money, so I thought I'd try it here before I ran out of my discharge money. Of course, when I got here, neither one of you was in sight, so I've been keeping the family fed by working on ships' engines all up and down the waterfront. I'm glad you showed up, because this," he pointed at the deck, "is the last job I have in hand."

"You could work for us full time," said Arundel.

"I thank you for the thought, sir, but you almost got my head separated from my shoulders too many times in the Baltic for me to want to risk the association again. I can do your machine work if you like, but none of the seafaring, if you please."

"Fair enough. Then we'll need to work with you to develop the specifications and figure out where we need to buy anything we don't have," said McPherson. "A couple of things come to mind immediately. Propellers are one. If either of you remember much about the size and pitch of those we had on the patrol boats, it would be helpful. The next is the gear box; it would be good if we could find a heavy duty one—possibly from a truck or large car—and adapt it. I think we'll only need it on the smaller of the three engines, for maneuvering close to shore. At those times, for the most part, we'll have the big engines shut down." He paused.

"How do you want to work, Jeff? Directly for the Takahashis, or for us?" asked Arundel.

"Aki pays me for my time, and I supply all my own tools," said Logan. "He buys all the parts we need. So far, it's working well."

McPherson nodded. "Leave it like that for the moment, and if something needs to be changed, we can look at it later. We have to go to Seattle again soon, and it's probably the place where we have the best choice in motors and props. Work out what we need, and we'll buy them."

"Another thing," said Logan. "These are large engines with big fuel tanks. We'll need some sort of electric fan to take away any fumes that build up in the bilge. You'll need to run them for about four or five minutes before you start the engines. If that doesn't work, we'll put a couple of fire extinguishers on clips in the front of the cockpit."

"It seems to me that if business is to start almost immediately, we need that packer," said McPherson as he and Arundel walked back out onto the street. "You didn't say whether your father had sorted it out with Harry."

"Sorry, yes," said Arundel. "We own the boat now, and the previous owner will stay working for us."

"What do you know about him?"

"Nothing."

"Better find out then. Where's the boat?"

"Moored in the outer harbour; her name is *Lady Jane*. I've got the car across the street, there," said Arundel, pointing. "We can drive."

"Hopefully you're benefiting from all the practice. We don't really want to be too obvious because you just miss hitting people."

"In that case, why don't you drive?"

"Thank you, I will." McPherson got into the driver's seat of the Crossley.

"You'll need this, then." Arundel held out a key.

"What's that for?"

"The key turns the lock, which allows the electrical system to fire when you turn the crank. Stops people from stealing your car."

"The last time I saw these cars working, they didn't have them."

"Welcome to the new world."

McPherson took the key and Arundel showed him where to insert it. McPherson meticulously inspected and tried every lever, pedal, and switch on the inside of the car, then got out again and walked around its outside. He opened the engine compartment and checked both the radiator and the measuring stick for the oil level. Once satisfied, he leaned across the driver's seat to turn the key and the small lever on the dashboard that advanced the spark for starting the engine. He pulled the switch to engage the self-starter, and the engine purred to life. He carefully reset the spark control lever, looked at Arundel, and said, "Where to?"

"Very thorough, Pilot. We're going to the Fisherman's Wharf by Erie Street."

McPherson gently released the handbrake, looked over his right shoulder, and pulled out smoothly onto the road. He changed gear without grinding. "Aren't you the clever one," said Arundel, with a barely concealed sneer. They arrived at the other side of the harbour, and he neatly reversed into a small space between two other cars without hitting either, or further grinding the gears. "You never told me you could drive so well," said Arundel as they walked toward the wharf.

"You never asked."

"Where did you learn?"

"In England, while I was waiting for other things to happen. It's really not that difficult—I'm surprised you have such a hard time with it.

"Can't explain it, Pilot."

"If we were back on board, I'd rip into you for inattention. You could start by treating the car more like a boat."

They reached the harbour wall overlooking the floating docks with hundreds of fishing boats rafted against one another. "So how do we find the one we're looking for?" asked Arundel.

"He'll probably be moored somewhere that lets him get out without too much trouble, so he's not likely to be on the inside of a bunch of other boats," said McPherson. "Let's concentrate on working from the outside in. What's her length?"

"Don't know—fifty feet or more."

They stood on the wall, and falling into the watch keeper's practice, each took an opposite side of the wharf area. Looking at the craft moored furthest away, they looked from the outside toward the centre. Without particularly thinking about it, each took a notebook from their pockets, sketched the outline of the wharf area they were examining, and marked the locations of likely-looking boats. When they finished, they compared notes and worked out the order in which they wanted to examine each one. When they found her, she was moored on an outer float with her bow facing the harbour. To get there, they had to pick their way over four smaller craft.

"If we like the arrangement, I'm going to suggest we go for a bit of a run tomorrow. I want to see if our new man is competent," said McPherson.

"I'll leave that part of it to you. I've an engagement for the whole day," said, Arundel, then he called out in the time-honoured nautical hail to a vessel before boarding it, "Ahoy, *Lady Jane*!"

"I hear you," came a voice from the cabin.

"It's Peter Arundel."

The voice, still hidden in the cabin said, "My new owner." A tall man, probably in his early forties, wound himself up the companionway from the cabin to the door opening on the deck. He wore a shapeless hat which had once possibly been black, with a peak at the front. His face was weather-beaten, and he spoke with the remnant of a Swedish accent. He leaned against the cabin and looked suspiciously at his two visitors. "I am Ollie Lindstrom. Who's Peter Arundel?"

"I am," said Arundel. "This is Dugald McPherson."

"I've been told about the pair of you but not much beyond your names. Where does it all go from here?" He crossed his arms. "I'm confused. A week ago, I bring the boat in with a load of fish, unload, and then moor behind some rich guy's yacht while I do a few running repairs. Next thing I know, he's offered me more money for my boat than I paid for it, as long as I stay on and run it for him. I guess he's not interested in fish, but as long as it's nothing too illegal I'm okay. All of a sudden, he shows up with this other guy and tells me he's sold the boat on, and I have the same deal. I guess you're going to tell me what the deal is, and I'm going to tell you whether it includes me."

"Fair enough," said McPherson. "Can we find somewhere to sit down and talk where everyone on the docks can't hear us?" Lindstrom opened the door to the wheelhouse, and they squeezed themselves inside.

McPherson looked around with approval as he saw the compass and engine controls were clean and no rubbish lay in corners. The chart rack was a vertical fixture fitted to the forward bulkhead on the starboard side of the wheel. Most of the slots were empty. The galley was three steps down from the wheelhouse and the table was down between two bunks.

"You're right," said Arundel, after they had settled round the table. "It's rumrunning, and the business is half-legal, at least the part of it in Canada. The other half is in the States, and there it is illegal, but enough people don't agree with it for us to make a bunch of money delivering liquor to them."

Lindstrom frowned. "Around the waterfront there's talk about problems in rumrunning with the American cops shooting at them, and loads being hijacked. Harry, the guy I sold the boat to first, said he'd lost a couple of loads already. I don't want to get into gunfights."

"Harry had a problem with picking people who knew what they were doing," said Arundel. "He saw you handling the boat and figured he needed a professional rather than the enthusiasts he'd hired earlier. We bought your boat because we wanted someone more competent than Harry in the boat-handling business. He's going to look after the land side, and we're going to do what we know about—which is boats."

"So why do you need me?"

"Dugald and I spent the war in small boats staying out of trouble. We think we can get a handle on this trade by doing the same. We need this boat because the fast one we want to use later isn't going to be ready for a few months, but we want to get the organization up and running before other people move into the market."

"We'll still need this boat later to help out the other one. If we like each other, we'll need you, too," McPherson added.

Lindstrom stood up and looked out over the bow. They rocked gently from the wash of another boat leaving the wharf. "I spent most of the war running up and down the coast looking for German battleships that weren't there. It was all volunteer, and the navy didn't want to have anything to do with us, so I'm not impressed with anyone saying they were part of it."

"The navy's not going to matter much from now on," said McPherson. "Before the war I was a second officer on coastal steamships, and Peter learned his boating from the Takahashis, a boat-building family with a yard in the Inner Harbour. I don't have much to go back to at the moment, and that's why servicing thirsty Yanks seems like a good idea."

"How much?" asked Lindstrom.

McPherson looked at Arundel. Arundel paused, then said, "Two hundred for each delivery, plus expenses. That will work out to a about a thousand a month at one run a week, and more as we expand."

"What do you want me to do?" asked Lindstrom.

"Get the boat ready for work," said McPherson. "Liquor crates are probably smaller than the ones you used for fish, so check the hold and make sure we can load without poking holes in the hull. I'll be with you on the first trips, but we'll probably need a reliable deckhand for later. I guess you can do most of your own engine work?" McPherson raised his eyebrows to emphasize the question, and Lindstrom nodded. "We'll need charts of the coast covering southern Vancouver Island, the Mainland from the Sechelt Peninsula south, and Puget Sound and the Pacific coast down to the Columbia River. How many do you have?"

"Not many," said Lindstrom, shaking his head, "and only the Straits and the San Juan Islands on the American side. For picking up fish I usually stick to the same routes and those places I know by heart. That includes every safe harbour in southern British Columbia and Northwest Washington, and I can find my way through just about any weather or sea condition."

"I'm sure you can, but you'll have to work with me or Peter, and it's better there's never any misunderstanding about what people mean; we use charts to make sure. The Dominion Fisheries Office has the Canadian ones, but they're handing most of that business to ships' chandlers, so get what you can there. We'll want to go back to Seattle with you and the boat next week, so we'll pick up anything more we need there." Lindstrom looked uncomfortable and grunted. "Problem?" asked McPherson.

"Never had a lot to do with charts; wouldn't know if I got the right ones."

"I'll do it," McPherson said. He poked around under the chart table, opening drawers and swinging open locker doors.

"What are you looking for?" asked Lindstrom. McPherson looked up.

"Where's your first aid kit?"

"What's that?"

"Basic medical supplies in case someone gets hurt."

"There's only ever been me. If I cut myself, I used seawater and a rag to stop the bleeding until I got to shore. You planning to get hurt?"

"First aid kits are for when you're not planning to get hurt and it happens anyway. It's a useful naval precaution. I'll bring one along. We'll do a run down to Seattle just to get used to one another, but I need some time to get everything together. Would Monday morning suit you?" He looked first at Lindstrom and then at Arundel.

"Yes," said Lindstrom, holding out his hand. Arundel shook it, and then McPherson. "I can use the time to clean her up. I'll fuel her and meet you in the Inner Harbour at ten o'clock."

Back at the car, Arundel said, "Why don't you drop me at the warehouse on the Gorge Road? My father has another of these cars ready and it needs to be picked up. You can keep this one for running about."

McPherson said, "That's very generous." He took the key, started the car, and pulled away from the curb.

The warehouse off the Gorge Road was a large building backing onto the waterway. Cars in various stages of completion were parked in orderly rows in front of it. The entire property was surrounded by a ten-foot-high chain link fence topped with barbed wire.

"Honk the horn, will you?" said Arundel, as they pulled up to the gate.

"A lot of caution for some broken down cars," said McPherson.

"We keep some of our stock inside." A man came out of a side door of the building and walked over to unlock the gate.

"If you have stock here, and I noticed more at the warehouse where I stored my trunk, there must be a fair amount of money involved in financing the trade. Although I assume the stock at the other warehouse belongs to someone else."

"Most of the financing comes from banks who put up the money over the short term and we pay them back when we sell the stuff," said Arundel.

McPherson noticed that Arundel did not comment on his assumption. "Must be some very patient banks, with all the stuff you've been losing."

"We make enough to keep them happy, and my father's insurance plan gives them a certain margin of comfort."

"Prohibition just got started. You must have got into the business quickly to get this much stock on hand this early."

Arundel opened the car door. "Markets respond to needs; it seemed obvious that this was going to happen, so once we decided to get involved, we had most of our stock ready to go in a month."

"You know a lot about the details of the business – are you sure you just got introduced to the details—or was that just more window dressing?"

Arundel left the car and walked through the opened gate. "Doesn't matter what you say, I'll be treating you as if you know everything," said McPherson to his retreating back.

McPherson found parking for his car behind the hotel and went up to his room. He needed the right clothes for a day on the boat so he took out a pair of his new canvas trousers and one of the mackinaw shirts. He pulled his travelling trunk out of the closet and opened it for the first time since he left England. A faint whiff of mothballs wafted up as he took out the top tray where he kept his ready-use linen. From below he took out each one of his spare uniforms carefully layered with brown wrapping paper separating them, until he found what he was looking for near the bottom, a light jacket, and a medium-weight woolen sweater. He carefully repacked the trunk, layer by layer. Last to go in was a canvas case where he kept his protractor, dividers, and navigation instruments; from this he took out a pair of eyeglasses with smoked lenses.

He put them aside and reached into the box he had brought from the storage company. From that he pulled out his seaboots, clasp knife, and cap. He carefully removed the company badge from the cap. It was better, considering how far the business had now come, that he did not look like he belonged to Canadian Pacific Steamships.

Chapter 15

Monday, September 7th,1919

Lummi Bay lay northeast of Victoria Harbour, and with the rising sun, it almost blinded them as it appeared high on their port quarter.

"Lucky we'll operate at night," said Lindstrom as they worked their way past.

"Lucky us engineers live below decks," said Logan, who had joined them for this run.

"Peter, since you're here, you can do a sketch of the routes around the shoreline," said McPherson. "We can add details from the chart later."

Arundel picked up a pair of binoculars, trained them on the shore and opened a notebook on the chart table beside him.

"Go around again, Ollie," he said, after they had done one pass through to the bay's southern end.

Lindstrom swung the wheel hard over to port and took up an opposite course.

"I'd prefer we didn't do that without looking at the chart—we never know what's inshore. If we have to turn for any reason, it's wiser to opt for sea room," said McPherson.

"You'd think I'd never been to sea."

"I'll bet you never willingly went near the shore at night. Calhoun had a bunch of loads go astray; it could have been rocks, bad navigation, or hijackers. The most important thing to do at sea is to stick to regular procedures. That way, when something unexpected happens, you've limited the number of options to consider. You steer away from the shore, you can spend your time looking at traffic. It's the reason why when you find yourself on a converging course with someone, both of you steer two points to starboard. If the other fellow does something stupid, you can deal with the issue directly, but you can expect anyone else in the neighborhood who does know what he's doing to follow the right procedures."

"Thanks, Admiral."

"You can be as snarky as you like, Ollie, but no boat I have anything to do with is going up on the beach because it isn't handled right." McPherson looked over at Arundel. "You have the deck."

"You carry much cash with you on the fishing grounds?" McPherson asked Lindstrom.

"Yup."

"Ever meet anyone more interested in your cash than the fish?"

"Yup."

"What happened?"

"They went away." Lindstrom reached into the top drawer of a locker mounted against the back by the door and took out a shotgun with two very short barrels, slung in a holster which allowed the ends of the barrels to protrude. "I always keep this slung across my chest when anyone's close. I've only had to fire it once."

"What happened to the man you shot at?" asked Arundel.

"Don't know—he fell over the rail and the guy he was with ran for his own boat. Maybe he got picked up; I never saw either of them anymore, and no one ever tried to hijack me again."

"It's probably a good idea to keep the shotgun, but I don't want us starting gunfights or even continuing them," said McPherson. "We're only going to be a target for the cargo. The plan is the liquor will be paid for before we leave, and our money for delivering it gets paid as soon as we get back to Victoria. We just have to make sure we deliver to the right people, and we'll identify them by them having the other half of a torn dollar bill. We get our half when we load."

"What do we do if someone takes a run at us?" said Lindstrom.

"First, we try to out-maneuver him and keep as much distance between us as we can. It's useful to know where rocks are, and we'll try to put ourselves on the other side of them. If he tries a shortcut to head us off, there's a reasonable chance he'll rip his bottom out. We haven't much speed, but most boats out there haven't much more, so we should always have alternatives."

Arundel made a couple of notes in his book after cross-referencing them with the chart. He looked out over his shoulder and then said, "Ollie. Bring her round to port, go south-south-west and then take up a heading on two hundred degrees." He turned to McPherson. "We can hold that heading almost to Seattle, unless you want to go inside Whidbey Island."

"No, we probably won't bring this boat down that far, and it'll be too easy to get cut off if we bring the fast boat in for deliveries. We could have a look at it later in case we need to hide behind it at some point. In the meantime, let's just get to Seattle. Do you have all you want for this part of the coastline?"

Arundel riffled through the index. "Charts are good for the water side, but we haven't got a lot of information on the land. We shouldn't have to hold the hands of the pickup crews. They need to be sure the places we pick have decent shore-side connections. I don't think we should rely on Calhoun to tell them to get maps."

"There should be something produced by the state of Washington," said McPherson. "If not, there's a new road atlas out—Rand McNally—it should have enough land information for them."

"We also need to find a way to signal each other," said Arundel. "Unless some of their people spent time in the American navy, they're probably not used to looking for lights flashing from the sea, and without a proper map, they're just as likely to show up on the wrong piece of coastline."

McPherson pulled out his notebook and wrote rapidly. "I'll see Calhoun as soon as we get in and get him to set up something with White tomorrow morning; I'd just as soon discuss business over coffee rather than when people are drunk and belligerent."

"I'll keep looking at the shoreline for a good practice spot until we get to Seattle," said Arundel.

Logan came up from the engine room. He was far more interested in the inner workings of the boat than navigation. "Your engine needs a little work," he told Lindstrom.

"Not my engine anymore. Talk to these two," Lindstrom replied.

Logan shrugged. "Doesn't matter who owns the boat, it's about whether we plan to use it to get back to Victoria."

"What's the problem?" asked Arundel.

"It's been maintained by a fisherman."

"What's that mean?" said Lindstrom aggressively.

"You're like every other fishing guy I've ever seen—you fix what's needed to get wherever you're going and only take the boat to the yard if you have to. Right now, the motor's loose on the mounts and the plug on the number three cylinder wants to fall out. We can probably get to Seattle the way we are, but I'll need a shop to mill a new plug before we try to go back home."

"Finnerty's will have that equipment; we spent enough money there—they should let you use it. We bought the engines there; it's in the alley behind the back gate of Boeing's yard at Elliot Bay." Arundel put his notebook back in his coat pocket.

"I've got a few things I can do here first," said Logan. I'll go and see him in the morning."

An hour later, McPherson entered the saloon of the *Eloise*. "Everything good on the way down?" Calhoun asked, looking up from the newspaper.

"Good enough," replied McPherson. "We'll be looking at a few mechanical things tomorrow, and Peter's looking for a practice landing spot we can use tomorrow night. We need to get together on some road maps so the pickup crews can get overland to the right place." He paused for a moment. "Are you happy with White doing that job?"

"That's what I'm going to find out now. I'm just about to leave."

"I'll come with you, but I don't want to talk business with these fellows over drinks," said McPherson. "They don't hold it well, so perhaps we can find somewhere to have coffee in the morning."

The two men walked together through the growing evening crowds on the downtown streets. They came up to the Alexis Hotel and took the route to the "Laundry" where White, Maureen and Burnand were at the same table. They sat down across from them.

"Jim!" said Calhoun, "how's things?"

"They'll be better if you have something real to tell me."

"We're here with the slow boat to look over some of the landing spots, pick up some engine parts, and sort out how you people will pick up from us," said McPherson.

"Mike here is going to do the pickup," replied White.

"We'll bring seventy-five cases, so unless you

can back a car up to the beach, you'll need a few extra fellows to hump the load to the cars." McPherson looked levelly at Burnand, who glowered back.

Maureen smiled widely, and McPherson followed her gaze over his shoulder to Arundel walking toward them. "Peter's going to be the one sorting out the land routes with you; he's had the most recent experience dealing with shoreline pickups and deliveries," he told White. "But let's talk about it in the morning." Arundel pulled out a chair. "The dining room upstairs is all right, but it will be more private if we meet on Harry's boat. We need you to lay your hands on a Washington state road atlas so we can look for a place to practice, as well as use for some for actual deliveries," he added.

"Sounds like you're still trying to tell us how to run our show," said Burnand.

"No," said Arundel, cutting in. "We're wanting to work out where we can get the stuff ashore and give it to the right people. Harry will have paid us for the merchandise before we leave the dock in Victoria, so he probably wants to get it to someone who's going to pay him."

Harry nodded.

"Which means we have to get to the right part of the right beach and hand the stuff to someone who can identify himself as the right party," said McPherson. "It also means we want to go over the shore-side information with you to pick places that work from the waterside. You bring an atlas, and we'll compare it to our charts. We should be through everything in an hour." He paused. "We need to work up a simple signaling process as well, so think about that while you round up your crews. We can do a practice drop when we leave tomorrow night." He stood up. "I'm heading upstairs now—I've been at sea long enough to get some sleep whenever I can. See you on the *Eloise* at...?" He looked at Harry, who looked around the table.

"Ten o'clock suit everyone?" Harry asked.

"Okay, if I have to," said White.

Burnand nodded.

"I'm with you, Pops," said Maureen.

Arundel smiled at Maureen and said, "I'm heading up as well. See everyone in the morning."

McPherson noticed the scowl White threw in Arundel's direction but didn't say anything. He headed for the elevator with Arundel and when they were out of earshot, he said quietly, "I hope you're leaving that woman alone. We're doing business with her father, and we don't need to complicate our lives. Besides, I thought you said you were spoken for."

"There's nothing happening there."

"I hope not. White looks like the kind of man who'd shoot us off just to make a point."

They checked out of the hotel in the morning and met in the dining room. McPherson said, "I think Peter should come with me to talk to White and his people. I'm not sure they understand what's needed to pick up cargo from a small boat. They've a long coastline to choose a landing spot from. Jeff, go on to Finnerty's and machine the engine plug. Take some dollars from Peter to cover everything we're likely to need as well as the taxi. If you want more, meet us at the *Lady Jane* before two o'clock and we can sort out the money and the pickup location then."

"I'll see you back at the boat then," said Logan.

The other two walked down Spring Street, which got steeper the closer they came to the waterfront. They could see the wharf where *Eloise* was berthed, and as they came up to her gangplank, McPherson asked, "Anything you particularly want to emphasize?"

"Just the signaling process. I'd prefer it be very simple, something like two long and one short from the boat and two short in return," said Arundel. "We should tell them to use a large light; in the Baltic we could get away with small ones, but we were used to doing it. These fellows aren't. We'll be sighting down a compass bearing, and I'm guessing they don't know what a compass is. A couple of practice runs tonight will at least teach them what they don't know, and we can start working from there. Plus, we need to get a copy of the map they plan to use."

They went on board to find Harry in the saloon, deep in the morning paper. There were a few minutes before the others were expected, so McPherson asked him, "You happy with Jim White still?"

"Why? Do you see a problem there?'

"We'll do a try-out tonight. If they show up with everything we asked them to bring, we can move ahead."

"Sure it's not because Peter here is hanging around with Jim's daughter and Jim's getting mad about it? You really shouldn't mix business with fun." Calhoun looked pointedly at Arundel.

"Maybe Jim shouldn't be so sensitive," said Arundel.

"It's not just Jim, it's Mike Burnand."

"I thought Jim had his sights on someone more eminent for his daughter, in which case, Burnand is the one with problems. He's already proved to be pretty incompetent with the boat. I can't imagine he's going to be much better with the shore operations. Jim may have to get someone else anyway."

McPherson interjected. "They're coming now."

White led the way with Burnand and two others behind him. He introduced the two newcomers. "This is Jed O'Brien and Jonas Schmid. Boys, meet Harry Calhoun. He's the guy we buy from, and these others are Dugald McPherson and Pete Arundel, his hired hands."

McPherson let the slur go by and nodded to the

new men. "Jim, we asked if you could lay your hands on a new Rand McNally Washington State road atlas. Any luck?"

"We found a road map of Washington and Oregon. It's got most of the major roads and all the towns marked on it." White pulled out the map and spread it on the saloon table.

McPherson looked at the publication date. "It's not a new one. Ours is back on the boat." He put his finger on a spot up the coast and said, "Let's try a chart showing Edmonds—here. Peter, you walk them through it."

Arundel went up to the wheelhouse and looked through the charts. He found the right one, and took it, together with the book of tide tables, back down to where the others were clustered around the table. He carefully folded the road map so it lay alongside the part of the chart that covered the waterfront. "It looks like there's a few roads coming into the neighbourhood," he said. "We need to select a reasonably clear stretch of beach to bring the load in. This bit north of Brackett's Landing looks like it should work. It has a railway track between the road and the beach which might be on a berm—that will keep stray cars away Anybody know the area?"

White shook his head and looked at the others who had come with him. All three shook their heads.

"Let's play it this way, then," said Arundel. "This is a practice run. We'll sail up this afternoon and turn to come in at midnight. You drive up, look at the beach and signal us if it's a go. There's a full moon tonight, so you should be able to see us at that time even if it's partly clouded over."

"I've never signalled anyone before," said Burnand.

"Okay. First, let's establish a code. We'll make it as simple as possible because it's easy to get confused at night. You flash your light twice; we flash once in return."

"You think we're stupid?" asked Burnand belligerently.

"No," said Arundel, "but there are enough things to do on a shore-side pickup. Make every job as simple as possible so you can get on to the next one." He paused, and Burnand's face seemed to relax, so he went on. "We're going to be lying about two hundred yards off the beach, just north of the breakwater at Brackett's Landing. We're not going to know what part of the beach you're on until we take a bearing on your light. At that point, one of us will start rowing the dinghy in and ground it on the beach. When we get there, everyone needs to turn-to and unload because none of us wants to hang around in an exposed location."

"So, who flashes the light first?"

"You do, and you may have to repeat the signal a few times before we see it. When we do, we know where to head for. Make sure the spot doesn't have any rocks or logs that would stop our dinghy from grounding. When we answer, flash twice again so we can get the bearing. After all the signaling, you just have to wait until we get to the beach."

"How long will that take you?"

"Just a moment." Arundel leafed through the tide table book. "It's slack tide this evening, so assuming the two-hundred-yard distance works, I expect it'll take us about twenty minutes to cover the distance in a loaded dinghy."

"Loaded? We thought this was a practice run."

"It is," said McPherson, "but we use some practice loads."

"Live bottles?" asked O'Brien.

"You'll find out when you open them."

"Anything else?" asked White.

"Yes," said Arundel. "At two hundred yards, a small light won't show. What's the largest one you have? We'll be using the searchlight on the wheelhouse."

"We could use a spotlight on the car, but that's another seventy-five yards from the shoreline on the other side of the railway track," said White.

"We'll leave that to you—if you have to, you might be able to run the car up onto the track. As long as there's no train coming, you should be okay. As we work our way through this process, we can get a little more discreet and use less travelled locations. Speaking of which," said Arundel, looking between White and his helpers, "let's get used to the idea that nobody says anything to anyone about this. The only way we get interrupted is if someone talks. No one who isn't on the beach to pick up the load gets to hear about it." He looked at White. "Are you bringing anyone else?"

"Not this time."

"See you at midnight, then."

"Are you happy with that?" said Arundel as they came back up to the shoreline walkway.

McPherson paused for a moment before answering. "I don't have a lot of confidence in them. They look like a bunch of thugs who're strangers to thinking. We'll just have to wait until tonight and make up our minds then. The job is simple enough, so there shouldn't be too much to confuse them."

At Fisherman's Wharf they met Logan getting out of the cab of a truck. "Found some stuff, Jeff?" asked McPherson.

"That, and a lot more information."

Arundel went round and looked at the load sitting on the pallet on the back. "What did you buy, half the American Army's stock?"

"Not quite, but once we've got this lot stowed and I've refitted our engine plug we need to talk."

The truck driver had a helper, and the pair of them used a hand-operated winch on a crane, mounted behind the cab, to swing the pallet onto a hand truck. Logan watched them and asked the driver, "Can you guys handle this down to the boat? I need to go down and wake the crew to set up to swing it aboard."

McPherson turned to go. "We'll leave you to it," he said.

"Officers! Leave all the hard work to the lower deck," Logan smirked.

"We could stay and help if you like," said Arundel.

"No, I can manage," said Logan hurriedly.

Arundel grinned and turned to join McPherson. They walked over the road to a restaurant and settled in to have lunch overlooking the harbour. "Not a lot of commercial traffic here either," said Arundel.

"It's noon on Wednesday. The locals are all at work offshore and foreign traffic is taking its time to recover. They're just like us—waiting."

On the *Lady Jane*, Lindstrom and Logan were finishing tying down the fastening on the main hatch covering. McPherson picked up the last rope-end that was draped over the railing, coiled it, and threw it over to Lindstrom. He looked at Logan. "You wanted to talk, Jeff."

The four of them went down to the galley and sat down around its small table. "I went down to Finnerty's and poked around the warehouse," said Logan. "There was a man running the shop who was prepared to talk once he got used to me being there. He was just out of the American Army Air Corps and had a lot to say about these engines. It turns out they were produced in volume at the end of the war, and less than two hundred actually got used in aeroplanes at the front. To build them, the government had assembled a bunch of people from the automobile industry who knew something about mass production. They stuck together a design that had bits of Rolls Royce,

Mercedes, and Hispano-Suiza in it, plus a few other parts they thought might fit, and shoved it onto a production line. They took a little while to find something that actually worked, but by the time they did, the war was over. They kept producing because they had some contracts running and they thought they might have some aeroplanes to put the engines into. They didn't, so now most of them are being sold off." Logan took out a notebook and opened it to where he had written down a list.

"You people are sure up on keeping notebooks," said Lindstrom.

Logan grinned and went on. "There were some problems with the water pump and the ignition generator. They tended to break crank shafts, but that seemed to be a vibration problem which the fellow said has been solved with the version we have. He also said the Army mechanics just replace engines when one breaks and don't bother repairing anything. He told me that, as far as he knows, none of them have passed a fifty-hour running test, so that's what I'm going to set up as soon as we get back to Victoria." He turned a page in his book. "They had a few in pieces, so I bought some crankshafts, pumps, and carburetors, as well another complete engine that I want to set up on a bench somewhere so I can try a few things out."

"How much of a risk are we taking with these engines?" asked McPherson.

"Some, but it'll probably be a lot less when I've had a chance to play with them a little. The Americans did everything in a hurry. The things they copied were good, and even when they changed their mind half-way along the process, it was to improve things. The aeroplane they were designed for isn't being built anymore, so they're not needed. We can use them, as long as we get ahead of anything that's likely to break. I didn't have enough money on me to get everything I wanted, but I got the impression we could help ourselves in exchange for a case of decent whiskey."

"What a coincidence," said Arundel. "I loaded some stuff before we left."

"You did?" said Lindstrom. "Lucky we didn't get raided when we docked."

"Since you've done it," said McPherson to Logan, "we'll drop down now and pick up the stuff. Did you make a list?"

"Yes, I have it here. I was also thinking on the way back—I haven't had a chance to look at the engines against the design that Hiro and Aki are putting together, but my first guess is we're going to have to do something about the radiator. In an aeroplane, it's out there on the nose, but in a boat, it's going to be below decks. We're going to have to duct some air from up top somewhere."

"I can see that," said McPherson. "Can you take us out now, Ollie?"

Lindstrom nodded, and Logan went down to the engine room to wait for the bell.

"Peter, a word with you," said McPherson, pointing to the stern. When they got there, McPherson paused for a moment and looked out over the harbour. "Peter, I never want to have anything loaded on a boat that I don't know about before it's put aboard."

"I thought it would be good to have some samples to help establish our credibility with White and his crew."

"It's White who needs to establish credibility with us, and at the moment, he's not doing too well at it. That's also nothing to do with the major issue—nothing goes on my boat that I don't know about first. I do not expect to raise this matter again. Is that clearly understood?"

Arundel was quiet for a few seconds. "Yes," he replied.

"How much did you put aboard?"

"Ten cases."

"And what did you plan to do with them?"

"Use them as a practice load."

"We'll give Finnerty one case for the stuff Jeff wants. We'll get them to throw in some loose pig iron to substitute for the weight of the bottles we're going to take out of the rest of the cases. You can give White's men one case as a tip if the operation goes properly."

"I'd promised them more."

"Better think of a good excuse then, because you're going to be in the dinghy."

Chapter 16

At five o'clock they cleared Seattle harbour, went north, and anchored out of the fairway a mile south of Whidbey Island three hours later. "We're just under seven nautical miles from Brackett's Landing," McPherson told the four of them squeezed into the galley. "We've got more men on board than we will when we do this regularly, so we can make it easy on ourselves. Ollie, keep the helm; I'll go with the searchlight and look for signals and any other traffic." He took a sip of coffee. "We'll give ourselves three hours to get there. Peter, launch the dinghy when we get to the area and we'll tow it. Jeff, you can pass the cases down when Peter gets in. We'll kill the navigation lights about a mile offshore, provided there's no traffic about. By the time we get down there we'll be about an hour off high tide, so that'll make the loaded runs in easier. We'll drop the anchor as soon as we see their light. The tide'll keep us stern-on to the shore—we can keep a shrouded stern light showing so Peter can find us again."

"Two hundred yards is a hefty distance at night—it's easy to lose track of my position. Do we have a compass we can put in the dinghy?" asked Arundel. "It'll be useless on the way in because all the metal in the load will throw it off, but it should be good on the way back."

"We should have thought of that one. We'll do that in the future, but I don't see one around. Ollie?"

Lindstrom shook his head. "We can live with tonight's full moon for the moment, and you should be able to see the north star," said McPherson to Arundel. "We'll be watching you through the night glasses and if things get too bad, we'll forget about being discreet and set off a flare. While we're waiting, why don't you check the chart and see if there's enough potential targets to give us sights for triangulation bearings?" Arundel nodded, stood up, and reached for the night glasses. "Everyone ready?" said McPherson.

The others nodded or grunted. "Let's give it a try."

McPherson stepped up to a position behind the wheelhouse with the searchlight at his shoulder. As they came out of the bay, he saw a freighter coming up on their starboard stern quarter. He went back inside; the Puget Sound chart was clipped to the folded-down board beside the wheel. He pointed to a position on it. "Steer another five points west for the next twenty minutes and then turn due south; hold the course until we're in range of the beach," he told Lindstrom. "There's likely to be more traffic coming up behind us and we don't need to wallow in their wash."

He watched the freighter pass them and saw its wash dissipate in the moonlit track of their own wake. Lindstrom turned on time. The shore drifted by with the occasional light showing from houses or farms. Another freighter passed them, but now they were well off its track. Half an hour later, a cluster of lights showed on the shore marking the town of Edmonds.

"We're coming up on Brackett's Landing," he called out from the wheelhouse. "Peter, how did you do on looking at those light bearings?"

"Not much for close work. There's a light on the breakwater at Brackett's and the prospect of a back-bearing on the light at Cultus Bay. I'll try another on Point No Point, but there's not enough to guarantee accuracy for a position two hundred yards offshore. Once we're in a rough position, I'll try Cultus Bay. After that we need to start flashing the shore."

McPherson grunted and turned to Logan. "Jeff, I'll help you put the dinghy overside now. We can tow it in. Once we're in contact, I'll give Ollie a hand at the helm so he can handle the engine controls while Jeff moves the crates."

They moved to the aft deck and threw off the lashings holding down the little boat. "Be easier when we get a dory; it's lighter and holds more stuff," said Logan.

They flipped the dinghy and launched it over the stern. McPherson grabbed the painter and wrapped it around a cleat. "Could use a longer one, otherwise it'll ride up over the stern if there's rough weather of any kind," he said as he went back to his spot behind the wheelhouse.

"Coming up to position now," Arundel called out. Lindstrom throttled back.

"Time?" asked McPherson.

"Two minutes to twelve," answered Lindstrom.

"Jeff, drop anchor!" said McPherson.

There was a splash from the bow, then silence as Lindstrom cut the engine. The boat slowly swung around as the tide took hold.

"Now we wait. Jeff, look to port of the stern, Peter, starboard, and I'll look directly over it," said McPherson.

Each took his sector of the shoreline and settled back into whatever comfort he could find. The shore loomed solid in the moonlight, but no movement showed. The land immediately adjacent to the beach seemed flat and no one could see a landmark or tree.

"Midnight," called Lindstrom, and they continued to wait.

"Got something!" said Arundel, just loudly enough to

be heard over the sound of water lapping against the hull. "One o'clock our position."

McPherson turned the searchlight and flashed it twice. Nothing came back in return. "I'll watch for another signal. Peter, you and Jeff load the dinghy."

Arundel unwrapped the painter from its cleat and hauled the dinghy up on their starboard side. He loaded the oars and climbed in. He settled himself onto the seat, made the stern line fast and took the first case from Logan. It was difficult to stretch and to place each case into position as well as keep the dinghy stable. "We should have practiced this when we were in the bay. It's different from the landings I did in the war," he said.

"I'm still happy us engineers stay away from the details of small boat handling," was the unsympathetic reply.

It took five minutes to pass the cases of the first load down and McPherson stayed in his position waiting for a signal that did not come. Finally, he saw another flash from a different part of the shore and returned the signal. The shore light kept winking.

"That part of the instruction didn't seem to work," said McPherson. "Do you see that, Peter?" he asked.

"Got it, but I'll just be guessing where it is if they stop flashing," said Arundel. Logan unwrapped the dinghy's mooring lines from their cleats and pushed the craft away from the boat. Arundel started to row toward the last position from which he had seen a light. The dinghy was painted white, so it showed up against the dark water as it crawled ever slower toward the shore.

McPherson could see a few figures start to gather at the point where Arundel would make landfall. He could hear some shouting as the craft broke through the line of phosphorescence which marked the shore. "Ollie, time the turnaround, will you?" He waited for less than a minute. "Mark the landing... now!" He could see the cluster of figures still moving around but there did not seem to be anyone up the bank. He waited for something to change and finally asked "Ollie, time?"

"Fifteen minutes."

McPherson leaned back against the wall of the wheelhouse, uncomfortable that he could do nothing about the delay. "Call out on each five-minute mark," he told Lindstrom.

The cluster on the shore did not seem to be changing. "Twenty minutes," called out Lindstrom.

Finally, he saw the dinghy separate from the shore and head back in their direction. "Jeff, uncover the stern light. He'll need it to see us."

The little boat inched over the water pushing against the still-incoming tide. When it had covered about half the distance, there was a flash from further up the bank, followed by the sound of a gunshot, followed again by another flash and another report.

"Who's shooting who?" asked Logan.

"Don't know; doesn't seem to be coming from the people on the shore."

It took another five minutes for Arundel to reach them, and when he arrived, they saw that he still had half his load on board.

"Unload and then leave the dinghy tied on aft. Let's put some distance on," said McPherson.

They all gathered in the wheelhouse after they got underway. McPherson raised his eyebrows at Arundel, who said, "That was fun. I made the beach and there was Burnand with about four others. I held the dinghy on the shore with the oars because none of them would grab the painter to pull the boat further up the beach. I called out for them to come and get the cases, and the first few refused because they'd get their feet wet. Finally, Burnand persuaded two of them to come out and get the load. I told them I could either hold the boat against the beach or pass them the cases, but not both. The two fellows on the shore finally grabbed the painter and held me in. It took us a long time to get five cases off the boat. Burnand complained there was no booze in them. I told him this was a practice run. Then I said, based on the way things were going now, we still had some distance to go. That made him madder and he pulled out a pistol. Fortunately, he was on the other side of the dinghy, and I hit his arm with the oar. That made the other fellows back off and gave me a chance to push the boat away and head back."

"And the shooting?" asked McPherson.

"Don't know who it was. Could have been Burnand picking up his pistol and letting it off, but the bullet went nowhere near me."

"We need to find someone else to work with," said McPherson. "I said it before, these people are just thugs, and incompetent ones as well. Ollie, head home. I'll relieve you when you get tired."

Chapter 17

Victoria, Thursday, September 11th, 1919

They had the Sound largely to themselves on the way back. McPherson stayed at Lindstrom's elbow marking their position from a bearing on each light they saw. Lindstrom had never bothered to use a logbook, so McPherson recorded each sighting in his notebook to avoid defacing their only chart. When they came abreast of the north end of Marrowstone Island and the point with the light on it that marked the entrance to Port Townsend, he said, "I'll take her now, Ollie."

"I'm okay," was the irritated reply.

"That's good, because if you rest a bit now, we've three boat handlers in good enough shape if something goes wrong." He took Lindstrom's position on the small seat behind the wheel.

"Not much went right tonight, did it?" said the fisherman as he moved over to lean against the locker on the other side of the wheelhouse.

"Not on the pickup side, anyway."

"How are we going to handle this boat if we have to use it again? We can get by with two hands, but three would be better."

McPherson paused for a moment and adjusted his position on the seat. "I'm guessing that the new boat won't be ready until November sometime, which means we use this one. We won't be going anywhere, though, if we don't get someone reliable to do business with."

"Any ideas?"

"I have one, or rather, you did," said Arundel, coming up the steps from the galley behind them.

"Oh?" said McPherson.

"Roy Olmstead. We looked into him after you suggested him. He runs a fairly efficient operation, but he's not doing any better on the seaborne delivery side than Harry was. His useless boat handlers out of Victoria and the clown princes of the western world on the shore parties seem to be the standard for that part of the business."

"You know him?" asked McPherson.

"No, but I know enough people who do to get him to talk to us."

"Can't do much worse than Jim White," said Lindstrom.

"Olmstead doesn't run a shooting war on the beach, and since he's still on the Seattle Police Force he can keep White and his thugs quiet," said Arundel.

"I wonder how long they'll let him stay on the police force?" asked McPherson.

"Hopefully long enough for us to get set up, and even if they were to boot him off after that, all his customers will still need deliveries."

"If we're planning to stay in business," said Jeff, appearing at the door leading to the galley, "we need to do something about those cases. They're a pig to load in a small boat. I could design some sort of a sling that would wrap around each one so loading's a bit easier."

"Unloading wasn't much fun either. I had to use both hands, and the chap on the receiving end hadn't a clue about what a small boat does when the waves are moving it about on the shore," said Arundel. "I think we all forgot that we need to keep one hand for the boat when we're moving a load."

"If we have some sort of improvised sling wrapped around each case, it'll get tangled up with the one underneath or beside and we won't be much further ahead. A decent shore crew will have someone to hold the boat," added McPherson.

"Even then a case is still a bit awkward to handle," replied Arundel. "We need to think this one through."

The sun was rising behind them when they came out into Juan de Fuca Strait and picked up a course for Victoria. No one had any new suggestions on the run in, but Logan reminded them, "I told you I wouldn't be running any loads. Anyway, for the next while I'll be too busy with the new boat to even load this one—that is, if you do decide to keep playing this game."

"I hadn't forgotten," said McPherson. "When can you round up Olmstead?" he asked Arundel.

"I think he's in Victoria today."

"Handy. Did you set that up?"

"Not me, Pilot—my eminent parent. He has these ideas about how things are about to play out. Must come from his life in insurance."

McPherson nodded and looked out at the entrance to Victoria Harbour, opening up off their starboard bow. "We'll pull into Fisherman's Wharf again. No sense in drawing attention to ourselves in the Inner Harbour."

He picked a convenient place to dock and expertly ran alongside it. Lindstrom went below and stood by the voice pipe in the engine room; together, they went through the complex process of putting the engine in reverse and maneuvered in.

"Jeff, even if we're using this as a tender in the long run, a reverse gear would be handy. What's involved in installing a gear box?" asked McPherson.

"Probably not much. We could use this to experiment on while we work one up for the next boat." When Lindstrom's head emerged above the galley steps, Logan asked, "Why no reverse gear,

Ollie?"

"Never saw the need. Had a deckhand standing about to do things like that. Nothing like the need to go backwards happens quickly on a fishboat." Lindstrom went forward to secure the mooring lines. Arundel took the stern ones and wound the spare length around a cleat.

McPherson moved back beside him. "When did you find out about all this?" Arundel had the sense to not ask him what he meant.

"The night before we left."

"And you didn't think to tell me that White was ropey?"

Arundel turned to look at him and paused. "I told my father about you having to flatten Burnand and about Jim being a bit aggressive during our last trip. He didn't think White was all that reliable, but we didn't want to upset Calhoun. The pair of them are a package, so if we had to replace one, we had to replace the other. You suggested we think about Olmstead as a back-up, and it seemed sensible. We asked him to come and meet us tomorrow—by that time we'd know how things had worked out on this trip."

McPherson turned and called over to Lindstrom, "Will you secure her, Ollie? We might need her tomorrow. Peter and I have a few things to talk over."

"I'll bet you do," said Logan quietly.

"I'll fuel her and clean her up a bit. Make sure it's not before tomorrow, though; some of us have to sleep," said Lindstrom.

McPherson grinned and turned back to Arundel. "Let's talk about this up on the wharf. I've made a career out of keeping surprises to a minimum, and this one has to be worked out."

They went up the ramp without speaking. When they got to the top, Arundel looked around and said, "Next time we should leave a car here."

"There should be enough taxis on Belleville Street. You can tell me more about the plans I don't know about while we walk down there." McPherson strode off and Arundel had to quicken his pace to keep up. McPherson continued, "Don't think I'm angry about you contacting Olmstead—it's just that I need to know what's going on."

"Fair enough. We don't have that many plans, actually. The market for booze in the States just crept up on us, and filling the need from our end has been an amateur effort. You've seen the quality of most of the people on the other side. Olmstead has been working with some other people on the Canadian side, but he's overwhelmed by the demand."

They came to the wharfinger's office, a small shack overlooking the wharf beside the path leading down to the inner harbour. Arundel motioned McPherson to stop.

"I can borrow the wharfie's telephone to call the house. I don't know whether Olmstead is going there or Father is meeting him in town somewhere. Usually, he likes to keep the two sides of his business separate."

He opened the shack door and called out "Wharfie!"

"Young Peter!" said an old man who shuffled in from a back room. "I heard you were back."

"I need to borrow your telephone. We need a ride home. This is Commander McPherson, whom you'll probably see quite a bit of—we're putting a freight business together and we'll need a bit of wharf space."

"That'll be a dime for the phone."

"Daylight robbery, as usual." Arundel reached for the stick-like instrument with its earpiece hanging from the cradle below the microphone. "One day, someone will come up with a better design for these things." He tapped the cradle a couple of times, and when the operator replied, said, "Arundel house on Hollywood Crescent, please. I don't have the number." He waited, tapping his foot, while the connection was made.

"Still impatient," said the wharfinger.

"Hello, Mother," Arundel said into the telephone. "We're at the office shack at Fisherman's Wharf. Where are we meeting Olmstead?" There was a rattling of a voice at the other end of the line; Arundel grunted acknowledgment at each pause. "My father is on the way," he said to McPherson after he hung up. They left, and Arundel called out over his shoulder, "Thanks, Wharfie!" They stopped at the side of the road.

"While we're waiting, you can tell me more about what has been arranged with Olmstead so far," said McPherson.

"Olmstead is a complicated issue. If we use him, we won't be using Calhoun, at least not under the present arrangements. I just hope Harry doesn't get wind of us picking Olmstead up at the Empress. We don't want him knowing about anything until we're all fixed with Olmstead."

"Sounds like we should slide up to the back door and send someone in to find him. We can sort out the employment details later, assuming you still want me around in this new situation—and assuming I want to be around with Olmstead." They both stood silently until Michael Arundel and the Crossley whispered up to the curb.

"I have to go by the terminal to pick up a friend of Sir James's before we go the Empress to find Mr. Olmstead," said Michael when they slid into the car.

"Who's the friend?" asked Peter.

"A Miss Campbell. She used to work for the admiral—communications or some such thing. He thought she might be useful to us."

"Miss Elise Campbell?"

"Yes. Do you know her?"

"I think I saw her in his office once," Peter said. McPherson recognized the code for discretion—*I can't tell you without breaching military confidentiality*, was what he was really saying.

Michael said, "Since you know what she looks like, you'd better be the one to get out and pick her out of the crowd."

"Hope I can recognize her still."

"I'm certain you'll manage," said his father dryly.

They pulled up at the terminal amidst the crowd of taxis and pedestrians moving in both directions. Peter swung down, and after a few minutes re-emerged, ushering an attractive, dark-haired young woman ahead of him. McPherson and Michael got out of the car.

"Miss Campbell, this is my father, Major Michael Arundel, and our colleague, Commander Dugald McPherson."

"Major. The commander, I know. How are you?" she spoke in a pleasant, low-pitched voice. Arundel opened the rear car door for her, and she climbed up into the seat, McPherson following her in.

"My wife will be pleased to see you," said Michael, moving out into the traffic. *I have no idea who you are or why you're here.*

"Admiral Romilly spoke most warmly of you," said Peter. *I know what you used to do; if there's anything we shouldn't talk about, tell us now before someone stumbles.*

"That was good of him. He said he was most impressed with the possibilities for a good life in this part of the world and suggested I come here and look around," she said. *I've been sent out to see things for myself and report back.*

"We're fairly busy at the moment. Are you looking for any sort of employment?" said Michael.

"I'm certainly interested in seeing what's available," she said. They motored down Belleville Street with the Legislative Buildings towering beside them; the Empress Hotel loomed ahead to their left. "This is an attractive town," she added.

McPherson turned to her and spoke quietly. "It's good to see you again. We're on the way to meet someone now. Perhaps you can give us a hand. None of us want to be seen with him just yet, so can we ask you to go into the hotel lobby and bring him out to the car?"

"Pick up a man, you mean. Some hotels throw you out for that."

He grinned. "You've been working for Admiral Romilly. I'm certain you know how to be circumspect." Louder, to the others in the front, he called out, "Miss Campbell doesn't mind helping us out of our current quandary."

"That's most helpful," said Michael, pulling the car into an unobtrusive slot on Douglas Street behind the hotel. "I think Peter has the most current description of Mr. Olmstead, the man we want to meet."

"He's in his mid-thirties, a shade under six feet, well-dressed, round-faced, bald, with his right ear set a little below the left and protruding out a little. He'll have taken a place in the lobby where he can see anyone coming in or out."

Elise got out of the car and went into the hotel. "You seemed to get an agreement from her fairly fast. How does she know you?" said Peter to McPherson.

"I met her during the war," McPherson said.

"There may come a time when you two need to swap reminiscences," said Michael.

They waited, talking about the trip down and the difficulties with Jim White for no more than fifteen minutes before Elise emerged from the hotel with Olmstead close behind her.

"That was quick," said Peter.

"I'm talented," replied Elise.

"Who is everybody?" asked Olmstead, getting into the back seat beside Elise.

"Sorry, we're a bit slow off the mark for politeness, Mr. Olmstead," said Michael. "I'm Michael Arundel, and this is my son Peter. The young lady you've just met is Miss Elise Campbell, and beside her is Commander Dugald McPherson. We thought you might like to come over to our house. It's quieter than most of the places we could meet in town."

"And less likely to attract the attention of other people as well. I saw you two guys in Seattle last month with Calhoun and his clowns," said Olmstead, looking directly at McPherson. "I hear you decked his biggest idiot. Hardly what I'd expect from one of His Majesty's officers and gentlemen."

"I was sailing on cargo ships long before I went into the navy. Aggressive drunks were common."

"Good that you handled the problem before it got worse, anyway. I tell my guys to do the same. If you drop someone fast enough, you don't have to deal with a gun or a knife."

They drove up the hill toward Beacon Hill Park. The noise from the air rushing over the canvas top made conversation difficult for a moment. McPherson turned to Elise, but she and Olmstead had their heads close together, deep in conversation. As they breasted the top of the slight rise beside the park and the noise died down, Peter turned around to Olmstead and asked, "Have you been to Victoria before, Mr. Olmstead?"

"Call me Roy. I suppose you're asking if I buy my booze here, and if we're going to do business. No, not often; I buy my stuff in Vancouver and most of it comes by land routes. The problem is there are only so many of those, and sooner or later the government's going to jump me."

"You understand government ways," said Peter.

"You stay alive in this business by changing your routine often. Any one of my contacts can change sides and buy off some grief by giving me up. If I were to disappear tomorrow someone would take my place, and that someone may already be planning how to do that. I'm interested in looking at moving stuff by boat because we have a lot more options for landing it than we have by just using roads." Olmstead shifted in his seat and looked out over the Straits as they came into view.

"We can certainly deliver to a lot of places, but to be successful needs careful organization," said McPherson.

"Sounds like a good subject to talk about over lunch," put in Michael, ending the discussion. They travelled the rest of the way in silence except for Elise and Olmstead continuing their private conversation.

At the Arundel house, Cynthia took charge of Elise, and the maid took her cases upstairs. Michael and Peter took Olmstead into Michael's study, and McPherson, irritated at being snubbed again, sat out on the terrace. He looked across the small bay and wondered which one was Emmaline Hemmingson's house.

"Deserted by everyone, Commander?" said Elise from behind him.

He turned to face her. "Apparently so."

"What's your part in all of this?" she asked.

"I'll know when they've finished their chat in the study."

"I sense some irritation."

"I was involved until now. The last buyer we had didn't work out too well. I don't know what will happen with this one. What about you?"

"As I said, the Admiral mentioned this was a nice place to live, and Mrs. Arundel is his niece. When the shooting stopped, I was at a loose end. I had a small gratuity from serving with the Women's Royal Naval Service, so I used some of it to come out here. It was better than staying and becoming a teacher or something else ghastly. Besides, the Admiral made it plain that the temptation to talk about the war had to be resisted; that will be easier to do here. You came from here anyway, didn't you?"

"Yes—to the extent that anywhere is home, this is. Would you care for a cigarette?" He pulled out his case and offered it to her. She took one and he lit it before taking out another for himself.

"I don't remember you smoking," she said.

"Only when I'm annoyed or bothered," he said.

She smiled and savoured the smoke for a moment. "Not that anyone has told me in detail, but the Arundels seem to be involved in running liquor into the United States. Isn't that illegal?"

"In the States, yes, but exporting it from Canada isn't."

"Splitting a few hairs, aren't they? There must be money in it. Are you involved for that reason?"

"I'm a merchant seaman and there aren't many merchant ships in need of officers at the moment. This happens to be the only alternative immediately to hand, although, based on what we saw of the American side last night, I'm not altogether convinced it's a good idea. That's why I'm prepared to see what the situation is with Olmstead before I commit."

"How much do you know of him?"

"Not much more than you do, unless there's something you're not telling me."

"He was as described, and he looked so confident. I asked if that was his name. He asked me who sent me and then he ushered me out of the hotel door. What do you plan to do with him?"

"He's a policeman in Seattle, and he runs the largest portion of the illegal liquor trade. By all standards I know, corruption is his middle name, and were it not for the fact it looks like he has most of the regulators in the city either on his payroll or buying his liquor, he'd be in jail. For that matter, most of their counterparts in Victoria seem to be on the other end of the business."

"Exciting times," she said thoughtfully. "So you haven't made up your mind either?"

"It's easy to convince myself the trade has a seal of approval on it, but in reality, the money's too good to say no. Besides, I'm a sailor. It's all I know, and at the moment, there are no other alternatives. If Olmstead is no better than the fools we dealt with last night, though, I have enough to wait until I find one."

Elise stubbed out her half-smoked cigarette in the cut-glass ashtray.

He turned at the sound of a door opening, and Olmstead and the two Arundel men joined them on the terrace. At the same time, Cynthia came out of another door and asked Elise, "Could you help me with putting some lunch together? If we don't get it out soon, someone's going to be talking about whiskey."

"My turn to leave the conversation," Elise said quietly to McPherson, and she got up to follow Cynthia.

"Thanks for the thought, my dear," said Michael to his wife's retreating back. "A significant lack of trust there," he continued to the other three men. Turning to McPherson he said, "We've settled our arrangements with Roy, so it only remains for us to find out whether you're likely to continue with us."

"That would depend on whether Roy can do better on the shore side than the last lot. I'd like to hear what his plans are."

"That's simple," replied Olmstead. "I don't have any detailed ones. I told you I've never successfully picked up from the water before, so I'm prepared to follow your lead there. Once we get the stuff to land, I can carry on as I'm doing now."

"The biggest difference is we deliver to beaches, so whatever you do has to involve moving loads over sand, mud and the odd bunch of rocks," said McPherson.

"Why not wharves? There's enough of them around."

Peter answered. "Occasionally, perhaps, but they're more likely to be at the end of a single road and too easy for the opposition to interfere. We also have to be careful that they're not in a cove, which would let the coast guard cut us off from the seaward side."

"Most beaches have a wide frontage, so both of us have a choice of exit routes," McPherson added. "I'd suggest we spend some time with the charts in the next few days and pick out some possibilities, as well as figure out how we let one another know when the loads are coming in."

Peter interjected. "We learned a lot about moving cases ashore during our ill-fated practice session with Harry's people. Cases are difficult enough to handle in a heaving dinghy, let alone passing them over to people on the shore. We need to work out a better way of moving them."

"It sounds like you've come to an arrangement," said McPherson.

"Yes," answered Michael, "we're going to be delivering to Roy and he's going to pay us on the shore."

McPherson frowned. "We need to talk about this."

"We can do that over lunch."

As the others walked into the house, McPherson pulled Peter to one side. "Miss Campbell will be with us at lunch. Is this the sort of detail she should be privy to?"

"She's one of Admiral Romilly's ladies; she's discreet."

"She was one of Admiral Romilly's ladies and

she was discreet. Remember Admiral Romilly's maxims? You don't tell anyone anything they don't need to know. No one needs to know anything about our operations who isn't involved with it. Unless something happened in the last thirty minutes I don't know about yet, Miss Campbell isn't involved." Peter said nothing and looked out over McPherson's right shoulder toward the bay. "So something did happen in the last thirty minutes, and you've added her to the crew. This isn't looking good, lad."

"It really doesn't have anything to do with you—she's not going to be on the boat."

"If I'm part of it, anyone who knows anything about what we're doing has something to do with me. However, if that's not to be the case, I'll just pull out now." McPherson walked into the house, heading for the front door.

"Goodbye then, Major Arundel, Olmstead," he said pleasantly as he passed each in turn.

"Not staying for lunch, then?" said Michael.

"No. Peter can give you the details. Is Mrs. Arundel available? I'll say goodbye to her on the way out."

"In the dining room, I expect. Are you sure you can't stay?"

"I'm sure," he said, and he went through the hall. Cynthia was by the window deep in conversation with Elise. "Thank you again for your hospitality, Mrs. Arundel. Goodbye."

"Not staying?" she asked.

"No, I'm sorry."

She looked past him. "Michael, Commander McPherson is leaving."

"Yes, so it seems. I wonder, Commander, could you wait a moment please? There seems to be a misunderstanding. Would you join me in the study?" He led McPherson across the hall into his study and closed the door firmly.

"You seem to be concerned about something."

"Presumably Peter gave you the details."

"Quickly, yes."

"And that would have included telling you of my concern about people being added to the group without my knowing."

"Yes."

"And presumably you share his view that people being added to the company is none of my concern?"

"We're the managers of this operation; we have to have the freedom to decide who becomes part of it."

"Indeed, you do; I simply insist on being informed beforehand and saying no if I don't like them. Of course, you can insist, but you should know that I'll only work with people I have confidence in." He indicated a chair, and when Michael nodded, he sat down. "Let's go over your success so far. You get involved with Harry Calhoun, who can't find Victoria without his steward steering his yacht here. He collects some delivery boys who mostly can't find Seattle or any other part of Puget Sound. His idea of customers in Seattle for the few loads that do make it through, as we found out last night, are a few drunken thugs who also can't find their way around a clearly marked beach and let off a bit of gunfire for no useful reason. How is it sounding so far?"

"Go on."

"You round up a substitute who might have some potential, but we really haven't had time to talk to him to find out if he has some bad points which might make him as useless as the last lot. We set up a convivial session over lunch, and then you add some cheerful young woman whose only recommendation is that she worked for the family's favourite admiral and is therefore discreet. I've spent my life at sea cutting down the occasions where I'm likely to be surprised. If I find myself in a situation where surprises are coming too quickly, I take another course. I have no intention of appearing to be rude, but it seems that if you want to continue along your present course, you don't need me."

Michael fiddled with his desk blotter. "You're quite direct."

"Indeed I am. You'll find that the sea requires it, as it's particularly unforgiving of anyone who's not competent."

"Hold on a minute, then." Michael paused and thought for a moment. "Do you have an issue with Olmstead?"

"I don't know. I would have been talking to him at lunch about selecting delivery points and how we would train his shore crews to work with boats. I confess that if I got the same answers Harry and his people gave, I would have walked out. I'm doing this job with you because, as I told Miss Campbell, the alternatives are very limited. There's some danger out there and I don't plan to get shot if I can avoid it."

"Ah yes, Miss Campbell. We asked for her to come out. There's a need for someone to do some administrative work and it seemed that if we got someone local, there would be a tendency to talk too much. Miss Campbell did a lot of unconventional things for Admiral Romilly, and while she's not a member of the family, she has a background we have confidence in."

"You knew she was on the way. You should have told me."

"We operate on the need-to-know principle, too. We didn't think you did."

"Now you know otherwise. That is, if you want me to continue working for you. I take it then that Miss Campbell is apprised of the details of the arrangements with Olmstead?"

"Just those she needs to know," said Michael with a slight smile. "Lunch?"

"I'm glad we understand each other. Yes." They

went back to the dining room, where Peter and Olmstead had joined the women.

Cynthia shut both doors and pointed to the sideboard where a selection of cold dishes was laid out. "We've set it up for a buffet so we can help ourselves without the maid having to come in and serve." Everyone served themselves, then sat down. Peter looked a little uncomfortable and took a seat beside Olmstead rather than McPherson, which left McPherson facing Elise.

"We've sorted out some basic items this morning, so we just need Dugald to set the scene for Roy to come in," said Michael.

McPherson nodded and said, "We'll need to show Roy around the Sound from the water side. Then he can look at some potential loading sites from the landward side. I'd like us to start on that this week, find a couple that are good for practice and a few more we can use for drops."

"What do we have to look for on the land side?" asked Olmstead.

McPherson laid his knife and fork parallel on the tablecloth to show the difference between each side. He used his finger to help explain.

"Access: the closer you can get cars or trucks to the beach, the less you have to carry by hand from the shore and the sooner you're out. Do you have anyone you can trust to look over likely spots?"

"I'd prefer to do it myself to start. That way I can tell someone else what's needed," replied Olmstead.

McPherson nodded approvingly. "You're getting there, Roy. We may not have worked out all our handling problems by the time we have our first run, so you may need a couple of extra fellows on the beach."

"How are we going to find out which beach you're delivering to?"

"We could make up a list and telephone you before we leave, or vice versa."

"There's no telephone in the world that can't be tapped," put in Elise. "We did it regularly during the war, even the field telephones at the front. As a matter of fact, that's how we knew the Germans were going to ask for an armistice. If you want to talk on the telephone, put some sort of a code together."

"It's going to have to be a simple one," said Peter.

"How do we do that?" asked Olmstead.

"There's a few around," Elise answered, "but most can be broken. There's not much to devising one that's difficult to break. I can probably do one up while you're out looking at beaches."

"You're a fount of surprises." said Olmstead.

"I try," said Elise. "A radio on board equipped to transmit voice messages would be better."

"But everyone will be able to hear," said Olmstead.

"Won't matter if it's coded."

"Let's stick to the immediate possibilities," said McPherson. "The point you make about telephone tapping is a good one. We should stay off the telephones with any sort of information we don't want anyone else to know about."

"You guys might have to worry about that sort of thing here, but in the US of A that is unconstitutional. I couldn't get away with it as a policeman," said Olmstead.

"If it can be done, someone will," said Elise. "I'll do you up a nice code to use."

"The only thing left is to work out how we make sure we are delivering to the right people," said McPherson. "What do you propose, Roy?"

"We pay cash on delivery," said Olmstead.

"Not really happy about that," McPherson frowned. "We either take a pouch of cash and trust it's okay or stand out there on the beach and count it, which I'm not keen on if there's rain or high wind. And

Roy, you have to trust the man you send to do the pickup."

"If there's a problem, we'll sort it out with Roy afterwards. I daresay he can deal with his own people," said Michael.

"One point I want to be quite clear on," said Olmstead. "I don't allow any of my guys to carry guns. If a shipment gets hijacked, they just let it go. We'll deal with the opposition later. What's your policy?" he asked Michael.

"Mine's the same as yours," put in McPherson before either of the Arundels could answer. "We'll have fast boats and the advantage of surprise, so hopefully that'll keep us safe. There'll be a shotgun in the cockpit, but that's for close quarters work at sea. If we change our mind, we'll talk to you. How long will you be staying in Victoria?"

"I've taken a few days off, but I was thinking of taking the boat on Sunday afternoon. I could add a couple of days to the trip if necessary."

"Would you like to see the boat we're using at the moment and also have a look at the one we're building?" McPherson turned to Peter. "I'm guessing the Takahashis don't believe in weekends when they have a project running."

Peter nodded.

"Tomorrow at the same door of the hotel at nine, then."

"I'd like to tag along, if I may," said Elise. "Apart from the excitement of playing in boats, I want to see how much space they have for radios."

"Peter?" McPherson raised his eyebrows.

"Yes, I'll call Aki and he can raise Jeff. I'll see Ollie this afternoon."

Chapter 18

Friday, September 12th, 1919

On Friday morning, McPherson did the rounds collecting everyone. He started at the Arundels and picked up Peter and Elise. She wore a naval duffel coat as well as cord trousers and canvas shoes.

"You're well-equipped," he said.

"I shipped most of my possessions here as soon as I made the decision to come." Arundel opened the rear car door for her before he climbed back into the passenger seat.

"You didn't have to be so quick off the mark agreeing with Olmstead about the guns. We haven't made our minds up," said Arundel quietly.

"It's your family that's making the noise about you, personally, running the risk of being shot at. If I agree to carry weapons on board, I'll tell you. As it happens, you've already made the decision to carry money back without telling me. I may change my mind, but if I do, it's only going to be something to defend us at close quarters, like Ollie's short-barreled shotgun, for example."

"We've had a couple of cases where returning boats have been hijacked and the crew's been killed."

"You really are going to have to get used to telling me these details. Speaking of details, have you told Calhoun he's out of the picture yet?"

"He's not really out, he's just back to our earlier

arrangements. He'll buy from us, but he's responsible for his own deliveries. We'll work with Roy because he can shift a lot more merchandise."

McPherson let in the clutch and pointed the car back down to the Dallas Road waterfront. "If volume is the answer, we'll need more than one boat, and soon."

"I don't really have an answer to that now," replied Arundel as the car swung up a slight rise and the view of the Straits opened up in front of them.

"I didn't really catch this yesterday," called Elise from the back. "I presume that's America over the water. Is that where you deliver?"

"Not entirely," said Arundel. "Puget Sound starts over your left shoulder and goes south about a hundred miles. We'll be going down there."

"Probably good radio reception if we get a good site for a transmitter."

"Ships did well with it before the war with powerful radio sets. The smaller ones we had toward the end of the war are just as good, and will probably work as well," said McPherson.

"Let's hope so. It certainly is pretty here," said Elise. They motored through the park at a slow enough speed for Elise to admire its gardens and the large houses that abutted it.

"You're not squashed together here," she said. "Even in the better parts of London, there's not a lot of room to move."

"It's part of Vancouver Island's charm," said Arundel.

Olmstead was waiting for them by the door of the hotel and walked quickly over the road to get in beside Elise. He was dressed warmly against the chill of the early morning, but in clothes more suited to the streets of Seattle than a Canadian fishing boat. "I forgot you people drove on the other side of the road. Damn near got run over last night."

"It's part of its English charm," said Elise.

Olmstead smiled down at her. "It's not the only thing that's charming," he said ponderously.

"We do our best. Besides, those clothes are very American; someone might have been aiming for you. I wouldn't worry, though; an hour on Dugald's boat will have them meshing with the background," she said brightly.

McPherson pulled back onto Douglas Street and turned the car around to head in the direction of Belleville Street, past the Legislative Buildings with their green domes almost shining in the morning sun. He sent the car up the slight gradient on Kingston Street and pulled over on a piece of gravel beside the wharfinger's shack. He led the way down the ramp and Arundel shepherded the other two. Olmstead was visibly nervous, and once they came to the float where the *Lady Jane* was berthed on the far side of two other vessels, he protested. "This ain't like getting into a car."

"Doesn't much drive like one, either," said Arundel unsympathetically, "but it's what's going to make your fortune."

Elise skipped over the two boats and deftly landed on the *Lady Jane*'s hatch cover. "I'm not letting her show me up," said Olmstead, and he stepped deliberately over the low rail surrounding the deck of the first boat. Slowly and steadily he climbed over the next one until he lumbered gracelessly, but safely, onto the deck beside Elise. They grinned quickly at one another. McPherson called Lindstrom out of the galley and introduced him.

"Miss Campbell wants to know all about the boat, so why don't you take her below and start the engine. I'll conn her out and Peter can take the lines. Roy, come with me into the wheelhouse and watch everything." He looked out over the stern and then forward round the floats in front of them. "Looks clear enough; We'll take her out in reverse. Ollie, will thirty seconds or so in reverse and then run her forward be okay?"

"Should give us enough headway to clear the floats."

"Okay, fire her up when you're ready." McPherson waited for Lindstrom to go below to the engine room with Elise, who had dropped her duffel coat in the galley. McPherson turned to Olmstead. "Shouldn't think he'll break any speed records in starting the engine with Miss Campbell down there admiring the process. It'll be easier when we have a reverse gear fitted and we don't have to reverse the engine." To Arundel, standing by the door of the wheelhouse, he said, "We'll go out stern first, so stern lines off now, bow lines on my signal." He raised his arm and lowered it rapidly.

"I assumed all you seafarers did things automatically," said Olmstead.

"If you want to stay alive at sea, never make assumptions."

"Speaking of which, I need to teach my land guys about working with boats."

"We tried with Jim White and his men. Listening didn't seem to be their strong point."

"My guys will be different."

"I'd still prefer to do a dry run. That way we can do it in daylight the first time and people will know where to put their feet. It also won't matter whether the police interfere." McPherson turned around and checked for boats coming up astern and then looked back at Olmstead. "How long do you plan to stay on the force? At some point your superiors may not want to overlook your other activities."

"I admit it's all a bit strange. Prohibition is something some brilliant politicians dreamed up, and one way or another got enough votes to pass it. There's a lot of people who don't agree with it, including some who voted for it. Don't ask me why—politics is too crazy for words. I'm selling booze to judges, politicians at every level, my bosses on the police force, and just about everyone in Seattle who describes themselves as respectable. It can't go on this way, but for the time being, I'll just keep doing it and see what happens tomorrow."

They waited idly for another five minutes and then McPherson called down the voice pipe to the engine room. "If you keep us waiting any longer, we'll miss the tide."

"With you soon," came the disembodied voice.

"How soon?"

A few minutes later, there was a rumble from below and the boat strained against the bow line. McPherson raised his arm and then dropped it. Arundel cast off and the boat moved out into the harbour. In a few seconds, the engine stopped and started again as Lindstrom changed directions.

McPherson swung the wheel to the left. "If you're coming to sea, this direction," he held up his left arm and pointed to a sidelight barely visible through the upper windscreen, "is port, and is signified by the colour red, like that one. The other side is starboard and signified by the colour green." He pointed to a similar one on the other side. "Every vessel has a permanent port side and a permanent starboard side. I'm going to turn full circle and go out of the harbour for a few minutes while we show you and Miss Campbell over this boat. It's going to be the one we use to make deliveries for the next few weeks so you're going to have to know what it can do."

He called Arundel over. "Will you take the helm? We can show what the town looks like from another angle, and then we'll slide over to Gonzales Bay and wave at your parents."

Elise came up from the engine room. "I don't see a generator that has enough power to run a radio if you want to put one in this boat."

"We haven't given that any thought so far—all the communications have been shore based, and this boat is a temporary one on the delivery side. We'll go over and look at the one being built shortly. Once it's running, we'll make the decision about what to do with this one. It can carry a lot, so we're thinking of using it as a supply ship anchored somewhere inconspicuous."

"How would we find it?" asked Olmstead.

"That's where coded radio transmissions come in, but that's something for the future," said McPherson. "Come and look at the hold," he told Olmstead, and led him out onto the deck. "Make yourself useful and throw off these lashings from the dinghy."

He demonstrated by unwrapping rope from a cleat on one corner, coiling it and hooking it back over the cleat. "We always like to keep things we can trip over down to a minimum." Olmstead leaned down and delicately unwrapped the opposite corner. After he had tried, unsuccessfully, to coil the rope and place it on the cleat, McPherson stepped over the hatch and did it for him. "I don't think we'll hire you for this part of the operation."

"Just as well. I've lost the touch since I left the farm. What do you want to show me?"

McPherson threw off the rest of the lashings, slid the dinghy toward the stern, and uncovered the canvas hatch cover. He cast off its tiedowns and rolled it off the opening. Olmstead looked down into the hold. "It's big," was all he could say.

"With the boxes we could carry on deck, we can manage about a thousand cases. We'll probably carry about one hundred or so in the shore boat, and we can use the gaff," he pointed to the spar attached to the mast, "if we have to load a boat lashed alongside. We still have the problem of transferring stuff to dinghies for a move to the beach and handling the boxes to the shore."

Olmstead thought for a moment. "When I was growing up on the farm, my daddy bought a small mill. It meant we could grow some crops that no one else did, put them through the mill and sell them direct. We'd put the flour in thirty-pound bags and sling 'em onto the wagon. By the time I was fourteen my brothers and I could pass the bags to each other and load a full wagon in fifteen minutes. Maybe you could unpack the cases and put the bottles into flour bags. It cuts the weight down to something you can handle in one hand. It also gives you a handle to hang on to. It'd make it a lot easier to move things from one level to another—up or down."

"We put bottles into bags on the way back from Seattle," said McPherson. "We packed them with straw to stop them banging into one another and breaking."

"Wood shavings would probably work better. Straw can blow around in the wind. Or you could wrap each bottle in cardboard."

McPherson looked at him with surprise showing in raised eyebrows. "I thought I was the shipping expert."

"Never make assumptions about farmers either—we have to invent things because we never have what we need when we need it."

"So, if we use the idea about bottles packed in bags, we'll put the dinghy overside and pass the bags down to it. The man rowing it heads for the shore, where one of your men grabs the painter—that's that little lead rope. He uses his other hand to pass a bag to a second man, who loads in onto something with wheels."

"Sounds about right. How close to the shore can this boat go?"

"Depends on the depth of the water near the beach and whether it's high or low tide. When we start picking beaches for landing, we can mark the distance we have to moor depending on the tide. When we get the new boat running, there may be places where it can nose in, but we need enough room to allow the propellers and the rudders to stay clear of the bottom."

To McPherson's surprise, Olmstead swung himself down into the hold and looked around it. "Lots of space here. How do I get out?"

"There's a hatch on the forward bulkhead leading to the galley. I'll get Ollie to open it—won't do your expensive clothes much good."

"They'll live."

"Roy getting used to playing with boats?" asked Elise, appearing through the galley door into the wheelhouse as he came in the other direction.

"Yes. Where's Ollie? I need him to open the hatch to the hold."

"I can do that." She turned and reached over to unclip the catch. "Open Sesame!" she said as Olmstead worked his shoulders, with some difficulty, through the hatch. "That will really do your suit in," she said when he finally made it out.

"Dry cleaning. It's the latest thing. It's supposed to make your clothes look like they're new again. I guess I'll find out."

"Coming up to Gonzales Bay," Arundel called from the wheelhouse. "I don't see any kind of an audience up there, but I'm coming about anyway."

"That'll give us enough time to show Roy what a chart looks like," said McPherson.

They made the Inner Harbour in just under thirty minutes. Arundel judged the approach to the Takahashi boatyard jetty well enough that the convoluted process of putting the boat into reverse wasn't needed.

Logan was waiting for them and caught the line deftly. "Still an almost-competent boat handler, I see," he called out. "Tak's made a good start," he told them as they walked up the steps. The outline of a boat could be seen under a tarpaulin, the edges of which were lying in several folds at the base.

"We keep a cover on her even when we're working on it. Tak has this idea that it keeps the temperature even while we're bending strakes on. I've never heard of it before, but whatever he knows about it, it's more than I do. I don't object because it also keeps the design and purpose of the boat out of sight."

"Hello, Peter," said a voice from above them.

Arundel looked up. "Hello, Aki," he replied.

"Okay if I lift the tarp?" said Logan. Aki nodded and Logan walked over to a rope hanging down in front of the bow. He pulled it down and there was a squeal from a pulley directly above him. Lines from the pulley went out to smaller ones positioned over the boat and larger ones attached to the body of the tarpaulin. Logan pulled steadily on the rope and wound the loose end round a large cleat beside him. The tarpaulin slowly rose. "Watch yourself. The tarp'll move over in your direction," he called out. "Just lift the edge over your head as it swings toward you and it'll flop down on the other side of the ramp."

When the tarpaulin was off, the skeleton of a fifty-foot boat lay in front of them. Aki, who had come down to join them, explained. "We found a length of oak for the keel and some good knuckles for the bow. They're doweled together and the oak ribs fit on it well. We've a steam box under the building so we can move each of the strakes out and directly onto the ribs. You can see we're about half done. We should finish the rest by the end of next week." He looked at Logan. "Jeff's been busy since you got back from Seattle. Jeff?"

Logan took up the explanation. "I set one of the Liberties up on a test bed once I found something that would quieten it down. I'm thinking of putting the exhaust pipes out underwater to keep the noise down when you're running. To start the engines—once I find out how to start the engines—I'm thinking a ten-gallon tank, down from the manifold, will act as an expansion chamber. If it doesn't work, we have the makings of a powerful explosion, so I need to play with it a lot more. We have to reduce the pressure on the oil pump at low speeds too. We might be able to manage this by doing something with the internal circulation system. That would reduce the pressure at low speeds but allow it to rise to the full sixty pounds when the engine runs full out. Right now, I'm just guessing."

He coiled the rope while he talked. "It's lucky we've had the experience with the Coastal Motor Boats, because otherwise we'd probably modify car engines for the job. It might be a bit easier because they come equipped with starting motors, gearboxes, proper cooling systems, and they're built for slow running. On the other hand, none of them have four hundred and fifty horsepower. There's lots I haven't worked out yet. It's all experimenting for the moment, but I should have everything solved when the hull's ready to go. We will definitely need more than one rudder, especially if we put in two engines. They're both very powerful, and on a full power turn, you could rip off a single one."

McPherson nodded. "I agree with that. We need to think about wheelhouse controls as well. We're adding a need for throttles and gear levers and readout dials. We could borrow some ideas from an aeroplane cockpit since we're using that kind of engine."

"Elise wants to talk about radios and the power to run them," said Arundel. "Are you putting a radio in the new boat?"

"Don't know, but we will put one in the *Lady Jane,* and she'll need to have more electrical power," replied Logan. He frowned for a moment, thinking, then changed the subject. "How are you going to handle the unloading? I thought for a moment we could use the same hydraulic ram that we used to launch torpedoes over the stern."

"Not a bad thought, but that would mean putting the stuff on a float of some kind. It might make it tricky for the shore parties to retrieve, and it would take up space so we couldn't carry as much of a load," said McPherson. "We also need a space in the cockpit for a first aid kit."

"What is that?" asked Aki.

"It holds basic medical supplies in case someone gets hurt." McPherson looked at Arundel and Logan. "We had a situation in the war where the kit was too basic, and someone lost too much blood. I'll pick one up. We need to store it somewhere toward the back of the cockpit, close to the deck and away from the engine."

"What will we call her?" said Lindstrom. "It should be something we'll recognize, but which other people have a hard time remembering because they can't pronounce it."

"Why does it need a name?" asked Olmstead.

"Quick identification. Our customers will be looking for it. Besides, boats should have names. It's good luck. I'll give it some thought," said Lindstrom.

"Don't want to push, but how long to get her finished?" asked McPherson.

"Can't be too precise," said Aki, "but we need our slipway back by early December."

They ran back in the *Lady Jane* to Fisherman's Wharf and Lindstrom stayed to secure the boat. "We need to talk about how the show's going to run," said McPherson as he loaded the other three back into the car. "Presumably, your father's house would be the best place for this," he said to Arundel.

"They're expecting us. My father was planning to go and see Harry this morning."

Michael took them straight into the dining room. "We've laid lunch out on the sideboard. Help yourself and find a place at the table."

Olmstead put himself next to Elise and the

other two men sat either side of Michael, who summarized the arrangements they had worked out with Calhoun. "How does that square with your plans, Roy?" he asked.

"I like paying in cash," said Olmstead. "I know there's security risks, but it's a lot better than tying transactions to records in banks. We have a federal income tax in the United States and if I start looking like I'm personally getting all the money from liquor sales, I'm liable for tax on it. How do I let you know what I want delivered, and where and when I want it?"

"I can accept the cash part of the operation, as long as I don't have to count it on the beach," said McPherson.

"The best way of handling it at the start is to keep every part of the business as simple as possible," said Michael. "As we get further into it we can get a little more elaborate, but at the moment I'd suggest we start by carrying basic loads of premium English whiskey, Buchans for example—that's Scotch to you, Roy—plus gin, rum, and Canadian rye. One brand of each; we can add others later. We deliver a standard load of one hundred cases on each run; that way we have the same amount of money for each load. We can do more if we add more boats."

"We still have to talk to one another so I can let you know where to drop off the loads," said Olmstead.

McPherson said, "I've been thinking about that problem. I suggest for a start we pick a bunch of locations in the Sound where you can get vehicle access and we can get in. We number each one and you tell us by radio which one to use. So, if Brockett's Landing was number fourteen on the list, you transmit "fourteen" on a regular radio watch schedule. We'd plan to arrive at midnight, transfer the load, pick up the money, and go."

"If we do this too regularly, people will know we're in the neighbourhood and we might have some problems," said Olmstead.

"That's where coding comes in," said Elise. "First we decide who we want to keep knowledge away from—our competition or the government? If it's the competition, a simple substitution code with the letters changed for every delivery should work for the first little while. If it's the government, we need to be more careful. They have people who break codes, and so will the competition as time goes on. I suspect we have a few months before we need to set up a really robust system, but in the meantime, I suggest we use a simple substitution code based on the days of the week."

"How does that work?" asked Michael.

Elise explained. "The days are numbered one to seven, Monday to Sunday. If we're using Brackett's Landing, whose number is fourteen, and if we're transmitting on Monday, we add one to the location number digit and send 'fifteen.' If we're transmitting on Sunday, we add seven to location number and send 'twenty-one.' Acknowledgment of the message will always be 'twenty-two'—two dots, three dashes repeated." She looked around the table to see if everyone was following. "Once we get going, we keep daily radio watches at a set time each day, with a fallback time in case the message is not acknowledged. We can make the process a little more obscure as we go along, but this should get us going. At the very least, it follows the two most important rules of radio transmission: keep messages short and give a positive acknowledgment."

"Well," said Michael, "that was most unexpected, and I, for one, am most grateful."

"So am I," said Olmstead.

Elise closed her notebook and slid it into a pocket of her handbag. "It adds some regularity to a business which'll probably have more surprises than we expect. The advantage is that we use a double code. The locations are coded, and that code is coded again. It doesn't mean that anyone listening can't break it, but if he does, it's difficult to use the information quickly enough to interfere with us. It'll do us for the time being."

"We'll have to float around the Sound fairly soon and pick out some locations," said McPherson.

"Which we then have to confirm as places we can reach from the land side," added Olmstead.

"And not draw attention to ourselves while we're doing it," said Peter.

"We would use cars to pick up from the beach," said Olmstead.

"One hundred cases are a lot to put in one car," commented McPherson.

"We use large cars and reinforce the back springs, but you're right, we'll have to use more than one for each pickup."

"What about trucks?" asked Peter.

"A large target, and too slow, and maybe too heavy to run over sand. We could use bakery, laundry, or milk vans. They have good reasons to be delivering in the early morning to the places where we sell."

"What about bringing in larger loads?" asked Michael.

"Takes too long to unload," said Peter.

"And I don't want to get into the warehouse business; what comes over the beach goes straight to the customer," said Olmstead.

"That only leaves the need to work with the land crews. We don't want a repeat of the 'Fred Karno's Army' show we had last week," said McPherson.

"Who's Fred Karno?" asked Olmstead.

"He's an English showman," Elise answered, "who puts on great noisy performances where everyone falls all over each other, just like Dugald told me Jim White's men did."

"I'd suggest we use some other boat than the

Lady Jane to do the exploring in the Sound if we can, preferably a pleasure boat small enough to get close to shore that we won't be using again," added McPherson.

"How would we find that?" asked Peter.

"Shouldn't be too difficult," said Michael. "There's a lot of warm-weather sailors amongst our acquaintances, and some of them are even investors."

"Change the name on the boat and the owner won't run into any problems afterward," said McPherson, "provided it's not particularly distinguishable."

"I'll look for a suitable boat available for us to borrow," said Michael. "We've taken the precaution of getting a photograph of every vessel we insure, so with Peter's help, we'll find something with the characteristics we need. Just tell me what you want."

"Diesel or petrol power is essential. We'll have Ollie and Jeff with us, but they won't want to be bothered with steam power. A radio would be useful, but not essential, and the cabin needs to be large enough to hold six of us without tripping over each other. We also need it to have some storage space in case we need to pick up engine parts," said McPherson. "We need a dinghy, too, but if the boat doesn't have one, we can sling our own. Peter will need to take a look over any likely boat, because if it's just something to play with, people leave off things they don't think are important like anchors and the right kind of mooring lines. It shouldn't have a draft of much more than three feet, otherwise we won't be able to get close enough to shore."

Michael made some quick notes and said to his son, "I'll spend the rest of the afternoon at the office looking at the insurance records for some of our acquaintances. Stop in this evening and if you like my choices, I'll talk to the owners in succession and take the first one who says yes. We don't need to make more noise about what we're doing than necessary."

"That gives us a day to organize everything. I can't leave before Tuesday," said Arundel.

"Why, in particular?" asked McPherson.

"My cousin, or to be precise, my mother's cousin will be coming in. He'll be joining us on the business side of things."

"Anyone I know?" asked McPherson pointedly. "I thought we were finished with unexpected additions."

"Sorry, Dugald. So did we. It's Admiral Romilly's son, John. I've met him and don't like him much," said Peter. "He's somewhere about my age, but beyond that I know nothing of him other than he was in the Navy. Elise, you worked for his father—did you know him?"

"Not much more than to say hello to," she said.

"Will he expect to travel with us?" asked McPherson.

"He'll expect to see something of the operations, I suppose, and he'll want to meet the people in Seattle."

"I presume he'll want to stay out of harm's way as well. Can you stay around until Tuesday, Roy?"

"I can manage that."

Chapter 19

Tuesday, September 16th, 1919

"Ahoy *Lady Jane*!"

A pleasure craft almost as long as the fish packer was drawing up alongside. "I have nowhere near the expertise of you naval types in driving this thing, but I did get here without sinking it," said Michael, standing at the wheel. "Now what do I do?"

"Keep your record going, Father," said Peter. "Kick her out of gear and let her drift up to us. I'll jump when you're close enough and grab the lines." They secured the lines and snugged the new boat against the *Lady Jane*. McPherson and Lindstrom hopped aboard her.

"We have her for two weeks, provided we take her back in good condition," said Michael. "Some fix-up and paint needed, which we're to do in lieu of payment. I took her over to Takahashi's. We've changed her name to *Rosalie*, and she's a common enough design to blend in. She has a Marmon engine taken from a pre-war racer, and Logan modified the cooling system to give her some reliability for a long-distance, high-speed cruise. He says she can reach eighteen knots, but fuel consumption will be high."

"Nice spacious saloon, well-equipped galley," said McPherson, as he looked around. "Four small cabins and a radio, too. Nothing needed that should stop her being ready to leave today."

Olmstead and Elise were standing at the back of the saloon beside another man. "This is John Romilly," said Michael. "I picked him up on the way over." McPherson turned to face the new arrival, a slight, well-dressed man about Peter's age with a disdainful look on his face. "This is Commander Dugald McPherson and Mr. Olav Lindstrom," said Michael. "Peter, you know."

Romilly shook hands perfunctorily. Lindstrom grinned and said, "Don't think anyone ever knew me by that name before. Call me Ollie or I won't know who you're talking to."

Romilly smiled back stiffly. "I've not been in America before, so your informality is a little strange to me."

"You haven't been in America yet if you landed in Canada and took the train across. We're different, and it's as well not to get the two of us mixed up," said McPherson. "What brings you here?"

"My father sees this as a place to form a base for managing business."

"That is thoroughly the Arundels' department; we're just in the sales and delivery end of it. How is the Admiral?"

"Busy as always." Romilly looked around the anchorage. "You do have your commercial areas close to home here, don't you?"

"Makes it easier for those who have to manage them," said McPherson.

"Most of the people doing this sort of work at home seem to manage quite well from an office in London."

"If things don't work well in a place like this, there's nothing to manage in London," said McPherson.

"I never saw myself as having to be this close to the coalface, so to speak."

McPherson was starting to share Arundel's misgivings about his cousin. "I've no doubt we'll think well of you when you leave," he said. He turned to

Lindstrom. "Ollie, can you round up the charts we'll need for Seattle and the east side of the Sound? I'll clear some space here." Lindstrom swung back to the *Lady Jane*.

"I can't imagine I shall be encouraging employees to address me by my first name," said Romilly.

"Ollie's not an employee. He works with us on an independent basis and gets a share of the takings," said McPherson. "Things are a little more formal in some places, but not here. We're off to Seattle now. You can come with us if you like, but we don't have room for all the luggage you have. Sort out what you need for a couple of days and just bring that."

Peter added, "We've booked you in at the Empress Hotel, so when we run round to the Inner Harbour to drop Father, you can go up there and leave anything you're not bringing with you."

"My father said I'd be staying with your family."

"Best laid plans and all that, we have a full house at the moment. You'll be very comfortable at the hotel—it's the best in Canada," said Michael.

They dropped Romilly at the wharf below the hotel. Michael went up and found a porter to help. "We'll be off in half an hour, so be back by then," said McPherson. They heard him giving instructions to the porter about the correct handling of his luggage. McPherson and Arundel settled back to wait in the saloon.

"He's still a nasty little shit," said Arundel. "He was supposed to stay with us, but I convinced Father to make the hotel reservations in case he hadn't changed from when I met him in London."

"He is rather. I take it he's staying here for a while. What are you going to do with him?"

"He's supposed to work for our London correspondents. They want him to have a look at our operation so he'll be less likely to cause any shipment problems on their end."

"Does that mean you want him to sail with us on deliveries?"

"Yes, if you can manage."

"After the last half an hour in his company, I have my doubts."

"May we be assured you'll try?"

"I will, but you may have to pick him off a rock somewhere if that's where I've dumped him."

Romilly barely made it back to the wharf before they left.

"Get used to being here when we tell you to be," McPherson told him as he stumbled inexpertly onto the deck. "I thought you were a naval officer." Romilly glared at him and went into the saloon as they cast off.

Once they pulled out into Haro Straits, McPherson asked Elise to look over the radio to see if it was a type which they should purchase for the *Lady Jane* or the new boat. A mast had been added in front of the wheelhouse and served as the forward support of the radio antenna. The radio was installed at the rear of the saloon, and Elise started by looking through the government regulations covering frequencies.

"We don't have much useful information here. This is an army set and it's designed to talk to other army sets—the owner probably has friends with similar sets on their boats. We should see what's available in Seattle and find one that can operate on American frequencies. We need a fairly new naval set because the transmitters and receivers are more compact, and their antennae are smaller. Our minimum need is for sets that can reach Seattle from Victoria. There were some new techniques in voice transmission that came available in the last few months, but I'd be surprised if that equipment was being sold off yet, so for the time being, it's still Morse code transmissions."

Lindstrom took the wheel once they crossed the international border. McPherson asked for suggestions for closer inspection of possible drop off points.

"I still want to stick to the east side of the sound," said Olmstead, "otherwise the run into Seattle is too long. I want to keep deliveries between four and six in the morning. I've decided on the bakery and laundry vans as delivery vehicles, and that matches the times they'd be out. Any time we use a car, I'd want it to be earlier still."

"The new boat will give us better range," said McPherson, "and with less time enroute we'll be able to run closer in, but I doubt that the *Lady Jane* or anything else like her will be able to do more than one trip every three days. Once we get more crews, we can do more runs, so that'll increase deliveries. Right now, we only have two choices: Bellingham Bay or something around Everett." He turned to Romilly, "Do you have any time handling boats?"

"Of course."

"Will you take the helm and give Ollie some time to work on the charts with me? Take her down Rosario Strait, and once we come out at Lummi Island, we can drop south again."

Even a boat fifty feet long could feel crowded with six people jammed into one part of it; it was more so when four of them needed to use the only table to spread charts around. Romilly followed the course without any incident while the other men discussed possible drop-off locations. McPherson took the helm again and they ran by twenty spots; on four of them they practiced a fast approach to the shore and a dinghy run to the beach.

"I think we should try both a dinghy launch from the deck and one where we tow it in, pull it alongside and load it," said McPherson. They tried each version of the operation in two more locations, and then sat down on the afterdeck to consider what worked the best.

"Towing's a little faster in getting the dinghy alongside and ready for loading, but if the tide's running the wrong way to the boat's heading, it might be a bit wild, especially if there's submerged rocks around," said McPherson. "We're not going to have a crew of more than two so they're going to have to work out how they want to do it each time."

"Delivery times are set by the pickup crew, so I suppose we just have to live with whatever the tide's doing at the time," commented Arundel.

"The 'we' in this case being Ollie and me," said McPherson sharply. "The big thing to worry about is rocks that are covered at high tide, so the best places are those where there's a reference point on shore which lets us take a bearing on which to run down. It's not a perfect solution but it'll have to do until we come up with a better one."

Dusk fell as they came abreast of the southern end of Whidbey Island. "We'll turn in here," said McPherson. "We're out of most people's way so it'll be anchor watch only overnight. It's a seaman's task, so Roy and Elise can have the night off get breakfast in the morning. John, you stand the first one. There are enough cabins for everyone, but the men will have to share. Elise, you can have that one at the stern all to yourself. Roy and Peter, take the first on the port side. Ollie and John, take the one opposite, by the engine, and Jeff and I can share the one closest to the saloon."

They managed a comfortable-enough dinner, though only Romilly helped himself to the liquor in the boat's generously supplied stock. "Where did that come from?" said an irritated McPherson. "Peter, I told you once that nothing gets loaded on a boat that I don't know about."

"Sorry, it belongs to the owner."

"I know the Customs guys," said Olmstead.

"It'll be okay."

Lindstrom was gently superseded in the galley by Elise and Roy. Conversation was desultory, as could be expected; Elise was not allowed to talk of her wartime life, Lindstrom had spent the war running his boat up and down a peaceful coast, and Roy, as a policeman, had avoided military service. Out of the galley, Romilly's contribution was about London high society, which excluded everyone else. The only subject left to talk about was their early years, which was a good reason for everyone to turn in.

McPherson briefed Romilly for the first watch; before he took over the next one he used the time to make notes about the knowledge gained on the way down. That done, he wondered about Emmaline. What was she doing tonight?

He woke Logan after two hours and turned in himself. It seemed only a minute before he was woken by Lindstrom, who told him dawn was showing over the coastal hills, and "there was some rustling sounds from Elise's cabin when I went out on deck. I think I saw Roy creeping out of it."

"Damn. I take it he's married."

"I believe so."

"That's all we need. I hope we don't have an angry spouse telling the opposition all about us. Nothing we can do about it now. We'll bring Elise back with us, in irons if necessary, and the Arundels can take care of the problem."

Chapter 20

Seattle, Wednesday, September 17th, 1919

After breakfast was cleared away, they took three hours to reach Seattle with *Rosalie* coasting at an easy eight knots. Between inspecting possible drop-off sites, there was nothing much to say except to keep on with the stilted conversation of people who were largely strangers. Olmstead and Elise seemed comfortable saying nothing to each other but listened in as Arundel, Logan and McPherson ran up a list of spare parts and tried to assess the need for radios. Romilly and Lindstrom shared the wheel.

As they came up to the Seattle wharves, Elise said, "We're going to need somewhere to base the radio. The higher it is the better."

"There's a couple of headlands close to the harbour, but it would be better to put the antenna on a building. There's starting to be a number of them as people talk to marine traffic, so it shouldn't be too obvious," replied Olmstead.

"What's that building?" she asked, pointing to a massive tower set amidst the downtown business district.

"It's the L.C. Smith Building—built in 1914. It has thirty-eight stories and reaches four hundred and fifty-nine feet from the curb to the top of its pyramid roof." When Elise raised her eyebrows, he added, "Us policemen like to remember details."

"We could put a radio antenna on the top and it would just look like a flagpole. Any office space available inside?" she asked.

"Probably."

"That's your show, Roy. We'll take whatever radio equipment is needed back with us and Elise can do the set-up at our end," said McPherson.

Elise protested, "It might be better if I stayed down here and did the operations work."

"Major Arundel has the final say on everything that gets done—we'll need to clear it with him," said McPherson. "He'll need to work out where the Victoria end goes. If he asks me, I'll suggest Gonzales Hill. Besides, it'll depend on the type of equipment we decide on."

Lindstrom took the boat into a vacant slip and McPherson secured the lines. "What now?" said Olmstead.

"It would be useful if you found an atlas," said McPherson. "We can spend this afternoon keying it to the charts. I'd like to leave here with drop-off locations and their codes settled. Jeff and Peter, could you go and search for naval radios? Maybe Finnerty's is a good place to start. Take Elise with you—she knows the right questions to ask. I'm staying on board while we're in port."

"I can show you around the town and then I'll take you down to Finnerty's" said Olmstead, turning to Elise.

"I'll go with you," said Romilly.

McPherson took Arundel to the other side of the saloon. "I'm not sure that's wise," he said quietly. "If John's spotted next to you by one of White's people, they'll know he's with us and they'll want to know who he is. The news that we're not using them might not have got through, or worse, it has and they're spoiling for another fight."

"I'll tell him to stick close to Roy."

"That includes you avoiding White's daughter. I don't plan to be there again to flatten someone with a prior claim."

"We'll be careful."

Olmstead returned two hours later, without Romilly, but with the book. "He left us at Rainier Square. Said he wanted to walk around downtown and meet us back here."

"Fine. We can go over the charts," said McPherson. He, Olmstead, and Lindstrom spent the next three hours poring over the atlas and its corresponding charts. They looked at each possible drop-off point for ease of access and its driving time from Seattle. They settled on the twenty best ones, and then worked out a schedule of deliveries.

"We can work out travel times to each location, but the key time is when you want to pick up. The *Lady Jane* will cruise at between seven and eight knots, and assuming an average distance of fifty miles to each drop off point, that means we have between six-and-a-half to seven-and-a-half hours at sea for each delivery—weather permitting. Add another hour for unloading and we'll take the same time to go back. That's a sixteen-hour day. We could do three runs a week based on that time frame, but it doesn't leave a lot of time if something goes wrong." McPherson thumbed through the atlas and made some notes in his book as he reconfirmed sailing times to a sample number of places. "How important are regular delivery times to you?" he asked.

"Right now, everyone's getting by on what they can get, when they can get it. You're not my only supplier, just likely to be my most reliable one. Despite the fact I don't want to run a liquor warehouse, we usually have enough to keep people happy for a couple of days. I generally move it onto the back of a truck and change the place I park it every few hours."

"Let's start with a weekly run to see how it goes. We'll up it to two when we're comfortable, and three if we can. We can handle it ourselves for the moment, but we'll need more men in the new year; once we're happy with them, we can alternate boats."

They added numbers to their preferred drop-off locations and Olmstead took one copy. "What about practicing your shore crews? We told you what happened with White's men," said McPherson.

"If you're leaving tomorrow morning, why not try a daylight delivery at Brackett's Landing at nine o'clock? You can follow it up with another nighttime one further north, and let us know the location after the first try?"

"Okay. I'll get Ollie and Jeff to put together some bags with something in them that weighs the same as bottles."

Logan, Arundel, and Elise came back before Olmstead left. A truck was following their taxi. The two men in it loaded a hand truck with three crates and trundled it down to the slip.

"We picked up three radios which should work—one for the base in Victoria, one for the boat and the third for the base here. Where do you want it, Roy?" she asked.

"I've been using my basement at home to store this sort of thing, but I'd better find somewhere different otherwise my wife will begin to ask too many questions." He thought for a minute. "We've got some spare space in the back of a furniture store in the old town; get it back on the truck and I'll take it up there now."

"Is that where you'll operate from?" asked Elise.

"Don't think so."

"Then while I'm here, why don't you take me round some likely places, and I can tell you if they'll work?" She turned to McPherson and asked, "What hotel do you use here?"

"The Alexis."

"I'll see her to it when we've finished our looking around," said Olmstead.

"Perhaps I can meet some of your chaps tonight," said Arundel. "Always helps to put a face to names."

"How about the Alexis dining room at seven tonight?" said Olmstead. "We can go from there. We could treat as a celebration of sorts—the Eighteenth Amendment goes into effect tonight." McPherson nodded.

"How remarkable," said Elise. "The American Congress changes their constitution in a way which, by prohibiting the manufacture and sale of alcohol, is the final piece of legislation that will keep our business going."

"Remarkable?" said Olmstead. "That's a real piece of British understatement." He paused as they turned to follow the delivery men back to the truck, then said, "I can pick Elise up in the morning and drive her over to Brackett's Landing."

McPherson watched them leave, turned to face Arundel, and said, "Remember what I said about staying out of trouble. This is becoming a serious business and we don't need it damaged by stupid behaviour."

McPherson left Lindstrom to find some storage space for the radios that wouldn't interfere with the boat's trim and went to find a newspaper to see if the legislation had really passed. That day's edition of the Post Intelligencer was sold out. He went back to the boat, just as Romilly appeared coming from the other direction.

"You found us," remarked McPherson.

"I got lost a couple of times, but yes."

Just after dawn on Thursday morning, with the coffee perking in the galley, McPherson heard a loud voice on the wharf calling for Arundel. He came out on deck and saw Jim White.

"You! Where's my daughter?" White yelled. McPherson stepped out onto the wharf and looked at him coolly. White carried on. "One of my guys saw her talking to your pal last night." He made to push past McPherson, heading for the boat.

McPherson handled him calmly but very firmly. "Don't do that, Jim. This is my boat, and you don't go one step further without my permission."

"Where's your pal?"

"Staying at the Alexis."

"I checked at the desk, and they said they knew nothing about him."

"If you had the same attitude there as you do here, I'm not surprised they wouldn't tell you anything."

White simmered down a little. Logan offered him a coffee which he took.

"Why are you guys down here anyway? he asked. "I thought we had a deal. You'd be delivering to me."

"Your arrangement's with Harry Calhoun. You should talk to him."

White sat morosely at the saloon table slurping his coffee. "You have kids?"

"No."

"Daughter's the only one left. I had a son, but he got shot in a fight a couple of years ago."

"I'm sorry," said McPherson.

"I just need her to keep the family hopes alive. My guy Mike Burnand should be the one for her, but she won't look at him."

McPherson said nothing. Logan and Lindstrom stayed close by in case there was another eruption. Finally, White grunted something which could be either thanks or an apology and left.

“What was that all about?’ asked Romilly emerging, yawning, from his cabin.

“A customer of someone we won’t be doing too much business with anymore.”

“Doesn’t seem to be happy.”

“They often aren’t. Coffee’s in the galley.”

McPherson waited until he was a few feet away and went forward to the wheel. “No sign of Peter?” he quietly asked Logan and Lindstrom who had gone there to avoid White. They shook their heads. “Hopefully, he’s got the sense to find us. He knows we’re due at Brackett’s Landing at nine. Let’s get some grub into us—we need to leave at seven.”

They made the boat ready to sail without Arundel and slipped the lines before anyone on the neighbouring craft was stirring. Traffic coming into the port was light and McPherson picked out the wharf that marked their destination by half past eight. They anchored off the point, staying out of the fairway and watching for movement on shore. No one appeared until half past nine. McPherson was irritated. They raised the anchor, and while McPherson kept his binoculars focused on the shore party, Lindstrom conned the boat in while Logan and Romilly cast off the dinghy.

“I see Elise,” said McPherson, “and now I see Peter.” He went forward and held the anchor until Lindstrom brought the boat in as close to the shore as he dared without risking it grounding. McPherson signalled Lindstrom to stop the engine and he let the anchor go. The boat drifted for a moment until the hook caught. “I’ll come with you, Jeff. We’ll pick up those two and I’ll talk to Olmstead to see if he wants to have his crews poke around a bit.”

He got into the dinghy and sat in the stern while Jeff gave a few powerful strokes. They reached the beach in under two minutes. Elise and Peter were standing quietly off to one side and McPherson ignored them while he talked to Olmstead.

"Would you like to have your people poke around the dinghy a bit? They should get used to getting their feet wet so they can dress for it. They'll also have to keep the bow hard onto the beach. The best way to do it is to have someone hold onto the mooring rope—we call it the painter—and keep it tight."

Olmstead motioned to a couple of men who were making hard going through the sand. "When you pick locations, keep the surface in mind," said McPherson, pointing to the two sloggers. "The closer you can get your cars or trucks, the sooner you can leave the beach, and we won't be looking for reasons to hang about. Never forget the tide's moving one way or the other virtually all the time. We'll make deliveries according to the time and not the tide."

"Got it," said Olmstead, and he waved his crewmen away from the dinghy.

"You shouldn't hang about the beach for any time after the pickup, either," added McPherson. "There's safety when you're moving."

McPherson motioned to Elise and Arundel to get into the dinghy and followed them. Logan took the oars and got them back to the boat in the same time it took him to go the other way, despite the increased weight of two people. When they arrived, McPherson got out first and Arundel followed him. Logan held Elise back momentarily.

"This is going to be ugly," McPherson heard Logan say as he made the dinghy fast to the stern and came on board as McPherson got to the taffrail.

"We'll ship the dinghy inboard in a while. Tell Ollie to get under way now," McPherson told him, and gave a pointed look at Elise. Logan understood and led Elise to the wheelhouse.

McPherson waited for them to move away

before he turned to Arundel. He didn't raise his voice, but there was a steely edge to it. "I'd call you a useless baboon except a baboon's got more sense. You brainless fop. There's hundreds of young women in Seattle and you have to pick the one who's the daughter of someone we're not going to do business with. I'm here because this operation was run by amateurs. We finally get a professional to work with us and you make a pig's arse of the operation. I'm taking you back to Victoria, but until I've cooled down, you're not travelling on any boat I'm running unless someone sends a nurse to look after you. In the long run, it'd be better if you did get your head shot off."

"What was that about?" asked Elise when McPherson came back to the wheelhouse.

He ignored her and turned back to Arundel. "You can ship the dinghy now." He was not prepared, until he had thought it through, to tackle the consequences of another illicit personal relationship that could wreck their business.

Chapter 21

Victoria, Friday, September 26th, 1919

McPherson met Arundel at the Consolidated Exporters' warehouse in West Bay at six in the morning and together they started packing the bottles from one hundred cases, using two bales worth of straw into two hundred sacks.

Romilly appeared at half past eight. "What's happening here?" he asked.

"All part of loading the cargo. You can help," said Arundel, throwing him a sack.

"What do I do with it?"

"Lay it flat, put in six bottles and pack it with straw. When it's full, twist a piece of string tightly round the top and make sure nothing falls out."

Romilly picked up a sack, carefully took bottles from a case and stuffed in the straw. "Not really used to doing this sort of thing, but I have to keep up with you chaps."

"Something happen to him?" McPherson asked Arundel out of Romilly's hearing. Arundel shook his head and shrugged.

"Why so many sacks?" Romilly asked.

"Easier to load into a dinghy," said McPherson. "If we transfer them at sea, we could be delayed due to torn or unstitched sacks, so it's easier to do here. We won't get all the bottles into sacks before we go, but we'll have a good start. We'll try six bottles in each and see how they handle. If it's too unwieldy we can cut the number down."

Just after nine a rattling diesel and a blast of fumes announced the *Lady Jane*'s arrival. Arundel helped berth her and when Lindstrom stepped ashore, McPherson handed him the cargo manifest.

"This says we're headed for Sointula. You ever been there?" said Lindstrom.

"No. Been past it any number of times."

"Will we always mark it as a destination?"

"Probably. We could use any small town well up the coast.'

"Why this one?"

"No reason, except the Arundels tell me it's far enough up there that Canadian Customs can play the game. It's unlikely they'd ever look at us, but it would be hard for them to check whether or not we actually went there. For the moment having a fish boat it makes it easier for us because she's the sort of boat that would go up that way anyhow. It allows everybody to say they saw nothing wrong with passing us through."

"Interesting to see if that continues," commented Lindstrom.

"We'll take the boat out as soon as she's loaded and anchor off Discovery Island. That way we can finish the repacking and we can watch to see if anyone's following us."

"Where are we going?" asked Lindstrom.

"Chuckanut Bay, south of Bellingham. We can pick the precise route when we get to Discovery."

"It's not really my problem, but how is this load going to be paid for?" asked Lindstrom.

"Whichever one of us has the last run in the dinghy picks up a pouch of cash from the people on the beach. We'll bring it back here and hand it off to the Arundels. I'll take your two hundred dollars out of it at the end of the run and give it to you—that's in addition to the money we give you for all the running around."

McPherson turned to Romilly. "You want to join us on this run?" he asked. "You can see how we do things."

"Thank you, no. I'll probably come on a later run."

"You can help us load then."

They left Discovery Island at four in the afternoon. McPherson set a course for East Point on Saturna Island. For early fall, the weather was not too bad—a stiff breeze out of the Sound, the water starting to get choppy. Visibility was reasonable and he kept the binoculars sweeping over the waters for any sign of the US Coast Guard. Fortunately, the *Arcata*, with her high superstructure and white hull, would be conspicuous. Boat traffic was light and there was only one other boat rounding the point out of Victoria Harbour behind them.

The packer's engine was noisy and the extra use they were making of it gave its tired cylinders more work than they deserved. "We should have leaned on Jeff to come along," said Lindstrom as they motored on through the evening. "He could have finished what he started in Seattle."

"I said he could promise his wife we wouldn't do that; it's the one thing that keeps him working with us. We'll try to borrow *Rosalie* again until this one can get a bit of an overhaul. I'll stay topsides. Will you go down and pack the rest of those bottles? Are the bags okay holding six bottles each?"

Lindstrom nodded. "They could be a little on the heavy side with us having to swing two hundred of them up from the hold. Have to try it first, I guess."

The slow bangs from the ancient engine and the fumes from its leaking exhaust made them both yawn. "I'll leave the hatch cover off," said Lindstrom. "It should stay dry enough in these seas. I'm more used to this than you."

"I'm grateful for that."

"After I've finished repacking the load, you stretch out on the bunk in the galley. Your job is to get us to shore and back again," Lindstrom said. "That's not going to happen if you fall asleep at the wheel."

McPherson thought about arguing; his sense of duty and the responsibility of an officer loomed high, but Lindstrom, with twenty years of practical seagoing experience behind him, made a stronger case.

"Okay. When you come up, I'll go down for three hours. Throttle her back to five knots and call me when we have Bedwell on the port beam. You can go down for the next three hours."

When Lindstrom called down, McPherson took the helm again. "Any sign we're being followed?"

"No, the boat that came out of the harbour after us swung up toward Sidney. There are a few boats with their nets out over by Port Townsend, but nothing to bother us at the moment.

Shortly after seven o'clock, McPherson changed course. The sea conditions were a little rougher. Lindstrom woke immediately with the change in the boat's motion and came up to the wheelhouse. The winds were piling the waves up over the shallower water as they ran down past Orcas Island. The coast was well provided with lights, so navigation was not excessively difficult despite the moonless night. McPherson sent Lindstrom back down.

He counted each light as they sighted it and confirmed their position on the chart. Any mistake could send them up on the rocks. Orcas Island had more than its share of reefs and rocky outcrops. By half-past-eleven, Bellingham Bay came up on their port bow. McPherson throttled back, called Lindstrom, and they started looking for the long spit that jutted from its southern shore.

Chuckanut Bay lay slightly to the south and McPherson reduced speed as they bore down on the spit. He had estimated their arrival for about one hour before high tide. Lindstrom kept flashing the Morse code letter "C"—dash-dot-dash-dot—with the small spotlight they had installed on the top of the wheelhouse. He used the control arm attached to the light to keep it trained toward the place on the beach where they expected to meet their pickup crew. He repeated the signal at thirty second intervals. McPherson throttled back further, only maintaining enough speed to keep steerage way.

The boat began to wallow in the troughs between the waves as they paralleled the shore, so he increased speed to take the craft in a wide circle away from the beach and headed into deeper waters where it was a little calmer. For a moment, as they turned back toward the beach, he saw a light reflected off the water off their port quarter. He marked the position on the chart as Lindstrom called down into the wheelhouse, "She's going to be a bit lively in these seas."

"And we may not be on our own here right now."

"What did you see?"

"Not sure—just a light out in the bay north-west of us."

"Not much we can do about it now."

"We don't have much room to spare with the sea this lively," said McPherson. "The skiff's only eleven feet, and round-bottomed to boot. She'll be okay in calm water but hard to control with a load on if the waves are up. Any ideas?"

"Not at the moment. Eleven feet is a good enough length—any longer and it'll be too hard to manhandle over the side. You said the dory would work better and we should have that for the next trip."

McPherson checked the chart again for hidden rocks. Lindstrom kept the signal going and as the *Lady Jane* breasted a wave and rode up over it, he got an answering signal from the shore. "Got 'em, Dugald," he said.

"They're a little south of where I expected," said McPherson, looking at the light and then at the chart. He checked the turn and pointed the boat toward the shore again. Lindstrom ran down to the engine room and throttled it back as they closed on the point they had picked to anchor. They kept watching the signal from Olmstead's men when it flashed every thirty seconds.

Lindstrom went aft to where the dinghy was lashed down over the hatch cover, threw off the ties and launched it, letting it drift back about twenty feet on its painter to stop it surging into the transom, and secured the rope to the deck railing.

They anchored about one hundred fifty yards from the beach so the ebbing tide wouldn't ground them before they finished the drop. Lindstrom pulled the dinghy back alongside, and once it was secured bow and stern and protected by rope fenders lashed to boat's side, he took off the hatch cover. McPherson stayed at the wheel until he was satisfied the hook had a good grip, then went down to stop the engine, and then aft to help with the offloading.

Once in the hold, he braced himself against the boat's motion and began to pass the bags up. Lindstrom piled them on the deck wedged against the railing. When they had extracted twenty-five sacks—McPherson's estimate of what the skiff could handle—Lindstrom stepped down into the skiff and McPherson came out of the hold and passed the bags down to him. The fishing boat's freeboard towered over the dinghy; there was no quick way of loading. Whichever way they did it, it was backbreaking work. In the event, their skiff could only take twenty sacks and stay afloat at the same time. Even then, it seemed dangerously low in the water, but Lindstrom dropped his oars into the row locks and started to pull powerfully for the shore.

The boat was pitching violently, and McPherson

went back to the wheelhouse to verify their position against the shore and check the anchor was not dragging. Periodically he caught sight of the dinghy as it crested a wave. When he saw the flashlights concentrated in one part of the beach, he guessed it had reached the shore. The boat's anchor was holding, so he went aft again and prepared the next load.

The shore crew made short work with the offloading. The little boat reappeared as if on wings. One second there was nothing except the waves, the next it was gliding down one to bump alongside. McPherson helped Lindstrom back onto the boat.

"Everything alright?" he asked.

"That thing is a pain in the neck. It's really hard to keep from yawing at the top of a wave. The only time it's any good at all is when we hit the beach and it stays upright."

"You okay to go again?"

"*Ja*—let's get on with it."

The first load had taken forty minutes from the time he had passed the first bag up to the time that Lindstrom had come back. They had one hundred and eighty bags left. If they could continue with their current pace, the man on the boat unloading the hatch while the other rowed, they would still have close to six hours before they could leave. It was going to be a long night and first light would probably find them still on the beach.

They swapped turns at the oars throughout the night and most loads went smoothly. They were both rapidly tiring and grateful the trips were getting marginally shorter as the tide receded. Lindstrom had the last trip. McPherson was watching through the night glasses and saw the skiff broach as it crested the last wave before the beach, then lost sight of the boat and Lindstrom. Then he saw waves breaking over its upturned hull and Olmstead's men reaching into the surf and pulling Lindstrom out.

They rescued the oars and righted the boat. McPherson saw Lindstrom take a package from someone, step back into the boat and start to row back. He arrived drenched and exhausted. He handed the package over and McPherson had to brace himself with the rail to almost lift him back aboard.

"Three of the bags broke open and their bottles were strewn around the beach. Not bad for the first try with the wrong kind of shore boat."

The watery September sun was just starting to gleam over the ridges of the hill to the east. "We need to get underway now," said McPherson.

"We've company out there."

"Where?"

"Can't see them at the moment, but I caught a flash of something a few minutes ago. If I were waiting to jump someone, I'd sit so the light fell on them first. My guess is they're close inshore to the north and they'll run down as soon as they hear us start the engine."

McPherson shielded his flashlight and focused a small amount of light on the chart. He pointed at a position on it.

"We've got a way to go to low tide, so I'd like to move us quietly to a spot on the other side of those rocks. They're awash most of the time so if we start the engine on this side and keep them between us and the other boat, they might just hit them as they run down. We need a bit of sea room between us and the rocks so we can do a hard turn as soon as the engine fires. I'll raise the anchor. Can you manage the dinghy and tow us back about twenty-five yards?"

"*Ja*. How will I know when to stop?"

"I'll point the flashlight down the tow line and give you three dots. Come back immediately—I'll be pulling on the rope as well."

Lindstrom pulled on the line holding the little craft bobbing in their wake, took the oars again and carefully boarded it. He rowed to the full extent of the tow line and kept the tension on the line waiting for the anchor to be lifted. In a moment he felt the dinghy move and he managed ten powerful strokes before he saw the light flashing in front of him. He reversed his strokes and was half pulled back to the boat.

"That should do us," said McPherson as he helped him back on board. "Light the engine as fast as you can."

Cold starts on diesels needed each cylinder to have a lighted fuse punk hammered in the top and fuel to be fed in. It took a minute and the noise and rattling that resulted must have been heard by any boat close to them. As the engine caught and the propeller bit, the boat leaned. McPherson checked the chart again and put the helm hard over to port. He called down to Lindstrom, "Open the throttle! Get as much speed as the engine'll give us."

Lindstrom did it, then climbed up the ladder through the galley and up to the wheelhouse. "I don't want to be caught below decks if someone hostile's heading for us."

McPherson was looking over the starboard side toward Governor's Point. "Looks like there's something on fire over there. Grab the night glasses—it's at..." he paused and centred the wheel, "...about eight o'clock."

Lindstrom swept the glasses over a narrow arc, delicately adjusting the focusing wheel. "Bloody hell, it's the bow wave of a boat heading for us. There's someone hanging out the cabin door. Looks like he's holding a rifle."

"Good luck to him with both of us bouncing around like this." McPherson moved the wheel to widen the distance between them. The white foam at the other boat's bow shifted in their direction. McPherson moved the wheel back. "Rifle's not going to be any more accurate at close range and they're going to find it hard to get their timing right at our combined speeds." He shouted to be heard over the thudding engine noise. "Go down to the galley, we may need to throttle back to turn in a moment."

They watched the oncoming craft close in. "At least he's not thinking of ramming us,' said Lindstrom, as he headed for the steps.

There was a sudden eruption of flame from the other boat's cabin and McPherson heard a rapid series of shots. The glass in the side of the wheelhouse shattered. McPherson felt a searing pain across his forehead. Blood gushed down over one eye. "Ollie—grab the first aid kit!"

Lindstrom hurtled up the steps from the galley, grabbed a wiping cloth from the ledge under the windscreen and shoved it into McPherson's hand. "Stick that against your head!" He pulled the shotgun from its slot on the bulkhead.

McPherson pressed the rag against his forehead. "Where are they now?"

Lindstrom looked aft through the wheelhouse door. "Looks like he's turning to starboard. Moving faster than we can, probably trying to cut us off."

McPherson wedged himself against the side of the wheelhouse and spun the wheel to port. "Go down and throttle back!"

"What are you doing?"

"Hopefully putting Chuckanut Rock between us. If he's moving at that speed, he's probably not keeping as good a lookout as he should."

"Hope you're right," said Lindstrom, going below again.

McPherson heard more than saw the boat fifty yards away and heading for their bow. Its roaring engine drowned out the sound of their own labouring diesel. It was too dark for him to see details, but he watched anyway. The other boat veered away as the helmsman saw the rocks. One crewman fell off the deck and thrashed around in the turbulent water.

"I think that was the man with the gun. Hope he can swim," said McPherson. "Give me a bit more speed," he called as he circled round towards the flailing man.

"What are you doing?"

"Going round to pick him up."

McPherson, with one hand still holding the rag to his forehead, edged the boat over to the other side of the rocks mindful of their own four-foot draft as the receding tide uncovered the reef. Lindstrom came up and moved to the bow, calling out to the man thrashing in the water, who still had the gun in his hand.

They came level with the other boat, and McPherson shone their spotlight over it, but they pulled up, cutting off the view of their own man flailing in the water. McPherson couldn't make out any faces, but he did another circuit as the other boat picked up speed, turned away, and headed round them to the south.

Lindstrom looked at McPherson. "Why did you want to pick him up? It looked like they were trying to kill us. I'd have let the bastard drown!"

McPherson took up the wheel again. "Two reasons. First, it's the law of the sea; you don't leave a man to drown if you can make an effort to save him. Second, we should try to find out who they are and why they just tried to kill us." He swung the wheel and picked up a course that would take them back round the north end of Orcas Island.

"Hope they got him. That's it, then," he said. "Now you can find the first aid kit," he said.

Lindstrom thought for a moment, opened a cupboard door under the chart table, rummaged around in it and found nothing. Then he opened the drawer above and pulled the kit out. "Better rinse the blood off before I wrap it," he said.

Between them they fixed a folded bandage as a

pad over the gash and taped it down with adhesive straps. "You take the wheel," said McPherson.

"Who was that?" asked Lindstrom as he picked up the new course.

"Don't know. Boat look familiar to you?"

"No." Lindstrom looked back at the other's wake. "Looks like someone's personal pleasure boat. Must have been moving pretty fast to come up on us like that. Wonder if it was the owner doing the driving or whether those fellows stole it."

"I've never seen anything like that gun, either. Maybe Olmstead can shed some light on it. I'm more concerned about whether they followed us in or whether they knew where we were going. They didn't hit us when we were loaded—they waited until we had the money."

"Didn't want to continue the fight, anyway. Maybe they didn't like the look of the shotgun," said Lindstrom, putting it back in its slot.

"Olmstead's men may have seen it happen, unless they cleared the beach as fast as we said they should."

"Could be they had people on shore who followed them and signalled the boat when we pulled out."

"I'll talk to Roy later. It's something he'll need to watch for."

"I'm going to get some dry clothes on and then stay as close as possible to the engine so I can warm up." McPherson did not want to meet the Coast Guard on the way home but figured they would not be awake and patrolling in the area yet. It was still a long haul back to Victoria, and rather than retracing their exact course of the previous day, he opted for a more direct route by heading west and going south of San Juan Island. He thought this would give them a slightly better excuse if a cutter hailed them. He could claim to have anchored on the west coast of Orcas Island, saying he was due to meet fishing boats from which he had contracted to buy the catch.

"Any coffee around here?" he called down.

Lindstrom lit the galley stove. "We've got to find a better way of doing this," he said yawning.

"The new boat will get us in quicker, but the whole unloading process has to be done better. That, though, is tomorrow's problem. Got anything to eat?"

Lindstrom pulled a loaf of bread from a cupboard, cut it into large slabs and handed half to McPherson.

Both men were desperately tired and they had at least another five hours to make Victoria. McPherson laid down in the boat's single bunk, and in a moment, was fast asleep. Lindstrom lit a cigarette and passed into an automated state that let him work the *Lady Jane* across the choppy straits to their wharf in Victoria Harbour without having to pay attention to anything that wasn't essential. When they finally made it in, it was almost twenty-six hours since they left.

McPherson woke when the boat nudged the wharf. The gash on his forehead felt like it was burning and throbbed incessantly. He sat up slowly and turned to let his feet swing over the edge of the bunk. Lindstrom was tramping the deck securing the mooring lines and poked his head into the galley when he had finished.

"Stupid question, but how are you feeling?" he asked.

McPherson grimaced as he leaned forward to shift his weight onto his feet. "Head's burning." He reached for the edge of the galley table to support him as he stood, "I feel dizzy." He sat back.

"You're beyond any fixing up I can do—you'd better head for the hospital. You're still bleeding a bit through the bandage."

"Give me a hand to change it before we go

ashore—there's no telling who I'll frighten if they see this."

Lindstrom carefully removed the bandage, washed the wound and replaced it. "The doctor'll have to do a bit of stitching on that one. There's a really deep gash there."

"I'm a bit too dizzy to be driving my car. Can you run me over to the hospital?"

"I've never driven one of those things in my life. I'd hit something and make the gash much worse. We can call a taxi from the office."

"... and call Michael to meet me at the hospital to get his money," added McPherson.

McPherson paid the cabbie, got out of the car, and grabbed a lamp post for support. The effort of walking into the hospital was almost as much as he could manage.

"Looks like you need someone to lean on." McPherson turned; Peter Arundel was coming up beside him.

"Thanks. The world's rotating a bit too much for me to be sure of making it through the right door. Where's your father, or are you collecting the money?"

"He's parking the car—be along in a second. I came to help you along. He can take the money." Together they made it through the door of the hospital and put McPherson onto a chair in the waiting room.

"You've had an interesting time." Michael came through the door and sat down beside him.

"Here—take this." McPherson handed over the pouch with the money. "I'll take the next couple of days off."

"Probably more than that," said Peter. "What happened?"

"Someone was waiting for us. They knew enough about our schedule to wait until we picked up the money and then they moved in. There must be a leak somewhere."

A nurse came and took McPherson into a treatment room. He sat down and a middle-aged doctor came in. "I'm Dr. Matthews," he said, reaching for the bandage. "This looks nasty, but someone has done a fair job of first aid. What happened?" he asked once he'd gently removed it.

"Flying glass."

"Umm," said Matthews, peering into the gash. "Won't ask you what broke it but there's a few bits left there. I'll need to pick them out before I can stitch it shut. My younger colleagues, home from the war, have taught us old pus-pushers some new techniques so you probably won't die from an infection, but I can't guarantee it. I've got some stuff that'll numb your skin, but it'll still sting a bit. You'll have a bit of a scar until your face gets enough lines to cover it up." He whistled tunelessly while he stitched the wound up. McPherson gritted his teeth as the needle pierced through the numbing medication.

"There!" said the doctor as he snipped the final thread off. "Keep the bandage handy until the scab dries. It'll go more quickly if you leave it off when you can, but it'll frighten the horses if you walk down the street with it in clear view. Get some aspirin. A couple of tablets every four hours should take care of most of the pain, but don't gobble any more than that—they can bite back." He stood up. "I'll need you to come back tomorrow, and then every couple of days for the next week."

McPherson protested. "I don't think it's that bad, really. I'll come back tomorrow, but after that I have work to do."

"Of course, I can't force you to come in, but do keep a close eye on it," said Matthews.

McPherson nodded and went out to the waiting room. Peter was sitting there. "My father paid the bill on his way out. I'll run you home."

"I'll need some supplies from the chemist's shop."

The chemist piled a selection of items onto the counter and wrapped them up. "Here's a couple of weeks' worth of supplies and some scissors. Let the hospital take care of the antiseptic part of the treatment. The doctor will tell you if you need to put any on yourself."

McPherson took the package and added a large bottle of aspirin.

"I'll organize someone to pick up your car and get it back here," said Michael when they reached the hotel and dropped him off. McPherson picked his way carefully into the lobby and up to his room. He looked at himself in the mirror. Leaving aside the days' worth of beard and dark rings underneath his eyes, the bandage taped to his forehead was surrounded by a bruise that seemed to get wider as he looked at it. He stumbled to his feet and fell into bed.

He slept for most of the next twenty-four hours. When he woke, the world was still heaving so he took a taxi over to the hospital. A different doctor looked at the wound, sniffed it and said, "No sign of gangrene. You'll live." He redressed the wound, grinned, and said, "You'll last for at least a couple of more days. Take it easy and we'll see you later."

Late Monday morning, McPherson went to the Takahashis'. Logan looked at his bandage and said, "That's why I'm not keen on going to sea with you."

Lindstrom brought the *Lady Jane* in at noon. Together they moored the boat to the float in front of the shipyard and then the three of them spent two hours crawling all over it. At the end of the session Logan said, "The engine needs a complete rebuild. It'd make more sense to replace it, especially if we're going to put in a reverse gear. We can look at the exhaust at the same time and put in a radio—or at least a place for one."

"We're probably going back out tomorrow night," said McPherson.

"Not in this boat you're not. I'm surprised you got home. There's a lot to talk about on the new boat but I need to get beyond the guess work I'm still doing. Besides, you're in no condition to listen to it with that head."

Chapter 22

Victoria, Thursday, October 2nd, 1919

They borrowed *Rosalie* again for a run on Thursday morning. Before they left, McPherson went over the contents of the first aid kit again and gave Lindstrom some more instructions on how to use it. "At least you know how to sew up gashes—it's the same as mending nets. If someone breaks an arm or leg, these metal bars are called splints. You brace the splint against the limb and wrap the whole thing with a bandage to keep the broken limb from moving. The iodine stops infection, and the brandy works as an anesthetic if you need one. I've put a book in the kit. It goes into more detail, and we can go over it together."

They replaced their dinghy with a dory the Takahashis had managed to build. Lindstrom looked over the kit, flipped through the book, then closed the lid. "Okay, now I'm a medical expert, maybe you can tell me why this dory's so much better than the dinghies that everyone else uses."

McPherson ran his hands over the boat's flat bottom with its planks laid lengthwise from bow to stern and sides sharply angled upwards. "It has good high sides, a deep bow and stern so the load will sit well inside. It doesn't treat the unskilled rower too well, but you'll find that even when it tips, these chines where the bottom meets the side will act like a keel and stop you making any leeway. You'll have a hard time turning her over like the dinghy, and the more weight we put in her, the more stable she'll be."

That night they were headed for the south end of Bellingham Bay, and even with the overcast skies making navigation difficult, they managed the journey in ten hours. The *Rosalie* could only carry one hundred cases and was also not as convenient for load handling as the *Lady Jane* because the load had to be stored in the cabin. It took both of them to pass sacks out of the cabin door and onto its roof. From there, one man had to balance on a narrow deck and pass each sack individually to the other who was standing in the dory. The advantage, however, was the dory was longer than the dinghy it replaced, and with its better stability, it could take twice the number of sacks, so their time rowing was reduced.

"This thing rowed like an ox-cart on the way in and behaved like a cork on the way out," complained Lindstrom.

"It didn't turn over, did it?"

"That's something, I suppose."

"I'll take the next run."

They alternated until the load was transferred, with McPherson taking the last one. Olmstead met him on the beach. He looked at McPherson closely. "Ugly gash there! At least there doesn't seem to be any gangrene," he said, handing over the leather money bag. "We heard the shots but didn't see anything of it because we took your advice and cleared the beach. We saw you heading out to sea and the other boat go north. I sent someone up later to check and he found a body washed ashore. It was Burnand. There was nothing on him to say who the others were. If they were just looking to grab the money, they certainly went about it stupidly. Some of our competitors aren't the brightest people, but no one boasted about it. There were no reports of a boat coming to grief afterwards or survivors being rescued." He shrugged his shoulders. "I don't know how they found us—I took the precaution of using a trailing vehicle to make sure we weren't followed when we left for the pickup. We posted sentries to watch for anyone approaching. And I talked to Calhoun. He said he had nothing to do with it. I believe him, if only because only White would be a more likely suspect and he denied it when I talked to him. He doesn't have a reason to start a fight with me."

"Do you think it could be an inside job?" asked McPherson.

"I've gone over everyone we're using, and no one stands out. I'm as concerned as you are."

"Someone could have been looking at us from the shore when we turned down to pass San Juan Island, but it would have been a lucky guess to have us at Anacortes. White's still the first suspect, and Calhoun's not that far behind. Any of your people in a position to know what they're up to? White has no reason to like us," McPherson said.

"That because of Peter and his daughter?"

"That, and we're not delivering to him. It could be the people who are, don't do it well."

Olmstead stopped and thought for a moment. "He's giving the Coast Guard and other federal people some easy targets, which probably means he likes us a lot less. My big bother is the gun they used on you. Even from where we were, I could hear that it sounded like a Thompson submachine gun. It's an experimental army piece, an automatic reloading, handheld gun. It has a magazine that holds twenty rounds and a bunch of them went missing from the U.S. Army at Camp Lewis. If one of them was used to shoot at you, I'm worried where the others are. They could just as easily be used to shoot at me."

"Or at us the next time we're here."

"I'm having my boys look around."

Victoria, Saturday, October 18th, 1919

McPherson and Lindstrom came in from a run on the second Saturday in October and Logan met them at the wharf. "The *Lady Jane's* ready," he said. "We replaced the engine with a Fairbanks Morse sixty-horsepower to give you a little more power. You have enough energy to come and have a look?"

"We took turns sleeping on the way in, so I'm good," said McPherson. "Ollie?"

"Sure," the Swede answered. "I'll call my wife from the wharf office so she doesn't worry."

Aki had the boat idling at the float, and they all went on board. In the engine room, Logan described the changes they'd made. "We found a truck amongst Arundel's cars. This is its hand brake lever and gear box. The spring-loaded clasp on the top is a clutch which lets you move it forwards and backwards to change gear. We attached the shaft through the third-forward gear in the box. I'm guessing it'll turn the prop at the right speed—it seemed all right when we took her out on the straits. The reverse gear is engaged when you move the lever ahead; you need to pull in the clutch to take it out of gear and release it when you've moved it." He did it twice to demonstrate, then continued. "The throttle's been led up from the engine room so you can control your speed from the helm position. To start it, you still have to go down to the engine compartment."

They went back up to the combined galley and saloon and Logan opened the small hatch that led to the hold. "We've put some temporary decking in that'll let you put the load closer to the hatch. It's clamped in, so it'll come out easily when you want to carry a larger load, but it means you won't have to stretch so far to move sacks to the deck." They pulled their heads back into the saloon where the engineer pointed to a new addition. "And we've installed a radio. There's both a transmitter and a receiver, but beyond connecting it to the boat's electrics and testing it, I don't have any idea who operates it and when."

"We'll keep a listening watch only until someone says we do it another way," said McPherson. "I'd like to take her out and try out the new stuff. Will you come with us?"

They cast off and went slowly into the harbour. McPherson tested the gear box by running backwards and forwards, keeping close to the shore before handing over to Lindstrom. When they passed the harbour entrance, they went to full speed. After a couple of minutes, Lindstrom said, "She's wallowing." He waited for a moment. "She's pushing more water than she should. Either the revs are too high or the propeller's wrong. The hull is designed for ten knots maximum—if we try to push her any harder, she'll just bury her nose."

"She's doing that now," said McPherson. "Jeff?" he called.

Logan poked his head into the wheelhouse. "I heard all that. I'll talk to Tak. We can either use another gear—there's three in the box, change the propeller, or put a governor on the engine. I never had this problem before. Our patrol boats had hulls that were made to go fast. We put in more power and the hulls handled it and went faster."

"I'm not too keen on using the engine at less than full power," said McPherson. "It's sometimes the only margin of safety we have, and we need the boat to act normally."

"The *Lady*'s an old boat; she'll do better by not being shaken apart," added Lindstrom. "I'll try her at three-quarter speed."

"Take her back to the yard," said McPherson.

"What now?" asked Lindstrom when they were tied to the float.

"I'll start today," said Logan. "If I have to change the prop, getting her ready will depend on when I can find a new one, but this is a holiday weekend so I'm unlikely to find anything before Tuesday. Even if I do, my wife'll kill me if I work through Thanksgiving. I'm off for the next two days."

McPherson drove Lindstrom home and went back to the hotel, at loose ends for two days. The thought of the Thanksgiving holiday hadn't occurred to him. It had never been a part of his early life—his mother only recognized events celebrated in Scotland and even then, only occasionally. The one exception, of course, was Hogmanay at the outset of each year. Shipboard life made allowances for Christmas, provided it didn't interfere with the running of the ship. It was the same with the wartime navy. For all their grousing, he envied Logan and Lindstrom their family life. It would be nice to build new traditions, but not yet. If he'd thought of it sooner, he would have called on Emmaline at the library. He hadn't seen her for a few weeks, not wanting to scare her off with the gash on his head. Too late now.

Wednesday, October 22nd, 1919

They pulled out of Victoria Harbour just before noon and set a course for Anacortes, a little closer than some of their other destinations. "Nice change to have a short clean run," said Lindstrom, looking up from the chart.

McPherson took the dory in when they arrived. The beach was a gentle slope which meant they had to anchor almost two hundred yards from the tide line, but they were able to transfer all the sacks in just five trips. Lindstrom and McPherson alternated at the oars, and McPherson had the last trip. He met Olmstead when he unloaded.

"When's the new boat going to be finished?" asked Olmstead.

"Won't be ready for testing for another month at the earliest."

"I'm getting nervous about having to stay up this end of the Sound," said Olmstead. "There's too much that can go wrong on the drive into Seattle."

"With the *Lady Jane* back, we can extend our range a little. I don't mind overnighting after we've done the drop off, but the more time we spend at sea, the fewer trips we can make, and I was just thinking we were ready to move up to three trips a week if all goes according to schedule. The radio gives us a lot more flexibility if we have to make changes after we've left, and the new engine, with its reverse gear, will make her a lot easier to handle in a tight spot. We'll think about bringing the occasional third hand on the boat, but there's lots of enthusiasts to work through before we let someone new close to the details. After our problems on that first run, I'm cautious about who's talking to whom, and always on the lookout for boats that could be following us."

"Three trips a week is good—I'll let my men know." Olmstead handed over the wallet with the money and McPherson rowed back. He swung back aboard and Lindstrom helped slide the dory over the stern rail. They lashed it down over the cabin roof. "Any sign of anyone taking too much interest in us?" McPherson asked when they finished.

"Nothing that I saw, but the tide's running fast and these flats are shallower than I thought. We don't have a lot of room left underneath us."

"Start her up and head for home. I'll get the anchor and then check for any new neighbours."

Lindstrom went down to the engine room. They still had to do the cold start routine, but with the new gear box they could do it without the boat surging ahead. When he got back to the wheelhouse, he put her in gear and ran her forward to give McPherson enough slack to raise the anchor. They eased round to the west on a heading to clear Lummi Island before turning south into Bellingham Channel, and from there, down to Rosario Strait. McPherson picked up the night glasses and did three careful sweeps around them. "All clear." He rechecked the chart and estimated another eleven miles before they could turn and make for Victoria, which lay about the same distance due west. "Zero one forty-five hours," said McPherson, looking at his watch.

"I guess you mean quarter to two," replied Lindstrom.

"Looks like five hours to Lopez and about another seven to Victoria."

"Can we crank her up a bit? Another twelve hours at sea doesn't appeal."

"Prefer not to hit a log," said McPherson. "This hull's strong but not really built for it. Wait for seven o'clock and if it's still clear then, we can speed her up a bit. It's clear enough out there. I'll take the first watch and call you when we reach Lopez."

"I'll sure like it when we get the faster boat for every run, or even another hand to share the load."

"The fast boat will come soon enough, and an extra hand will go well for handling the cargo. Peter and I have been looking, but I haven't seen many we could trust to stand a lone watch while we're running."

"I agree on the problem of reliable help. I'll get the coffee going so you're not part of today's problem."

McPherson grinned as he took the Rosario Strait chart out from the rack under the table. He pulled out his cigarette case and fiddled with his lighter while he looked it over. He lit an unaccustomed cigarette, took out his notebook and rechecked their route against the tide tables, savouring the smoke while he reread the notes he had made against points along their course. They were heading into Bellingham Channel for a two-hour run to meet the Strait. Lindstrom pushed a steaming mug toward him.

"Why so far north?"

"I prefer not to go too close to Port Townsend on the American side. There's nothing to be gained from attracting the Coast Guard's attention."

Lindstrom nodded. "You ever do anything without that notebook?"

"Nope. It's where I keep track of all the minor details. It's more important now than it ever was on a larger ship because there we never sailed this close to rocks and weren't as likely to be bothered by eddies or tidal currents."

"You keep notes about each time you deliver liquor and about all the places you go to do it. Isn't that dangerous if someone else gets to see it?"

"I keep the book in this weighted cover when we're at sea so that if it looks like we're going to be captured, I can throw it overside."

"Isn't that a lot of information about your past that you might lose?"

"Better that than letting someone use the information to make our future uncomfortable. However, on the last trip I came to the same conclusion. This book has too much information in it, so I'll be taking a new one to sea every time now, and I'll make notes in a second copy when we get back. Then, if I have to throw it overboard, I only lose that day's notes."

"Never worried me much when I was fishing."

"You were in waters you knew, and I don't suppose you travelled much in the middle of the night." Lindstrom went back down to the saloon and climbed into the bunk.

McPherson took a tentative sip of the scalding hot coffee and adjusted their course further to the east side of the Channel. He did two more careful three-hundred-and-sixty degree sweeps with the night glasses before settling in behind the wheel. He kept his feet firmly planted about thirty inches apart and his left foot slightly in front of the other, bracing himself against the boat's movement in a light swell. The moon was at seven-eighths coverage and just starting to show over the hills to the east. A hint of fog came off the shore when, two hours later, they passed the south end of Cypress Island. He swung the helm south-west to clear Fidalgo Head and caught sight of a red flash slightly down the coast. He guessed it was a port-side running light of something, and he kept their heading clear of it. As they came closer, he made out three white lights running up the mast of a tug, the signal of a tow behind the boat. He throttled back to four knots, and he made out a log boom crossing in front of them; he swung further west to pass behind it.

"That would not have been good if we were moving faster," he said out loud to himself, and he picked up speed again to offset the tidal current that was pushing them closer to the shore.

A few minutes later he picked up the original course when the same current pushed the boom out of their way. His days on the bridge of larger ships had taught him how to stay awake in the tedium of the night watch. As a young seaman he had the officer of the watch standing behind him, checking his every move. Now he had to do both jobs. He ran his eyes from the compass in front of him, up to the waters ahead from starboard to port, the opposite to reading so as to slow his pace down. Periodically, he would look back at their moonlit wake and shift his feet to keep his blood circulation going. He marked various waypoints as they passed, using his notebook rather than defacing the chart.

They made the southern tip of Lopez Island at five-fifteen, and he left the wheel to wake Lindstrom. "Do you want to get yourself a coffee before you take over?"

Lindstrom grunted something unintelligible but was at McPherson's elbow with his coffee mug in hand fifteen minutes later.

"We're here," said McPherson, pointing to the chart. "Deception Pass is due east, so you can set a course west. Crank her up to whatever speed you want, don't hit anything, and call me when we make Victoria Harbour."

"Aye, aye, sir."

"Lay off!" said McPherson. He stumbled below and knew nothing more until Lindstrom woke him after they had berthed in Victoria.

"Why didn't you wake me earlier?"

"You're not the only guy who can drive a boat, but you are the one who deals with the big money. Get out and take the cash with you. I'm going home to bed." McPherson looked at his watch—it was a quarter past twelve.

"Not bad time," he said. They walked up through the yard and stopped at the gate. McPherson reached into the wallet, took out two hundred dollars and gave it to Lindstrom. He looked up and down the street while he shrugged himself back into his oilskin coat. "I doubt we'll find a taxi around here at this time of the day. We'll need to walk."

As they turned toward downtown, a car came up level with them and stopped. Peter Arundel called out, "Need a ride somewhere?"

"Ollie needs to go home, and I need to pick up my car at the warehouse, since you ask." John Romilly was in the front passenger seat, so McPherson and Lindstrom climbed into the back. Arundel drove through the industrial properties lining Store Street, turned onto Bay Street, and over the bridge.

"Go right here onto Skinner and then onto Tyee, Peter," said Lindstrom, "and I'm two houses down when you go over Regatta."

"The properties seem very narrow," said Romilly.

"They're called fisherman's lots," said

Lindstrom. "They can be anywhere from thirty to fifty feet wide to accommodate different types of boats on the waterfront but stretch back sometimes as much as three hundred feet to the road. I needed sixty feet on the waterfront for the packer, so I bought two lots. I built my house over the pair of them, so we have lots of room for the family."

They dropped him off in front of the house, and Arundel, with a clashing of gears and a roaring engine, managed to turn the car around. "I'm not sure how you run a business with people who all do it on the side," said Romilly.

"In the first place, it's a business that's just getting started," said Arundel. "No one has been doing it full time so far. In the second, it wasn't until Dugald joined us that we had anyone reliable to organize the operation. We've a long way to go yet as far as getting the right people involved, and the right kind of equipment as well."

"So, I'm supposed to tell the partners in London that everyone here is still stumbling around not knowing what to do?"

"I don't care what you tell people in London." Peter stopped the car on the road beside the warehouse.

"Thanks for sparing us the crashing gear sounds, here anyway," said McPherson as he stepped out.

"Where are you going now?" asked Arundel.

"Your father's office."

"Before you go," said Romilly, "how much did you collect last night?"

"Enough." McPherson looked at him coolly.

Romilly started to turn red. "That's no answer. I think you need to understand my place in this endeavour."

"You don't have one until Major Arundel tells me what it is," countered McPherson.

Romilly turned to Arundel. "This is most

unsatisfactory, Peter," he blustered. "I require our employees to follow my instructions."

"As Dugald says, take it up with the Major."

Over the next five weeks, the coast was fogbound for three and for the other two, it rained—hard. On the first night the fog came down, McPherson crouched over the chart looking at his watch and estimating their course, adjusting it for time, tide, ocean currents, and the *Lady Jane*'s uneven engine speed.

"I'm not sure what you're doing," observed Lindstrom.

"It's called dead reckoning navigation."

"I've done the same thing, but I look for seaweed and sniff the wind for a hint of scent from trees so I know where I am."

"I thought you said you stayed in port when things got difficult."

"Didn't mean that we couldn't get caught out there when the weather came down. Just had to remember that if I saw kelp, it usually meant rocks and if the tree smell was strong, I was closer to shore and should either anchor or poke around for a bit more."

McPherson grunted. "Keep your eyes open then. I'll rely on you to keep us off the rocks."

Despite the weather slowing them down, they were never late, nor missed a place where they had to deliver, but three times Olmstead's crew lost themselves on the landward side and once had a road accident on the way in. "I need competent help," Olmstead erupted on the telephone after the last event.

"You'll have to spend a bit of time training them," said McPherson unsympathetically.

Chapter 23

Victoria, Friday, November 28th, 1919

By the end of the last week in November, McPherson and Lindstrom were exhausted and the *Lady Jane* was complaining about the heavy use they'd put her to. They took the boat into the shipyard for Logan to look over, and after tying it up and talking to him, walked up the ramp to Store Street.

"I'll tell Arundel we're cutting back to twice a week and carry bigger loads," said McPherson. "I'll get him to increase your take for the extra workload—it won't make up all the difference in pay from three trips a week, but you probably knew we couldn't keep this pace up forever."

"*Ja*. This money has been a nice bonus, but I'm beat," said Lindstrom.

"The new boat's speed and bigger load will make things easier, but we're not there with it yet. When it is, if they want more stuff moved, we'll have to train up a new crew for this one." They left the wharf and walked over to Government Street, staying together in companionable silence until Lindstrom hopped onto the streetcar that would take him home.

McPherson waved and continued up Government Street to Arundel's office. Despite the lunch hour, Michael was in. McPherson handed over the wallet with Olmstead's payment in it.

"Ollie's had his two hundred out of this, and we

need to talk about the delivery schedule. I don't mind twenty-six-hour days, but I'd like to limit them to two a week. The radio communication is working well, but we may need to bring Miss Campbell along to develop more codes."

Michael spread the bills out on his desk and cast a practiced eye over them. "You haven't had to pay anything else out of this, have you?" he asked l.

"No, why?"

"I don't want you to take this the wrong way, but the payment is always short a significant amount."

"You've been paying me on time so I wouldn't be helping myself, and Ollie always gets his two hundred dollars and no more."

"I've been checking with some of the other people who have dealings with Olmstead and they report the same problems. We give him a very advantageous price because he can move a great deal of merchandise, but it doesn't help if we don't get paid," said Michael.

"How much are you short?"

Michael flipped through some papers on his desk. "Two thousand, three hundred and fifty dollars."

"Whew! How much are we supposed to pick up on each run? I've never counted it."

"Should be twelve thousand dollars. We talked to Olmstead and he refused to make up the missing funds. We talked to Miss Campbell and she hasn't been able to shed any light on the matter. Olmstead appears to have used his position on the police force to take a number of his competitors out of business. Our investors are naturally concerned, and at the moment, I have nothing to say that would reassure them."

McPherson looked out the window for a moment. "Does this conversation mean you want me to be more involved in the money side of things? Perhaps we should sit down and talk this issue through."

"By all means. Do you have some suggestions?"

"Certainly some experiences that might be adapted." McPherson paused again and sat down. "It's not uncommon in the shipping world for people to try things on." He grinned. "Even ship's captains can be convinced to take on an extra piece of cargo, like motor cars, without telling anybody, and then pocket the money from transporting it. Manifests can be altered to conceal some cargoes, and from what I saw as second officer, I can attest that crew members and dockers can steal goods in transit. The biggest problem is the shippers themselves, especially if they're large. They think you need them, so they sometimes pay very late, or even not at all. So, they take a few liberties. Olmstead is simply following a well-trodden path, except he seems to be making more money off it than most."

Michael frowned. "What did you do? If you let people take advantage of you, you're out of business."

"Several things, starting by asking for the account to be settled. If they don't, it often works to do something unexpected. Sometimes we'd unload something totally valueless, like worn out tarpaulins, and send that to them."

"How would you handle Olmstead?"

"Two thousand, three hundred and fifty dollars is too much to let go. I'd suggest we deliver some bottles filled with water. That'd be enough to get his attention. In the meantime, start looking for some alternative buyers. There seem to be some potential ones around. I don't think it's a good idea to stick with just the one buyer."

"He can bite back, and we still don't know who organized the ambush on you in September," Michael pointed out.

"His ability to bite back probably doesn't work too well outside Seattle, and the ambush might have been more his problem than ours. As to his ability to distribute lots of merchandise—it doesn't mean much if he doesn't pay for it," countered McPherson.

"I'm pleased to see you keep that part of the business in mind. The people who put up the money for us aren't greedy, but they like to see a return on their investment. Let's go at it slowly, then. We'll get Miss Campbell down there again to see if she can improve things. If nothing happens, we'll deliver a few bottles of water and see what happens. Peter can hunt around for someone to fill his shoes, or at least, broaden our market a bit."

"I'm assuming you're aware of Miss Campbell's relationship with Olmstead?"

"John told me."

"He was paying more attention than I thought."

"That's gratifying, I suppose." Michael waved his hand over the banknotes on the desk in front of him. "Help me count, please," he said.

It took them the best part of an hour to plod through the pile of crumpled paper. "Some of these have had a hard life," said McPherson, separating a clump of bills. "There's every kind of note you can think of in here. I hope they're all real."

"I suppose you didn't have a lot to do with managing the money on board ship."

"No, that was the job of the purser."

"Well, it's something we have to think about now, especially as Olmstead's proved he's less than reliable when it comes to paying bills. Half of these bills have been issued by individual banks, and the rest by the national government. The Americans hate their own banks, so they end up using anything the other party will accept." They continued counting for a few minutes.

"While you're thinking of what you want to do with Olmstead—and with him not paying up—this seems a good time to cut the number of deliveries."

"I thought you sailors worked a routine that lets you sleep and work in quick succession."

McPherson shifted in his chair and stretched his

legs, still aching from the long night behind the wheel. "Just because we can do it, doesn't mean we should. On the present schedule, we're becoming too predictable, and also too tired. With someone possibly waiting for us again, it's not good if they have a regular time to find us, and a tired sailor is an unsafe sailor. That's a dangerous combination, especially taking into account the *Lady Jane's* relatively low speed. Besides, I think we can fit up to a hundred and fifty cases on the *Lady Jane*—if we do two runs with that instead of three runs with a hundred, it will be more cost-efficient all around. Only thing is, Ollie will need a bit more money, since he gets paid per trip but he'll be doing more work."

"How do you want to organize things, then?" asked Michael.

"We'll take the next four days off. I'll have a word with Miss Campbell and see if she'll run down to Seattle and come back before the next delivery. We could leave her down there, but we'll need someone else to run the radio here. Perhaps some of the discreet young women in your circle here might be useful. Millie Anstruthers comes to mind. I don't think Miss Campbell will be in too much danger when Olmstead discovers what we've done, but she can claim to have known nothing about it. "

"I'll warn her first and give her the option of turning the arrangement down, but if she worked for Sir James, she's used to lying for her country."

McPherson got up. "We can keep the same set of arrangements with Olmstead about the drop off point, and Ollie and I will plan another twenty-four-run. When the new boat comes on stream, I'd like to switch the *Lady Jane* to a supply role and feed other delivery boats. Other people can pay to build and run them; it spreads the risk about and the more we restrict our role, the less exposed your investors are."

He walked toward the door, then turned back. "Speaking of investors, what are your plans for young

Romilly? I haven't seen him for a while, doing so many trips, but he's obviously still involved. He's no great boat handler so he won't be any help there, and he manages to annoy just about everyone he meets."

"You, too?"

"I have the easiest part. I don't have to let him on a boat."

"There are some business complications about having him here and I can't move him along at the moment. I'll keep him out of the way."

"Thank you for that—I think if he has a surprise waiting for us, it will be a nasty one.

Saturday, November 29th, 1919

McPherson left his car at the bottom and climbed up Gonzales Hill in the middle of the morning. He knocked on the door of their new radio station in a house the Arundels had bought for the purpose. Elise opened it and grinned at him.

"This is a pleasant surprise, Commander."

"I'm trying to get used to being Mr. McPherson, but it's not coming easily," he replied, "so, thank you for the recognition, Miss Campbell."

She took him upstairs where the radio had been set up in one of the bedrooms. "Nicely done," he said. "How are we doing for codes and broadcast times?"

"Roy has a man on his end who handles the set, and we do a regular check in at five each evening."

"Why five?" he asked.

"There's a lot of commercial traffic on frequencies all around us at that time. I like to use word codes where possible. It makes the messages easier to handle for someone who's not used to them. Major Arundel telephones the information about the delivery and Roy's man sends back the location. If there's nothing to talk about on the day, I just put in a code word to that effect and the man knows that we're just sending dummy messages. It's not a perfect system, but it'll hold us for the time being. I'm going down to Seattle in a few days to put a better system together and train Roy's men in it."

"I was never close to the signals side during the war. Did you do it this way then?"

"Yes. Sir James always thought that it was more suspicious if you didn't transmit regularly."

"We'll be changing our schedule and probably the amount and composition of the loads. Can you adjust the codes to handle that?"

"Yes."

"We'll probably need you to get someone to help you with the radio, particularly if you're going down to Seattle. Do you have any thoughts?"

"I've been thinking about that. I'd like to have someone who understands the need for secrecy and won't gossip."

"Someone from the Arundel circles would be a good start. There's lots of naval people around and some of the wives and daughters might be suitable. I was thinking about Captain Anstruthers' daughter, Millie." He paused. "While on the subject of naval children, what do you know of John Romilly? As you have seen, he seems to be more trouble than he's worth."

She looked back at him levelly. "I know little of the Admiral's family circumstances, but I believe his son went to Oxford before he entered the navy during the war. His decision to go to university rather than follow a naval career was a severe disappointment to the family. It may well be that he was sent here to keep him out of London for a while."

"Interesting. We also we have another problem we'd like you to help solve."

She raised her eyebrows in a question. "Oh?"

"Olmstead has been paying short on each delivery and he now owes too much money for us to ignore."

"Oh!" The intonation went downwards.

"The Arundels tell me they've talked to him and he hasn't made up the difference yet."

"Why tell me?" she asked defensively.

"You'll be going down there in a few days, won't you?"

"I'd want to stick to the signals side of the operation."

"You seem to get on quite well with Roy."

"I'm not sure that would extend to the business side of things."

"You know who's involved with this operation, and Olmstead should be told what they might think if they end up in business with people they can't rely on. We're going to do something that gets Olmstead's attention. All you would have to do is ask if he's done something to cause it. So far, they're happy with the deliveries we've made, but that only works if he pays for it."

Elise nodded. "I'll tell him, but there's no guarantee he'll do what you want. There are other people he can do business with."

"There's no one who can give him the volume and the decent brands we can, and anyone else wanting to sell to him might have difficulties with us. Olmstead has things his own way in Seattle because of the police, but I don't think that'll work the same way outside the city."

He left her standing at the front door watching him as he walked down the hill. "I hope I got that point across," he said under his breath. He looked back up at her and waved; when she went back inside, he turned and walked the short distance to Emmaline's house.

Monday, December 1st, 1919

Two days later, McPherson picked up Lindstrom in the morning. "We're going to need a telephone installed in your house if you want me to not bang on the door and wake everyone."

"Telephone bells do that, too," Lindstrom replied.

"Something in that, I suppose. I told Michael we're on a different schedule, and about the change to your pay to accommodate the larger load."

"Any argument?"

"No."

They drove down to the boat yard and found that Logan had built a crank arrangement he planned to mount onto the side of the engine cover. It was to be attached to a lever in the wheelhouse and would let them do a warm start from the helm. He had installed a flywheel that disengaged when the engine started.

"Interesting," said McPherson. "How long have you been playing with that?"

Logan picked up a piece of metal strapping and measured it against the lever. "I'll use this as a bracket to hold it against the bulkhead," he said, almost to himself. "About a week," he went on. "I thought of you fellows having to start the boat in the middle of the night with a bunch of other things to do at the same time."

"We'll be running on Wednesday night. Will she be ready then?" asked McPherson.

"We'll test her tomorrow to make sure she is."

Lindstrom and McPherson walked back up to the street. "What are you going to do with two more days off?" asked McPherson.

"I'm going to keep quiet about it, otherwise my wife will have a few ideas," said Lindstrom.

He drove Lindstrom home, then he went home and looked through his notebooks for any more information which might be useful in the coming weeks. The new boat would need different ways of handling loads, and he spent time thinking about that.

The other job was to have the warehouse crew make up the dummy load for Olmstead. He thought about it for a while and phoned Michael.

"We need some empty bottles, and the only places where I can think we can get them are the clubs and hotels in Victoria."

"That should keep Peter busy for a day or so," said Michael.

Chapter 24

Wednesday, December 17th, 1919

At dawn on Wednesday, McPherson and Lindstrom cast off the *Lady Jane's* lines and ran her over to the Arundels' inconspicuous warehouse at the head of West Bay. McPherson had already packed the load in straw-padded sacks filled with six bottles each.

"We've been having some difficulty in getting Olmstead to pay us," said McPherson. "We've put bottles with water in them amongst the others." He picked one up from a pile on the side and handed it to Ollie, along with a regular bag, to weigh against each other. "No difference in the weight, as you can see," he said, "but I didn't want to go without telling you beforehand."

"Cagey!" said Lindstrom. "Load them first so they'll be the last out of the hold. We need to be clear of the beach before there's any chance of someone finding this out."

"Finding what out?" The voice came from the warehouse door, and John Romilly walked out.

"Nothing to do with you," said McPherson.

"I believe you'll find everything in this operation has to do with me. I insist you tell me what's going on." Romilly moved closer to inspect the bags they'd put to the side.

"Leave those alone!" barked McPherson. "If you have a problem with anything we're doing, talk to the

Major." He leaned toward the younger man.

"The London office will hear about this," Romilly said, but he backed away.

"That's fine. Meanwhile, unless you're going to help load these sacks onto the boat, go back to your office and stay out of my way." Romilly sniffed but left quietly. The warehouse crew loaded them in half an hour, and after a last check of the charts they pulled away from the wharf. They fueled up at the float moored by the Point Ellis shipyard and were clear of the outer harbour by ten o'clock.

There was a slight swell at the entrance to the Straits. Their delivery was to the north end of Whidbey Island, so they stayed in Canadian waters over the top end of Puget Sound to avoid the likely patrol route of the Coast Guard. McPherson had the first watch as they headed northeast, eventually sighting Sidney Island off their port bow. He did regular sweeps with the binoculars, ahead and behind.

At the end of one, he thought he caught a glimpse of the *Arcata* over by Port Townsend, but the increasing swell and intermittent mist gave him no chance to confirm it. At dusk, the winds picked up. They turned into Spieden Channel and Lindstrom came up to take the helm. He sniffed the air and looked around.

"It'll be better to take waters where we can get a bit of shelter when we need it. There's probably a south-easter brewing up."

"That weather used to cause us to look for more sea room. You happy about staying this close to the shore?" asked McPherson.

"Done it often enough before, but not in these waters." Lindstrom reached for the chart, spread it out, and pulled the light down a little. "I'll stick to San Juan Channel down to Friday Harbour. After that, and all being well, we can go north-east up Upright Channel. If the wind gets up, it may funnel up the channel and we may have a time of it, but it shouldn't be anything we can't handle."

"I'm glad you're confident; I'll trust you. Leave the running lights on—there's no need to break laws we don't have to, and we don't want to run into anyone coming the other way. I saw what looked like the *Arcata* over by Port Townsend, so there's no Coast Guard around here."

McPherson went down to the galley and turned into the bunk. Despite the boat pitching and rolling and the need to wedge himself into the bunk, he slept. He only woke up two hours later because the boat's motion changed. He went up to the wheelhouse and found that Lindstrom had throttled the engine back to give bare steerage way.

"What's up? Why so calm?"

"I pulled into Odlin Bight; it's fairly sheltered here. If you take the helm, I'll put some grub together. It's better to set it up now before we head out round the point into the channel between Lopez and Blakely Islands where it might get brisk again."

He went below and McPherson eased the boat up the channel until he felt it start to lurch as the wind came over the island. He turned back into sheltered waters. Lindstrom came up with a steaming mug of coffee laced with sweetened condensed milk. "Ever use this?" he asked.

"Ships live on it," said McPherson.

Lindstrom came back from the galley a few minutes later with two corned beef sandwiches with blocks of cheese on a plate beside them. While they ate, McPherson held the boat on an easy circular course. When Lindstrom finished, he took his plate and mug back to the galley. "Time check?" he called when he reappeared.

"Twenty-one, twenty."

"I'll guess that's twenty past nine; I'm still not that deep into navy talk."

"Keep trying." McPherson swung the wheel to take them out of the Bight. "Put your head down. It'll probably only take us an hour and a half to get to the other side of Thatcher Pass." He pointed to a place on the chart between Blakely and Decatur Islands where the channel intersected with the Rosario Strait.

Lindstrom looked at the place McPherson was pointing to. "That's where the wind will really thump us if it's still blowing at this rate." He looked down at the chart again. "I've not been here, as I said, but did you big-boat fellows ever worry about tidal rips? That's where the tide is running on the opposite direction to the wind."

"We call them tidal rips, too; they can be pretty bad if you're too close to shore or a mid-channel rock, but mostly we could power away from them. Why?"

"Thatcher Pass is a place I'd worry about one, especially in this wind."

"Get some rest then. We'll worry about it when we get there."

McPherson headed the boat out into mid-channel and they took the wind first on the starboard bow. He took as much sea room as the channel gave him until he had a feeling for the wave pattern, then he swung the bow into the oncoming wind. The channel leading to Thatcher Pass ran south, south-east by south, or one hundred forty degrees. He did not have a good fix on his position and no lights were visible through the driving spray. He checked the chart again and eased the helm over closer to the Blakely Island side to avoid Frost Island, which lay about two- thirds of the way down.

The wheelhouse windows were misted over so he switched off the light on the chart table to cut down on the reflection. He met each wave as best he could, trying to take each successive one on the port bow so he could roll over them without having the propeller clear the water and start to race. He opened the side windows, latched them back and looked out each in succession for the loom of the land on either side. His seat was firmly anchored to the deck, but still creaked ominously as his weight was thrown against its arms on each roll.

After an hour, land appeared on the starboard side and he adjusted the course slightly to stay well clear of it. He hoped it was Frost Island, and for a moment thought about whether it would have been more sensible to have kept Lindstrom up as a lookout. The idea passed as rapidly as it had arrived—the next nine hours needed for the delivery and return trip would keep them both occupied. He saw a flash off the port bow and needed to check the chart to confirm the source. That meant getting down from his chair, looping two rope rings over spokes on the wheel to hold it firm on their course, and turning on the light over the chart which was now wet from the spray coming in the open window. He confirmed they were coming up to the south end of Blakely Island and the entrance to Thatcher Pass. He held the course until the light was directly abeam and then slowly turned into the pass, gradually changing their heading through south-east to due east. As he came up to the north end of Decatur Island, the wind eased, and their motion settled to a gentle roll.

The change brought Lindstrom up from his bunk. He walked around the wheelhouse and closed the windows. "You've had a good time," he said, mopping the loose water off the chart.

"For a moment I thought it might take two of us, but I managed."

"Welcome to small boats. Sometimes the fellows who aren't careful don't manage." Lindstrom picked up the tide tables for the sound and looked at his watch.

"Any suggestions for the next bit?" McPherson asked.

"Let's poke our nose out into the Straits. These winds will funnel up them and the tide's ebbing, so there could be a strong current running. It's the sort of place where gusts can run to seventy knots or more—if it's that bad we're staying inside. Let me take the helm—it's going to be tight."

McPherson looked at the chart, still readable after its soaking, and confirmed the heading they needed. "Hold her on one hundred twenty degrees. I reckon the wind will keep pushing us to the north and we should pick up the light at Ship Harbour. If we get the one from Fidalgo Head first, we're too far south."

Lindstrom gripped the wheel and aimed their bow into the waves. The boat lurched against the tide rip and the wind took them on the beam. "I hope you're right. This weather is when I usually run for cover."

"I don't blame you. We had more engine power to get through it and some captains still ended up on the rocks. We'll take cover if it gets really bad."

It took another hour for them to sight the light at the entrance to Ship Harbour, where Anacortes skirted the bay. The wind eased as they rounded the point and the water calmed. McPherson went out the wheelhouse door and stood by the searchlight. "Chart says there should be some pilings here from something that was built over the water, so keep running very slowly. I'll look out for a signal." He braced himself against the back of the door and flashed the three long dashes the shore party would be expecting. After fifteen minutes, flashing at regular intervals, he received an answer. He banged on the wheelhouse roof to tell Lindstrom to stop engines before going forward to let the anchor go. He reached into the wheelhouse and Lindstrom passed him the night glasses.

"I hope we've figured the distance right. I don't want us to ground," said Lindstrom.

The boat swung on the anchor as the still-ebbing tide took hold. McPherson went aft and threw off the lashings from the dory. Lindstrom came back to help put it over the side. The hatch covers came off quickly and McPherson went down to the hold and started passing sacks up to the deck. They set a spring-mooring on the dory to keep it firm against the boat and then cinched down three bumpers to stop the two hulls from grinding together. He saw Lindstrom, despite years spent on boats, struggling to find his balance on the heaving dory. Whichever way he tried to work it, he could not steady himself while reaching up to the sacks piled on the *Lady Jane*.

"You have to come up and pass them down," he called out to McPherson, who raised his hand in acknowledgment. He put a few more sacks up to the deck and followed them up himself. He knelt and held on to the hatch coaming with one hand and used the other to pass down sacks. The dory's flat bottom gave them enough room to pile forty sacks and leave enough for Lindstrom to row.

McPherson cast off the lines and pushed the dory away from the side. Lindstrom put the oars in the water and was immediately lost to sight. McPherson watched him go, then jumped back into the hold.

Fifteen minutes later, the dory bumped against the side and Lindstrom threw the bow mooring line to him. He jumped out of the hold and wrapped it round the stern cleat. He had to scramble round the load piled on the deck to take the stern line forward and secure it there. He crawled back and started passing down the next load. He was able to talk without shouting over the wind. "I guess everyone was there—four of them."

"Olmstead?"

"Didn't see him." It took ten minutes to load the boat each time and another four trips to the beach.

McPherson took the last load in and collected

the leather pouch with the money from a man on the shore whose name neither he nor Lindstrom knew. The tide was turning when he got back, and the boat was starting to come broadside to the beach. He turned the dory to bring it alongside when the boat rolled and almost capsized him. He escaped by pushing one oar off the side and pulled toward the stern.

"Ollie, catch!" he shouted, and threw the painter over the stern rail. The dory lurched backwards and the line came loose. McPherson dived toward the bow to retrieve it and lost an oar over the side. He got his hand onto the painter but kept making more sternway. The *Lady Jane* was still held by her anchor and Lindstrom had no way of helping quickly. Fortunately, there was a dim light showing from the wheelhouse so McPherson at least had a point of reference. He used the remaining oar as a paddle and dipped it quickly from one side to the other. There was enough light to see the loom of the boat and he managed to get the dory close enough to throw the line again. This time Lindstrom caught it, reeled him in, and wrapped the line around a stern cleat. McPherson was relieved to feel the engine already throbbing through the deck. "Get her underway. I'll get the anchor," he said.

When he got back to the wheelhouse, Lindstrom was doing a wide turn out into Guemes Channel and setting a course west into Rosario Strait.

"This is my first time on a small boat in nasty weather. For a moment I thought we might not make it," said McPherson.

"That was nothing really unusual. Were you scared?"

"Yes."

"Good! Nothing more dangerous than a brave guy on a fishing boat."

They came out past the headland guarding Ship Harbour. "Water's pretty calm now. What route'll we take home?" asked Lindstrom.

"This wind should die down as fast as it came up. I think we should head out into Juan de Fuca. It's an easier route and without the wind we're not going to be knocked about." McPherson looked at his watch. "Zero five hundred," he called out. "First light on the water in about an hour. It means we'll be sailing in plain sight and it'll take us just over two and a half hours to get into Canadian waters. The Coast Guard's likely to be awake so we might be intercepted."

"We're not carrying anything we shouldn't." Lindstrom waved his arms around the wheelhouse.

"What about the money?"

"Lots of reasons we could have for it."

"Canadian boat, American money?' said McPherson. "Probably better if we hid it. That way we don't have to have any discussion at all."

"They can search us."

"Probably a good idea to leave something they can find."

"Such as?"

McPherson thought for a moment. "They're always hot on having the right papers on board and their rules call for running lights. I'll loosen the bulb on the starboard running light. They can find it easily and probably won't bother us too much more. We've got their Marine Rules hanging over the chart table, our Canadian registry is in the slot behind it and all the other running lights are working."

"What's our excuse for being out?"

"We're looking to buy some ice chests and the weather came up, so we laid up in..." McPherson looked at the chart, "...Whatmough Bay, until it passed."

"Where were we going for the ice chests?"

"Nowhere in particular, we're just getting

reorganized after the war and need to get our kit together. That's as good an excuse as any for not having this thing smell like fish. They can see it's just been refitted. Where can you hide the money? We can keep some available but not nine thousand."

Lindstrom reached over to the chart table, opened the top drawer, reached underneath the counter and felt around. There was a click and a wooden board fell down with its edge resting on his wrists. He pulled his hands back and the board fell the rest of the way to the stack of charts resting in the drawer. McPherson handed him the wallet and he slid it over the board and clicked it back into place. "I was a fish packer, had money all over the place in the boat and my sawn-off shotgun clipped to the panel beside the wheel."

"We haven't had it out since that boat tried to jump us. Check it now?" said McPherson.

Lindstrom pushed the wooden panel between the wheel and the bulkhead; it swung outward pivoting on a vertical rod. The shotgun appeared, clipped to the face.

"Looks like you keep it oiled. It's part of your regular operations. What are you going to say if they ask you about it? Presumably the shells are changed occasionally."

"After every trip."

"Let's keep it that way—and hidden as well. Now let's find the short way home." Lindstrom closed the gun slot and turned back to the wheel.

They came out of the Strait by the south end of Lopez Island at six o'clock and turned west on a course that would give them Victoria Harbour in two-and-a-half hours. Half an hour into it, with the south end of San Juan Island on their starboard bow, McPherson spotted the white hull of the *Arcata* steaming purposefully to intersect them.

"Here they come," he called. Fifteen minutes later a signal light blinked out from its bridge. "Heave to for inspection," he read. "We might just as well admit to being able to read Morse Code; save him the bother of shooting at us." He flashed an acknowledgment slowly. "Don't want to seem too competent."

They watched a boat swing down from the cutter's side and start to row purposefully toward them.

"Four oarsmen and a cox'n," said McPherson.

They watched the boat move steadily toward them. When it came within hailing distance, the coxswain lifted a megaphone to his mouth. "*Lady Jane*, we're coming aboard."

McPherson waved them over. The bow oarsman threw the painter over and McPherson cleated it in. The coxswain threw over the stern line as the boat's crew brought it expertly alongside and then swung himself on board.

"Where've you been and where're you going?"

"Around the San Juans looking for gear, and now we're heading home to Victoria." McPherson leaned easily against the wheelhouse door.

The coxswain pushed past him and headed into the wheelhouse. "What gear?"

"Ice chests and anything else we like the price of."

"Where are they?"

"Didn't like the prices; you people are as short of stuff as we are."

"Open the hatch." Lindstrom came aft and helped McPherson launch the dory to get at the hatch cover. They folded it forward and the coastguardsman looked down into the hold. "Doesn't smell like fish. Why is that decking so close to the cover?"

"It was there when we bought the boat. We left it in. Might be handy if we pack prawns or crab."

"Looks like there's bits of straw around."

"Boat just came out of the yard; stored the cover in a barn. Probably picked it up there." The man looked back at them suspiciously. "Let's check your paperwork."

They went back to the wheelhouse where the guardsman riffled through the Maritime Regulations and checked the boat's registration documents. "You Canadians sure are law abiding; if this was an American boat, all these papers would be missing." He looked at the registration papers. "How come it says 'Consolidated Fishing' here?"

"They lent us the money to buy the boat; registration's in their name until we pay them off."

"When will that be?"

"Depends on what happens next year; could be then, maybe the year after," said Lindstrom.

"Switch on the running lights." Lindstrom leaned over the wheel and pushed the toggle switch forward. The guardsman went forward and peered at the bow light, came back, circled the wheelhouse and went back to look at the stern. "Everything's good except the starboard one."

"Was okay last night," said Lindstrom frowning. He reached into a drawer, took out a spare bulb and went out to change it.

"Where's your gun?" the coxswain asked. McPherson pushed the panel by the wheel and swung it out.

"Why do you need that if you're not carrying money?"

"We're a packer, we're always supposed to have money aboard. The men you have around here don't know we're running empty and they do have guns. It's better to be safe until you get them under control."

"Not my job," said the government man. "It's okay, you can go now."

He went back to his boat and McPherson uncleated his lines. They both nodded to one another as the boats diverged in the gentle morning swell.

"Don't think he believed a word we said," he

told Lindstrom when he went back into the wheelhouse.

"Nothing he could prove, anyway. Nice catch with the story about the hatch cover and the barn."

"Seemed the right thing to say."

Lindstrom grinned. "You've done well for someone who just strolls around on a ship's bridge."

"Never heard it called doing that before."

"Keep doing it that way and we'll survive."

"Only as long as you keep rolling us over the right wave."

Chapter 25

Thursday, December 18th, 1919

They pulled into Victoria at half past seven. McPherson got off in the Inner Harbour from where he could walk up to the Arundel office. "The boat doesn't need any attention," he said to Lindstrom. "Why don't you dock her at your place? I'll see you at Tak's tomorrow at eight."

"What about changing her name and appearance? The coastguard got a really good look at her."

McPherson stopped and thought for a moment. "I don't think we need to do it right now. There's nothing special that would make her stand out at long range, and if we do get stopped again, they'll be more suspicious if they see us on a boat with a changed appearance. We can give it some more thought if we change the crew."

He waved as Lindstrom reversed the *Lady Jane* and turned her toward the Gorge. He walked up Government Street, very hungry and extremely tired. He stumbled a little as he crossed a curb.

"Careful!" said a voice behind him. He looked round and saw Michael Arundel.

"I'll be in to see you after I've had something to eat."

"I'll join you. Murray's is over here and open."

They walked in and settled into a corner table at

the back. McPherson handed the wallet over. "Less the usual two hundred to Ollie. I didn't get the name of Olmstead's man on the beach so I've no idea whether he helped himself to the missing money. I hear Roy doesn't treat those who cross him too well, but when he complains about the short load, we could always ask whether his own people are dipping into the money."

Michael took a quick look in the wallet before pocketing it. "I'll count it later. In the meantime, Elise will go down to Seattle on the morning boat. Peter'll have to go later to talk to other buyers, including White."

"I'm not sure White is the man Peter should be talking to."

"Why not?"

"I take it Peter hasn't told you the story about his last trip down and why I won't let him on the boat."

Michael frowned, "No. What happened?"

"Peter's got too friendly with White's daughter. The first time we were down there, I broke up a fight with one of White's men over her. When Peter showed up last month, he and the daughter disappeared together and the fuss started all over again. I gave him a ticking off for it."

"I wish he wouldn't do this sort of thing. He's a married man, after all."

"Really? Who's his wife?"

"Her name is Tatania. She's a Russian he met in the war."

It was McPherson's turn to frown, but he had a moment to think as their waitress took their order. When she left, he said, "I know of her. He brought her back on board our ship in the Baltic. His boat was badly shot up and his first officer was dead. The skipper hustled the pair of them out of sight and kept them there until we made London. They left the ship there and I was immediately posted out to the Middle East. I didn't see Peter again until I got back here. I asked

Peter what happened to her and he said he'd never seen her after we landed them. What's the need for secrecy, and where is she now?"

"We don't know. There were some complications and she had to leave Europe by another route. She may have come out through Shanghai."

"Scarcely a direct route."

"A lot of refugees from the revolution went that way."

"I hope she makes it."

"So does Peter. Where are you going now?"

"To sleep right now. Tomorrow at eight o'clock, Ollie and I are meeting Jeff at Takahashi's to give the new boat a run."

"Assuming it works well, when can we start using it?"

"The likelihood that it won't have some problems is nil. The earliest I would expect to have it is a week from now—and probably not then."

The waitress brought their food and Michael took a bite before asking, "Who's coming with you for the trial run?"

"Just those two. Why?"

"I'd like Peter there, if you don't mind."

McPherson paused before answering. "Nobody's daughter's going to be there, so he could make himself useful. We are going to need more crewmen fairly soon. Ollie and I still need to slow down the pace. In a few months, the more boats running around Puget Sound, the more stretched the Coast Guard will be."

The next morning, McPherson left his car at the hotel and walked through a light drizzle to the shipyard. Arundel was parking his car beside the walkway. "Not a lot you can muck up if you stay on this side of the border," said McPherson.

"No," said Arundel.

"Remember that if your father, against the advice I already gave him, sends you down."

Lindstrom joined them and they walked down the boardwalk beside the slipway together. The boat, with the tarpaulin off, sat waiting for them with Logan and both Takahashis standing beside it. The new boat had a cramped cockpit; it would feel all the more so if they were all to board for the trials.

"Quite a crowd," said Logan. "Someone's going to have to ride in the back."

"Ollie and I will be in the cockpit with you," said McPherson. "Everyone else in the hold—the cockpit's too snug. Is there enough room back there to stop you all bouncing over the stern?"

"Probably," replied Arundel, folding back the cover.

McPherson looked at Hiro and asked, "What would be the proper way to launch this boat?"

"We make a special axe for each boat and use it to cut the rope holding it to the shore.
We give you the axe so you carry it in the boat for good luck." He reached over the foredeck in front of the windshield and picked up a canvas-wrapped bundle. He unwrapped it, revealing a one-piece, unfinished-metal axe with a shining edge annealed to the blade. McPherson felt it and a small line of blood appeared on his thumb.

"Whew! Didn't expect that," he said and handed it to Logan. "You do the honours." Logan moved to the bow. The rope was tied to a ring attached to the boat's stem and stretched taut from where it was wrapped round a bollard set into the concrete base of the dock. He made one economical preliminary chopping motion.

"Wait a moment," said Lindstrom, "she can't be launched without a name." Everyone nodded agreement, but they hadn't discussed it properly so no name had been chosen. Finally, Lindstrom said, "I had a thought." He paused, holding out a grubby piece of paper. "When the Coast Guard pulled us over it would have been useful if we had carried a name that was hard to remember and hard to copy down. It's a small advantage, but if we go by someone quickly and they can't get our name, it's hard for them to pass it on. The Salish people around here have a language that uses a lot of hard sounds and gaps. I wrote this down as something we might use." He passed the paper around.

"R-i-t'w-a-x-l," Arundel spelled out. "How do you pronounce it?"

"You don't," replied Lindstrom.

"Anyone have a better idea?" asked McPherson. No one did. "Do you have a piece of chalk?" he asked Hiro. Hiro nodded to Aki who ran up into the office and came back with one. McPherson laboriously wrote out the name on the bow and then called out to Logan, "Let her go!" To Arundel and Lindstrom, he said, "Grab a stern and bow line and walk her down the slipway."

Logan chopped the retaining rope and the boat moved down the ways on its carriage. "She's a little heavy at the bow, but she'll be okay when she's loaded and also when she's at speed," said Hiro.

"Everyone on board," called McPherson, and there was a rush as men dived in. Hiro stayed on the float to throw off the lines. "Crank the diesel." Logan, with Lindstrom watching, lit the punks and hammered them into the cylinders. Lindstrom swung the flywheel and the diesel started with a puff of smoke from its exhaust pipe which led out on the port side at deck level. "I'd be happier if we could lead it out further aft and I wouldn't object if we took it out of the side of the boat," said McPherson.

"I thought that might be the case." said Logan. "This set-up is temporary, anyway. Wherever it comes out it has to be below deck-level, otherwise the pipe gets damaged."

"I have the conn," said McPherson. "Everyone holding on to something solid!" Everyone nodded. "Let go for'ard!" He set the throttle to one quarter ahead and pushed the control lever forward as Hiro threw the bow line inboard. The propeller started to turn slowly; he put the helm over and the boat strained against the stern line. "Let go aft." Hiro threw that line inboard and followed it himself.

"No sense annoying the harbour master by going out too fast." He moved the throttle ahead to half speed and guessed at their pace through the water. "Five knots, six maybe. Wake's a bit heavy." He turned to Hiro.

"All your hull's in the water. Be different when she's at speed."

He gave a couple of twitches at the wheel. "Nice and responsive; two rudders are good at this speed."

They came out from under the Johnson Street Bridge and had to slow a little to pull in behind a fishing boat on the same course. McPherson marked the time and estimated speed in his notebook.

"Does everything go in that book?" asked Aki.

"Most things."

"Why?"

"When something happens, I know what we were doing up to that point. It does away with a lot of unnecessary guesswork."

The fishing boat held them up for a few minutes before they reached the harbour opening so they had to swing either side of their course to avoid overtaking him. "Probably doesn't make much difference, but the less attention we draw, the better," said McPherson.

They used the time to check every control in the cockpit and McPherson, leaning against the back wall, marked each one in his notebook. "Start the Liberties when we get on the other side of Trial Island. We'll run them full out for ten minutes, then test the throttles at each speed setting, run some tight turns in both directions, and last of all, try running one in reverse and the other forward and see how well we do a fast turn. Keep the diesel turning over and its propeller disengaged once the mains have caught."

Logan took station at the engine controls when they came round the island. "Course is due east," called McPherson. "Peter, keep a look out forward; at the speed we'll be going, anything on a converging course isn't going to be out of our way by the time we get there."

"Can't see over Ollie's head," Peter called back.

"We need seats in the helm and engine control positions," said McPherson, making another note.

"Padded and with seat belts, the way this thing gets chucked about in anything more than mill-pond conditions," said Logan. "We can use the ones they put in aeroplanes to stop the pilot from falling out during a roll."

"Everyone ready?" asked McPherson, looking round. Everyone nodded. Aki wedged himself into one of the front corners of the hold; his father looked unconcerned. "Go!"

Logan pushed the throttle on the diesel to 'Full,' waited for the engine to respond, and turned on the ignition switches of both Liberties. He set their throttles to 'Full' and pulled back the lever connecting the diesel's gear box to the ratchets on the flywheels installed on the engines' crank shafts. The port engine started with a roar, the starboard one stayed quiet. Logan cut the running one and tried again. The result was the same. "I'll need to get in and have a look."

Lindstrom put the diesel into gear and throttled it back to maintain steerage way in the gentle swell. Logan took a toolbox down from the ledge in the diesel compartment and opened the hatch that gave him access to the engine from the side. There was only enough room for Logan to stretch out on the cockpit deck, so McPherson moved into the hold. "Could look at the design of those hatches to see if we can make the engines a little easier to work on," he told Hiro, who nodded.

Logan ran a check on the fuel lines and ignition systems. He also took out each spark plug and checked its gap. "Looks all right. Step back everyone—I'm going to pull up the deck. The connecting rod from the diesel's gear box may have come loose." He used two pull rings countersunk into the deck planks to take out the front half of the cockpit floor. Underneath lay the mounting for the engine starting lever with two rods protruding from its side. Logan felt along the length of the one leading to the starboard engine. "Feels loose," he said.

He reached into his toolbox and pulled out a small fitting identical to the one on the end of the rod. He unbolted the bracket holding the rod to the rib of the boat and replaced it. He reached up, pulled the starting lever back and tested the fit of the rod. "Should work," he said and stood up. He replaced the deck piece and said, "Let's try again." He looked at Lindstrom who was standing at the back of the cockpit. "You take the engine controls."

Lindstrom went back to the wheel and pushed the throttle on the diesel back up to 'Full.'
He turned on the two ignition switches and pulled the starting lever. This time both engines thundered to life and the boat surged forward. Lindstrom disengaged the diesel's propeller. The bow came up and the hull rose smoothly up onto its step. Once they had reached cruising speed, Logan pushed two other levers located under the control panel and the engine noise dropped abruptly. At the same time, the hull rose in the water, but they ran a little slower. The noise of hull thumping through the water was still loud enough to prevent

normal conversation.

"What did you do to make that happen?" asked McPherson, bending to talk into Logan's ear.

"I wasn't sure it would work, but the exhausts have been diverted to come out through the hull. It's dropped about ten knots from the cruising speed, but probably added back five because there's less bulk being pushed through the water. We could install a speedometer if you need to know how fast you're going for estimating the time between two points."

"We'll think about that later. It could help us work out a precise time of arrival if we do a long run down the Sound. Making less noise certainly means we won't get noticed as much. Let's go on with the rest of the test and see if anything breaks." McPherson put his hand on Lindstrom's shoulder and said, "Ten minutes!" in his ear, then pointed to his watch. Lindstrom nodded and pushed both throttles to 'Full.' The propellers churned and as the bow came up, the boat, first slowly and then rapidly, picked up speed. McPherson motioned Arundel and Aki to positions beside Lindstrom, pointed both forefingers forward and said "Logs!" They nodded, took the best vantage points they could find, and looked out intently over the waters ahead. McPherson made more notes in his book.

They passed Discovery Island after eight minutes, and two minutes later McPherson said, "North!" Lindstrom went into an easy turn up into Haro Strait. McPherson waited until they were steady on the new course, then shouted in Lindstrom's ear, "She doesn't have any list that I can feel. Let's go through the maneuvering run." He motioned everyone else to hold tight, then turned back to Lindstrom and shouted, "Bring her back to cruising speed." He waited a moment as they slowed imperceptibly and then ordered, "Starboard thirty!"

Lindstrom swung the wheel over and watched the compass card spin. The boat leaned into the turn and they skittered a little to port as their reduced draught gave them less grip on the water. At twenty-five degrees, he brought the wheel back amidships and they came up on the new course. They were heading into American waters, and while there was no American government boat that could match their speed, McPherson did not want to get close enough to any shore for a pair of idle binoculars to identify them.

"Let's try a hard one," he told Lindstrom, and then signaled to the others again to hold on. "Port one hundred and eighty degrees." Lindstrom started the turn easily and the boat came off the course, leaning into the turn.

Suddenly, it lurched and there was a clattering noise from the stern. "Meet her, slow ahead both," shouted McPherson, holding up two fingers to reinforce the order.

Hiro Takahashi was leaning over the stern. "We've ripped off a rudder," he said.

"All stop!" shouted McPherson. Lindstrom turned off both ignition switches and the boat was suddenly silent except for the diesel, still quietly popping.

"He does speak all the English he needs," said Lindstrom.

Logan pulled out his toolbox and went to the stern. "The bottom rudder pintle's broken off at the hasp," said Hiro. "Can you hold the rudder while I cut it away?" He leaned over the stern and held onto the wrecked piece. Logan took a hacksaw from his box and handed it down. Hiro felt around the damaged piece. "Someone hold my legs," he called, "otherwise I'm going overside." Aki was the nearest and he moved over to do it. Between them, it took five minutes to get the damaged rudder clear.

They held an impromptu conference at the back of the cockpit. "There's too much power coming out of those two engines," said Logan. "There's not enough of the hull in the water to spread the force around and hold the extra lift given from the exhaust modification, although I think we'd have the same results if it was just the effect of the two engines without the exhaust change."

"Suggestions?" asked McPherson.

"I'll think about it," said Hiro.

"We've got one rudder to take us home, so we'll do that on the diesel," said McPherson.

An hour later they pulled in against the float at the shipyard. "She'll have to come back up on the ways," said Hiro.

Aki jumped out and reached for the bow line when they came up to the float. After the morning's launching ceremony there was only a short length left. Arundel swung himself out, ran up to the yard and found another. It took all of them half an hour to maneuver the boat over the slipway carriage and haul it up using the hand winch.

When the boat was snugged down, they all crammed into the office. "All suggestions, please," said McPherson.

"How fast were we going?" asked Lindstrom.

"No idea," said Arundel. "Faster than any of the Patrol Boats I had."

"Probably touched fifty knots when we got up on the step," said Logan. "That's a lot of drag on the rudders during a turn."

"We could try a third rudder. Maybe all of them have to be bigger with stronger fittings," said Hiro.

"She's really heavy on the wheel," said Lindstrom. "It'll be worse if we add any more weight onto it."

"We could put geared steering into her," said Aki. "Big ships have it, so it should be possible. Jeff, you took that gearbox apart for the reverse gear. Some of it's left over—we could have a large gear wheel drive a small one and have that turn the rudders."

"Try it, then," said McPherson. "Jeff?"

"While we're at it, we could add separate starting rods for each engine. That would mean you don't have to shut the other down if one doesn't start."

"I can see us doing that if we start the Liberties in an emergency. We don't want to slow down if someone's chasing us. Any idea what kind of speed we would be running on one engine only?"

"Probably sixty percent of full, maybe more, but you wouldn't be able to use the exhaust to lift her either."

"Why?"

"Lack of balance, mostly. The exhaust comes out under the engine so you'd be up on one side, and that, combined with the torque from the one engine running, would cause you to list. I'm also not sure about the effect of exhaust pipes coming out of the water when we heel on hard turns. I'd like to test for that when we go out again."

"We're stacking up some jobs," said McPherson. "All of them should be done before we test her again. What about the oil pressure?"

"We're still playing with it," said Logan. "It's okay at cruising speed for long periods, but low revs, such as when you're close to shore on a delivery, cause oil pressure to fall and the plugs to foul. That'll severely reduce performance, not to mention having the whole engine overheat. It'll probably be better to do all the close-to-shore work on the diesel."

Aki was having a quiet conversation with his father in the back of the room. They both nodded and Aki turned to them and said, "The propellers and the rudder also need more protection than they have. We would like to put steel bracing struts in front of all of them. It should help if you run over a log. Watching Jeff on the deck fiddling with the engine controls tells me I want to redesign those engine compartment hatches, and perhaps alter the cockpit deck planking so it's easier to get to those connecting rods. You and Ollie will need to learn how to make running repairs like checking fuel lines, ignition, and plugs."

McPherson nodded agreement. "What about a box of spare parts?"

"We can work up a list. We don't need too much because if something serious breaks, you can always heave to somewhere inconspicuous and come home when it's quiet."

"Okay. When you look at her tomorrow, will you have a look at the tanks and see what our fuel consumption was? I don't expect a surprise, but it's important to know." He made a tick in his notebook, closed it, and looked over at Hiro. "How long to do the work?"

"Three days to make the rudder and the rest of the hull work. Engine hatches, perhaps we make gate-fold doors that can hinge back on themselves, two days. Jeff?"

"I can get the starting assembly and the steering done at the same time."

McPherson put his notebook back in his pocket. "That takes us to Christmas Eve." He looked at Lindstrom. "I'm assuming your family will want you then." The Swede nodded. McPherson said to the group, "Shall we make it next Friday, then—the 26th at 10:00 here?"

To Lindstrom on the way out he said, "We'll need to do the next run in the *Lady Jane*. I'll see you Monday morning."

Later that afternoon, McPherson walked into Arundel's office.

"Did you hear anything from Olmstead?" he asked Michael as he came in.

"Certainly did; he was furious."

"Do you wish us to go ahead with another delivery on Monday?"

"Yes. Will the new boat be ready?"

"No. We'll take the *Lady Jane*."

"Just as well. With the new boat and a load of liquor, he might be tempted to hijack them both. Be extra careful anyway. He likes us because we're the only supplier of the brands he wants—Seagrams and the Reifels can give him a limited range, but most of their stuff is committed elsewhere—but coppers can be unpredictable. Watch your back!"

"How's the radio link working?" asked McPherson.

"Well enough—Elise is down there; she transmitted his order and set up the delivery point."

"And she's keeping Olmstead close to us?"

"Seems so."

McPherson thought for a moment. "I'd like you to change the delivery point at the last minute. Give them just enough time to get there from the place we set initially. It'll make it unlikely that he'll be able to lay on any extra help if he wants to rough us up and it'll make the point that we're in charge of deliveries. If he wants a reason, don't give him one. Where's the drop?"

"Richmond Beach."

McPherson unrolled the chart on the table under the window. "Richmond Beach is here," he pointed. "We'll change to Edmonds, here," he pointed again. "They'll be expecting us at midnight, so make the call an hour before that, at 11:00. Who will be on the radio here? Will you be able get the change down to them then?"

"For the moment it's Peter, and yes."

Chapter 26

Monday, December 22nd, 1919

McPherson got to Lindstrom's at ten in the morning. "You fuel her?" he asked.

"Yes."

"Just so you're absolutely clear on the risk, this run might be a bit difficult, and if you don't want to do it, tell me. Olmstead's furious. Those bottles filled with water got his attention. He has the idea that he's the king of Seattle and we should think ourselves lucky to do business with him. As far as we're concerned, we'll keep supplying him as long as he pays up, but if he doesn't, we won't. We're pulling a last-minute change of destination, in case he's set up something nasty on us, but this trip might end up with some shots fired. I'll understand if you don't want to take the risk."

"You know I ran around with a lot of cash, so that's something I'm used to." Lindstrom grinned and pulled a box of shotgun shells out of his pocket.

The night was overcast, but occasionally the clouds parted enough so they could see the sliver of a new moon. McPherson looked at the luminous dial of his watch. It was coming up to six o'clock. "Stay on this course. I'll check the lights on the way down. Thank God for this wind—there's no fog."

McPherson checked his guide paper regularly. As they approached the drop point, he tapped

Lindstrom's shoulder and signaled with an outstretched hand with palm downward for him to slow down. He looked at the chart carefully with a flashlight. Lindstrom did a three-hundred- sixty-degree sweep with the night glasses. "No traffic in sight except a freighter, two miles northwest, inbound. I'm guessing we're about three hundred yards, due east, from the beach," he said.

McPherson gripped the small searchlight that served as their signal light. The signal for the day was an innovation from Elise, the Morse code letter 'L.' He flashed dot-dash-dot-dot, waited a minute, then flashed again. They kept moving parallel to the shore, scanning the beach from end to end, turning back every sixty seconds. "While we're waiting, let's try a spin turn by running the engine on the inside of the turn in reverse. We'll give them another thirty minutes and then we'll go," he said.

They ran five times in both directions before Lindstrom called, "Flashing light from the shore, about ten o'clock from us."

"What signal?"

"Dunno. Didn't get it all. I'll get the bearing when they do it next time."

McPherson changed the direction of the light to the new location and flashed the signal again.

"There it is," shouted Lindstrom.

"Got it." He spelled out the flashes. "Dot-dash-dot. 'R.' That's it. I'll go in with the dory. Keep circling." McPherson looked at the chart again. "We should be alright here with our draft. The tide's not going to bother us one way or the other as long as you keep the circle tight. There's no rocks that'll cause us a problem. Keep the night glasses on me, and if you see anything go wrong, get out. Your wife doesn't need an early widowhood. If everything works well and you see me push off the beach, put the side lights on so I can find you, drop the anchor, and start bringing out the load."

He went aft and unhooked the lashings holding the dory, slid it over the stern, and climbed in. He settled himself at the oar locks but took the precaution of facing forward and pushing the oars so he could keep a bearing on the flashing signal light and see who might be waiting for him on shore. He stepped carefully over the side of the dory when it grounded and pulled it up above the wave-line. Four men trudged through the darkness and reached down to reach the cases.

"Hey, what the hell?" said the one holding the light when they discovered the boat was empty.

"Olmstead?"

"Who else do you think it is?"

"You're short money."

"I told Elise I'd pay you when I'm ready."

"So she said, but I'm not giving you any more booze until I'm ready."

"Who else are you going to sell to? I run Seattle."

"Then you can give them all the rotgut our competitors will sell you and we'll sell the decent stuff to your competitors in Tacoma and other places up and down the Sound. All those judges, prosecutors, and other cops you have on the payroll aren't going to be happy with the second-rate slop you give them, and then you're not going to be worth protecting."

Olmstead stood there silently. "You bastard. You got stuff on board?"

"You have money?"

"Yes."

"If it's nine thousand six hundred dollars plus the missing two thousand, three hundred and fifty dollars, I'll unload the boat."

"I can raise it up to ten thousand dollars by borrowing back the money I gave out to the guys on the shore here and have the rest to you by Wednesday."

"Give me the money. I'll trust you for the

balance in cash, in Victoria, but only until Wednesday."

Olmstead made the rounds of the crew he had standing by, collecting money from each. He came back in ten minutes and handed over a heavy canvas bag. "You guys have the easy part of this trade. Liquor gets sold for coins. I have to change it for paper money without people noticing. It takes time."

McPherson reached in and riffled through the contents. "It feels like money. If it is, I'll be back with the first load in twenty minutes." He paused for a moment. "We're both making enough on this trade to live with a little inconvenience. Our problem is that you stuck us with a big one."

He pushed the dory out through the waves and looked for a red or green riding light. He found a red one off to his left and rowed toward it. He was alongside in five minutes and he and Lindstrom set the mooring lines and fenders to hold the dory tight.

"If this is money in here, we need to load as many sacks as we can without capsizing. I don't want us hanging around here for much longer than two hours."

"It is money," said Lindstrom shining the flashlight into the bag. "Here comes the first load then." He passed down two bags.

Even though the dory was snugged into the boat, the wind kept the hull swinging around the anchor. There was enough of a sea running to make the sides pitch against one another sometimes causing Lindstrom to suddenly need to reach up to pass bags over.

The difficulty in rowing a heavily-laden dory showed immediately he cleared the lee of the boat. As he came closer to the shore, the waves grew larger over the shoals and the boat grounded after it planed down the front of the roller before it reached the beach. He got even wetter when he jumped out to steady the craft with the painter; the shore crew got wet in the four inches of water that surrounded the dory, and nobody's temper improved as the night wore on. McPherson had to bail out the dory when he came back empty. "I'm glad one of us remembered to put in a bucket," he said to Lindstrom when he returned to the *Lady Jane.*

"Fishermen remember these things."

"I don't like overloading boats but this one is a lot more stable with a load in her than she is empty."

It was exhausting work and they changed shifts at the oars after each trip. Lindstrom came back from his first run and said, "It's a little easier if you can ride in behind the crest of the wave. You still slap down on the beach but you're a little further up it."

"I'll try that," said McPherson. He took the last run and made sure Olmstead did not see how tired he was. They ran off into the channel with the dory trailing behind to get going faster. When they looked back and no one was following them, they considered it safe enough to haul the dory aboard.

"How did he take it?" asked Lindstrom once they were on their way again.

"Without a lot of grace. I told him if the money wasn't there in the right amount on Wednesday, we'd be doing business with someone else."

"Do we have someone else?"

"At the moment, no, but that's Arundel's problem. You and I can take our money and wait for a solution to appear. The big thing is to find more guys to do the running around. Other than us, everyone the Arundels have turned up have left something to be desired."

Victoria, Tuesday, December 23rd, 1919

McPherson drove over to Arundel's office, went upstairs and found Michael waiting for him.

"How did it go?" asked Michael.

"Well enough." He put the wallet on the desk. "I haven't counted it, but less the two hundred I just gave to Ollie, Olmstead said there was ten thousand in it. I told him if the balance wasn't here in cash by Wednesday—tomorrow—we'd cut him off. I think it's too risky to have him as our only customer. The other side of that argument, as Ollie pointed out on the way home, is that to service more customers, we're going to have to expand our operation a bit, both with more people and more boats."

They stacked the money in common denominations regardless of their issuer. Arundel looked at some of them with increasing distaste. "I wish the Americans would get their money straight. I have to take all these bills to the bank, and they go over each note to make sure it's legitimate. Sometimes as much as ten per cent of them are duds and we have to decide whether we chase our customer for the shortage or just accept the loss."

"Olmstead was complaining he sells liquor for coins and he's got enough problems just getting the right kind of paper money from his customers that he still ends up paying us short. That's the excuse he gave me for paying that much less again."

"He is inventive."

"Did Elise help?" asked McPherson.

"We suspected a problem and confirmed it after you suggested we might use her in this way. As you can see, delivering liquor is just one part of the operation. Our customers need to organize much more than just selling to their buyers." Michael expertly bundled the bills into standardized amounts.

"No wonder everyone is so discreet about the nature of the trade. Ten thousand American dollars is a lot to be taking into a bank. It's enough to buy five moderately priced houses."

"The banks are quite pleased to see them. At this point where the Canadian dollar is starting to sink in value against the American one, we have a nice margin to work with. We price our liquor in American dollars and pay for it in British pounds, but we pay our taxes in Canadian dollars. At the same time, we have a lot of money at stake. We need to buy the liquor in Britain and have it shipped out here. That involves paying for the transportation, insuring the cargo, and organizing everything that goes into the local operation, including, in this case, building a special boat. That's a lot of money to put up and we don't get it back until this happens." He picked up a bundle of notes and slapped it against the desk. "We're feeling our way around. We organized our operation last year, but it wasn't until you appeared that we got things in order. As you might imagine, our investors are anxious to see some return on their money."

McPherson handed more bills to Michael. "All of which means we need to be careful who we take on as a customer. I assume that will be Peter's job?" Michael nodded. McPherson went on. "While he does that, why don't I look for the men to do the deliveries—Peter's not had much luck yet, or else he's not trying very hard."

"Yes, that's a good idea. You can get started once the new boat is up and running."

"Hopefully, that will be next week. We're meeting at the Takahashis' for the next trial on Friday. When are we making the next delivery?"

"Saturday, and Olmstead would like a quick turnaround after that to stock up for New Year's."

"Fair enough," said McPherson. "I told Ollie he was off now until after Christmas so he could spend the time with his family."

"Speaking of which," said Arundel, "would you like to join us for Christmas lunch?"

"Thanks, but I have other plans." McPherson stood up as he straightened the last pile of notes. "And right now, I need to go and buy a toy truck."

Friday, December 26th, 1919

McPherson was at the yard early on Friday morning and sat on the float looking at the traffic moving around the harbour. An eclectic array of tugs, fishing boats, log booms and coastal freighters jockeyed for space. Two Canadian Pacific passenger ships lay at the company dock and he thought for a moment about how his life might unfold if he ever got an appointment to the bridge of one of them. Things were looking up in Victoria on a personal level, and he wasn't sure he wanted to spend weeks at sea anymore.

Hearing footsteps on the walkway, he turned to see Lindstrom and Logan walking down the ramp.

"Anyone see Aki?" he asked.

"Here," said a voice from above.

"Is she ready for the water?" asked Lindstrom.

"Be right down. Pull the cover off her."

Logan pulled on the rope hanging down at the bows. A block squealed and the tarpaulin rose, brushing off the edges of the deck, and the boat appeared from under it.

McPherson walked up from the float, stopping first at the stern where three newly-installed rudder blades hung firmly at the base of the transom. He ran his hand over each one. "Nice and tight," he said.

"Expect it any other way?" asked Aki.

"No," he said with a grin. "Let's try the wheel before we put her in." He swung into the cockpit and cast off the noose that was looped over a wheel spoke. He turned the wheel forty- five degrees.

"How much on the rudder?" he asked Lindstrom.

"About five degrees to starboard."

He turned the wheel the same amount in the other direction. "Now?"

"The same going the other way."

"We know what to expect then. Ready to go?"

he asked Aki. He looked around the yard. "Is Hiro coming?"

"No. He thinks we can fix our own problems now. We'll wind her down on the winch. We've got her on a cable." Aki grinned and walked over to where the winch was mounted at the head of the slipway. He turned the crank handle and *Rit'waxl* slowly moved down the ways. Lindstrom jumped onto the foredeck, leaned over the bow, and took out the steel shackle that held the cable to the ring bolt on the stem. McPherson pulled the boat over to the float with the stern line and loosely cleated it in.

"All aboard!" Logan and Takahashi scrambled on and took places in the hold.

The other two settled onto the new seats and strapped themselves in. "Comfortable," said Lindstrom. "What did you anchor them to?"

"Put some steel plates along the ribs, riveted a base plate to them, and then bolted the seats on. They'll hold," said Aki.

Lindstrom started the diesel and they moved out into the fairway.

"Jeff, we'll do the same as we did last time, except we'll try the steering on the diesel first and then on the Liberties," said McPherson.

It took them fifteen minutes to work their way through harbour traffic to the entrance, and another ten to the other side of Trial Island. "I'm not really happy about winding our way through the harbour when we have a load on board," said McPherson. "Everyone can see us, and we could get jumped when we hit open water."

"With the speed of this boat, we can pick our departure times and then use a different patch of water each time we go out," said Lindstrom.

"Perhaps. Anyway, let's deal with the immediate problems. Jeff, let's you and I swap places. I want to look at the wake as we steer." McPherson went aft and sat in the stern with his notebook out. "Forty-five degrees of port wheel on," he called out.

"Forty-five degrees of port wheel on," confirmed Lindstrom. McPherson drew a sketch of the boat's curved wake and added his estimate of its angle. He called for ninety, one-hundred- and-eighty, two-hundred-and-twenty-five, two-hundred-and-seventy, and three-hundred-and- fifteen degrees of port and starboard wheel turns and noted the results.

"Interesting exercise," he said when he came back to the cockpit. "The results will probably be different with the Liberties running but it looks like we'll have to take the wheel through two full rounds to get our maximum turn in. It means no close high-speed maneuvering with the main engines close to shore; we won't have time to spin the wheel to get ourselves out of trouble.

McPherson flicked back two pages in his notebook. "Anything new on the engines, Jeff?"

"I think I've solved the low-speed oil pressure problem, so I'd like us to run for about twenty minutes at low revs to see if I'm right. We ran her around the harbour and it worked all right, but sometimes it works differently when there's motion from the sea."

"What did you do?" asked Lindstrom.

"Drilled a small hole in the bypass valve."

"Simple solution," said Lindstrom.

"We'll see when we run her at those speeds."

"Now we start the mains. Which way does the lever go?" asked Lindstrom.

"Left and right," said Logan. "Opposite way to the engine you want to start. Port engine, pull the lever to starboard; starboard engine, pull it to port."

"I'll start engines," said McPherson. "Full ahead." He reached for the ignition switches. "Port engine now." He pushed the lever away from him. The engine started and the noise from it was deafening. Lindstrom could see him mouthing, "Starboard engine," as he pulled the lever toward him. They could not hear the second engine start over the roar of the first, but they felt its vibration through the deck. McPherson pushed the two levers for the exhaust bypass and they could hear again. They ran it at full speed for twenty minutes.

"Ready for the low-speed test?" he asked Logan, who nodded. McPherson gave him his seat.

Logan put his hand on the throttles and nudged Lindstrom on the arm, making a lowering motion with his hand and then ran both levers to the quarter speed position. At the same time, he disengaged the exhaust bypass and the noise level increased again. They ran for twenty minutes while he stared at the oil pressure gauge.

"Looks like it's fixed," he said finally.

They ran up the engines and reengaged the exhaust bypass. McPherson signaled Lindstrom to turn the boat for home. "Any problem using her for a run tomorrow?" he asked Logan.

"None that I can see; you can always bring her home on the diesel."

Twenty minutes later they were passing Ogden Point and moving quietly through the harbour. McPherson said, "We'll put her under a tarp at the warehouse dock and moor the *Lady Jane* in front of her just to keep her safe from wandering eyes." He turned to Lindstrom. "We can load her tomorrow morning. Will you fuel her before we do that?"

Saturday, December 27th, 1919

"I've been thinking about loading the boat," McPherson said to Lindstrom when he picked him up the next morning. "We're going to need a bit of help on the warehouse side. I'll get Jeff to set up some sort of a gantry and load her in one go."

"Most gantries are used to pick up boxes, which

would add extra weight to the load," pointed out Lindstrom. "If we were a bigger ship with a hatch and a way of moving the boxes around in the hold, it might work. Worth thinking about anyway. We'd need to put a crane of sorts out there, too. Hopefully the men in the warehouse did as we asked and put the sacks together so we can just have 'em wheeled to the dock."

They drove into the warehouse yard, but there was no one to be seen. The warehouse doors were locked shut and blinds were drawn on the office window where Romilly worked. "What's going on?" asked Lindstrom. "They knew we were going out today, didn't they?"

"They did," said McPherson. His face was grim. "What's more, they knew it was the first run out for the new boat. I think Romilly's trying to sabotage the operation."

Peter Arundel's car drove in. He got out and said cheerfully, "I came down to see how all this weight fits into *Rit'waxl*."

"So did we," said Aki, getting out from the passenger side.

Logan got out of the back seat at the same time. "We want to look at the trim of the boat when it's loaded."

"Welcome to the party," said McPherson. "Now if only we had something to load."

"What do you mean?" asked Arundel, looking around. "Where is everyone?"

"That's what we want to know," said Lindstrom.

"I suspect young Romilly is up to something," said McPherson. "Do you have a key to the warehouse, Peter?"

"Of course," said Arundel. He went to the office door and unlocked it. A moment later the large warehouse doors swung open from the inside and he returned to the group.

"We'll have to load her up ourselves," McPherson said. "Good thing you're all here—you can get some first-hand experience with how the loading works. Right now, let's get the load on something with wheels and move it dockside. We need to get away by three."

It took them almost four hours to finish. Lindstrom went to find some food to pack for the journey. "This boat doesn't have a galley or a head, so we need to get prepped up before we go," he'd said. "Fishermen have to remind naval officers of basic stuff. We could at least use a spirit stove to heat water."

McPherson spoke to the others while Lindstrom was gone. "We were looking at using a gantry of some sort to move the stuff to the dock, and a winch to put the load into the boat. While it's not an onerous job if we have the men to do it, we've just seen what it takes if we don't. Aside from that, the less the bottles get jockeyed around, the less breakage we'll have. We would need something that would fit precisely into the hatch and be small enough to let us close the cover." This time it was Arundel who produced the notebook. McPherson grinned. "Let's put that on the list of the next problem to solve."

"I have an idea about the loading system," said Logan. "We could make a box to fit into the hatch and make the sides short enough to let the hatch cover close over it. If it had shackles on all four corners, a crane could sling it down directly. That means it could be loaded in the warehouse and wheeled out onto the dock. I'll think about a crane that could lift it." He sketched out a rough diagram and wrote down the results as he worked out the weight. "The problem is that one hundred fifty cases weigh four thousand, five hundred pounds. Installing a crane on the dock to move that weight would be a big structural job, but I think I can modify a truck with a crane on the back to handle that kind of load. It'll need a counterweight on the front to supplement the weight of the engine, but it's possible."

McPherson took the sketch and turned it around to look at it from a different angle. He gave it back and said, "Would the weight of the box added to that be problematic?"

"All things considered, it wouldn't be that much more," Logan replied.

McPherson nodded. "Can you start working on that as soon as we leave? The *Lady Jane* can load with her own gear, but you might think about modifying the crane—especially if we decide to use her to carry larger loads. Peter—when you get back to the office, tell your father he's got to do something about Romilly. I'm sure he's behind this."

Arundel nodded and McPherson and Lindstrom got into the cockpit. McPherson took the connand strapped himself into his seat. Lindstrom opened the forward hatch and swung down under the foredeck to start the diesel. It took them almost five minutes to work their way out from behind the *Lady Jane.* It needed both Arundel and Takahashi on the packer and Logan on the dock, alternately freeing them from mooring lines and fending off with boat hooks.

When they gained the harbour, Lindstrom came from under the deck and strapped himself into the second seat. "That was complicated," he said.

"Moving the boat around or loading it?" asked McPherson. "Both bits of the job need to be improved."

"I think there's enough space to put in a dock alongside the warehouse that can give us two berths. *Rit'waxl* can take the inside one and be shielded from view," said Lindstrom.

"Good idea. I don't see the harbour master complaining—we'd be well way from the fairway. Jeff's idea looks like it would work. Hopefully he'll have something done about it when we get back." McPherson pulled out his notebook and started writing.

They came out into the Straits at four o'clock. Lindstrom pushed the diesel to full power.

The swell was heavy and the load in the stern weighed them down. The diesel couldn't bring them up to planing speed and they wallowed uncomfortably. "Useful to know what the boat'll do," said Lindstrom.

"Let's go faster, then," said McPherson.

Lindstrom went through the starting procedures and both Liberties fired. He cut in the exhaust bypass for each engine and pulled the throttles back to cruising speed. The bow rose for the most part over the oncoming waves. Occasionally they ploughed through one and the spray came over the windshield, blasting their faces.

"What do you figure the wind is?" asked McPherson, raising his voice to make himself heard above the engines.

"Fresh breeze like this, probably no more than twenty knots."

McPherson pulled the peak of his cap down and escaped the worst of it. Lindstrom had spent his seagoing life in a closed wheelhouse and his woolen toque, though warm, sopped up water and did not protect his eyes from even the smallest blast of spindrift.

"You need a cap like mine," shouted McPherson into his ear. "Stay low until this settles down a bit."

Lindstrom ducked down behind the windshield, but that offered very little cover. "Let's put up the cockpit cover."

They pulled it out from its locker behind them and tied it down over the windscreen and sides. "Throttle her back a bit, maybe this thing won't blow all over the place then," said Lindstrom.

The improvement was minimal. "We need a fixed cover," said McPherson. The extra lift from the exhaust bypass brought more of the hull out of the water, but as they bounced over the wave crests, their propellers broke water and the engines raced. "There's a choice here," he shouted. "We run with little noise and possibly damage our propeller shafts, or put up with the roar and keep the engines safe."

They compromised by slowing down, which let the boat ride easier and reduced the spray coming over the bow. McPherson unrolled the wax paper on which they had marked the details of their course, and through the night glasses, spotted the light houses at Port Wilson and Admiralty Head. When he estimated their position to be approaching the east side of Haro Strait leading down the west of San Juan Island, he gave Lindstrom a heading of south by south-east. They were still in a heavy swell and running into the teeth of the wind. "I'm guessing we're doing thirty to thirty-five knots," he said.

"Dunno. I've never been this fast in a boat. Before I met you, not even in a car neither."

Victoria, Sunday, December 28th, 1919

A watery dawn broke behind them as they passed well to the west of Sheep Island. McPherson cut the Liberties once Lindstrom had raised his arm to signal that he'd started the diesel. "Didn't know I could sleep in a wet cargo hold."

"The starboard Liberty is hiccupping a bit. Better get Jeff to look at it before we take her out again," said Lindstrom.

"Is that one jinxed? We'll go into Takahashis' now then. Arundel wants us to do a quick turnaround and go out again tomorrow so they get extra for New Year's, but it will have to wait until Tuesday."

The sea had a mild swell, but the rain slashed over the windscreen. "I'm glad we'll get a cockpit cover. There's going to be nights worse than this one in the next couple of months," said Lindstrom. They came into the harbour behind the Canadian Pacific night boat and swung round it to turn into the Inner Harbour and the float in front of the boat yard.

"Ahoy Takahashi!" McPherson called as he wrapped the bow line to the float's nearest cleat.

There was no immediate reply. He cut the engine and threw the stern line to Lindstrom, who made it fast on the next cleat. Carrying their oilskins, they walked up the ramp alongside the slipway where a seiner had replaced the *Ritw'raxl*. They reached the end of it and started up the steps to the workshop. "Hold it right there!" came a voice from above them.

McPherson looked up. "Get you up too early, did we, Aki?"

"Dugald! What's the matter?"

"Starboard Liberty's making some noise—doesn't sound too good. Can you call Jeff in to look at it?"

"Suppose so."

"We also need a fixed cover over the cockpit. We didn't do too well in rough water and the canvas one leaks. We'd like her again tomorrow, but we need her again by the next day, so if all you can get done is the engine, that's okay. If you need to talk to me, I'll be at the hotel. Leave a note if I'm not there."

"I'll do my best on the cockpit cover, but I'm not guaranteeing it—getting in and out of the cockpit might be a problem."

"Olmstead won't be happy, but if there's a problem with the boat it can't be helped, I suppose." Michael reached into his desk drawer and took out some large envelopes. He wrote the denominations of bills and dollar amounts on the outside and they loaded the bundles of bills in the right ones.

"Jeff's having another look at the starboard engine, and I asked Aki to put a fixed cover over the cockpit. The weather's too unsettled these nights to risk having a wave wash over an open boat. We could take the *Lady Jane* if absolutely necessary, but I'd like to get *Ritw'raxl* running regularly as soon as possible."

"That makes sense. Work on that then and let me know when and where."

"I'm assuming, then, you want me to take over the delivery scheduling," said McPherson when they had cleared most of the desk.

"It might work better that way."

"I've had some thoughts about it. We've had the experience with building *Rit'waxl*, and there's going to be enough money in the delivery business for other people to build their own boats. We have the choice of keeping her running ourselves or selling her off to someone else. On balance, I'd prefer it if we stayed in the supply business. The *Lady Jane*, or something like her, could carry a full load, station off the coast in Canadian waters, and transfer loads to shore boats. All we'd need is a radio link."

McPherson thought for a few seconds before adding, "If we do that, we could stick to the brandy, whiskey, rum, and gin we now have and sell to the delivery men. How many cases has Olmstead said he'll take in the next couple of months?"

"We have a thousand cases in the warehouse now and another five thousand on order; he wants them all. I'd like to move it as soon as possible when we get it—I don't want to have to store goods in a place that's less secure."

"That would be about thirty trips in *Rit'waxl*, a little heavier loaded than the last run. We could boost the load to two hundred cases, but that's six thousand pounds. The hull would stand it as long as the weather was reasonable, but it's a lot of extra loads with the dory, and that's what takes the time on landing. It's too much for just Ollie and me—I'd prefer to take the *Lady Jane* in with a couple of extra crewmen and go alongside a dock. We'll need all of Olmstead's police influence to make sure no one's noticing."

"I'll talk to Olmstead. You look for more crew."

"I was thinking some of the men at the warehouse might work. I'll talk to them. Speaking of which, would you mind telling me more about why young Romilly's still here? He's been a right pain, and that mess at the warehouse yesterday cannot happen again. Elise told me he might have been sent here to get him out of London."

"I'm not that sure myself. The family connection is on my wife's side, and his father won't disclose his plans for lunch unless he thinks you need to know."

"Yes, I did work for the Admiral."

"So you did. And my wife tells me John was involved in something political when he was at university before the war, but that was just something that passed. It could be he made some undesirable friends who may have resurfaced. He's like a lot of young Englishmen who get sent out here for a fresh start."

"From what I've seen of him so far, I'd prefer the fresh start didn't involve our boats. He certainly won't impress any of our potential customers. Everything he says irritates someone in Canada. God only knows what will happen if we let him loose on the Americans."

"Peter will keep him under control."

"Peter may be fully occupied in keeping himself under control."

Michael grunted. "Where will I find you if I need to?"

"I still have a room at the Strathcona Hotel. I'm headed there now."

Chapter 27

Monday, December 29th, 1919

Jeff was waiting at the shipyard. "*Rit'waxl* won't be ready until we put some new bearings in," he said. "All that experimenting with the oil pressure must have caused the old ones to wear out. We have some spares, but I'd really like to take a good look at the rest of both motors and see if there's anything else that's likely to need replacing. We can't expect to have this market to ourselves for long and there'll be a shortage of motors when everything starts to break. We should get a couple of spare full assemblies."

McPherson nodded in agreement. "We'll take *Lady Jane* down tomorrow then for the delivery—they want the liquor for New Year's Eve. That will give you a few days to get *Rit'waxl* back into good shape. Why don't we plan another trip with *Lady Jane* on Sunday when all the festivities are over? We can do a one-night layover and pick up parts in the morning. You'll have to come with us, though. Neither Ollie nor I would have a clue about the details of engine parts."

"I'll tell my wife I'm going up the coast for the night, but not until Saturday, otherwise I won't hear the end of it."

They spent the next hour looking over the engines and making notes about improvements that could be made to the controls in the cockpit. After a short discussion with Aki about when the work should be scheduled, McPherson drove over to the Arundels' house and found Peter out on the terrace with Romilly.

"Quick word, please," said McPherson to Peter. Peter led him into the living room. "We need to change some delivery arrangements for tomorrow night and get some money for motors."

"What's the problem?"

"The starboard Liberty's a bit shaky and Jeff thinks the bearings have had it. He wants to tear it down and see if there's anything else likely to go. While he's doing it, he'll have a look at the other one and see if there's anything there that needs work. Remember, these things were churned out at the end of the war and quality sometimes suffered."

"We're committed to Roy for tomorrow night."

"We can do that in *Lady Jane*. Then on Sunday we'll do another run with her with Jeff on board, lay over for the night, and pick up the parts on Monday morning. It would help if we could meet Roy earlier than midnight on that run."

"That should be enough notice even for him. Where do you want to deliver?"

"One of the more northerly beaches for tomorrow night—with this quick turnaround, Ollie and I will both be tired. Then for Sunday, Brackett's Landing—we haven't been there since that try-out with Calhoun. We have to go into Seattle for the parts anyway."

"We'll send a signal during the regular watch time tonight."

Tuesday, December 30th, 1919

McPherson brought the money in to Michael Arundel's office shortly before noon. "How did it go?" Arundel asked.

"The weather was a pig. We were glad it was a short run, but Olmstead wasn't too happy about it," said McPherson.

"He'll live," said Arundel dryly. "Tell me about this next trip you're making. You wish to buy more engines?"

"Yes. It makes financial sense to pick them up sooner rather than later."

"I'll take your word for it. What's your plan?"

"I'll set up for loading early on Sunday—it will be a long run with a slow boat. Jeff will be with us; he's going to lie to his wife about it so if you happen to hear from her, he's gone to Nanaimo."

"Why should she call us?"

"This is Victoria—everyone knows who's in the trade, even your nasty nephew."

"He already knew. We do need to introduce him to the American side of the business. Peter will take care of that. We'd like you to take them with you on this trip."

"Peter—fine, but why don't you send Romilly down by the regular boat?"

"Don't want him to be seen going through American Customs."

"You or the Admiral?"

"Both of us. We don't want the Admiral's efforts to be directly connected."

"He could have picked a better messenger. I saw a few people in his office who could do a much better job of being unobtrusive."

"John isn't part of his official life."

"Let's leave it this way, then—I'll get him down there, but since it's part of a regular run, he's going to have to help row the boat. We don't have room for passengers with the sort of load we're carrying and the way we need to handle it. I trust you'll tell him, because if I have to, it'll be brutal."

"I'll take care of it. That gives you a few days off. Do you have plans for New Year's Eve?"

"Yes. A quiet evening."

"Alone?"

"No."

"Still seeing Mrs. Hemmingson, then?"

"As often as I can. Tell Peter to bring the son and heir with him to the warehouse on Sunday."

Sunday, January 4th, 1920

The clang of an engine telegraph bell woke him. He lurched out of bed looking for the ship's helm station, directly in front of the captain's sea cabin, two steps up from the door. He came up short by the hotel window which looked out over Douglas Street and the streetcar that clanged by below.

It took him a full minute to orient himself and wonder why he was in the captain's sea cabin. Then he remembered the dash home through the Oresund Strait between Denmark and Sweden after they picked up Peter Arundel and his bullet-ridden patrol boat with its shattered first lieutenant and Tatania. He came slowly back to the present and laid out his seagoing gear.

By the time he had something to eat and got outside, it was seven o'clock. A stiff breeze was circling the hotel's yard, and with it a light rain. He pulled his cap peak down over his eyes, sunk further into the collar of his roll neck sweater and kept his hands in the pockets of his duffel coat until he had to take them out to open the car door. He was very grateful for the car's self-starter, particularly when it started on the first push of the switch. He drove down to Store Street along the harbour, stopped before he turned onto it, and looked at the flag in front of the Legislature Buildings to get some idea of where the wind was coming from. It was facing partially away from him, so he guessed it was from the southeast—scarcely an unusual direction at this time of year. Better than if it was blowing in the other direction; a northwester would bring Arctic weather, and with it, snow.

Fifteen minutes later, he was honking the car horn outside Lindstrom's house. The Swede came out immediately. "We need to pick up Jeff," he said as he got into the front seat, "but if his wife sees this car, she'll guess he's travelling with us."

"Where does he live?"

"On Battery Street in James Bay."

"We'll drive over. I'll park out of sight of the house. You walk over and get him. We'll be close enough to Fisherman's Wharf for it to look like you're walking from there."

A block from the house, Lindstrom hopped out and came back with Logan wearing his oilskins and carrying a tool bag. "Family all right with the story?" asked McPherson.

"Yes, but I'd better not try it too often. The money you're paying is better than I could get anywhere else, but I'd just as soon have the wife find out about it after we're past the need for me to take runs south."

"The next time we'll send you down on the ferry and you can take her with you. That might ease the strain a bit."

"Maybe."

"Speaking of strain, John Romilly's taking this trip with us." Two grunts were all he got for an answer.

They arrived at the warehouse gate and honked the horn. The watchman came shuffling out and unlocked it. There was no sign of either Arundel or Romilly, so they went into the warehouse to organize the load. "We've made a platform which will let us use the boat's gear to lift the cargo into the hold," said Logan. "It's over here on a small wagon we built to hold it."

"Any more ideas on a better kind of loader for the dock, Jeff?" asked Lindstrom.

"Should have it done in a week or so, but for now we can wheel the load onto the dock and use *Lady*

Jane's gear to swing it over."

"Can the boat's lifting spar hold the load? It was only designed for nets," said Lindstrom.

"We've strengthened the base of the mast and mounted the base of the spar on a collar that rests on a plate we attached to the deck. We've replaced the spar itself with a steel one."

"Let's give it a try, then," said McPherson, and he leaned down to push. The others got behind the wagon and pushed as well. Logan held the steering bar, and they worked the load out onto the dock.

"Be handy if this thing had brakes," said Lindstrom.

"Hadn't thought of that," replied Logan, "but you're right. Three-and-a-half thousand pounds doesn't stop easily. I've got blocks for the rear wheels once we get the load in place by the boat." Between them they maneuvered the wagon to the right place on the dock. Arundel and Romilly came out of the warehouse, each carrying an overnight bag and dressed for business.

"As well you didn't show earlier. Your suits would have got dirty," said McPherson sourly.

"Sorry. John takes a long time to get ready," said Arundel.

"You should have hurried him along. You know we're meeting Olmstead's men early tonight. At least you can see how well Jeff's latest invention works. Ollie, will you run the loading operation?" Lindstrom nodded. "Peter—you and Jeff get the hatch cover off. I'll put the shackles on the load." McPherson pulled the spar over to the shore side and checked its rigging. "You've put a different block on, Jeff."

"I felt a four-to-one pull would be safer."

"Four to one. Powerful gear! Get on board, then," he told Romilly, who was looking distastefully at his surroundings and managed to avoid the hard shove Logan aimed at his back to help him along the way.

They came out into the Straits at ten o'clock and laid a course to take them down the west side of San Juan Island. Once they were on it, McPherson called Arundel. "Peter, since you're here, take the lookout. The *Arcata's* around here somewhere. She's got a lot of water to cover and the captain has to be as concerned about boats coming out of Vancouver as he does us. She could be over closer to Rosario Straits. I'd prefer a straight run into Brackett's, so it wouldn't be good if we met her coming out as we're going in. We're supposed to be there by 9:30 tonight and we don't have a lot of spare time."

Time passed slowly for five men on a slow boat in a heavy swell with rain keeping them inside the wheelhouse. "Keep the running lights on," said McPherson as dusk fell. "Otherwise, we'll look suspicious."

Arundel shouted, "Ship off starboard bow!" A cargo ship coming out of the Hood Canal almost cut them down.

Lindstrom swore. "So much for running lights," he said as he pulled the helm over to take them inside the other vessel's turn and they ran port side to its starboard. "Almost left some paint there. Time check?" he asked.

"Twenty forty-three!" called McPherson.

They came abreast of the south end of Whidbey Island, picking up the lights at Point No Point and Possession Point. Arundel and Logan launched the dory and they towed it in.

"John," said McPherson, "you can pass the sacks up from the hold."

"I'm scarcely dressed for this sort of thing."

"You can get the hotel valet to make you pretty again. Get in the damn hold!"

"First time I've heard you swear," said

Lindstrom. Logan grinned.

Romilly stepped gingerly into the hold and started passing up sacks to McPherson and Logan. Arundel, continually estimating their position from sights on the two lighthouses, finally called out. "We should be in position."

McPherson moved to the back of the wheelhouse and took down the spotlight. He flashed the Morse letter 'X,' the signal for the day.

"It's all very well to run on moonless nights, but local navigation isn't helped when you can't see anything," said Arundel from the after deck.

"You managed in the Baltic, and there were no lighthouses on the German coast."

"Had another officer on board to drive the boat so I could take star shots, and we didn't have to worry about getting cases of whiskey to the shore."

"Tide's ebbing," said Lindstrom. "I'm taking her out on another circle. Don't want to ground her and be left stranded on a dry beach when daylight comes."

"Roy make up the money yet?" McPherson asked Arundel quietly.

"I don't know."

"We'll treat him as if he has. It'll save embarrassment. I'll swap runs in the dory with you, Jeff can run the loading, and John can stay in the hold—provided someone answers."

He kept flashing the recognition signal in the direction of the beach. "Even if they can't see the signal directly, they should get the flash of it on the sand." McPherson frowned. "What's taking them so long? I want us to be off this beach quickly and we don't want to lay over in Seattle with a full hold."

"There's a light," called Lindstrom. "Off the port bow."

"I'll get the hook." McPherson walked carefully forward and uncleated the rope holding the anchor to the deck.

"Dash dot dash dot," read out Lindstrom.

McPherson dropped the anchor over the side and went back to pull the dory alongside. "I'll take the first run. Let's do fifty bags per load, so six runs in total."

They managed the fifteen-minute turnaround for each load. McPherson had the last one and Olmstead was there holding the canvas bag with the money. McPherson pointedly did not ask him whether he had settled up with the Arundels or whether this bag held the right amount.

"Just under two and a half hours. Not too bad—we'll do better with practice. Are you coming into town tonight?" said Olmstead.

"Wasn't thinking of it. I planned to stay on the boat."

"Elise wants to talk to you."

"Peter's going in."

"It's about changes to the radio schedule. She wants you."

"See you later then. Same place?"

"Yes."

McPherson took the money bag, got into the dory, and rowed back. Lindstrom had the engine running by the time he came aboard. They hauled the anchor and brought the dory inboard.

"Not before time. We'd have had to shift anchor if we took any longer on shore," said Lindstrom.

"Set course for Seattle. Are you all right staying on the boat alone?" McPherson asked. "There should be over nine thousand dollars in that bag. Elise wants to talk to me, but I should be back in just over an hour."

"I'll be fine."

As they pulled up to the wharf in Seattle, Arundel said quietly to Lindstrom, "There's more money in the bag. Roy made up the shortfall. I counted it; there's over eleven thousand in there. Better tie up where there's lots of light."

"Lucky I kept the shotgun," said Lindstrom.

"If the Customs show up, we're down here for engine parts and we'll be going in the morning."

Arundel turned to Logan. "When can I promise *Rit'waxl* for deliveries again? She gives us a lot of options for places to bring loads in. If they're not all going to Olmstead, I have to know where I can promise."

"She's ready to go anytime now," said Logan. "Between the trials and that run down here, I've an idea of what parts we need to stock to keep her running. I don't think Aki has done the fixed cover yet, though."

"So far, we're the only ones running Liberties," said Arundel. "Once people see us doing it, we can expect some copycats and the price will go up."

"I'll go over to Finnerty's and lay in some spares," said Logan. "Can I have them delivered to the boat tomorrow, and can you pay for them when they get here?"

"Yes," said Arundel.

McPherson cut in. "I'm heading for the Alexis. You two coming?"

"Dressed like that?" asked Romilly.

"Unless you have anything better that would fit me."

"No."

"It's all right," said Arundel. "It's after midnight. The cream of society will have left and it'll just be us ugly ones."

Chapter 28

Seattle, Monday, January 5th, 1920

Arundel led McPherson and Romilly rapidly down the alley at the back of the Alexis Hotel. "Olmstead has ramped up the security," he said, in answer to McPherson's puzzled look. The smell of tobacco was almost overwhelming, but they could not tell where it was coming from.

They knocked at a door inset in the wall beside a loading dock. A peephole opened at eye level and a voice on the other side said, "Okay!" The door opened enough to let them in one at a time. They squeezed into a small corridor where the doorman looked disdainfully at their disheveled appearance.

"If Roy hadn't told me to expect you, I'd have left you out there," he said.

"We'll do better next time when we're not so rushed," replied Arundel.

The doorman gave no reaction but nodded at the door at the other end of the corridor. Arundel went first and pushed it open. "No surprises here," he said. "There's another peephole and the door's heavy."

There was another man waiting on the other side who said, "Check your guns here, gents. We don't want any misunderstandings getting out of hand." Behind him there was a counter with a glass top, beneath which were rows of pistols and knives with tags attached. They let him feel the outside of their pockets before they were allowed to go through a steel gate separating them from the main floor of the club. "Lieutenant Olmstead don't like guns, or people messing up the furniture by fighting."

"Reassuring," said McPherson.

The main room of the club was noisy even at this late hour. McPherson had not noticed when he was here before how free of smoke the room was with the number of people puffing on cigarettes and cigars. A slight breeze running through it told of an electric extractor fan that took the smoke out into the alley, which explained the smell out there. They looked around for Olmstead and found him in a raised corner of the room. A band was playing noisily in another corner. They pushed their way through the crowd toward Olmstead's table.

Olmstead grinned as they walked up and said, "We'd better let Elise get Dugald out of her system. She's been going on about what we need to do with the radio, and I don't understand any of it. Peter, there's a couple of guys I want you to meet over here." Arundel tried to protest, but Olmstead pushed him in the other direction.

McPherson sat down and leaned in toward Elise so he could hear her over the band. "What's up? We could have found a quieter place to talk."

"It's better if we stay here. Roy gets a bit jealous if I talk to a man and he can't see me."

"Do all American men get so possessive? I've not come across that before."

"Like anyone, they have their merits and their drawbacks. I go along—Roy's married and that makes it complicated enough."

McPherson didn't want to get into a conversation on that subject, so he moved on. "What's the problem with the radios?"

"It's nothing to do with the radios, and Roy doesn't know anything about this. It's John Romilly."

"He's an annoying prig, but we seem to be stuck with him."

"When I told you I didn't know anything about the Admiral's family life, it wasn't true. I do know something about John. Before the war, he was up at Oxford and got involved with a student club that was very sympathetic with the people who became the Bolsheviks in Russia. His father put it down to the sort of stupidity that students always get themselves involved in. The war started and he went into the navy, and everyone thought that was the end of it. That's why I didn't say anything. But two things have happened to change my mind. The first is, I got a note from Captain Anstruthers in Victoria last week saying John's name had come up as a contact for a group of people in Shanghai."

"Shanghai?"

"A lot of people fleeing Russia come through there. Where the old regime goes, the new one follows. They're usually looking for things of value that the old owners are taking with them."

"I don't see the connection."

"The Bolsheviks have a lot of people involved in the labour movement here, and if you look at the papers, you see a lot of strikes happening throughout Europe and North America. Most are local grievances. They were papered over during the war but they're boiling back up. The people coming to power in Russia are very interested in making their movement international, and they think that stoking any kind of political dispute will help their cause."

"How would chasing down members of the old regime help the new one to encourage labour problems here?"

"Many of the White Russians—the old regime—are carrying large amounts of valuables. Some know the identities of the of the people in the new regime—at least, so the Admiral thinks." The band stopped between sets and it was easier to hear her. Elise continued, speaking more quietly. "I wouldn't have been concerned, even with Captain Anstruthers's warning, other than making sure John knew no more about the details of our business than he could find out by asking anyone on the street. But then the second thing happened two days ago. A couple of young men with strange accents showed up and knew enough about our business to start hanging around Roy's drivers. We only found out they were Russians when one of our men, whose family came from there, heard them talking to one another."

Elise looked around the room, saw Olmstead and waved. "We don't have a problem with the labour thing—it's even good for business when the workers go on strike because they get together and drink more, at first anyway. But the two Russian lads didn't get involved with the local agitators; they only seemed to want to talk to our men. One of Roy's policemen saw them at it and talked to our men afterwards. Turned out they were looking for information on what we do. Roy's policemen found the Russians and told them to move along. These two showing up after I had the note from Captain Anstruthers about John all seemed too much of a coincidence."

"How long have they been here?" asked McPherson.

"A couple of months, perhaps. I only just heard about them, but I've asked Roy to have his policemen check."

"Roy still hasn't found out who it was behind that ambush in Chuckanut Bay last month. We never saw any faces other than Burnand and he wouldn't have been leading it." McPherson thought for a moment. "John associated with some odd people at university, and everyone thought he'd moved on. Now we find the same sort of people hanging about and asking questions, but John himself hasn't given us any reason directly to cause any suspicion. Has he?"

"The one issue doesn't necessarily follow from the other. One thing I learned in intelligence was, never trust a coincidence until you're sure it is one—or isn't."

"Have you told Peter all this?"

She paused before replying. "They're cousins, and the family's all tied to Admiral Romilly. I wasn't sure what the reception would be like."

"You work for the Arundels, though."

"Not entirely. I was sent by Admiral Romilly to help the business run smoothly. There's a lot of money tied up in it."

"So, you're telling me as a way of kicking the problem upstairs."

"The Admiral was quite clear about my telling you about any concerns I had."

"He didn't know I'd be involved in all this, at least not before you left England."

"You'll find he's been in on this from the beginning."

"And now we find it's his son who may be the big concern. Speaking of co-incidences, I met Peter unexpectedly on a boat coming home when the Admiral would have known my travel arrangements. It seems a lot of thought has gone into getting me involved, not just Captain Anstruthers's explanation of having to look after local, well-connected pirates." McPherson leaned back in his chair and took a long breath. "That explains some things. I wonder if they'll make me guess the rest?" He looked out over the room. Olmstead was in a group in the middle and Arundel was off to one side talking to a woman who had her back to him. There was no sign of Romilly. He stood up for a better look and still couldn't see him. "John's not here; would you go round the room and have a look? I'll go down to Roy and check there."

He went down the two steps to the main floor, checking the room as he went up to Olmstead. "All sorted out," he said. He looked around again and moved next to Arundel. "See Romilly anywhere?" he asked quietly.

"No," answered Arundel.

"Hello, Dugald." Maureen White, standing beside Peter, spoke pleasantly.

McPherson looked at her and saw, over her shoulder, Jim White coming toward them. McPherson ignored Maureen and stepped past her, cutting off her father.

"Hello, Jim. Not going to have another fight, are we?" he asked.

"Can't you keep this bastard away from my daughter?"

"Easy Jim, they might be talking business."

"We don't do any business."

"We might do, if you want to buy from us and use your own boats for delivery."

White cooled down when Arundel turned his attention away from Maureen. "Olmstead gives us problems in Seattle," he said.

"And I'll give you more if you put your nose in here," said Olmstead, who had come up behind them.

"Don't do business in Seattle," said Arundel. "Roy here could use someone to take the Coast Guard's attention away from him, and if you service towns up and down the Sound, they're going to be spread pretty thin."

Olmstead grunted, looked at White and said, "Stay out of my town." He turned away.

"I'm not sure he likes to be reminded about the limits to his influence," McPherson said quietly to Arundel.

Elise came back from looking around the room and shook her head. "We seem to have lost John again," said McPherson. "We're leaving by midday tomorrow, if anyone sees him to tell him. I'm tiring of his habit of going missing when we want him, and showing up when we don't."

"I'll get my boys on it," said Olmstead, turning back to them.

"Thanks. I'm going back to the boat," said McPherson, "Now I am worried," he said quietly to Elise on the way out.

Arundel walked up the wharf at noon, still without Romilly. He was wearing the same suit and whistling. "Pilot!" he called out as he stepped aboard.

"Go get changed, will you? Logan should be back soon, and we'll need your help with the parts. Wouldn't want to get your clothes dirty," said McPherson.

Logan came back to the boat with a truckload of engine parts and Finnerty, who wanted the money for them. They moved the boat to a part of the wharf where they could load it. Lindstrom looked over the load and asked Finnerty, "Did you weigh this?"

"Four thousand, three hundred and twenty-eight pounds, and less than five ounces."

"Nice and precise."

"I'm a scrap metal dealer. I buy and sell by weight, with an allowance for packing."

"What's in here?" asked Arundel.

"Three engines in crates plus a bunch of spare parts Jeff thought you might want."

"Those engine crates need to be stowed properly," said Lindstrom. "We'll take out the mid-level planking from the hold and use some of them as shims under the crates. We can put two forward and one toward the stern. The rest of the stuff can go wherever it fits, with as much in the forward locker as possible to keep the bow down. Come and have a look."

"You two settled up?" McPherson asked Arundel when Finnerty went back to his truck and Logan went aft with Lindstrom. Arundel shook his head. “There’s two men standing on the sidewalk over by the restaurant at my eleven o’clock. Don’t make a big point of it but look round as if you’re counting off the load and see if you recognize them.”

Arundel took his notebook and pen out of his pocket and made as if he were counting items on Finnerty’s truck. “No,” he said, “but they just pulled back and into a doorway out of sight, although they might be able to see us through the corner of that restaurant window. Why are you concerned?”

“We’re carrying over eleven thousand dollars in cash. Ollie and I took turns staying awake last night and we had a Seattle cop standing guard at the wharf’s gangway. This town’s as good as Victoria when it comes to knowing who’s moving stuff around. When you’ve finished with Finnerty, come on down to the aft deck. I need to ask you about something, but not here.”

Twenty minutes later Arundel settled with Finnerty and came back to the wheelhouse while the others started to load. McPherson had unclipped Lindstrom’s shotgun and was watching people passing on the street alongside. “Elise is worried about young Romilly,” he said. “How much do you really know about him?”

Arundel looked out over the harbour before answering. “What’s her concern, and why did she raise it with you?”

“She’s had a warning from someone that people in Shanghai are asking about him and she’s kicked the problem upstairs.”

“Is that someone Captain Anstruthers, and were the inquiries from someone who seemed to be Russian?”

“A pair of young Russian men have been hanging around Roy’s drivers asking about our operations. One of the drivers has Russian parents and he confirmed the language. Roy heard about it, sent some of his men to find them, and moved them along.

Now they've disappeared—unless they were the two hanging around on the street over there."

"John went a little off the rails at university before the war, but the family thought he had settled down."

"Elise knows about his university days and she's not about to put this information down as a coincidence. Do you have any idea about what two stray Russians might be looking for?"

"No."

McPherson frowned. "Not very convincing, but this is no place to argue about it. Are you coming back with us?"

"No. I'd better find John. Can you drop me by the Pike Place Market? It'll be faster than walking."

"I'll tell Ollie."

It took them another hour to finish loading. McPherson and Arundel put the hatch covers back and secured them. They cast off immediately and got underway. When the diesel rumbled to life and the boat reversed away from the wharf, they stood by the hatch coaming holding on to the mast. McPherson automatically faced aft, looking for anything that might obstruct their way.

Lindstrom took them out from the boats moored ahead of them, switched the engine to slow ahead, and swung out toward the fairway. McPherson came forward into the wheelhouse. Arundel followed him, saying, "I saw a boat pull out from the wharf ahead and move into the lineup in front of us. Might be nothing, but..."

McPherson grabbed the binoculars and used them to pick out the boat off their starboard bow. "He's just pulled out of the line—looks like he's trying to hide amongst that crowd of work boats while waiting for those two ahead of us to pass him. He looks familiar—might be the same one that ran at us in Chuckanut Bay."

Lindstrom eased the wheel over slightly and let the boat behind them come up on the starboard side, giving them another screen behind which they could maneuver. "I'll try speeding up to see if that has him make a move," he said. He pushed the throttle to Half Ahead. "He's certainly going to be faster than us. If we have any luck, we can confuse him before we head in to drop Peter off. Where's the Pike Place Market wharf?"

"About a mile ahead," said McPherson, looking at the shoreline.

Lindstrom pushed the throttle to Full Ahead and kept the boat alongside between them and the other craft. "The extra weight we're carrying makes her a bit sluggish. Maybe losing as much as a couple of knots," he called out.

McPherson shifted the glasses to the other boat. "He's speeding up and trying to get ahead of the boat beside him. He's trying to keep at least one boat between us all the time. Let's assume he's got the glasses on us." He waited for a moment. "That's not working. He doesn't have the speed to get in front and cut over. At least we know what speed he can make." He paused again. "He's dropping back—looks like he'll try to come up behind us. We've got two boats between us now and he's going to be too busy trying to work his way through traffic. See if we can move in front of this boat. If we can lose him now, it's our best chance."

"Harbourmaster's going to love us," said Lindstrom as he swung in front of the boat beside them. "We've got enough speed to get by him anyway." They waited for five minutes while the boats settled into new positions.

"It worked," said McPherson. "There are two boats between us and he's coming up fast on the other side of the far one. He's lost us for the moment. Anyone else we can hide behind?"

Lindstrom slotted in behind a tug coming out from the docks and pulled back to Half Ahead.

"The Pike Place wharf'll be up in another five minutes," said McPherson. "That tug'll cover us for the run up to it." He trained the glasses on the wharf. "Nothing else moored to it. Peter—we'll do a slow approach and then a brush pass at the wharf so you can jump off. We can still use the tug to keep our friends out of sight." Arundel nodded.

Lindstrom brought the boat up slowly and Arundel braced himself on the deck beside the wheelhouse. When they were a foot away from the wharf, he jumped, landed on his feet, and waved as they pulled away.

"Let's go home, Ollie," said McPherson.

They came out from behind the tug and ran up into the long line of boats heading out of the harbour. The other craft appeared about two miles ahead of them, coming toward them.

McPherson called out, "Everyone into the wheelhouse. Jeff, get down into the galley. We don't want them counting heads, then they'll know we dropped someone off. We just want them to guess. Ollie, if he comes near us, move over and shunt him; he's more fragile than we are." He kept the binoculars focused on the oncoming boat. "I count three heads in the wheelhouse." They approached each other rapidly even at the regulation speed for the harbour. McPherson kept the glasses on the other boat as it moved sharply to starboard. "I can't be sure, but one of those heads looks like Romilly."

"Have to leave that to Peter to work out—he'll have Olmstead to help if he needs it," said Lindstrom.

Chapter 29

Victoria, Tuesday, January 6th, 1920

The wind picked up as they breasted Port Townsend. The extra weight they were carrying made the *Lady Jane* wallow so she was harder to handle than usual. The loss of two knots from full speed brought them to the warehouse almost eleven hours after leaving Seattle, shortly after midnight. McPherson and Lindstrom had shared the helm and Logan had spent a wet and cold time on the foredeck, looking out alternatively for floating logs and the Coast Guard. The *Arcata* had passed them coming into Port Townsend, well past her usual docking time, but had left them alone.

"Too close to quitting time," said Logan.

"We'll unload her in the morning," said McPherson. "I'll be talking to the Major, but I'll stop by afterwards. We should do a test run in *Rit'waxl* before we take her down again. Noon work for everyone?"

The other two nodded. They secured the boat and McPherson drove them home. He went back to the hotel. He dropped into bed utterly exhausted, but even then, could not sleep as he tried to work out what Romilly was doing.

In the morning McPherson woke, not particularly refreshed, but a shower and breakfast helped. He walked over to the office at ten o'clock. He had the canvas sack with the money inside slung over his shoulder and covered by his duffel coat. He handed it over to Michael Arundel when he walked in.

"Peter counted it, said it brought them up to date. There are chits in there for Ollie and Jeff. Peter paid for the engines and parts from another pocket." Arundel took the sack and McPherson continued. "I need to talk to you about young Romilly again. The first problem is Elise is nervous about him and kicked the problem up to me; the second is that he disappeared the night we pulled in and didn't show up again on the wharf when we left. The third problem is that we had a boat trailing us on the way out which looked like it might have been the same one that ran at us in Chuckanut Bay last month. I can't swear to it but it looked like John was one of the three people in its wheelhouse. The fourth problem is that Elise told me two young men, identified by one of Roy's people as Russian, were hanging around his operations in Seattle."

Arundel put the sack in a desk drawer and locked it. "I know. Peter telephoned me yesterday. It's all part of a larger problem we have been unable to discuss with you."

"Sounds big enough; Elise said she got a warning relayed directly from Captain Anstruthers. How deep does all this go?"

"I can only tell you what I know. You'd better sit down—this will take a while." McPherson took the offered chair, and Arundel continued. "I have to go back a bit. Admiral Romilly took you to meet the King in London."

"Yes, but I'm surprised you know about it. The Admiral told me to keep quiet about what I'd been doing. He had a box in his desk that contained the British War Medal, the Victory Medal, and the Naval General Service Medal with a clasp on it which said NW Persia. He took them out and gave them to me. I asked about the clasp because I'd never been there."

"And the Admiral said the government wished to preserve the fiction that it had not been fighting in Russia," said Michael.

"How do you know that? The Admiral told me if that ever came out, he'd come and find me."

"As you know, the Admiral only gives information to people who need to know it, and, as you can see, I've been let in on part of the story. Presumably the visit to His Majesty came soon afterwards?'

"Yes. I was sent to a tailor in the Admiralty basement to have the ribbons put on my jacket, and the next morning, Sir James took me personally through a small door at the side of Buckingham Palace. That led to a staircase, a long corridor and into a study where the King looked up from his desk at me, and said, "You again!"

"Yes, I'm told he has a direct manner of speaking."

"I didn't know what to say so I just said, 'Sir!' The King took a small case from his desk drawer and took out a medal, pinned it on my jacket, and said, 'I'm told this is more than well deserved.' I looked down and saw I had the Distinguished Service Order. That was a surprise because I knew junior officers didn't get it too often."

Arundel said, "And then he went on to say, 'I'm told we have no further immediate need for your services, Commander, and that you will be returning to that delightful part of our Dominion.'"

"I could ask," said McPherson, "how you know all this?"

"Sir James wrote to us and gave the details, because after you said, 'Yes, Your Majesty,' he said, 'I've no doubt your career will continue in a profitable manner.' I believe you replied, 'I hope so, sir.'"

"You have almost the entire conversation."

"Let me just talk about what the Admiral told you and you'll know how far I've been brought into the picture. He would have said that the King was unusually talkative, and that often means he's marked you for future service. You must have had difficulty imagining how you'd ever be in his path again."

"That's right."

"The Admiral will have told you the one valuable lesson to learn here is the King reigns over more than four hundred and fifty million people and he concerns himself about what they're thinking. Two thirds of his relatives just got booted from their comfortable perches and one got murdered by his less-than-grateful subjects. The King is surrounded by people who tell him what they want him to know, and he knows that if he wants to survive, he needs a network of people whom he can contact for different opinions. As often as not, those people might be considered 'junior officers'—it helps with continuity if they don't all retire at the same time."

Arundel got up, walked over to the window, came back, and sat down again. "He will have told you about wars being handy in one way because they give the King the opportunity to meet people who have done good deeds and proved themselves reliable. He told you the King may never call you, but you're on the list and it may be one of his yet-to-be-born grandchildren who needs you. What he didn't tell you was it was he himself who recommended you to the King. From reports the Admiral got from your immediate superiors, he deemed you were just the sort of man the King would want—competent, careful, and discreet."

"This is gratifying, but I'm a bit out of my depth in this kind of company," said McPherson.

"The Admiral, and by extension, the King, appears confident in your abilities, and above all, your discretion."

McPherson sat back in his chair and took a moment to think of a reply. He looked back at Arundel and said, "It's only because you're quoting the admiral and the details of a conversation where it was only he and I in the same room that I find any of this believable. I assume, then, you're on his list, too."

"I'm simply retired, and though Peter has his competent moments, no one would consider him uniformly discreet. I was just called out for the war to tidy up some loose ends where my erstwhile colleagues needed help. I understand, at the end of the conversation, when you were outside, Admiral Romilly told you the list contains the names of, perhaps, little more than a hundred people whom His Majesty has decided are sufficiently reliable for him to entrust with some of his most sensitive concerns."

"Yes," said McPherson. "That's exactly what was said."

"Peter and I are aware of the list's existence, but we are not among those included on it. We may, however, by making a request through the Admiral, avail ourselves of the services of its members. Your meeting Peter on the night boat was not a coincidence."

"I had worked that out. What I don't understand is how your business causes you to ask for help from the king?"

"You will, I am certain, appreciate that the particular business in which we find ourselves engaged requires a good deal of money to initiate and maintain it. The profits are immense, and as you have noted, the risks are extensive. You will also know from reading any newspaper that the world is in much turmoil. Of his relatives who fell from their places of eminence, His Majesty's cousin, the German Kaiser, is of no concern to him, but the fate of another, the Tsar of Russia, who was, after all, on our side in the war, distressed him.

"He was requested to arrange a place of refuge for the Romanov family somewhere in the Empire. The King's advisers deemed it to be unwise to do so publicly. The Royal Navy's, and your, presence in the

Caspian Sea was initially ordered so as to have a force on hand to aid in his extraction should it have been necessary. That part of the operation was superseded when the family were murdered by their captors last year. What was not superseded was the need to do something with a large sum of money sent by the Tsar to the care of His Majesty prior to the revolution. His Majesty has been good enough to refer it to the Romilly family bank in London for management. The directors of the bank decided it was desirable to segregate those funds in every respect from any others they administer on behalf of our royal family."

McPherson was slowly absorbing the scope of the information. "I certainly knew there's money and influence behind this trade, but I thought it was the usual collection of merchant bankers who show up here from time to time. Isn't there a risk this information can leak out?"

"There is no direct link to our relationship with His Majesty's funds. As you say, it could be only the kind of people who are often active here. On one hand, this particular relationship closes several options for conventional investing, but it does open up opportunities for their use in less orthodox ways."

"Are you telling me the King is the financier for this business?"

"In a manner of speaking, and among others, yes, although I'd be surprised if he knew it. His instructions to our bank are clear; he requires that the principal and a sum equivalent to an adequate annual return be held in trust until such time as a suitable heir to the Tsar is identified."

"Isn't this business an enormous risk for that purpose?"

"No greater that being a 'name' on a syndicate at Lloyd's and it does have the advantage of being comparatively liquid, so if an heir is determined tomorrow, funds can be made available."

"He must trust the Romillys."

"We've earned it over several generations."

"We? Are you part of the bank? I thought you just married into the family."

"I hold no formal appointment, but since the bank is a private one, the directors are free to involve anyone they trust in managing its activities. They've been good enough to give me a role."

McPherson took a deep breath and looked at the ceiling. "Coming back to the immediate difficulty, what about John, then? He doesn't seem to fit too well in any of this."

"The family has had other bad ones along the way, not unlike the royal family in that respect. They've always made good on any deficiency."

"So, what do we do with him? And the two men he seems to have joined in Seattle? And why, then, are they shooting at us?"

"If John is involved, it has to be a political issue along the lines suggested by his pre-war associations. We must assume these two men are associated with the new regime in Russia. If they're here, it's likely that someone has discovered the Tsar's money is involved. They would have to know these dollars are actually located in London and the only part of it that's here is what we collect."

"They might be looking for the cash Roy pays us, but that can only be a minor fraction of the total amount, so they have to be looking for some leverage to gain the whole sum by other means," said McPherson. "They haven't been around for a long time, but they did discover we were doing business with Roy. They asked too many questions and presumably one of Roy's men was quite forceful with them, so they slunk back in a hole and only re-emerged when John appeared. One advantage is that with John having joined them, we at least know who they are."

"That's an excellent point," said Arundel,

looking approvingly at McPherson. He stopped and moved an inkwell around on his desk while he thought. "I don't know much about the motivation of criminals," he went on, "so I can't think what items of value would force the Romilly family to hand over money entrusted to its care, unless it was something of greater value. Like a person, for example."

"That would be a family member or someone they saw to be of value," replied McPherson, "and at this moment, the most vulnerable one is Peter. If they tried to get him in Victoria, they knew the authorities would arrest them almost on arrival. He's in the United States now, where they have much greater freedom of movement even with Roy's men on the lookout." He frowned. "We need to get him out—now—and now means using *Rit'waxl*. Jeff assured me she ready to go, so I can leave immediately."

"Peter's there to pick up his wife. She landed in San Francisco a few days ago and is heading for Seattle. We have to wait for him to call in. I don't even know where he is at the moment."

"I can't think of anything that's more important than dodging kidnappers and if we have Peter and his wife to worry about, the problem just got much larger. Can't you use an emergency call to Elise? She could get Roy to help round them up. He's not likely to be keen on having the Russians in the neighborhood either."

"I'll do that. Why don't you go over to the warehouse, get the boat ready, and I'll phone through when I get word."

"It would have been handy if the radio could have been installed, but we can keep that in mind for later. I'll do this run solo. I don't want to be risking Ollie's life, and no one else knows enough about handling *Rit'waxl*. The boat should be tested after the repair job, but we'll just have to risk it. I don't want to be out in the Straits when the call for a pickup comes in. I'll pick up my working rig from the hotel on the way.

Pass the message over to the warehouse if it comes in while I'm on the way."

"I could come with you."

"Not to be impolite, but a boat's no place to be if you don't know what you're doing. If I pick up Peter, he can help on the way back. That'll ease the load a bit."

Lindstrom was at the warehouse with Logan when he arrived. "What are you doing here so early?" said Lindstrom.

"We thought we'd get the boat unloaded and fixed, then disappear before you showed up," added Logan. "We were just about to leave. Why the working rig? We're just going to test the boat."

"Have to delay the test for a while. I might have to do a run."

"I'll get set and come with you," said Lindstrom.

"I can handle it, Ollie; this is going to be a rough one. I have to pick Peter off a hostile shore. Jeff knows what that means."

"I'm the one who can handle the shotgun, and my wife's a lot more understanding about the risks of the business than his," said Lindstrom. "You need help. I'm your man. Tell Arundel to put some money aside, so if I don't come back, my wife'll have something."

"Thanks, Ollie. I'll arrange it," McPherson said. "Let's get the tanks topped up, then."

Logan and Lindstrom checked the engines and all the control linkages, ran the blower for a minute, then started the diesel. Logan took it over to the fuel float.

"Would be nicer if Aki had got that fixed top together," said McPherson. "When Jeff gets back, let's roll the canvas one up and stow it behind the cockpit. Have you got some extra shotgun shells? This is the kind of show where we might need them."

"They're in the *Lady Jane*. I'll get them."

Lindstrom walked up the dock just as the watchman came out the other way from the office.

"Major Arundel's on the telephone for you, Commander." McPherson diverted over to the office and picked up the receiver.

Michael didn't waste any time. "Elise called—Peter's ready for pick up."

"Where is he now?"

"In Seattle."

"In any immediate danger?"

"Olmstead's men are watching the outside of the building, but we've no way of knowing whether there's some local help we don't know watching, too."

"It's worse than you thought then?"

"Yes."

"In that case, we need to arrange a pick-up point where anyone trying to interfere can be easily spotted. It's a daytime run at full speed, so even if we can run on the quiet rig, someone's likely to see us. Is it absolutely necessary that we get them today?"

"Yes. His wife arrived and we need to get them out now."

"I'll not argue, then." Lindstrom came into the office and stood against the wall. "Just a moment, Ollie just came in." McPherson turned to him. "Ollie—Puget Sound chart? We need a place with good road links to Seattle that both Peter and *Rit'waxl* can reach in about the same length of time."

"Thought you'd need it." Lindstrom unrolled it on the desk and opened the road atlas they kept in *Lady Jane.*

"We need a place with a wharf. It'll be the same sort of brush-pass pickup that we used to drop Peter in Seattle. We'll need a recognition signal too. A light's no good in the daytime." McPherson traced the coastline with his finger stopping at possibilities. Lindstrom followed them in the atlas, shaking his head at most of them.

"How about Meadowdale?" McPherson said finally. Lindstrom nodded. "You hear that?" he said into the telephone, waited, and nodded at Lindstrom. "If we run at full speed, it looks like about two and a half hours from here," he told Arundel. "It's close enough to Seattle and remote enough on the coast to give us what we want. If we get anyone trying to cut us off, we can use the islands to screen us on the way out. Looks like it has a town wharf."

Lindstrom nudged his elbow. "Signal?" he asked.

McPherson nodded and paused for a moment. "That just leaves some way of recognizing each other," he said into the telephone again. "We'll be navigating our way in and hoping any fog will have blown off by the time we get there. I think a large white towel waved from a pole would do. They'll recognize us by the sound of our engines. It's not perfect, but it's the best we can do at short notice. Peter will know enough to have a fallback if they miss us on the first run."

He waited for another moment. "Will you repeat this back, please? You'll need to repeat it to Elise, so we need to keep the instructions as simple as possible to avoid confusion." He listened as Arundel repeated the instructions and then added, "A large white towel on a pole and listen for our engines." He looked over at Ollie. "He'll call it down and confirm back to us."

McPherson waited at the office while Lindstrom went to meet Logan coming back from the fuel float. McPherson joined them five minutes later. "They'll be there," he said. He threw off the lines and Lindstrom headed the boat toward the Outer Harbour. "Our secret existence is now officially over." He stowed the chart in the locker and put the Puget Sound Pilot in the chart table drawer. He took out his notebook and marked bearings from the chart to major landmarks around Meadowdale. He worked out a triangulation pattern that would confirm their location when they arrived and drew it in his book.

"Okay. It's now eleven forty-five hours. Estimate fourteen fifteen arrival. Let's start the mains as soon as we hit the Outer Harbour marker."

Chapter 30

There was enough of a swell running when they started the engines and sailed out into the Straits to make the run uncomfortable, but not enough to slow them down. They cut in the exhaust bypasses and ran quietly. Sitting continuously was tiring. The seats, even cushioned, amplified the shock of the hull cutting through the waves. For much of the journey, they both found it less restrictive to stand on the shuddering deck, where their bent knees absorbed part of the shock.

They turned south into Puget Sound, keeping closer to the west side of San Juan Island, curbing the chance that they might catch the attention of someone at the Coast Guard Station at Port Townsend. The *Arcata* was nowhere in sight, and a mile down the Sound they moved closer to mid-channel. When they passed the two-hour mark after leaving Victoria, McPherson started taking bearings on shore landmarks.

"Half-speed both engines, Ollie," he called, as he rechecked bearings and picked up the binoculars to examine the shore. "Cut out the bypass both engines." The noise increased substantially. "Take her in southeast by east. We'll run into position about two hundred yards from shore and then circle if there's no signal." McPherson handed over the binoculars and pointed. "Do you see the wharf?"

"Got it. We'll go in a little closer so I don't lose it against the background." Lindstrom handed back the binoculars, sat back into his seat and fastened the safety belt. They circled again, now about one hundred and fifty yards from the shore.

McPherson kept watching through the binoculars. Another ten minutes passed. "It's fourteen fifteen hours," he called out. They did two more ten-minute circles. "There's some movement on shore," he called. Lindstrom cut the circle short and pointed the bow at the shore. "White towel flying," McPherson said. "See it?"

"Got it."

"Two people coming down to the lower wharf—it looks like a float. Can you handle both throttles and put the engines in reverse?"

"Yes."

"I'll do the deck and drop them both on the hatch cover when they come aboard. Can you do port side in?"

"Yes. Give me a second to set up." Lindstrom swung the helm to port and then to starboard as he lined up on the wharf. He throttled back to Slow Ahead when he was about twenty-five feet away, closing to three feet off the wharf. McPherson climbed out of the back of the cockpit and threw two fenders over the side as Lindstrom brought the boat in fast. The fenders touched and scraped along the dock as he put both engines in reverse.

McPherson, although crouched on the deck and holding on to the coaming around the hold, was almost catapulted over the side. As the boat came nearly to a stop, he called out, "Now!"

The two on the dock leapt and stumbled onto the deck surface, McPherson pulling them down onto the hatch cover. Lindstrom watched him, and as soon as they were down and holding on, pushed the lever back to Half Ahead and sent the boat back out toward open waters.

McPherson checked that both were uninjured

after the jump, then looked at the second one. "Tatania, I presume?"

"Yes," said a woman's voice, McPherson turned toward her and saw the blonde hair and profile of the woman he had last seen leaving the Cabot Cove almost two years ago.

"Full ahead," called McPherson to Lindstrom. "If it's a clear run we'll go straight home." Lindstrom pushed the throttles forward and the engine noise momentarily rose before he engaged the exhaust cut-outs. "No reason for us to go deaf," McPherson, turning back to Arundel. "Now, Peter, I'm certain there's a story here."

"Dugald, this is my wife, Tatania Gregorovna Shevchenko. You last saw her coming aboard the Cabot Cove in April 1917."

"And what does that have to do with what's going on now and why we had to come screaming down here to pick you up?"

"It's all a bit complicated and not the sort of thing I can easily shout over the sound of this boat hammering over the waves, even if it does have a muffled exhaust."

"*Arcata* on the port bow!" called out Lindstrom as they were passing Port Townsend.

McPherson looked over in that direction and levered himself into the cockpit. Arundel and Tatania came in after him.

"Give me the wheel, Ollie," he said, cinching himself into the seat. "They're blocking us from our direct route to Victoria." He started zigzagging slightly toward the cutter. "Everyone, hold on! With a boat like this, he's going to ask questions about what we're doing—and maybe impound the boat until he gets some answers. I'm not sure we'll have any he'll like. Hopefully he won't shoot first."

Arundel trained the binoculars on the cutter.

"What's he doing?" Lindstrom asked.

"Signaling for us to heave to. Don't know why he thinks we can read Morse Code."

"He'll back it up with a cannon shot, probably near our bow!" McPherson shouted to Arundel.

"His gunner's going to have a hard time resetting his range finder at the speed we're closing in on him," replied Arundel. "He won't be able to depress his barrel without blowing his own bow off before long. Biggest danger will be the machine gun on the bridge, but if he's cranked up to maximum speed he'll be heaving and probably corkscrewing a bit. Makes it hard to maintain his aim."

"What happens when we get close?" asked Tatania.

"The machine gun's on the port wing of the bridge. We'll go up the starboard side close enough for our wake to rock him a bit more. He'll probably try to swing to starboard once he sees what we're doing and he may try the machine gun as we get closer, but he'll still have a hard time keeping the sights on us, especially until he figures out our speed."

The cannon on the cutter's foredeck boomed. "Look for the fall of the shot, everyone!" shouted McPherson.

"One hundred yards off the starboard quarter. That's his warning one!" shouted Arundel.

"See how he does in reloading and adjusting the range." Another thirty seconds passed as McPherson kept weaving toward the cutter. "We're about three hundred yards off his bow, he's starting to turn to starboard, wants to bring the machine gun to bear." The cannon boomed again. This time the shot fell short, one hundred yards in the other direction.

"Hard to maintain an aim when the skipper doesn't warn you," shouted Arundel.

"Probably doesn't have a voice pipe down to the gun. Relies on hand signals from the bridge. That only works if you practice—a lot," replied McPherson. "Swinging to starboard a little quicker, digging his bow in a bit, must be corkscrewing. That machine gun's going to have a hard time bearing on us. I'll swing in as close as I can, but it's not going to be a sure thing."

McPherson had no idea whether Arundel heard him over the roaring engine. He aimed the boat at the bow of the cutter, now noticeably rolling toward them. He saw the gunner on the bridge trying to lift his barrel as the roll of the ship forced him up against the breech. McPherson swung the boat along the cutter's starboard side. Their wake forced its bow up. They heard the machine gun stutter as they came alongside, the hulls clearing each other by inches.

"Missed us!' shouted Arundel.

McPherson turned round and looked to the *Arcata's* stern; another machine gun was aimed at them. He punched Arundel on the shoulder and pointed at it as he swung the wheel to starboard. Tracer rounds snapped by them on the port side.

"Ollie's hit!" Arundel yelled. Lindstrom slumped down in the corner with blood emerging from his right side. Arundel grabbed the first aid kit from the locker on the aft bulkhead. Tatania knelt beside him and opened Lindstrom's jacket. Blood was flowing steadily from a wound just above his waist. She ripped his shirt, folded it into a wad, and pressed it against him.

"The bullet went right through," she shouted and pointed to the exit wound. She pushed her fists against both, while Arundel unwrapped a large bandage. Between them they stopped the blood flow, and as carefully as the lurching boat would allow, moved him back over the cockpit edge and onto the hatch cover.

McPherson kept up an irregular zigzag course to throw off the machine gunner's aim until they were out of range, then throttled back. "He won't try to follow us anyway. Tatania, will you look after Ollie?" To Arundel he said, "Was that a stray bullet or was anything else hit?"

"Looked like we got stitched a bit along the outside of the deck."

"Better have a closer look once you've got Ollie settled."

The *Arcata* was well behind them. McPherson swung north into the group of islands at the south end of Lopez Island to screen them while they looked after Lindstrom. He slowed once the cutter was out of sight.

"Ollie!" called Arundel, "can you hear me?"

Lindstrom nodded and said through clenched teeth, "I'll live."

"Hang on, we'll crank on speed and get you home to a doctor. Peter, check for any more damage," called McPherson.

Arundel crawled away from the hatch cover into the cockpit and ran his hands over the side of the boat. "Looks like some holes here."

"Open up the engine hatch, I'm not keen on the results of tracer rounds near our fuel tanks."

Arundel opened the hatch and peered inside. "Dugald, this doesn't look good. We've taken a bullet by the port engine's fuel tank inlet. Petrol is splashing over the manifold."

"Take the helm."

Arundel slid over and strapped himself in while McPherson took his place. "Ouch. Cut the engine!" McPherson ordered. Arundel leaned forward and threw the ignition switch on the port side. The boat slowed and took on a list from the force of the torque on the starboard engine. "It's enough to get home. We can do about twenty-five knots on the one engine. Can't really go out into the Sound again, though; we'd still be in range of the *Arcata's* cannon and she'll be ready for us. We'll go up San Juan Channel; it won't take us much more time. Ollie all right?"

Arundel looked over at Tatania, raised his eyebrows and looked down at Ollie. She nodded.

"She competent?" asked McPherson.

"She looked after Wilkes when we were limping back to the Cabot Cove."

"Okay! You keep the helm. I'll look at the chart. We'll go out by Friday Harbour and over to Sidney; we can get help for Ollie there. Castle Pass is ahead, turn north when we get to the headland over there," McPherson pointed. Arundel eased the throttle forward and headed for the point of turn.

"We've got company," said McPherson ten minutes later, looking over their port bow.

"It's the same one that was following us out of Seattle," said Arundel.

"They must have worked out we'd be meeting you somewhere on the coast and waited for us off Whidbey Island. If the Coast Guard hadn't appeared first, they'd have hit us already," said McPherson.

"They don't have our speed," Arundel pointed out.

"With us on one engine we don't know that, but they can cross us," McPherson countered.

"Probably be best to run bow to bow until we get some maneuvering room," suggested Arundel.

McPherson agreed. "Let's try that first. Hope he's not carrying anything nasty. There's a few too many rocks around here for us to have much room to dodge him." He pulled out the chart and ducked down to the deck to fold it to where their position could show. "Tell Tatania what we're going to do—she'll need to hang on to Ollie if we have to jink around a bit. What are they looking for?"

"Me," said Arundel. "It's a long story and I'd just as soon wait until we get to shore."

McPherson nodded and clipped the folded chart to its board while holding the wheel steady with his knee. "Can't say I'm surprised. Your father told me some of the story. How's Ollie doing?" Arundel leaned over the back of the cockpit.

"As good as can be expected," he shouted in McPherson's ear when he turned back. "He's hurting a lot, but Tatania got the bleeding stopped for now, anyway."

"There's a rock which is mostly covered at high tide, there," McPherson pointed at the chart. "We'll try the same trick as before and hope they haven't learned anything. I'm going to start edging over a little to see if we can get them to think they can cut us off. Grab the glasses and see what you can make of them."

Arundel picked up the binoculars and wedged himself against the front corner of the cockpit. The bouncing hull made it difficult for him to keep focused on the still-distant boat. "I can see three heads by the helm. He's probably running full out. Difficult to estimate speed, but he's holding steady against the shoreline, so he's probably matching us."

"I'll slow down a bit. I want to pick the place to meet him."

The other boat was clearer at three hundred yards off their port bow. McPherson pulled out the chart again and looked round for landmarks. He took rough bearings on each and adjusted his course and speed again to keep the other boat heading in the direction he wanted.

Arundel put the glasses up again. "John Romilly is definitely one of them. One of the others is wedged against the rail... he's holding a gun of some sort."

"Shotgun?" asked McPherson.

"Can't see."

"If it's a rifle, they'll never get a good aim. If it's a shotgun we need to keep our distance. If it's that sub-machine gun they hit us with before, we need to get something to happen to them before they can open up.

Let's just work on surviving, shall we?" They watched the other boat narrow the distance for a minute.

"Be nice if we could do something other than guess where those rocks are," said Arundel. "Chart makes them about there," replied McPherson, estimating a bearing from two landmarks and pointing over the starboard bow. "It's not very precise, but it's all we can do. I'll pull her over a little to port and make it look as if we're trying to make him overshoot us." The other boat did not adjust its course. "Awful boat handlers," he said. "Looks like they expect to just drive onto us—which they will do if we can't pull them over those rocks." He put the wheel over in the other direction and slowed a little more. "What do you see now, Peter?"

"About the same. The man with the gun is still wedged in place. There's one other who's conning the boat, and Romilly's just leaning on something at the stern. With all this bouncing, can't make out a lot more."

They were closing now, down to fifty yards. The other boat swung over to pass port side to their starboard. The man holding the gun fired a burst. No one saw where the bullets went.

"That's the same one they used before. If it was Burnand shooting either he dropped it before he went overside, or they have more," shouted McPherson. "Hang on!" He whipped the wheel over, putting the rocks between the two boats.

They heard the crash even over the roar of their own engine. The other boat's bow rose, showing the full length of the underside of the hull before it fell back and rolled away from them. McPherson went far enough forward to clear the rocks, eased back the throttle, and turned back to the wreck, now floating upside down with no sign of its crew anywhere on it.

"See anyone?" McPherson asked.

"There's someone in the water twenty yards

ahead, just off the starboard bow. Looks like he might be moving."

"Can you get a line over him?"

Arundel took a coiled rope hooked over a cleat inside the cockpit and carefully worked his way along the deck. He knotted a large, fixed noose at one end and held it over the side of the boat as McPherson, leaning out from behind the windshield, tried to gauge the distance to the now slowly flailing man.

"Hold my feet, Tatania, I don't want to join him in there," Arundel called out. He managed to loop the noose over the man's head and one of his arms and started to drag him behind the boat. McPherson pushed the gear lever to neutral and the engine, losing the need to turn the propeller, raced until he settled the throttle to idle. He went back to help bring the man aboard. It took the two of them to haul him over the rail and settle him on the hatch beside the wounded Lindstrom. He was bleeding heavily from a gash on the forehead, and he screamed as they moved his leg.

"You check him over, Peter. I'm going back to look for any more survivors and then get us some sea room. The *Arcata*'s around here still. With any luck she'll think we're long gone, but you never know."

He did two wide, slow rounds of the area but there was no sign of anyone else in the water. The upturned hull of the other boat was mostly submerged and floating free of the rocks. When they came out into Castle Pass, he had a careful look around and saw the *Arcata* heading south toward Port Townsend. He headed up the pass and into Griffin Bay. He slowed the engine to idle again and looked over the shoreline on both sides of the pass. The occasional light twinkled in the looming dusk and a tug towing what looked like a log boom moved slowly in the other direction. He checked the chart and moved closer to the shore where anchoring seemed possible. He found a site about five hundred yards off a log strewn beach. He cut the engine, went forward to let go the anchor, and came back to join the others.

Tatania was using the remaining bandage from the first aid kit to staunch the flow of blood from the man's head. "He's still bleeding from his arm as well," she said. "He's drifting in and out of..." she searched for the word.

"Consciousness," said Arundel as he put his ear to the man's mouth. "He's breathing, but it's very shallow." Blood seeped through the man's clothes and onto the hatch cover. "It's coming from his back." He leaned down again. "We're going to turn you over." The man's eyes flickered and his lips moved. Arundel put his ear closer. He sat back up again and put his finger to the other's neck to find the carotid artery. He left it there for a minute then looked back up again.

"He's gone."

"Did he say anything?" asked McPherson.

"Just 'Liesel.' That's a German girl's name."

"German? Elise Campbell said you were being chased by Russians."

"Can't explain that. I'll search his clothes, see if there's anything that says something about him."

"Don't take a long time about it," said McPherson. "Right now, we have a dead body we can't explain and I'm not keen on either carrying it around foreign waters or bringing it home. It'll be dark enough in thirty minutes for nobody to see us bury him at sea. I want to do that quickly. Every minute we stay out here makes it harder for Ollie. Our choice is to make a run directly for Sidney, where we know we can get help, or stop at a succession of towns on San Juan Island on the basis that we might get help." He refolded the chart to show their course out. "We'll head for Sidney. I'll get the anchor to wrap around him, so he doesn't float."

"Why don't we just dump him overside?" asked Arundel. "There's an upturned boat to explain a body."

"Didn't you learn anything in the navy? We don't leave casualties floating if we can avoid it." He went into the cockpit, took out the ready-use toolbox and found the monkey wrench. He went forward and unshackled the anchor, together with the leader that was attached to the chain that led to the capstan.

"Any idea of who he is?" he asked when he got back.

"No sign at all," said Arundel. "How's Ollie?"

"Seems to be stable." McPherson knelt down beside them. "Ollie," he called, quietly but firmly. Lindstrom opened his eyes. "We're taking you home. We've got one engine, but we're running light. We can probably get up to thirty knots, so it'll be at least another hour before we make Sidney. It's faster than heading for Victoria. Hang on."

"Okay."

"We need to keep him warmer." McPherson told Arundel. "Help me move the cockpit cover over him," Between them, they levered the unwieldy piece of canvas, unwrapped one side and stretched it over. McPherson took off his sweater from under his duffel coat, rolled it into a pillow and put it under Lindstrom's head. "Are you comfortable staying beside him?" he asked Tatania. She nodded. "We need to put our foreign friend here over the side." He took out his notebook and wrote down the approximate location.

"I hope you don't go into too much detail. What if someone finds your book?" asked Arundel.

"Just the place, date, and time. I'll remember why. The water's deep enough here; it'll look less suspicious doing it now rather than starting the engine, moving the boat, stopping, then starting again."

"We should say something, shouldn't we? I don't know what, though," said Arundel.

"Do you remember what the captain said when we put Wilkes's body over the side off the Danish coast?" asked McPherson. "I was up on the bridge watching you, but I couldn't hear anything."

"I was barely listening, and it went so fast; we gathered on the deck, you stopped the engines, the captain said something, and Wilkes's body slid off the plank."

"I'll think of something. I'll wrap the anchor to him. You pull a plank off the hatch cover and get set to put him over the stern."

Arundel carefully avoided disturbing Lindstrom lying on the other side, and ten minutes later the hatch cover was off. He leaned it against the taffrail, and they moved the body onto it. McPherson was sweating despite the cold, brisk breeze. He took off his hat, put his duffel coat back on and left it open. He sat by the body's head. Arundel took his place on the other side and each of them grasped a cleat mounted at the edge of the cover.

"O Lord, we commit this man's body to the deep and your eternal care." McPherson intoned. "We don't know who he is or why he's here, but he said a woman's name, Liesel. Please protect her because he's no longer there to do it." He put his hat back on. "Okay, Peter, lift and let go!" They lifted the edge of the plank and the body slid away.

They put the plank back in its place over the hold. Arundel knelt on the deck to help Tatania hold Lindstrom. "You managing, Ollie?" he asked.

"*Ja.*"

"I'm going to have to start the diesel to get the Liberty running. The boat's going to shake a bit while we fiddle around." He reached into his inside pocket and pulled out his cigarette case and offered them around.

"Put them away," croaked Lindstrom. "You're going to have to run the extractor fan. There's more gas in the bilge than there is in the tank. One spark and this thing will blow up."

"Thanks, Ollie. I wasn't thinking. Peter, will

you crank up the diesel?" Arundel came into the cockpit, opened the forward hatch, and crawled into the engine compartment.

"Hold on for five minutes while I get the blower going. There's probably no danger from the diesel, but why take chances?" said Arundel. He turned the blower switch and almost passed out from the fumes that vented out of the bilge area. "Need to do something about that."

"Be happy to stay alive long enough to get back so we can point the vent in another direction," said Lindstrom.

They waited the full five minutes, timed on McPherson's watch, before he said, "Start engine!" The diesel chinked to life. "I'm starting starboard engine now," he called as he turned on the ignition. He moved the connecting lever over and the engine coughed a couple of times and then went silent. McPherson silently prayed and disengaged the starting lever. He waited another two minutes to allow the carburetor to drain and then tried again. The engine roared and the boat listed to port as the torque took hold.

He looked back at the hold cover. Tatania was trying to stop Lindstrom from rolling over but his weight was about to overwhelm her. "Peter!" he shouted over the noise of the engine. Arundel poked his head out. McPherson pointed back and then set the engine back to idle. Arundel swung over the back of the cockpit and reached them just in time. Lindstrom's wound had broken open and they'd run out of bandages. Arundel ripped his shirt off from under his sweater and used it to tighten the dressing. McPherson left them to handle it and started to work out the course to take them home.

Piloting a boat hurtling through dark waters at night while the other pair of hands he needed to help him were trying to save a man's life was difficult. The night sky was overcast, although some moonlight was reflected on the clouds and from them onto the water. He picked up the night glasses and looked around him, trying to fix their position. The chart table was a fold-up off to his left and no help if he had to leave the helm to look at it while maneuvering the boat in tight waters. He pulled out his notebook, opened it to two facing pages, and copied out the principal points along the way. He then drew a copy of the route with the turns, bearings and way points marked on it. He had just enough space on the dashboard to clip the open notebook to it and a ledge to hold a flashlight.

The shore lights along the route were minimal. He had one on Cattle Point behind them and Turn Rock in front, which gave him starting bearings. The rest of the trip would be a matter of dead-reckoning based on speed and bearings, as well as his best estimates of tidal currents in unfamiliar waters. He cinched the seatbelt tight, opened up the throttle, and set the boat to the best speed he dared. Cutting in the exhaust bypass made the noise manageable. He looked back to see how his passengers were faring. Arundel gave him a thumbs-up signal.

The channel was a thirteen-mile dog leg, and he veered northwest at Turn Rock, approximately the midpoint. The lights from the town of Friday Harbour coming up on his port side made him feel safe enough in the mid-channel. He estimated their speed was holding at twenty-eight knots. He rechecked his route marked in the notebook with the help of the flashlight. They passed Rocky Bay and he slowed, looking for the entrance to turn west by Spieden Channel. He kept sea room to make sure he got the centre of its half-mile-wide opening.

"You all right, Pilot?" said Arundel's voice in his left ear.

He nodded and said, "We're heading for the north end of Sidney Island. It's about ten miles from here and if we stay on this bearing," he pointed to the compass, "we should be there in just over half an hour. How's he doing?"

"Holding on; it's easier to talk to him with the noise down."

Without warning, the boat lurched, and the bow pointed up for a moment. There was a sound of scraping along the keel, then the bow went down and buried itself in the sea. The engine roared as the propeller came out of the water. Arundel was thrown back onto the rim of the cockpit and landed in a bruised heap on the deck. The boat settled and floated evenly.

McPherson stopped the engine, unclipped himself from the seat and went back to check first on any damage to people.

"Ollie, Tatania—you all right?" he shouted.

"Stupid flaming navy man. We hit something," said Lindstrom weakly.

"I'm alright. The ring around this part of the boat stopped me from sliding into the water," said Tatania.

"Peter?"

"Don't think anything's broken."

"Stay there for a moment. I'll look around." He found the flashlight rolling in a corner of the cockpit deck and crawled up to the bow. He leaned over the side and made his way back to the stern pushing at something alongside in the water.

"There's a log caught on the starboard side," he said when he came back to the cockpit. "It won't go anywhere when I push it, so it's caught on something."

"That something is most likely the propeller," said Arundel. "I had that happen once or twice when I ran little boats around before the war."

"We'll try the diesel. The log might have gone right past its propeller. Peter, you do the start-up if you can." Arundel went into the engine hatch and after a moment, the diesel came to life.

"Try reversing to see if the log comes out," said Arundel. He looked over the side as McPherson put the boat in gear. "It's moving out at an angle, try a bit more speed." McPherson went to Half Ahead. "It's clear."

"I'll try the starboard main now," said McPherson. He moved the starting lever and the engine caught. He moved the gear lever forward. There was a grinding sound from the stern. "Propeller's wrecked," he said, shutting down the ignition. "That log must have bent the shaft. Sorry everyone, we're going to head for Sidney instead of Victoria. Better see if Ollie's comfortable—if not, we might have to drop in at Roche Harbor. It's big enough to have a local doctor and the hotel is bound to be somebody's customer in the rum trade so they'll be friendly."

Arundel went back and returned almost immediately. "He says no to Roche Harbor; he thinks he'll live but if he doesn't, he wants his family around."

"Logic there. Tell him it'll be forty-five minutes to an hour."

They made the dock in Sidney in just over forty minutes. McPherson told Arundel to find a telephone and get some medical help. He tied the boat up on his own and then went back to check on Lindstrom, who beckoned him to come closer. He knelt down beside him. Lindstrom whispered, "Peter pulled something out of that guy's jacket, looked at it and put it in his pocket."

McPherson turned to Tatania and said, "I'll stay here with Ollie. Can you go and wait at the end of the pier to make sure the help comes to the right place?"

"Yes, of course," she said.

McPherson watched her walk away and then turned back to Lindstrom. "What did it look like?"

"Looked like it was a small leather case."

"Did he look inside?"

"No."

"I'll have a talk to Michael. We'll never get the entire truth about anything from him, but I think we've been shot at enough on this trip to be told how much of a risk was involved."

Chapter 31

Sidney, Wednesday, January 7th, 1920

Tatania came running down the dock, a trench-coated man carrying a canvas bag behind her. "This is the doctor," she said breathlessly.

The man swung down easily onto the boat and dropped to his knees beside Ollie. He pulled the makeshift dressings carefully away. "Haven't seen one of these for a year or so," he said. "I'll stitch him up, but we need to get him to hospital." He worked on the wounds for a couple of minutes and then looked up at Tatania. "Will you ask your young man to have the operator call the ambulance?" She went back up to the shore. The doctor looked at McPherson. "Who are you?" he asked.

"I'm Dugald McPherson. I run this boat. This is Ollie Lindstrom—he helps me."

"I'm Ewart. He's probably not in too much danger, although infection can always set in. It's good that you had a first aid kit on board. We only need to keep him stable while we move him. None of my business, but I suppose you're in trade of some sort?"

"Yes," said McPherson.

"Does he have any close relatives around here? They should be told, and they'll probably want to be at the hospital as soon as possible."

"Get Greta and bring her," said Lindstrom quietly.

Tatania came back with Arundel. "Ambulance is on its way," he said.

"Better meet it at the top of the wharf. They'll have to move him on a stretcher," said the doctor.

"I'll go," said Tatania.

"I phoned my father," said Arundel to McPherson. "He's coming to pick us up."

"Have him stop and get Mrs. Lindstrom on the way back. I'll go with you, Doctor, and stay with him until Mrs. Lindstrom arrives," said McPherson.

Ewart's nose wrinkled. "Been a while since I've smelled that combination of fuel and seawater. Hope it doesn't annoy the patient when he gets inside the ambulance."

"He's a fisherman. We're both used to it."

"Help me prepare him to move. I don't want him getting any colder than he is now." They rearranged the canvas tonneau cover. Lindstrom took the moving stoically and only grunted when the covering touched the outer side of the bandages. They waited another half an hour before Tantania came back down the wharf with the ambulance crew. Four of them carried the stretcher up to the shore and gently moved him into the back of the car.

"Nice to have a proper ambulance," said McPherson.

"Yes," replied Ewart. "I don't how they managed to get all these ex-army Crossleys over here, but it's been tremendously useful."

McPherson took a closer look and saw the military markings still showing against the vehicle's white paint but said nothing. There was no sign of Michael Arundel yet, but a Customs Officer appeared from a shed at the head of the wharf. "You people can't go without clearing customs," he said.

McPherson replied, "We're taking this man to St. Joseph's Hospital. This lady is coming with us," he added, pushing Tatiania into the car in front of him.

"Mr. Arundel," he said, pointing, "will take care of the proper procedures."

A cold breeze caught them from the side as the door to the emergency room opened. Cynthia Arundel walked in, a frown creasing her forehead. McPherson stood up and said, "Mrs. Arundel. Good evening."

"More like morning, it would seem, Commander. My son appears to have got himself into some danger." She looked around for Peter.

"This is Dr. Ewart, Mrs. Arundel," said McPherson. "He's been attending to Ollie Lindstrom, who got a bullet hole in him in the process of extracting Peter. He and your husband have gone to pick up Mrs. Lindstrom and bring her here." Tatania came forward. "And this is Tatania Gregov..." He stumbled over the name.

"Tatania Gregorovna Shevchenko, Mrs. Arundel," Tatania said.

"Hello, Tatania. You're my daughter-in-law. What a strange way to be introduced." She put her hand through the younger woman's arm and paused for a moment and took a deep breath. "I beg your pardon, Tatania, Commander. As you may well find in the future, regardless of their age, children remain a parent's first concern. I am sorry about Mr. Lindstrom. How is he?"

Dr. Ewart stepped in. "As well as can be expected, Mrs. Arundel. It's now a matter of waiting."

Michael and Peter Arundel arrived half an hour later with Mrs. Lindstrom. It was the first time any of them had met her and the introductions were a little stilted as a result. McPherson was not prepared for the attractive blonde, who appeared to be no more than thirty years old and very pregnant.

The doctor spoke first. "Mrs. Lindstrom, I'm Dr. Ewart. Your husband is resting comfortably. Presumably Mr. Arundel told you the circumstances involved in his injury? He just needs to rest now."

"It's probably not visiting hours," said McPherson wryly, "but I'm certain Dr. Ewart can get the rules bent for you. Would you like to see Ollie now? Then we can arrange a hotel room for you and a taxi to bring you back in the morning."

"Or you could come to our house, and one of us can drive you here in the morning," said Cynthia.

"I would be grateful for your hospitality, Mrs. Arundel," she said in a heavy Swedish accent. "Perhaps Dr. Ewart could take me to my husband, and we could leave when I have seen him?" Ewart led her into the interior of the hospital.

"Thank you for that, Cynthia," said Michael. "Would you take Mrs. Lindstrom back with Peter and Tatania? I'll give Dugald a ride to his hotel now. He's almost dead on his feet." He took McPherson's arm and propelled him out the door. "It's time for you rest now, sailor. Everyone you're responsible for is being taken care of by someone else—you need sleep."

While they walked to the car, McPherson said, "I told the customs man in Sidney that Peter would explain everything. I hope that part worked."

"It's a complicated story," said Michael. "He was happy enough when I got there. He didn't want to ask too many questions, otherwise he might get answers. Our trade gives the government money and there isn't anything coming back over the border except cash, and that does everyone some good." He changed the subject. "You had a bad time."

"It was reassuring that Miss Shevchenko arrived unscathed," said McPherson, stumbling involuntarily and reaching for the door to steady himself.

"It's probably a good idea to leave the discussion of details until tomorrow. Would you join us for lunch?"

McPherson scarcely knew whether he answered but kept himself under rigid control to keep from reeling as he left the car and made for the elevator in the hotel lobby.

At nine o'clock, McPherson stepped out into the grey, drizzly morning to walk to the shipyard, clarifying the day's jobs in his mind.

He walked up Store Street and in ten minutes reached Takahashis'. Aki was there cleaning up the office.

"Hear you had a time of it yesterday." Aki barely looked up.

"Nothing's a secret around here. The boat's in Sidney, parked at the end of the dock. I'd like Jeff to get up there before people get too curious about it. We took some bullets, but the main damage happened when we hit a log. Shaft's bent and there's some propeller damage. We came in on the diesel, so he could probably do some running repairs and sail it back, but he'll need help. We'll have to look at the shaft mounting—it shouldn't haver bent like that."

"How's Ollie?"

"He has a hole in him and the hospital's hanging on to him for a while. I have to get busy putting crews together—we won't be able to count on him for a few more weeks yet, assuming his wife will even let him go out with us again. I've been given the go-ahead to hire and I have a few leads, so hopefully we'll have more people involved fairly soon."

"Don't know too many who could handle *Rit'waxl.*"

"Neither do I, but it might be that we put most of our efforts into supplying American shore boats. I'll give Jeff a ride out to Sidney, but I have to get back to town by noon, so we'd better leave fairly soon. Will you come with us? You may have to find someone to tow the boat." Aki nodded. Jeff was in the workshop under the office. They loaded him and his tools in a dinghy and rowed up to the warehouse dock to get

McPherson's car.

McPherson pulled up outside the Arundels' house at ten minutes past noon.

Cynthia was at the hospital with Greta Lindstrom. The rest of them were in the dining room clustered at the end of the big table. "Miss Shevchenko," McPherson said. "It was a surprise to see you."

"She's come a few miles since I last saw her, too," said Peter.

"Perhaps you can enlighten me as to why you were the target of at least two Russians hanging around Seattle? Now one of them seems to have been German, and they were being helped by the renegade son of my most recent commander. As you said, Major Arundel, it was all a little complicated even when it just involved some money belonging to the Tsar of Russia. Now it's more so." McPherson smiled bleakly "Perhaps the leather case Peter lifted from our dead German friend might shed some light on it all."

Michael raised his eyebrows at Peter. "I thought it might give us a clue as to who he was. It was empty," said Peter.

"Indeed!" said McPherson. He paused before going on. "Last time we spoke, you said Peter had something he needed to finish in Seattle, Major. I'm assuming that was Miss Shevchenko."

"Tatania and I were married in 1918," said Peter. "Tatania was being sent back to Russia with money as part of an attempt to rescue the Tsar. The Admiral thought it would be better if she were issued a British passport in my name, that it would help her to travel unhindered. No one thought Russia would sink into chaos at the speed it did, or that the Tsar would be murdered by his captors." He paused.

"As I told you, Commander," Michael added, "that rescue attempt was part of the reason you were sent to the Caspian Sea. The plan was to bring the Tsar though territory controlled by Loyalist forces, and eventually into an area held by the Empire, possibly India. We may never know whether the Bolsheviks found out about the plans and forestalled them by murdering the Russian royal family. In any case, your performance there led to Admiral Romilly suggesting to the King that he should keep note of you on his special list."

McPherson sat down. "Presumably, that's why you offered me this job."

"Yes, the Admiral asked us to keep you close. We knew when to expect you to arrive, and it seemed a good idea to have Peter meet you."

"Where did John Romilly feature in all this?" McPherson asked.

"That was a surprise," said Michael. "In retrospect, it might have been him who warned the Russians to intercept Tatania back in the Caspian; however, it's highly unlikely John would have known the details of the undertaking, and so that may have caused the Bolsheviks to take the drastic measures they did."

Peter stepped in. "After we dropped Tatania off in England, she was sent back into Russia. When the new regime got wind of it, they went after her. She made it to Shanghai with other White Russians and has been trying to get to Canada ever since. She managed to get to San Francisco and contacted me, but she knew she was still being followed."

"John would certainly not have known details about the bank's role, but he might have suspected some involvement and would have passed that information on to the Russians," said Michael. "They would have used his position within our family to get to Tatania, but I suspect they never thought Roy Olmstead's people would get involved. I think, at the end of it all, John was just a sad amateur trying to find a place in a new world order."

"How are you going to explain his death?" asked McPherson.

Michael answered him. "I'll let the Admiral know. I think we can ask Roy Olmstead to arrange an item in the Seattle papers about a young Englishman drowning in a boating accident. The British Consul can make the necessary arrangements for burial should the body be found."

The four of them sat quietly for a moment.

"Where does it all go from here?" asked Peter.

"To lunch for a start," replied his father.

The sound of the front door opening got their attention and Cynthia came in. "Mr. Lindstrom is being kept in hospital for a few more days. His wounds have been stitched up, but they don't want to let him out until the doctor is sure it's not infected. I took Mrs. Lindstrom home, and we'll arrange for a taxi to pick her up twice a day so she can go and see him. I told the hospital secretary we will pay any costs associated with his stay."

"Hopefully he'll be out soon, anyway," said Peter. "Not that we're being niggardly about it," he added hurriedly. "We need to look at our crew lists. We don't have anyone other than us doing deliveries."

"Don't you mean me?" said McPherson. "We need good seamen who buy from us and deliver reliably. That's next week's job."

The maid came in to bring lunch and conversation stopped while they arranged themselves around the table.

"It was over a year ago that we stopped fighting in France," said Michael.

"And in April, it will be three years since Nicholas went," said Cynthia.

When they'd worked their way through the meal, Peter looked up and said, "I assume you'll stay with us, Pilot."

"There's nothing else in the offing, and now I'm used to a bit of law breaking, it doesn't seem as much of an issue, especially since we're in the King's service—however remotely," he said with a smile. "Besides, Emmaline and I settled some things at New Year's, which gives me a reason to stay in Victoria now, so yes—I'll stay with you for as long as this thing lasts."

Historical Notes

While this is entirely a work of fiction, its characters represent much of the reality that prevailed in a tiny corner of Canada in the years immediately following the First World War. Prior to that conflict, Vancouver Island had been a comfortable refuge for people who prized the anonymity it allowed to escape scandal or worse in the place from which they came.

The declaration of war sent many young men to enlist for the cause of "King and Empire" in Canadian army units whose traditions, forged in those days, endure to modern times. Many older men sought forgiveness for earlier sins by travelling "home" to rejoin the ranks of former regiments.

The background material was extracted from events that accompanied the end of the war and from the collapse of empires. Prohibition in the United States provided a major business opportunity throughout Canada, including a major revenue source for governments. A contemporary cartoon showed a map of North America with Canada leaking liquor from the north.

The events described in this novel are fictional but are likely outcomes of the circumstances that prevailed in the era. Some of the characters are real, including Captain James Troup, Roy Olmstead, and Elise Campbell, although the circumstances describing the beginning of Roy and Elise's relationship are likely not. The conversations in respect to the King are inferred, although I would be surprised if he did not maintain some sort of independent information network, given the kind of information often made available by his conventional advisors. The Liberty aircraft engine was used by rum runners, albeit a few years later than the period covered by this book.

Dugald McPherson is based on a number of real-life counterparts, both as a self-educated Canadian man of exceptional competence and as an example of the Royal Navy's need to rely on skilled officers from the merchant service.

Acknowledgements

This novel is the result of a twenty-year exercise in writing and rewriting and would never have appeared without the help and encouragement of family and friends. These ranged from a cheerful “How’s it going?” to “Isn’t it done yet?” My wife, Judith, who read and edited at least seven drafts, deserves the most credit, because without her, it would simply not exist.

Ron Chudley, the accomplished writer of several Canadian scene mystery stories, and the other beta readers who willingly accepted the antepenultimate draft of one hundred and forty thousand words, gently suggested places where continuity needed attention and details were surplus to the needs of the plot, and which characters were not entirely believable. I owe much to my friend and daily dog-walking companion Leigh Mair, who politely put up with listening to many proposed alternatives of plot and character.

Nora Bryant took on the commission of a painting for the cover; the original hangs proudly in our sitting room and I smile whenever I look at it.

I was fortunate to find an excellent editor, courtesy of fellow writer Darrell Duthie, the author of the Malcolm McPhail Series of Canadian World War One stories. That editor, Dexter Petley, was most definitive in his opinions and showed me how it was possible, and indeed desirable, to lose forty thousand words; I almost managed it.

My daughter, Helen Burbank, took her father’s efforts seriously and responded with her usual frank advice. My sons, Curt and Mark, were invaluable guides to the techniques and capacities of social media promotion.

I am grateful for the Canadian Authors Association, a major support for embryo writers. Alan Waddy and Rick Dewhurst were two other writers who guided me through the early challenges of publication, including the indelicate art of selling, and Tanis Bapty's proofreading skills proved invaluable.

Having collected the requisite number of rejection slips from conventional publishers, I came to rely increasingly on Suzanne Anderson, the author of *Self-Publishing in Canada*, and the members of the Cowichan Writers Group for advice and encouragement over the last few months of preparation. Hugh Stephens, author of *In Defence of Copyright*, guided me along that tricky path.

In particular, the greatest group who deserve acknowledgement are the members of the Royal Canadian Navy, the Canadian Army, and the Royal Canadian Air Force, whose exploits and enduring sacrifices from Canada's earliest days provide the meat with which storytellers make meals.

References

Baltic Episode, A Classic of Secret Service in Russian Waters. Captain Augustus Agar VC, DSO, Hodder & Stoughton 1963

Exploring the San Juan and Gulf Islands. Don Douglas & Réanne Hemmingay-Douglas, Fine Edge Nautical and Recreational Publishing 2011

The Royal Navy in the Caspian Sea 1918-1920. John Guard, Great War Primary Document Archive

Don't Never Tell Nobody, Nothin' No How: The Real Story of West Coast Rumrunning. Rick James, Harbour Publishing 2018

Slow Boat on Rum Row. Fraser Miles, Harbour Publishing 1992

Rumrunner, The Life and Times of Johnny Schnaar. Marion Parker and Robert Tyrrell, Orca Books 1988

Those Beautiful Coastal Liners. Robert D. Turner Sono Nis Press 2001

Wikipedia

Archives of the Victoria Colonist

Manufactured by Amazon.ca
Bolton, ON

39981186R00231